He must have sensed her approach for he suddenly turned

When their gazes connected, his eyes lit, then turned dark and smoldering. The small thrill became a rushing river of awareness. All at once, Adele knew why Ty had called her to meet him and what he wanted. She didn't hesitate going to him.

Dropping the reins, he came forward. Luckily, Hamm was placid by nature outside the arena because another horse might have spooked when Adele flung herself into Ty's open arms.

"I've been waiting a week for this," he said as his mouth came down on hers.

Only a week? It felt to Adele as if she'd been waiting forever. For this kiss. This moment. This man.

Dear Reader,

We hope you enjoy the Western stories
The Comeback Cowboy and *The Accidental Sheriff*
by *New York Times* bestselling Harlequin American
Romance author Cathy McDavid.

The Harlequin American Romance series
celebrates all things Western! These stories are
heartwarming contemporary tales of everyday
women finding love, becoming part of a family or
community—or maybe starting a family of her own.

And don't miss an excerpt of *Having the Cowboy's
Baby* by Harlequin American Romance author
Trish Milburn at the back of this volume.
Look for *Having the Cowboy's Baby*, available
September 2013.

Happy reading,

The Harlequin American Romance Editors

The Comeback Cowboy
&
The Accidental Sheriff

———

CATHY MCDAVID

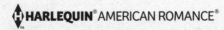
HARLEQUIN® AMERICAN ROMANCE®

ISBN-13: 978-0-373-68914-9

THE COMEBACK COWBOY
& THE ACCIDENTAL SHERIFF

Copyright © 2013 by Harlequin Books S.A.

The publisher acknowledges the
copyright holder of the individual works as follows:

THE COMEBACK COWBOY
Copyright © 2011 by Cathy McDavid

THE ACCIDENTAL SHERIFF
Copyright © 2010 by Cathy McDavid

Recycling programs
for this product may
not exist in your area.

Printed in U.S.A.

www.Harlequin.com

CONTENTS

ABOUT THE AUTHOR

Cathy makes her home in Scottsdale, Arizona, near the breathtaking McDowell Mountains, where hawks fly overhead, javelina traipse across her front yard and mountain lions occasionally come calling. She embraced the country life at an early age, acquiring her first horse in eighth grade. Dozens of horses followed through the years, along with mules, an obscenely fat donkey, chickens, ducks, goats and a potbellied pig who had her own swimming pool. Nowadays, two spoiled dogs and two spoiled-er cats round out the McDavid pets. Cathy loves contemporary and historical ranch stories and often incorporates her own experiences into her books.

When not writing, Cathy and her family and friends spend as much time as they can at her cabin in the small town of Young. Of course, she takes her laptop with her on the chance inspiration strikes.

THE COMEBACK COWBOY

To Libby and Connie. I always knew you would make great critique partners. What I didn't know was how much your friendship would enrich my life. Thank you for making the last ten years not just a journey but an adventure. I love you both.

Chapter One

Welcome to Seven Cedars Ranch, Home of Cowboy College.

He sat immobile, staring at the large sign with its horse-head logo, his jaw tightly clenched.

Up until the moment he drove through the main gate, he'd been able to deny how really low he'd sunk in the last six months and how really far he'd have to climb to get back on top.

No more. The time to man up had officially arrived.

He reached for the door handle on his pickup—only to have it abruptly wrenched open. Startled, he turned to look into the face of a kid no older than eighteen or nineteen.

"Welcome, Mr. Boudeau. We've been expecting you." The kid waited, a gosh-I-can't-believe-it's-you grin plastered across his freckled face.

"The name's Ty." He removed the keys from the ignition and climbed out.

"A real pleasure to meet you, Ty." They shook hands. "Folks 'round here call me Stick." The kid stepped back, and Ty could immediately see how he'd earned the nickname. Stick could get lost standing behind a flagpole. "Right this way. Adele's waiting for you."

Ty hesitated, the doubts he'd successfully kept at bay during the four-hour drive across Wyoming gaining ground. He needed help, that was a fact. But from a woman? One who made a living instructing amateurs at a glorified dude ranch. For a professional tie-down and team roper like himself, the idea was ludicrous. Certainly not "genius," as his younger sister had professed.

And yet he'd come.

"Okay to leave the truck parked here?" His Ford F350 dually and horse trailer blocked all six of the available spaces in front of the rustic two-story lodge.

"No problem."

Being a minor celebrity, even an undeserving one, had its privileges, he supposed.

Grabbing his wallet, Ty followed Stick up a stone-lined walkway, across a sprawling porch and through the front entrance of the lodge. With each thunk of his boots on the hardwood floor, his gut clenched tighter. This place was his last-ditch effort. If it, and Adele Donnelly, couldn't figure out what he was doing wrong, then he might as well kiss his roping career goodbye.

"Here's the main lobby and that way is the business center," Stick informed him as they crossed the spacious room with its vaulted ceilings and pine beams. Ten-foot-high windows looked out onto rolling green grounds dotted with thick stands of trees. "The front desk is where you check in and out, get the weekly schedules, sign up for classes." He shot Ty a guilty look over his shoulder. "Not that you need any."

"You never know." He definitely needed something.

"There's a lounge with a TV over there for guests." Stick pointed. "It's got satellite."

"Oh, good. Can't miss my daily dose of CNN."

His attempt at sarcasm went right over Stick's head, who didn't stop talking long enough to take a breath.

"The dining hall's that way. Breakfast is served from five-thirty to seven, lunch from eleven-thirty to one and dinner from six to seven-thirty. Social hour starts at five.

'Course, if you're hungry, Cook's always got a pot of stew or chili on the stove."

"I'll remember that."

Ty didn't anticipate doing much socializing during his four-week stay. He was here to rope. Though competent in other rodeo events, steer wrestling and team roping mostly, tie-down roping was what he excelled at.

Make that *had* excelled at. Everything had changed last December.

Stick escorted him to a long counter resembling a hotel registration desk, only on a much simpler scale. "You in there, Adele?" he called.

Ty caught a glimpse of a desk with a phone and computer through the open door behind the counter.

When no one answered, Stick tapped the bell on the counter. It promptly dinged. "Huh." He pushed his cowboy hat back, revealing a shock of red hair, and scratched his forehead. "Guess she's not here."

"We can come back," Ty offered, in no hurry to meet the owner and manager of Cowboy College.

In the next instant, he mentally kicked himself. He hadn't come all this way to chicken out at the last minute.

"But we have to get the key to your guest cabin. How else you gonna unpack your stuff?"

"It'll wait," Ty assured him. The poor kid was trying so hard and deserved a break. "How 'bout we head to the barn and unload my horse. Maybe Adele will show up by the time we're done."

Stick immediately brightened. "Sure thing," he said, only it sounded more like "shore" thing.

Back outside, they hopped in Ty's truck, and Stick directed him down the dirt road to a row of three barns. Across the open area in front of them was a large arena complete with holding pens, boxes, chutes, bleachers and an announcer's stand. A handful of riders were honing their roping skills with the help of some wranglers. Situated behind the barns were two smaller arenas, a pair of round pens, and endless acres of fenced pastures in which dozens of horses grazed on fresh spring grass. About a half mile beyond that, at the base of a valley, afternoon sunlight glinted off a large pond.

"How's the fishing?" Ty asked.

"Plenty of bass and bluegills. But if you're hankering for some serious fly-fishing, Little Twister Creek's the place to go. It's not far, about a mile or two from here. My cousin and I go every chance we get."

"You up for some company sometime?"

Stick's face exploded into a huge grin. "Just name the day." As they approached the row of barns, he indicated the largest one. "Here we are."

Ty pulled up in front of an old-fashioned hitching post and parked. His horse, Hamm, greeted him with a shrill whinny and a bang on the trailer sidewall when he went around the back and unlatched the gate. Eager to be free after the long drive, the large gelding piled out of the trailer. Once on solid ground, he raised his head high, took in his new surroundings and whinnied again. Mares with young foals in the far pasture ran to the fence for a closer look at the newcomer.

"He's a beaut!" Stick gazed at Hamm admiringly.

"That he is." Holding on to the lead rope with one hand, Ty patted the horse's neck. Plain old sorrel didn't begin to describe Hamm. With four perfectly matched white stockings and a three-inch-wide blaze running down the entire length of his face, he was striking.

"Bet he can chase calves down like lightning streakin' across a meadow."

"He's fast all right." Ty didn't elaborate. His problem, the reason he'd come to Cowboy College, had nothing to do with Hamm and everything to do with him.

"This way." Stick started toward the barn opening. After several steps, he turned, gave Ty's horse another adoring once-over and whistled low. "That big boy can sure walk out."

The barn housed at least forty horses. Every one of them charged to the door of their stall and hung their head out to observe the visitors. A few of the braver ones stretched their neck out to either sniff Hamm or give his rump a quick nip. Ty assumed some of the horses belonged to Cowboy College and the rest to guests like himself.

Midway down the aisle, Stick stopped and opened the door of an empty stall. "Here you go."

Being accustomed to traveling, Hamm entered his new quarters without balking. He quickly inspected the stall's perimeter, then buried his head in the feed trough. It was empty, and a second later his head shot up in obvious displeasure.

Given it was late afternoon, Ty supposed the stable hands would be feeding soon. Still, he asked, "You got a little grain or pellets we can give him until I go over his diet with the barn manager?" Hamm liked to eat, and a snack would help him adjust to his new surroundings.

"Be right back." Stick took off and promptly returned with a small bucket of oats.

Fifteen minutes later Ty and Stick were parking his trailer behind the barn. When they were done, Ty pulled his truck around front.

Stick sat forward in the passenger seat. "There's Adele." He hitched his chin toward the arena. "Come on, you can meet her."

Horses and their riders had gathered at the south end of the arena. Ty picked out a trim young woman astride a stout paint mare, a blond braid snaking down her back from beneath her battered cowboy hat. Despite the distance, he recognized her immediately. No surprise; he'd been staring at pictures of her on Cowboy College's website for weeks while deciding to come or not.

"She looks busy."

"Naw." Stick dismissed his concern with a wave. "She won't mind."

They selected a spot along the fence and settled in to watch, their forearms resting on the top rail.

"Hey, folks."

Stick's friendly greeting was returned by all except Adele. She was preoccupied with lining her horse up in the box. The mare, obviously new at tie-down roping, didn't like being enclosed in such a cramped space. She danced nervously, snorting and pulling on the bit. With firm hands and a honeyed voice, Adele brought the animal under control.

"Good girl." She placed the pigging string in her mouth, checked her rope and shifted in the saddle. Ty knew she would cue the wrangler manning the chute only when she and the horse were completely ready. That moment came a second later.

"Go!"

The wrangler slid open the gate, and the calf bolted for freedom, running in a straight line away from the chute. Adele's horse might not have much experience, but its instincts were right on the money. The mare exploded from the box at a full gallop, following the calf with the persistence of a heat-seeking missile. Adele's arm came up. In the next instant, she threw her rope. The noose landed right where it should, squarely on the calf's horns, and she leaped from the saddle even before the mare had come to a complete stop.

Ty watched, completely captivated as she raced to the calf and dropped it effortlessly to the ground, securing its legs with the pigging string. She worked efficiently, not a single motion wasted. And yet there was a natural, fluid gracefulness about her.

It was then Ty noticed the mare. Rather than backing up and stretching the rope taut, as was her job, she moved aimlessly, allowing the rope to hang loosely. The lack of assistance, however, didn't appear to hamper Adele's performance. She threw her hands in the air, signaling she was done—in less than eight seconds, according to Ty's internal stopwatch. The students watching at the end of the arena broke into applause. He and Stick joined them.

Stick beamed. "Isn't she something?"

"Pretty good." Ty rocked back on his heels, absorbing what he'd just seen and thinking how much he hated admitting his sister might be right about Cowboy College.

Adele stood, exhibiting that same dancer's grace from earlier. The calf, now free, trotted off, only to be rounded up by one of the wranglers. Suddenly, Adele turned and glanced in Ty's direction. Their gazes connected, and the same recognition he'd experienced when he first saw her was reflected in her dark green eyes.

"Glad to see you made it, Mr. Boudeau. I'm Adele Donnelly."

"Glad to be here."

"Did you get your horse situated?"

"Stick's taken fine care of us."

At the compliment, Stick puffed up his skinny excuse for a chest. "Ty still needs to get checked in."

"I'll be up to the main lodge in a bit."

She walked over to her horse, calmly collecting her rope and winding it into a coil. With the ease and confidence of a practiced athlete, she swung up into the saddle and rode out of the arena.

Ty stared after her. Despite hearing of her skill, he'd half expected—make that half hoped—the stories about her to be hype.

They weren't.

Adele Donnelly could not only show him a thing or two about a sport in which he'd been a top World contender mere months ago, she could quite possibly beat the pants off him.

"HEY, DELLIE." ADELE'S grandfather joined her behind the registration counter. "What are you doing?"

"Hi, Pop." She straightened from her hunched position and rolled her cramped shoulders. "I'm just going over these schedules."

"I heard Tyler Boudeau arrived."

"About an hour ago."

"You meet him yet?"

"Briefly, at the arena."

"Which cabin did you assign him?"

"Number twenty-two."

Pop grunted. "The honeymoon cabin is bigger."

"It's booked. Number twenty-two is our next largest cabin, and the view from the back balcony's the best on the ranch."

"It's kind of far from the barn."

She studied him curiously, wondering what was up.

He rarely concerned himself with a guest's accommodations, preferring to leave the administrative functions of the ranch and roping school to Adele. On most days, when his acute arthritis didn't confine him to bed or the couch, he could be found at the barns and arena, teaching classes, overseeing the livestock and supervising the ranch hands. He still put in a full day's work when he could, but the last few years he'd come to depend more and more on their barn manager to pick up the slack.

"So, what do you think of him?"

Adele paused before answering the question, unsure of her response. Having a professional roper stay at the ranch, particularly one of Ty Boudeau's caliber, was certainly a boon for business. But the explanation he'd given for his month-long stay, that of training his new horse, hadn't rung true.

"We exchanged only a few words, and those were pleasant enough."

"Humph." Pop seemed disappointed.

"He should be here any minute."

His eyebrows shot up, momentarily erasing the deep wrinkles creasing his brow. "You don't say?"

Adele almost laughed, with surprise, not humor. Her grandfather was starstruck and couldn't wait to meet their semifamous guest.

"In that case, guess I'll get me a cup of coffee in the kitchen and wait for him."

"Decaffeinated," Adele called after his retreating back, and resisted adding, "You know what your doctor said."

A few minutes later, she looked up from her work to see Ty stride through the lobby door. She had to admit he wasn't hard to look at. And taller than she'd expected. Picking up the house phone, she paged the kitchen and said, "Tell Pop he's here," when Cook answered.

Reaching the counter, Ty removed his cowboy hat, and an unruly lock of sandy-blond hair promptly fell across his tanned forehead. His attempts to push it off his face were wasted…and also charming.

"Welcome again, Mr. Boudeau." She gave him her best professional yet friendly smile.

"Please, call me Ty."

"And I'm Adele."

The registration process didn't take long. When she finished, she put together a stack of papers, including a brochure, maps of the ranch and the nearby town of Markton, the current week's schedule of classes and events and a list of rules and regulations.

"Please read through this the first chance you have." She pointed to the papers stapled together on top. "You can't begin using the facilities until we have a signed copy on file."

"Tell me, am I signing away all my rights?"

Adele thought she detected a twinkle of amusement in his dark brown eyes. Perhaps he wasn't all-business, as she'd first suspected.

"No. You're just agreeing to abide by the rules and regulations. Very standard stuff. We already have the liability waiver and insurance certificate you faxed last week."

Ty signed the form without reading it and slid the papers across the counter.

"Let me make you a copy." She went into the office, where she kept a desktop copier, and returned shortly. "Here you go."

"Thanks." Ty folded the sheets in thirds and slipped them in his shirt pocket, again without reading them.

Oh, well, she'd done all she could.

Her grandfather appeared from the entryway leading to the kitchen, his chronic limp barely noticeable for once.

"Hey there, young fellow." He extended his right hand. "I'm mighty glad to make your acquaintance."

"Mr. Donnelly." Ty's glance fell for the briefest of seconds on Pop's hand before clasping it in a firm shake. "It's a real honor to meet you, sir."

Adele liked that Ty didn't appear put off by her grandfather's missing right thumb, a casualty of a roping accident that had happened long before she was born.

"The honor's mine," Pop said. "I've been watching your career since you were competing in junior rodeo."

"And I've studied yours."

"You have to go back a lot of years for that." Pop laughed, but it was filled with warmth.

"I'm counting on you teaching me a thing or two while I'm here. It's one of the reasons I came."

Pop stood a little taller. Most of their guests were recreationists and wannabe cowboys. Some were high-school students hoping to eventually compete on the professional rodeo circuit. Almost none of them knew about her grandfather's once impressive and long-ago rodeo career. Not until they got here and saw the photos and framed buckles on the lobby wall.

"I doubt there's anything I can teach you." Pop chortled. "Now Adele here, she's likely to have a trick or two up her sleeve you can use."

"I saw her earlier at the arena," Ty said. "She's good."

"She's the best in the state, man or woman." Pop's voice rang with pride.

Adele loved her grandfather, but at the moment she wanted to cringe. "Mr. Boudeau is one of the best in the world, Pop."

"Doesn't mean he can't learn a thing or two from you."

"I agree," Ty answered good-naturedly. "Getting help, from both of you, is the reason I'm here."

Adele wondered if he'd added the "from both of you" for her grandfather's sake, considering how hesitantly the words had rolled off his tongue.

"Pop, why don't you show Mr. Boudeau to his cabin? You two can swap stories on the ride."

"Nothing I'd like better. Except I'm due to meet the boys in thirty minutes."

His regular Thursday-night poker game. She'd forgotten about that. "I'll call Stick."

"Adele, maybe you can take me?" One corner of Ty's

mouth lifted in a grin. A very potent grin. "I'd be much obliged."

"Certainly."

"Good," Pop said, with more satisfaction than the situation called for. "That's settled, then."

As Adele left the lodge with Ty, she couldn't shake the feeling that her grandfather had set her up. She should be mad at him, but when she hopped onto the truck seat next to Ty, being mad was the furthest thing from her mind.

TY SLANTED A glance at Adele, wondering what she was thinking. They'd both been relatively quiet during the five-minute drive through the main part of the ranch, except for the occasional item of interest she pointed out.

"Is this my home away from home?" he asked when she directed him to an attractive cabin atop a rise.

"Yes." She removed an old-fashioned hotel key from her pocket. No key cards for Cowboy College. "You'll love the view from the back patio."

They climbed out of the truck, and Adele led him along a split-fence-lined walkway to the front porch. Unlocking the cabin door, she swung it wide, and went ahead only when he indicated for her to precede him inside.

Ty took in the cabin's spacious and charmingly appointed interior, which appeared to have every amenity he could possibly want. "Very nice."

"If you aren't happy here, we can always move you to a different cabin."

"Are you kidding? This is great."

"It's a little far from the barn and arena." Adele walked over to the drapes on the other side of the living room and opened them, revealing a sliding glass door that looked out onto a calendar-perfect view of the nearby pond and distant mountains.

He joined her at the door and scanned the horizon. A glorious red sun was starting to dip behind one of the mountain peaks.

"It's worth the extra distance just for this."

Adele eased away from him, piquing his interest. Women generally acted the opposite, hanging all over him if possible. It was either a hazard or a perk of his profession, depending on a guy's perspective. Ty mostly found it wearisome. Except in Adele's case. Sharing the same air space with her had definitely been enjoyable.

Apparently not so much for her.

"There are two bedrooms," she said, walking past the fully equipped kitchenette. "The master and a small guest room. The couch also folds out into a bed. Your rental agreement allows for overnight guests up to three consecutive nights, but you have to report them."

"Dana will be glad to hear that." Was it his imagination or did a glint of curiosity flash in Adele's eyes? "My little sister's been bugging me to come here and take lessons from you."

"Oh, really? We'd love to have her," Adele said, so smoothly that Ty figured he'd been mistaken.

Perhaps because she was so different from the women he usually met, or that she was a roper like himself, he found himself trusting her. Enough to reveal the real reason he'd come to Cowboy College.

He hadn't expected he would, the idea of enrolling in a roping school for amateurs being hard to swallow. Taking instructions from a woman made it worse. But she'd impressed him in the arena, demonstrating a core of steel.

Like the one he had lost.

"It's not just my horse," he said abruptly. "It's me."

"What?" She turned to face him, her expression puzzled. He cleared his throat, freeing the words stuck in it. "The horse I'd been riding the past four years suffered a fractured metacarpal last December in a fall. Right before the National Finals Rodeo. I was ranked second at the time."

"I know, I read about it in *Roper Sports News*."

"I lost more than a gold buckle and a title that day. Iron Grip Ropes had signed me for a sponsorship deal. A very lucrative sponsorship deal."

"Which was contingent on you winning," she correctly guessed.

"I competed on a friend's horse, but lost the championship by one-point-eight seconds." Ty swallowed. Six months later, the bitter defeat still stung. "I bought Hamm in February after an extensive search. He's an incredible horse. Big, athletic, strong, fast and smart as a whip. Everything I could want." Ty paused.

"What's wrong, then?"

"That one-point-eight seconds. No matter what I do, no matter how hard I train, whatever trick I try, I can't seem to perform any better on Hamm than I did on my friend's horse. And I don't know why."

"Sometimes the partnership between a rider and horse is off."

"I'm hoping that's all it is. Because the alternative, that I've somehow lost my competitive edge…well, let's just say it's not acceptable."

He went to Adele and took her hand in his. The calluses on her palm from years of roping were in stark contrast to the silky smooth skin on the back of her hand. *Like her*, he thought—tough on one side, soft on the other.

"This isn't easy for me to ask, Adele. But I need your help."

She gazed at their joined hands for several seconds, then lifted her eyes to his. "I'll do my best."

"Good. Because the Buffalo Bill Cody Stampede Rodeo is less than four weeks away, and I *have* to win."

Chapter Two

Adele stood with Pop on the fence beside the chute and watched Ty position his horse in the roping box. People who weren't involved in rodeoing had no idea how many hours were spent training for the sport by studying others from the sidelines.

"What do you think?" Pop asked.

"Good-looking horse."

"Real nice looking."

So was the rider, but Adele kept that opinion to herself. Ty sat tall in the saddle, his Stetson angled low over his eyes, his Western cut shirt stretched taut across his broad shoulders. She wondered if he'd object to having his picture taken for their next website updates.

Almost immediately, she changed her mind. Ty had come to Cowboy College because of a problem, one he hoped to correct. It would be thoughtless and insensitive of her to take advantage of his misfortune in order to advance the ranch.

Ready at last, Ty signaled the wrangler, who pulled back the gate on the chute and released the calf. Ty's run, over in the span of a few heartbeats, was a good one. Not, however, spectacular. And spectacular runs were needed to win World championships.

"What do you think his problem is?" Adele asked her grandfather as Ty exited the arena.

"Not saying yet." Pop waved to Ty and pointed at the box, indicating for him to take another run.

Ty's admiration of her grandfather yesterday afternoon wasn't unfounded. Pop had been National tie-down roping champion for three years straight in the late 1950s, and again in 1963, before permanently retiring. Granted, things were done a little differently in those days, but the basic sport had remained the same.

One aspect not the same was the popularity of tie-down roping. That had grown tremendously in recent years, especially among amateurs. Not only did horse people with an interest in roping participate, so did thrill-seekers looking to try something new, urbanites wanting to experience the cowboy life, and even companies offering team-building retreats for their employees.

The increase in popularity was what had given Adele the idea to start Cowboy College. Her business savvy combined with her grandfather's experience made a winning combination. Together they'd turned a run-down ranch into a thriving enterprise.

Seven Cedars hadn't always been in trouble. For three decades after her grandparents bought the place, they'd run a modestly successful cattle business. Then, during Adele's junior year at university, her grandmother had died unexpectedly from an aneurysm. Pop sank into grief, letting the ranch go. Adele's father wasn't able to leave his job and move his second family from Texas to tend the ranch. Until Adele arrived after graduation, no one realized how bad the situation at Seven Cedars, and Pop's depression, had gotten.

Cowboy College not only breathed new life into the ranch, it gave her grandfather a purpose again. Within a year, they'd opened their doors, and had grown steadily in the six years since. Guests came from all over the country now, spending anywhere from a long weekend to weeks on end.

Ty Boudeau, however, was their first ever professional roper.

His horse, Hamm, lined up in the box with only the smallest amount of urging. "Go!" he shouted. As on the first run, the wrangler released the calf and Ty successfully roped it in a respectable time.

"He could do this all day and it wouldn't be any different," Adele commented.

"I'm afraid you're right." Pop rolled the toothpick stuck in his mouth from one side to the other. He was rarely without one since giving up chewing tobacco years earlier. Another of his doctor's mandates.

"The horse isn't taking one wrong step," Adele commented, "and Ty's doing exactly what he should be doing."

"But the magic just isn't happening."

"Could his problem be lack of confidence?"

Pop shrugged. "Possibly. Losing a world championship when you're as close as he was could set anyone back."

"Except Ty doesn't strike me as lacking confidence." *In or out of the arena*, thought Adele.

But then, he'd lost much more than the championship. Sponsorship deals, good ones, didn't grow on trees, and had launched more than one athlete on a successful post-competing career.

"You never know," Pop mused out loud. "He could be putting on a good front. My guess is it's the horse."

Adele shot her grandfather a sideways look. "You just agreed Hamm's a nice horse."

"But he isn't Ty's other horse. Don't get me wrong. The boy was always a good roper, one to watch since he began competing in junior rodeo. He didn't come on strong until four years ago, when he got that horse. It was a perfect partnership. Now he's lost that partner."

"I think Hamm has the potential to be every bit as good as Ty's other horse."

"Maybe even better."

Adele nodded in agreement. "He just has to realize that."

"I'm thinking he already does." Pop's expression became pensive. "Recovering from a loss isn't easy, be it someone you've loved or a dream you've held. Something inside dies. There's no miracle cure and no set timetable for recovery. Ty will come back when he's ready." Pop turned a fond smile on Adele. "Or when someone shows him the way."

She patted his hand in return, recalling their early days of Cowboy College. "You could be right."

Stepping off the fence, she pushed a damp strand of hair off her face. The temperature might be only in the low seventies, but the bright morning sun beat down on them, warming her through and through. "If he were anyone else but Ty Boudeau, I'd recommend the beginners' class. The best way to get to know your horse is by starting with the basics."

Pop also stepped off the fence. "Why not Ty?"

"He's…one of the best ropers out there. He doesn't need a beginners' class."

"Are you sure? Could be just the ticket."

"He'll laugh in our faces, then pack his bags."

"He won't laugh if he's committed." Pop moved the toothpick to the other side of his mouth. "And Ty strikes me as a man with a mission."

"Excuse me for disagreeing."

"Relax, Dellie. You know it's a good idea. Ty Boudeau has everything it takes to be the next World Champion. And when he is, he's gonna be thanking you and me."

"Okay," she grumbled. "But I'm not going to be the one to tell him he has to take the beginners' class. *You* are."

"Isn't this place great? My husband and I arrived just a few days ago. We've never been here before. Have you?"

The woman astride the horse standing beside Ty had been rambling nonstop for five minutes solid, not caring if he answered her question or not before going on to the next one.

It was different being around people who didn't recognize him. Different and unsettling. When had he become so accustomed to the attention?

"How'd you get into roping? My husband rodeoed some when he was growing up. We saw a show on cable TV about couples roping, and decided to give it a try. And now we're hooked. Me, not so much."

The woman paused to take a breath. Ty used the lull to observe Adele.

She stood on the ground giving instructions to the group, which was comprised of about a dozen beginner ropers. Ty only half listened. He was quite familiar with the training technique she described—a fake calf head attached to a bale of hay and pulled by a wrangler driving an ATV. The group had assembled in one of the smaller arenas beside the barn, away from the ropers practicing in the main arena, in case the ATV spooked their horses.

"I can't believe I'm actually taking a roping class." The woman untangled her reins for the third time.

"Me, either."

When Pop had proposed the idea that Ty participate in the afternoon beginners' class, he'd balked. Then he learned Adele would be teaching it. That, and the arguments Pop had presented about getting back to basics, convinced Ty to give one—and *only* one—class a try. He told himself it wasn't because he found Adele attractive. Rather, he wanted to see if she could teach as well as she roped. His decision to remain at Cowboy College depended on the outcome.

She continued explaining how the wrangler would take

off on the ATV, and that the riders should allow their horses to follow the calf head and bale of hay, rather than attempt to direct them.

Yeah, yeah. Ty suppressed a yawn.

His cell phone rang a minute later, coming just when he thought he'd reached his boredom threshold. Unclipping the phone from his belt, he checked the screen. A photo of his younger sister appeared with her name above it.

"Sorry, I need to take this call," he told the students nearest him, and nudged Hamm into a fast walk away from the group. Stopping about twenty feet away, he answered the call. "Hey, Dana."

From his chosen spot, he could see Adele frowning at him. Too late, Ty realized there was probably something in the rules and regulations he hadn't yet read about no cellphone calls during class. Oh, well, he'd already screwed up.

"How's it going, bro?"

"Not so great."

"Why?"

"Because I'm sitting here in a beginners' class."

"Really! Doing what? Showing the students how it's done?"

"No, attending. Actually, attending as little as possible."

"I guess a refresher course never hurts."

He should have figured Dana would agree with Pop's suggestion, being it was her idea to come to Cowboy College.

"Right. I could be doing this in my sleep."

"So prove it."

"You're not serious." He laughed.

"I am, Ty. You need to figure out what's not working, and fix it. Taking a beginner class might seem ridiculous, but you need a new perspective, and I'm all for trying anything. You should be, too, if you want to win that championship."

Ty tamped down his rising annoyance. It had been a long

time since anyone had lectured him. A long time since he'd felt he deserved a lecture.

A quick glance at Adele confirmed yet another talking-to might be in store for him. She looked about as happy with him as his sister sounded.

"This isn't easy for me, Dana." The admission came with an uncomfortable tightening in his gut.

"I know, honey. But I'm one of the people who has your back, remember?"

"And I appreciate it."

"You couldn't have two better experts there."

"I agree with you about Pop Donnelly. And I wouldn't mind half so much if he was teaching the class."

"What's wrong with Adele Donnelly?"

There was nothing wrong with her that Ty could see. It was his ego having the problem. Granted, he'd asked for her help yesterday, but that was in a weak moment. This morning, when he'd faced himself in the bathroom mirror, he wished he'd asked Pop for help instead.

It wasn't too late. He'd get through this one class and seek out the older man. Maybe then he wouldn't feel like so much of a loser. Or have an entire group of people witnessing his shame.

"You practice with a woman roper," Dana prompted.

"It's different with you."

"Because I'm not competing against you in the same sport?"

"Yikes." Ty grimaced. "That smarts."

"Give Adele a chance before you hightail it out of there."

How did his sister know he'd been contemplating leaving? "Fine. I promise to stay another couple days."

"You said a month." Her tone dared him to defy her.

"Okay, okay. You win."

"Call me if you need anything."

"I will." They disconnected after saying goodbye.

Ty silenced his cell phone and walked Hamm over to the group, smiling apologetically to his classmates and Adele, who blatantly ignored him. All right, he deserved that. Leaning forward and propping a forearm on the saddle horn, he made an effort to really listen to her. After several minutes passed, he had to agree she knew her stuff. She certainly had the attention of all the students.

"Are we ready to try? Who wants to go first?"

Hands shot into the air, none of them Ty's.

"All right, how about you, Mike?" She picked the husband of the woman Ty'd been talking to earlier.

He sat quietly on Hamm, watching Mike and the others take their turns one by one. He easily and quickly spotted the errors with each student. Adele did, too, and patiently explained it to them in laymen's terms the students could comprehend. When everyone had done it, Adele's gaze landed on him.

"You're up next, Ty."

He moved into position behind the bale of hay. Hamm pawed the ground, far more eager to get started than his owner.

"Wait. We're going to do this a little differently with you. Put up your rope."

"My rope?"

"Then drop your reins and kick your feet out of the stirrups."

"You're kidding."

"No hands, no legs."

"Why?" he asked.

"You don't think you can stay seated?" Her green eyes flashed up at him.

He attached his lasso to his saddle with the rope strap.

"Ma'am, I can break a green horse riding bareback and with one hand tied behind my back."

"Then this should be a cakewalk for you." She stepped away from him.

With a shrug of his shoulders, his hands resting on his thighs and his legs dangling, he waited for the wrangler to take off on the ATV.

"One more thing," Adele said, the lowered brim of her cowboy hat partially hiding her face. "You have to do it with your eyes closed."

"Excuse me?"

"Eyes closed, Mr. Boudeau."

Was she smiling?

Ty decided to go along with her rather than put up a fight. He'd promised Dana, and besides, the students might learn something from watching him.

"Go!" he told the wrangler.

Hamm took off after the bale of hay as if it were the real thing. Because the wrangler didn't drive the ATV very fast, Hamm's gait was an easy lope rather than a full-out gallop, as it would be in the arena.

Ty set down deep in the saddle, adjusting himself to the horse's rhythm. Trying to, he amended. It wasn't as easy as he might have guessed. Not with his eyes closed and his legs dangling. As the driver zigzagged, mimicking the course a calf might take, Ty felt—*really* felt—the nuances of Hamm's muscles bunching and releasing when he changed directions. Ty shifted accordingly, to compensate for the horse's movements, thinking about it rather than doing it instinctively as he should.

After thirty feet, the wrangler slowed to a stop. Hamm also slowed. Opening his eyes, Ty used the pressure of his legs to guide his horse in a circle and back toward the group.

Once there, he stopped and rubbed his neck, contemplating what had just happened.

"You look perplexed," Adele said, studying him.

"Not that so much," he answered.

She'd put him through a very basic exercise, one, he realized in hindsight, he should have tried himself. Perhaps if he had, the results wouldn't be quite so startling.

Ty trusted himself as a rider. What he'd learned today was that he didn't trust Hamm. Not entirely and not enough. His other horse's accident had robbed Ty of that vital component to a successful rider-horse partnership, and the tiny fear that it would happen again was causing him to hold back.

"Ty?" Adele asked.

He grinned suddenly and waved to the wrangler to come back around.

"I want to go again."

"HEY, ADELE, HOLD on a minute."

Hearing her name, she stopped and turned to see Ty hurrying after her.

Uh-oh. He was probably annoyed at her for what she'd pulled on him during class earlier. Squaring her shoulders, she waited for him to catch up, committed to defending her actions.

"Can I help you with something?" She smiled, pretending she didn't notice the Ben Affleck–like perfection of Ty's strong, dimpled chin or the fluttering in her middle that ogling his chin caused. "Perhaps a copy of the rules and regulations you obviously lost."

"I guess I deserve that." He returned her smile with a healthy dose of chagrin. "No more phone calls. You have my word."

She was glad to see he didn't take offense at her more-serious-than-humorous jest. Rules were rules, in place for a reason, and Ty Boudeau didn't get to break them just because he was a professional roper.

"You're allowed one mistake before we start giving demerits. Ten demerits, however, and you're kicked off the ranch."

His startled expression was so comical, she almost laughed. "I'm joking."

The hint of a twinkle lit his eyes. "You're good, you know."

"I've had a lot of practice keeping unruly students in line."

"No denying I'm one of those unruly students in need of lining out, but that's not what I meant."

"Oh?"

"You're good at spotting what a person's doing wrong. Me included."

She knitted her brows in confusion. "I didn't notice you doing anything wrong."

"Maybe not exactly. But the exercise helped me understand some things about myself. Things that need fixing."

"Not many competitors at your level would admit to that. I'm impressed."

"Don't be. I'm usually thickheaded. A good suggestion could be driving a Mack truck straight at me, and I'd ignore it."

"I'll remember that next time."

He moved closer. "I just wanted to thank you for the help."

"You're welcome." She worried that he was going to take her hand again. Relief flooded her when he didn't. One intimate encounter was more than she could handle. "Have a productive remainder of your day, Mr. Boudeau."

"If you don't mind, I'd like to pick your brain sometime when you have a minute."

She debated refusing his request. In the end, she decided

to grant it. He was a paying guest, after all, and part of the fees they charged entitled students to "pick her brain," as he said.

"I'm heading over to check on one of our expectant mares. You can come with me if you like."

His dark eyes, arresting to begin with, lit up. "I would."

"I'm not keeping you from anything important, am I?"

He fell step in beside her. "Only the horde of adoring female fans waiting for me in the lobby."

She momentarily faltered. "If you have to go…"

"I'm kidding." He flashed her his heart-stopping grin.

It appeared she was just as gullible as him.

He surprised her during their walk with the questions he asked, which were detailed and thought provoking. Did tie-down straps really help horses stop faster, or hinder them? How did she feel about the new Professional Cowboy Association regulations, and did they affect her teaching methods? What kind of personal fitness regime, if any, did she recommend for her students?

More than once, Adele found herself examining the techniques of roping from a different and enlightening perspective.

"Here's where Pop and I keep our private stock," she told Ty when they entered the smallest of the ranch's three barns. At the end of the aisle, they came to a double-wide stall separated from the other horses by twenty feet and a six-foot wall.

"And this is Crackers," Adele said by way of introduction.

Upon seeing her, the heavily pregnant mare nickered softly and lumbered over from the corner where she'd been standing, to hang her shaggy head over the stall door.

Adele stroked the animal's neck. "She was my first barrel-racing horse. Gosh, was that really fourteen years ago?"

"Did you compete professionally?" Ty asked. He stood beside her, his elbow propped on the stall door.

"A little in college."

"Any good?"

"All right."

"Why'd you quit?"

She absently combed her fingers through Crackers's mane. "I came here after graduation to help Pop with the ranch. He'd turned seventy, and his arthritis was getting bad. He needed help, and I needed a job." She didn't mention her grandmother's death. "I've always loved Seven Cedars, and spent a lot of time here when I was growing up."

"Did your parents rodeo?"

"My dad. Though he never did all that well, and moved to Texas years ago. My mom traveled the rodeo circuit considerably longer than Dad, but not to compete."

Adele didn't elaborate. Despite Ty's friendliness, she wasn't ready to confess that her mother had taken up with whatever cowboy would have her, dropping Adele off with her grandparents if her father wouldn't have her. As her mother aged and her looks faded, those cowboys went from being competitors to bullfighters to stock handlers. In between men, she'd find a small place to rent for herself and Adele, but only until another man came along. For a young girl feeling unloved and unwanted, Seven Cedars became a haven in an otherwise turbulent childhood.

"So, Pop taught you to rope."

"He was a man ahead of his time. In those days, women didn't rope. Period." She opened the stall door and went in to give Crackers a closer inspection.

"She looks close," Ty observed.

"Soon." The foal had dropped considerably in the last week, but otherwise, Crackers showed no signs of delivering. "She's due this week."

"Her first?"

"Second. Up until a few years ago, we used her steadily

for beginner students. When her stamina began to fade, we decided to breed her." Adele patted Crackers's rump, then left the stall and shut the door behind her. "She's got good lines, and she's a good mama."

"And she's your first horse."

"Pop bought her for me when I was a freshman in high school. There were always plenty of horses to ride wherever I lived, but she was the first one that was truly mine." Latching the stall door, she met Ty's gaze. "Cook will be serving dinner soon, and I need to get back to my office first."

"Will I see you in the dining hall?"

"Absolutely."

Adele made a point of sharing dinner each evening with the students, often moving from one table to another. That way, she got to know them on a more personal level. Breakfast and lunch, however, were hit-or-miss and often consumed on the run.

At the entrance to the barn, she and Ty separated, each heading to their own vehicle. Hers was parked closer, and she hesitated before climbing in, stilled by the sight of Ty striding to his truck.

It had been a very long time since Adele had met a man who gave her that uncomfortable yet deliciously thrilling feeling every time she got within ten feet of him.

She silently warned herself to proceed with caution. Ty Boudeau had all the makings of a heartbreaker, and as much as she might want to get to know him on a more "personal level," she was far better off keeping her distance.

Men who spent inordinate amounts of time on the road didn't make good husbands. It was one of the many lessons her parents' failed marriage and her mother's endless stream of lovers had taught Adele.

Chapter Three

Ty drove through the small town of Markton, the closest community to Cowboy College. It could hardly be described as a metropolis, but he liked its grassroots country charm, its one stoplight at the intersection of Main Street and Brown, and the way everybody waved at everybody else.

Markton was a far cry from Santa Fe, where he'd grown up. He couldn't say *lived* because once he'd left home to rodeo full-time, he traveled six to nine months a year. When he needed to crash for a while, he stayed at his older sister's place. His fifth-wheel trailer parked behind the barn was, sad to say, the closest thing he had to a permanent residence.

He drove along Main Street at the posted speed of thirty-five, enjoying his free afternoon and taking in the various sights. The Spotted Horse Saloon. The feed store. Bush's General Store. The elementary school. The barbershop and its counterpart, Goldie's Locks and Nail Salon.

He'd often thought he might like to settle down in a town like Markton, and as he drove through it—end to end in less than five minutes—he contemplated where to stop first.

The feed store, an always familiar stomping ground, looked to have possibilities. Ty pulled into an empty space across from a sign advertising a popular brand of dog food. Inside the store, he was greeted by the middle-aged man behind the counter, whose double take was almost comical.

"Ty Boudeau?" he asked with raised brows.

"On a good day," Ty joked.

"We heard you were in town." The man came around from behind the counter carrying a pen and piece of paper. "Name's Henry Parkman."

"Pleased to meet you."

"If it's not too much trouble, the wife would sure love to have your autograph."

"No trouble."

It felt good being asked. The requests for autographs had tapered off since he'd lost at Nationals. Ty preferred to think it was because he hadn't been competing of late, not that he'd fallen from grace.

As he scribbled his name on the notepad, Henry Parkman produced his cell phone, held it at arm's reach, leaned in close and snapped a picture of him and Ty.

"For the wife." He grinned sheepishly. "Anything special I can help you with today?"

"Just browsing."

"Holler if you need me," he said to Ty, returning to his place behind the cash register.

Ty gravitated to the back of the store where the saddles and a rather impressive assortment of lariats hung on the wall. Though he wasn't in the market for another one, he removed several from the wall display and tested them for weight and flexibility.

For reasons he chose not to address, he avoided the Iron Grip Ropes—though it probably had something to do with the face smiling at him from the rope's cardboard wrapper. Garth Maitland. The man who'd beat out Ty for the championship last December.

"Mr. Boudeau?" The cracking voice belonged to a teenager who bore a striking resemblance to Stick.

"Hi."

"Hate to bother you, sir," he said, his exceptionally large Adam's apple bobbing as he talked, "but could I trouble you for an autograph?"

"Are you by chance related to Stick over at Cowboy College?" Ty asked as he signed the kid's ball cap with a black marker.

The teen's eyes went wide. "He's my cousin."

"Well, he's a pretty good worker. But don't tell him I said so."

"I—I won't," the kid stammered, and made a beeline for the door.

Ty wasn't in the market for a new pair of boots, either, but he checked out the selection just for something to do. The front-door buzzer went off every few minutes as customers came and left. Deciding he could possibly use a new leather belt, he picked one out and headed to the counter.

While he completed his purchase, the door buzzer went off again. Bidding the store owner goodbye, he turned…and came face-to-face with Adele.

"Oh!" She drew back. "Hello. I didn't know you were here."

"Just seeing what the town has to offer." He glanced at the attractive young woman beside Adele, whose stylish clothes and painful looking four-inch heels were more suited to a stroll down Hollywood Boulevard than Main Street in Markton. "I'm Ty Boudeau."

"This is my friend Reese Carter. She's engaged t-to…" Adele stammered, then recovered. "She lives on the ranch next door."

Ty's chest suddenly constricted, and he cautioned himself not to jump to conclusions. Markton boasted more than one rodeo family; Seven Cedars had more than one neighbor.

"Nice to meet you," he said, and shook the hand Reese offered. "Are you ladies in the market for horse pellets?"

"We were just killing a little time before going for lunch at the Spotted Horse."

"They serve food?"

"Surprisingly good food." Reese smiled brightly.

She sure didn't look as if she'd grown up on a ranch, not with her high heels and the designer sunglasses propped on her head.

"Well, it was nice running into you." Adele looked ready to bolt, and clamped on to her friend's arm. "See you later at the ranch."

"Would you like to join us for lunch?" Reese asked.

"I'm sure he's busy," Adele cut in before Ty could answer.

Because she seemed in such an all-fired hurry to get away from him, he answered, "I'd like that very much. Appreciate the invitation."

Adele's mouth, usually lush and pretty, tightened.

Finding her discomfort amusing, Ty followed the ladies to the door and held it open for them. They crossed the street at the corner and went up half a block to the saloon entrance.

Inside, Reese informed the hostess her fiancé would be joining them.

"I'll show him to your table."

"That won't be necessary." Reese peered past the hostess, her face alight. "Here he comes now."

Everyone looked over to see a handsome cowboy making his way toward them, his swagger confident.

The same anxiety that had gripped Ty that first day at Cowboy College, the one he thought he'd successfully conquered, returned with a vengeance. Too late, he realized his mistake—he'd misread Adele completely. At the least, he should have asked Reese her fiancé's name before barging in on her and Adele's lunch date.

Then he wouldn't be stuck sitting across the table from the man who had beat him in team and tie-down roping last

December, stealing the title of World Champion and the Iron Grip sponsorship deal from him.

EACH BITE OF Ty's Swiss-cheese-and-mushroom burger tasted like paste and sat in his stomach like a lead ball. He couldn't fault Garth Maitland for his unappetizing meal. The guy had been nothing but decent all during lunch. He always was, even when Ty lost to him at Nationals.

Until then, Ty and Garth had been friendly rivals, getting along well, real well even, when they weren't competing. Not the same could be said when they were in the arena. Both of them were out to win, and a mutual liking and respect of each other's abilities went only so far. After losing the title, Ty had kept his distance from Garth. Not because he resented the man; Garth had won fair and square. The problem was Ty's, who felt he was staring his personal failings square in the face each time he looked at Garth.

The lunch conversation, stilted at first, soon settled into a congenial rhythm, carried mostly by his companions. Ty injected a comment every now and then just to keep anyone from noticing his discomfort.

Except one person did.

"I'm sorry," Adele whispered under her breath, when Garth and Reese were busy speaking to each other and momentarily ignoring them. "I tried to—"

"Not your fault," Ty whispered back. They were seated together in the booth, the only positive thing about lunch as far as he was concerned. "It's okay."

"Really?" She appeared genuinely distraught.

He flashed his best interview smile, hoping to reassure her. "Really."

She'd tried to avoid this disaster earlier at the feed store. He had no one to blame but himself.

"What brings you to Cowboy College, Ty?" Reese asked, her demeanor curious but friendly.

Instantly, silence descended on the table. Adele gnawed her lower lip. Garth's eyebrows raised in curiosity.

Ty got annoyed—with himself and the situation. Okay, he'd lost the world championship title and a profitable sponsorship deal. To the man with whom he'd just eaten lunch. No reason for everyone to act as if he had an incurable disease.

"I apologize if I said something wrong." Reese looked contrite.

"You didn't." Ty gave her credit for not ignoring the sudden tension. "I came to Cowboy College for Adele's help with my new horse." The glossed-over explanation sounded better than the truth.

"It was a shame about your other horse," Garth said sympathetically. "And bad timing."

"It was. But these things happen."

"They do. My old partner fell and busted his kneecap last September. He won't be competing again until this fall, and even that's iffy."

"Here's to this season." Ty lifted his mug of beer in a toast.

"To this season," Garth repeated, and lifted his own, a glint in his eyes. He was obviously looking forward to the next time they went up against each other.

Determination surged inside Ty. Residing next door to his rival might have some advantages. At the very least, the constant reminder would help motivate him and keep him focused on his goal.

Reese's glance traveled from one man to the other. "Is something going on here I don't get?"

Garth chuckled.

Ty wanted to but wasn't able to let his guard down enough to explain.

The remainder of their meal went well, until it came time to pay the server.

"I've got it." Ty reached for the bill.

"No problem." Garth beat him to the punch by a scant second. "I already told the waitress lunch was on me." He signed the slip with a flourish.

"All right. I'll buy next time."

"Deal." Garth grinned, and for a moment they were friends again.

Outside the saloon, they made plans to go their separate ways.

"You need to head back to the ranch right away?" Reese asked Adele.

"If you don't mind. I've got a bunch of work at the office stacked up."

"It's Sunday. Don't you ever take any time off?"

"I just did."

"You work way too hard," Reese scolded, and slung an arm around Adele's shoulders. "Come on, we'll drive you home."

"She can ride with me," Ty offered. He'd assumed Adele had driven herself, or he would have offered earlier.

"You don't have to," she answered a little too quickly.

"No problem. I'm going that way."

"I hate cutting your trip to town short."

"You're not. I was just thinking of heading back to the ranch." In truth, he'd been planning on driving down the road to Little Twister Creek and the fishing spot Stick had mentioned earlier. Noting Adele's hesitancy, Ty couldn't help himself and pressed the point, if only to see if she'd rather inconvenience her friends than ride with him.

"Why don't you come by one day for a visit?" Garth suggested. "Have a look around."

Ty had seen pictures of Garth's place in various rodeo

publications. It was a roper's dream. Part of him wanted to go, just to check out the setup and salivate. The other part of him resisted. He would, after all, be walking into the enemy's camp.

"Thanks. I may take you up on that one day."

"Bring your horse. When you and Adele have worked out the kinks," he added.

Ty bristled. With competitiveness, not anger. He recognized a challenge when it was issued, and would like nothing better than to take Hamm over to Garth's and show him what he could expect to see on the circuit next month.

"I'll do that. Soon."

"I'm looking forward to it."

"I don't know about you," Reese said to Adele with exaggerated weariness, "but I've had just about as much testosterone as I can handle in one day." She looped her arm through Garth's. "It was really nice meeting you, Ty. And I do hope you'll come for a visit. With or without your horse. Bye, sweetie." She blew Adele a kiss. "Call me tomorrow."

"You okay?" Ty asked Adele as they were heading to his truck. "You've been awfully quiet."

"A little tired. I ate too much at lunch."

"We can walk a bit if you want."

"I really should get back to work."

He was pretty certain there was more to her subdued mood, but didn't ask, opening the passenger side door instead.

"Sorry about me and Garth back there," he said as he drove. The ranch was only about a fifteen-minute ride from town. Ty didn't intend to spend it all in silence. "We probably got a little carried away."

"It's understandable. All things considered, I think you two behaved quite well."

"Meaning he could have rubbed his championship belt buckle in my face?"

"That, and you could have retaliated with something equally petty. It had to be hard for you, sitting there, pretending you weren't bothered."

"Not as hard as watching him win last December. You have no idea how much I wanted his rope to land short that day."

"I do," she said absently, staring out the window. "I've watched men compete in roping for years, and known that no matter how good I was, no matter how hard I trained, I'd never be allowed to compete against them."

"Do you want to?"

"I do and have. In local jackpots where women are allowed to enter. But it's not the same as a professional rodeo."

"You're the exception. Not many women can go head-to-head with a man in this sport."

"Not yet."

Ty had to smile. He had no doubt if a member of the fairer sex could break into professional tie-down roping and pave the path for others, it would be Adele Donnelly.

Which was why he should probably give her every opportunity to help him with his problem.

"Selfishly," he admitted, "I'm glad you're not competing professionally."

"Why's that?"

"Because after the last few days, I'm thinking you're the only person who can help me." Her expression softened. So did a place in Ty's heart. "Unless you think it's a conflict of interest. Garth's your neighbor and friend."

"No conflict. He understands business is business."

"Just out of curiosity, have you ever beaten him in a one-on-one match?"

Her green eyes sparkled. "Frequently."

Ty burst into the first true belly laugh he'd had in months.

Moments later, they pulled up in front of the main lodge. He put the truck in Park but left the motor running.

"Thanks for the ride." Adele had her hand on the door handle but made no move to open it.

Was she also reluctant for their afternoon encounter to end?

"Thanks for letting me tag along during your lunch," Ty said.

"Are you serious? It couldn't have been that much fun for you."

"There were a few high spots." Like the seating arrangement.

"Next time I try to warn you—" she gave him a stern look "—pay attention."

"How 'bout next time we go to lunch just the two of us?"

The pause that followed lasted a little too long.

"I…uh…" She inhaled slowly and squared her shoulders. "Thank you for asking, but I don't date guests."

He hid his disappointment with a joke. "Is that one of those rules on the list I haven't read yet?"

"No, a personal one. Less messy that way when the guest leaves." Without another word, she pushed open the passenger door and hopped out, giving him the briefest of waves as she climbed the steps to the lodge entrance.

Her abrupt departure had Ty wondering if she'd been there and done that, and been left behind with a wounded heart.

And since he was leaving after the Buffalo Bill Cody Stampede, he certainly couldn't argue the logic behind her rule.

"WHAT'S WRONG?"

"Nothing, Pop." Adele had practically steamrolled her grandfather in her haste to get inside.

"You sure?" He studied her with concern.

She suspected he'd been watching her and Ty from the lobby window. "Absolutely. Why would you think there was?" She made her way around the registration counter and into the sanctuary of her small office.

Pop followed her, shutting the door behind them except for a narrow crack—just in case someone rang the bell.

"You're upset, and Ty looked none too happy, either."

She was never any good at hiding her feelings. "Reese and I ran into him at the feed store. He wound up joining us for lunch. Garth was there, too."

Pop harrumphed. "Guess I can't blame the boy for being a touch prickly after that."

"Actually, he handled it pretty well." She gave her grandfather a brief account of the lunch.

"Then why are you acting like you two tangled? Is he mad about taking the beginner class?"

"Not at all."

Pop lowered himself carefully into the office's single visitor chair, wincing slightly. When he was settled, he let out a long groan. "Damn hip's giving me fits today. Must be the rain."

It hadn't rained in over two weeks and didn't remotely look like it was going to anytime soon. "You taking the new medicine your doctor prescribed?"

"Yes, and quit nagging me." They both knew he should have hip-replacement surgery, but Pop insisted he wasn't going under the knife unless it was a matter of life and death.

Adele thought his refusal had more to do with her than any fear of hospitals. He worried about leaving the entire responsibility of the ranch and Cowboy College to her.

"And quit changing the subject," he scolded.

"What?"

"From you and Ty." His wizened features softened. "You like him."

Hoping to distract her grandfather, she shook her mouse and roused her computer from its hibernation. "He's just another guest."

"You don't date enough. You need to get out and have a little fun now and then."

"I went to lunch today."

"With friends. That's not the same."

No? It had felt a little like a date. Part of the time, anyway.

"You've haven't gone out with anyone since that Joe kid from Phoenix."

"Yes, I have."

"When? Who?"

Adele searched her brain and came up blank. "I'm sure I have."

Pop just grunted. His way of saying he was right.

She skimmed the contents of her email in-box, hating to agree with her grandfather. Joe had been her last relationship, and it could hardly be called serious. In fact, none of her relationships since she'd graduated high school had been serious.

"Ty's a good man," Pop continued, oblivious to her diversion tactics. "And he's taken a shine to you. I can tell by how he looks at you."

"I'm not interested in him except as a guest of this ranch and a student in my class."

Pop chuckled. "I guess that's why you were walking away from him earlier like a bee flew up the back of your shirt."

"I was not!" Adele's heated denial was met with another grunt. She clicked on the unopened emails in earnest, ignoring her grandfather.

He abruptly sobered. "Is it because he's a professional roper?"

She didn't respond.

"They're not all bad," his said, his gravelly voice dropping in pitch.

"I know." She turned and gave him a soft smile. "But men like you are the exception, not the rule."

"It's been a lot of years, Dellie. Time you moved on. Put your parents and what they did behind you."

"I don't want to talk about them. Not now."

"Just because your mom and dad were lousy parents is no reason to shut yourself off from love. I won't be around forever."

"Don't say that!"

"You need someone besides an old coot like me to dote on. A husband. Children."

"You're more than enough."

"Get to know Ty. Don't let him being a professional roper put you off."

Her grandfather had hit the nail on the head, and they both knew it. Work was simply an excuse. The main reason Adele didn't date much was because the vast majority of single men she met were unsuitable. Markton was a small town and the pickings slim to begin with. Making it worse, she didn't date employees or, as she'd told Ty, guests. Most others close to her age were either rodeo men or wannabe rodeo men.

After watching her parents destroy each other's lives *and* hers, she'd vowed not to become involved with anyone remotely connected with "the business."

"He's leaving in a few weeks, Pop. Even if I wanted to give him a shot, I wouldn't."

Before her grandfather could comment, the bell on the reception counter rang. Adele sprang to her feet and called, "Be right there."

As there were no new guests scheduled to arrive today,

she fully expected to see one of their current students standing at the counter, waiting to inform her of a need. At the sight of the lone, middle-aged woman wheeling one small suitcase, Adele came to a sudden stop, every thought flying instantly out of her head.

"Who is it?" Pop asked, hobbling out the office door. He, too, drew up short. But unlike Adele, he wasn't at a loss for words. "What the hell are you doing here?"

Adele wanted to know the same thing.

"Oh, Pop," Lani Donnelly chirped. "Is that anything to say to your daughter-in-law?" She turned to Adele, a too-sunny-to-be-real smile on her face. "Don't just stand there, baby girl, come give your mom a hug."

Chapter Four

Adele didn't move right away. She couldn't. Waves of hurt, anger and resentment hit her all at once and kept her rooted in place. She was vaguely aware of a guest coming out of the business center and leaving through the lobby entrance. She was *acutely* aware of her grandfather standing beside her. For a man with debilitating arthritis, his spine had snapped as straight and rigid as an iron bar.

"Please, baby girl." The pleading in her mother's voice penetrated the haze surrounding Adele.

She shored up her defenses, only to discover they weren't as impenetrable as she'd hoped. The sad and neglected little girl inside her still longed for the comfort of her mother's arms and the reassurance that she was loved.

"You okay, Dellie?"

At Pop's question, Adele glanced down, to see that her hands were shaking.

"I'm fine." And she was fine. Pulling herself together, she wrung the tremors from her fingers and raised her chin. No matter what, her mother wasn't going to hurt her again. Not after Adele had worked so hard to create a good life for herself.

"Hello, Mom."

They each took a step, then two, and met in the middle.

The hug Adele offered was reserved. Not so for her mother, who clung to her, then burst into great racking sobs.

Adele wanted to remained unaffected, but couldn't. Years of mistrust and disappointment, however, enabled her to extract herself from her mom's desperate grasp.

"What's wrong?" she asked.

"Nothing." Lani dabbed at her eyes. "I'm just so happy to see you. It's been months."

Almost two years, but Adele didn't bother correcting her.

They were about the same height and had once possessed similar figures. A weight loss during the last two years had left Lani painfully thin. Combined with her rough-around-the-edges appearance, she looked years older than her actual age. Her green eyes, highlighted with too much makeup, darted around the lobby with the desperation of a starving animal seeking its next meal.

"You should have called to let us know you were coming." Adele struggled to keep bitterness from creeping into her voice. Her mother may have hit rock bottom—the only reason Adele could think of to explain the unexpected visit—but that didn't erase all the bad memories.

"The battery died on my cell phone, and I haven't had a chance to replace it."

She was lying. Adele could feel it in her gut. Her mother had probably been unable to pay her bill without the help of a man.

Was else was she covering up?

"You look good, Pop." Lani smiled at Adele's grandfather, though her eyes were still filled with tears.

"You don't." Leave it to Pop to cut to the chase.

"This last year's been pretty hard on me." She swallowed.

He hobbled closer. "Is that why you just showed up out of the blue?"

"I, ah…"

One of the housekeeping staff entered the lobby pushing a cart laden with cleaning supplies, fresh linens and a vacuum. After a hesitant glance at them, she changed direction and went into the TV lounge to begin her work.

Lani rolled her suitcase from one side to the other. Uncertainty clouded her features, and she blurted, "I need a place to stay for a few days. Maybe a few weeks. I know it's a lot to ask, and Lord knows you have every reason turn me away, but I've got nowhere else to go. I'm willing to work off my room and board."

Adele took a step back, stunned by her mother's request. She didn't know what shocked her more—that her mother had the gall to show up unexpectedly and ask for a favor, a big one, or that she was actually willing to work. Lani hadn't voluntarily sought employment that Adele could recall.

"I don't know, Mom," she hedged. "We're kind of full right now."

"I can always sleep on your couch." The offhand remark came across as desperate. "You'll hardly know I'm there. I swear."

Adele almost choked. Her mother sleeping on her couch? Not in this lifetime. "Mom—"

"She can stay in room nine." Pop stepped around Adele.

She started to protest, not wanting her mother anywhere near Seven Cedars, only to shut her mouth when Pop took hold of her mother's suitcase.

"Come on, we'll take you there now. Dellie, grab the key and bring the golf cart around."

Though they ran the ranch together, it technically belonged to Pop. Adele might disagree with his decision, and would tell him later when they were in private, but the choice to let Lani stay was his to make.

She promptly spun on her heels and fled to her office without glancing back.

In addition to eighteen fully equipped cabins, they had a building with nine hotel-like rooms behind the main lodge. Number nine was on the end, the smallest of the rooms, and contained only a twin bed. For that reason, it was usually vacant. The room had been reserved for the upcoming weekend, but the guest had canceled.

It looked to Adele as if they wouldn't be renting number nine out even if they did get a last-minute request.

Removing the room and golf cart keys from a cabinet in her office, she exited the lodge through the kitchen's back door. The cart was parked under the large cedar tree where she'd last left it. She preferred driving ATVs, and used the golf cart mostly to transport guests and their luggage.

Not once had she imagined that her mother would ever be a guest.

The reason Lani had given for her unannounced visit didn't ring true. Though it was obvious she was in dire straits, Adele couldn't shake the sensation there was more going on than a run of bad luck. The question was what?

"Here we are," she announced when they pulled in front of room nine.

The three of them climbed out of the golf cart's one bench seat with noticeable relief. Pop insisted on removing Lani's bag from the back and wheeling it inside.

Adele opened the door to the room and handed the key to her mother with some reluctance.

"Thank you." Lani's voice cracked and her eyes welled with fresh tears. "Both of you."

"Come on, Dellie." Pop patted Adele's shoulder. "Let's give your mother a chance to get settled. Dinner starts at six," he told Lani. "If you want, after you eat, you can go to the kitchen and help the staff clean up. They're always shorthanded. Cook will tell you what to do."

Lani simply nodded and quickly shut the door behind them.

Her mother's hurry to be alone might be because she was going to start crying again, Adele thought, and her determination to remain unaffected battled with concern. Not caring was easier when Lani lived hundreds of miles away.

"She's in sorry shape," Pop said once they'd gotten back in the golf cart and were putt-putting down the road to the lodge.

"Is that why you agreed to let her stay on?"

"Partly."

"You're not usually such a softy. Especially where Mom's concerned."

In fact, the last time Lani had dropped Adele off at Seven Cedars, Pop had told Lani that Adele was staying with him for good and for her not to set foot on the place again. Adele had been fourteen at the time, but she remembered their huge fight as if it had been last week.

Lani had respected Pop's demand and never come back. Until today. Adele had finished out high school in Markton and then left for the University of Wyoming, seeing her mother only on occasion. When she'd returned to Seven Cedars after graduation, it had been like coming home.

"Maybe it's time to let bygones be bygones."

Adele wasn't so sure about that. There were too many bygones to let go of easily.

They reached the lodge, and she parked the golf cart under the same tree. Pop started to get out, but she stopped him with a hand on his arm.

"Considering the way Mom's always treated you, you have no reason to show her the tiniest kindness, much less forgiveness."

Pop sighed, removed an unused toothpick from his front shirt pocket and stuck it in his mouth. "Your mom's made a lot of mistakes in her life, but she did one thing right. For which I'm very grateful."

"What's that?"

"She gave me and your grandmother legal guardianship of you back when you were fifteen. She didn't have to do that."

"She gave you guardianship?" Adele's jaw went slack.

"Your dad signed off, too."

"Why didn't you tell me?"

"Lani didn't want you to think your parents had abandoned you."

"But they did," Adele insisted. A year after that dreadful day and terrible fight.

"Depends, I guess, on how you look at it. They weren't such bad parents that they didn't realize you needed a real home and someone to take care of you."

With that, her grandfather left Adele sitting alone in the golf cart, reeling from her second shock that day.

All this time, she'd believed her grandparents had wanted her. Had fought to have her.

Instead, her mother and father had simply handed her over, like an old set of golf clubs or a broken TV.

Worse, none of them, not even Pop, had had the decency to tell her.

A WALL OF CHILLY AIR greeted Ty the moment he stepped outside his cabin. For a moment he considered driving to the barn, then decided a brisk walk would jump-start his sluggish system.

Normally an early riser, he was up and at it even earlier than usual thanks to a restless night. The reason for his tossing and turning was the same as his trip to the barn at half past the crack of dawn. Hamm hadn't been himself yesterday and appeared to be favoring his right front leg. After having his other horse suffer a debilitating injury, Ty was cautious when it came to Hamm. Some might say overly cautious.

In his mind, he had good reason. He couldn't afford another setback. Not this far into the rodeo season.

He briefly considered stopping at the dining hall and grabbing a cup of coffee. They weren't scheduled to start serving for another twenty minutes, but as Stick had promised on Ty's first day, Cook was very accommodating to the guests. Ty's concern for Hamm took precedence, however, and he made straight for the main barn.

The ranch hands had just begun feeding when he got there. While Hamm was happy to see him, he was more interested in breakfast. The big horse paced back and forth in anticipation as the feed wagon moved slowly down the aisle. Ty used the opportunity to observe the worrisome front leg.

Hamm grabbed a bite of hay even before the thick flake was dropped into his feed trough. He then ignored the hay in favor of the grain that followed, snorting lustily.

Now that he was standing still, Ty entered the stall and ran his hand over Hamm's front leg, paying particular attention to the knee area. It looked normal. No swelling or bruising. Next, he hefted Hamm's foot and, using a penknife, checked under the shoe. Hamm didn't so much as blink during the entire examination. Could be because he was fine. Could be because he was too busy eating to care about a little tenderness.

After another minute and a pat to Hamm's rump, Ty decided to get that cup of coffee in the dining hall and come back when the horse had finished eating. Then he'd take him to the round pen, work him a few minutes and get a better look at the leg, just to be one hundred percent sure.

Maybe he'd ask Adele to join him and give an opinion. She had a good eye when it came to both riders and their horses. It also gave him an excuse to see her. She'd missed dinner the previous evening. He assumed whatever work she'd mentioned at lunch with Garth and Reese must have kept her busy.

In the dining hall, the aroma of breakfast proved too tempting to resist. When one of the waitstaff brought out a tray of freshly baked cinnamon rolls, two somehow made it onto Ty's plate before he realized it. He no sooner sat down to eat then he noticed Adele cutting across the large and noisy room toward the kitchen.

Her gaze didn't waver from the floor in front of her, which was certainly strange. She was often in a hurry, especially in the mornings. But she always had a wave or smile for the guests. Ty's curiosity lasted only until she disappeared behind the kitchen's double doors and he took his first bite of the warm and gooey cinnamon roll.

Thirty minutes and one full stomach later, Ty was back in the barn. Haltering Hamm, he led the horse to the round pen. There, he put him through his paces, mostly satisfied that whatever had been bothering him yesterday, if anything, was no longer an issue. Nonetheless, he'd watch Hamm closely during morning class.

After walking him several times around all three barns to cool him down, Ty returned the horse to his stall. Class didn't start until nine, leaving a good hour to kill. Not really enough time to go back to his cabin. Ty supposed he could grab another cup of coffee in the dining hall.

It was then he saw Adele heading into the small barn where she and Pop kept their private stock. Even at a distance, she still appeared distracted. Then it hit Ty. Her mare—Crackers?—was due to deliver any day. That could explain Adele's unusual behavior, especially if there was a problem with the birth.

On impulse, Ty followed her into the barn and, as he'd guessed, found her at Crackers's stall. She had her arms resting on the door and was staring, unseeing, at the mare and newborn foal standing by her side.

"She had the baby," Ty said, approaching quietly.

Adele started at the sight of him but recovered quickly. "Sometime last night. A filly."

The foal, initially wary, relaxed enough around her human visitors to begin nursing. Ty noticed she stood straight and that her weight was good. A blanket of white spots covered her hind end. "She looks healthy."

"Seems to be. The vet is coming out later this morning to check on her."

"Nice markings, too. Going to be an Appaloosa like the mare."

For the first time that morning Adele looked Ty fully in the face. He was momentarily taken aback by the dark smudges beneath her eyes. She hadn't slept well, either.

"Are you okay?" The question slipped out automatically.

"I'm fine." She tried to smile, but it was lopsided. Then it wobbled.

"Adele."

All at once, she let out a sob. Her attempts to swallow a second one failed.

Ty responded without thinking. Reaching for her, he pulled her into his arms.

Her immediate response was to stiffen and draw back, as if she suddenly realized what she'd done.

"It's okay," he murmured, and she relented, burying her face in his shirt.

"I'm sorry."

"Don't be." He patted her back.

Normally, Ty avoided crying women, or at least kept his distance. Like a lot of his male brethren, he supposed, he didn't know what to say or how to act. His confusion was ten times worse if he was the cause of the woman's distress.

For some reason, it felt different with Adele. And not just because he was relatively certain someone else was responsible for her being upset.

He guessed she didn't often let down her guard. That she did so in front of him, allowed him to offer her comfort, showed just how much she trusted him and—was it possible?—liked him.

Tilting her head back, she looked up at him, blinking back the last of her tears. "I can't imagine what you think of me." Her damp lashes had formed tiny spikes that surrounded her liquid green eyes.

Ty was captivated. Driven by a force he couldn't resist, he lowered his head and pressed his mouth to hers.

Just one taste. One tiny sip of her petal-soft lips. He wanted more. Any man in his right mind would. But even this infinitesimal piece of heaven was more than he was entitled to. Whatever upset Adele had left her vulnerable, and he wasn't one to take advantage of that.

With a last featherlight brush of his lips against hers, he drew back—only to have Adele stop him with a tug on his jacket. Clutching the thick fabric in her hands, she drew him closer.

Clearly, her emotions had gotten the better of her, and she wasn't thinking straight. If Ty were a gentleman, he'd tactfully disengage himself from her embrace. At the first touch of her tongue to his, however, *his* emotions got the better of *him*. When he heard Adele's soft moan and felt her arms circle his neck, he was a lost man.

The longer their kiss lasted, the more difficult it became for him to restrain himself. She felt exquisite, a maddening combination of taut muscles and soft curves. She tasted even better, like biting into another one of those freshly baked cinnamon rolls.

Just when the last of his restraint threatened to snap, she

broke off their kiss, stepped back and placed her palms on his chest. Both of them were breathing hard. Her tears, he noted, had dried.

"Adele."

She shook her head and shushed him with a finger to her lips.

He hoped she wasn't planning on apologizing, because he sure wasn't sorry about what had happened. No way.

"If you're—"

She silenced him with another head shake, and cut her eyes to a place just over his shoulder.

All at once the hairs on Ty's neck rose, and he sensed they weren't alone.

"Shoot," he muttered.

"Yeah," Adele agreed.

A moment later Ty heard a loud voice say, "What in tarnation is going on here?"

He turned, expecting to see Pop.

What he didn't expect was the woman accompanying him, her face an older, harsher version of Adele's.

Grinning saucily, she gave Ty a thorough once-over. "Well, ain't you something."

Behind him, Adele softly swore.

"Is she your mother?"

"Yes."

"You look kind of alike."

Adele grumbled to herself. If Ty had so easily spotted the resemblance, so would everyone at the ranch.

"She here for a visit?"

"Sort of." After only two meals, dinner last night and breakfast this morning, Lani was fast becoming useful in the kitchen—a surprising turn of events that didn't make Adele one bit happy.

"How long is she staying?"

"Not long." *Better not be.*

"I'm sorry about putting you in a, ah, compromising situation back there," he said.

They were walking toward the main arena, though walking was a loose term. Adele was practically running, and Ty, even with his six-foot-plus height, was forced to take long strides in order to keep up with her. She didn't want him accompanying her, but after getting caught kissing him, by her grandfather and mother, it didn't seem fair or right telling him to beat it.

"You weren't the only one participating in…what happened."

He chuckled. "For which I'm damn glad."

"I shouldn't have—" She swallowed to clear the lump in her throat. Allowing her emotions to run amok was what had landed her in this jam in the first place. Why had her mother chosen now to show up? Why had she shown up at all? And why did Ty have to be such a good kisser? "I shouldn't have allowed things to go as far as they did."

"What now?" There was a hint of amusement in his voice. "Are we going to pretend we didn't kiss?"

Adele would like nothing better. However, she was relatively certain she'd remember kissing Ty for the rest of her life. In vivid detail.

"I think we should try."

He laughed out loud.

She frowned and trudged ahead.

They reached the main arena and went in through the gate. Beginner class was scheduled to start soon. Some of the students were already warming up their horses in the adjoining, smaller arena.

Ty followed Adele to the holding pen that housed the calves, and busied himself checking on the gate while she reviewed a list of instructions with the wrangler. When they were done, she made an effort to shake Ty by suggesting, "Go ahead and saddle up if you want. Class starts soon."

"What about your horse?"

"Stick's supposed to be taking care of that for me." Fingers crossed, the kid was doing his job. Adele dreaded going into the barn, just in case Pop and her mother were still there.

And speaking of Pop and her mother, just what the heck were they doing together? In her embarrassment and haste to get away, Adele had forgotten to ask. Anybody else and she'd have believed they were wanting a peek at the new filly. But Pop and Lani didn't take strolls around the ranch together.

As soon as class was over, she intended to find her grandfather and pester him until she got an answer.

But before then, she was going to have to relieve herself of Ty's company. Covering the last item on her list with the wrangler, she left him to join Ty at the gate. Subtleties hadn't worked, so she tried being direct.

"You need to leave now," she told him. "To get ready."

"I will leave." He flashed her that killer sexy grin again. "As soon as you agree to meet me after class. We need to talk."

She cast a furtive glance at the wrangler, who appeared to be occupied with his task of separating the calves, but was probably hanging on their every word. "I thought we agreed to pretend that didn't happen," she hissed.

"I meant about your mother."

She drew back, completely caught off guard. "Hell no."

His grin widened. "You owe me that much. For allowing things to go as far as they did," he said, quoting her.

"You started it."

"I admit, I'm a man and a pushover when it comes to a crying woman."

She glanced over her shoulder at the wrangler and grimaced. How long until this piece of juicy gossip made the rounds of the ranch?

She conceded to Ty's request only to get rid of him. "I'll meet you in the barn office at eleven-thirty."

"I have a better idea."

She didn't like the glint in his eyes.

"Take me on a tour of the ranch."

"A tour?"

"Our horses will already be saddled. And I've been wanting to see the place since I arrived."

"Fine," Adele reluctantly agreed.

She just wished part of her wasn't thrilled and eagerly anticipating a ride with him.

Chapter Five

Ty collected Hamm from where he'd left him tethered in the barn. Tired of standing, the horse practically knocked Ty over in his haste to get outside. Ty didn't mind. He admired the horse's natural athleticism and endless energy. If they could just get in sync like him and his last horse, they'd be unbeatable.

A quick stop at the water trough proved to be a waste of time. Hamm wasn't interested in drinking. He did no more than splash water with his snout, reminding Ty of that old saying about leading a horse to water.

Adele hadn't specified a meeting place, so Ty led Hamm toward the open area in front of the barns, figuring he'd see her eventually. He ran into two of his classmates near the smaller practice arena—Mike and his wife, the woman who talked a lot during class. Thankfully, her name came to Ty a split second before she hailed him.

"Hey there, Ty."

"How you doing, Sandy? Mike? Getting some extra practice in?"

The couple was taking turns tossing ropes at a stationary practice dummy.

"Yeah." Mike grinned sheepishly. "I can't quite figure out what Adele was trying to show us this morning." He wound his rope into a loose coil.

Sandy laughed. "I can't figure out *any* of it. But it's still a hoot." Of the two of them, she was the less serious and the less coordinated. That didn't stop her from enjoying herself, a trait Ty admired.

He wondered what it would be like to have the kind of affectionate and supportive relationship Mike and Sandy did. He met a lot of women on the rodeo circuit, but most were either competitors focused on their own careers or buckle bunnies with a personal agenda that didn't appeal to Ty.

Like Adele's mother.

He hadn't said anything to Adele, but he'd recognized Lani the moment he saw her. No surprise, really. Rodeo folk might be spread from one corner of the globe to the other, but they were also a small community unto themselves. Everybody knew everybody, or at least had heard of them. Lani had been a member of the rodeo world far too long for Ty not to have run into her now and again through the years.

He was no authority on reading people, but he'd wager Adele wasn't close to her, judging from the look she'd given Lani earlier.

"You think you could watch me throw a few and see what I'm doing wrong?" Mike asked.

"If you don't mind," Sandy hurriedly added. "We don't want to keep you."

"Sure. Why not?" Ty was early and Adele was nowhere in sight. "I can spare a few minutes."

"Taking a ride?" The woman's attention strayed to Hamm, who was pawing the ground impatiently.

"Thinking about it."

They didn't need to know he was touring the ranch with Adele. And if she failed to show up as promised…well, he could always ride around the ranch by himself.

Tethering Hamm to a nearby post, he perused the open area one last time. No Adele.

"Go ahead." Ty turned his attention to Mike. "Show me what you've got."

The man raised his arm over his head and swung his rope in a circle before tossing it at the fake cow head. The lasso just missed.

"Dang." Mike shook his head in disgust. "I think I might need glasses."

"Do it again." Ty studied him closely while he repeated the exercise, and came to the same conclusion he had the first time. "This time, try shifting your weight just slightly to your left foot."

Mike did and his next toss landed where it should, if a little lopsided.

"All right!" He beamed.

"One more time."

Mike threw the rope again with the same results.

"Good job." Sandy clapped.

"Can you feel the difference?" Ty asked.

"Yeah." Mike rolled his right shoulder as if testing it.

"Your center of gravity was off."

He laughed and shook his head. "Sounds too simple."

Ty didn't comment. He was too busy replaying his statement to Mike over and over in his head.

Center of gravity. He should have picked up on that in the beginners' class, when Adele had had him riding with his eyes closed. He'd repeated the exercise several times since, until he felt he knew which way Hamm would turn even before the horse did. But Ty hadn't paid attention to his center of gravity while throwing the rope.

Another point-two second gain in his time was staring him smack in the face.

What was wrong with him that he hadn't seen these mistakes before? He was hardly a novice. Blaming four years of competing exclusively on one horse was beginning to sound like a lame excuse. In reality, Ty's inflated ego and over-abundance of confidence had gotten in the way, convincing him he needed to retrain Hamm rather than retrain himself.

While Ty was absorbed with this latest revelation, two things happened. Mike continued to throw more successful tosses and Adele emerged from the barn astride the paint mare she'd usually rode.

"Hey, I've got to go," he told Mike and Sandy.

"See you at dinner?" Hope shone in Sandy's eyes.

"You bet."

"Thanks for your help." Mike extended his hand, and Ty shook it.

"My pleasure."

And it was. Ty had enjoyed giving Mike pointers. On top of that, he'd learned something valuable about himself.

From the corner of his eye he spotted Adele riding in his direction. Memories of their kiss returned, and he forgot all about Mike and Sandy and roping and pretty much every-thing else except her.

Riding to meet her halfway, he ignored the stares of nearby wranglers. He couldn't be the first guest Adele had taken on a tour.

"Where would you like to start?" she asked, as Hamm tried to make friends with the mare by stretching his head out and sniffing her. The mare responded by pinning her ears back and playing hard to get.

"How far is Little Twister Creek?" Other than that one afternoon in Markton, and walking to and from his cabin, Ty had seen almost nothing of the countryside.

"A few miles. More than we can fit in this afternoon."

"Then how 'bout just around the ranch?"

She took him through three gates. At each one, she opened the latch and swung the gate wide without dismounting. When they were both through, she pushed it shut and relatched it, also without dismounting.

"You've been working with her," Ty said as they rode across the big pasture.

"Bella can be a bit flighty, but she's learning." Adele nudged the mare into a slow trot, but not before he glimpsed her eyes warming with pleasure at his compliment.

"How long have you had her?"

"A month or so. I'm training her for a client."

"You do that often?"

"Sometimes. Depends on the horse and the client."

With Adele riding in front, they picked their way along a winding trail toward a manmade stock pond.

"Did your grandfather raise cattle long?"

"A lot of years. He bought Seven Cedars back in the sixties after he retired from rodeoing. The ranch isn't as large as some of the other ones in the area, but he did pretty well until about eight years ago."

"What happened? The economy?"

Adele hesitated briefly before answering. "My grandmother died."

"I'm sorry."

"It was hard on Pop."

It had been hard on Adele, too. Ty could tell. "When did he lose his thumb?"

"Oh, gosh, over forty years ago. That was the reason he quit rodeoing."

"A roping accident?"

"Yeah. His thumb got twisted in the rope. The horse went one way and the calf another."

"Some guys still compete without a thumb." The loss of a digit wasn't entirely uncommon with ropers.

"Pop says he was ready to retire, anyway."

"Well, this is a nice place to retire to."

Winged insects, buzzing in the warm midday sun, flitted over the pond's glassy surface, dipping occasionally to take a sip of moisture. Suddenly, there was a small splash in the center of the pond. Ty had the urge to bring his rod and reel another day and go after one of those bass making a meal of the flying insects.

"So, when did you come here to live?"

"I visited Pop off and on ever since I was a kid. We didn't start Cowboy College until after I earned my business degree." More hesitancy before answering. Whatever else there was to the story, she wasn't saying.

They'd passed the pond and were now on a slightly wider trail that allowed Ty and Adele to ride side by side. The arrangement also pleased Hamm, who continued trying to win Bella over with little love nips. Unfortunately for him, she remained indifferent.

"I like what I do." Adele gave Ty a shy smile. Her eyes, however, were lit up, their brilliance captivating him. "Technically, it's work, but most days it feels a whole lot more like playing."

"Can't blame you. This is a great place to work. Wish I'd thought of opening a roping school."

"We're a little remote for some people."

"That's what makes it so nice. I could see myself living here." His gaze traveled to the distant mountains, their tops peeking through a blanket of wispy white clouds.

"Not some big fancy ranch?"

"If you're referring to your neighbors, no." He gave her a wry smile. "Though I admit I wouldn't mind heading over to Garth's place one day just to check it out." His grin widened. "Maybe you can take me."

"We'll see." Her expression instantly closed.

Had he pushed her too far, reminding her of their kiss

earlier? He wanted to talk about it, but gut instinct told him she wasn't ready.

After several minutes of riding in silence, Ty asked, "Do you have any other family in the area?"

"You mean besides my mother?"

He didn't react to the bitterness in Adele's voice. "Here or anywhere."

"My dad's in Lubbock, Texas. He moved there about fifteen years ago after marrying my stepmom."

"Did your dad rodeo, too?"

"For a while. He quit when I was young."

The careful answers Adele delivered told Ty more about her and her childhood than the sparse and rehearsed information she provided.

"Do you see much of them?"

"No," she answered, with a finality that implied the subject was closed.

He took the hint and gave her some space.

"I read somewhere you're from Santa Fe," she said after a few minutes. "Is your family still there?"

"Most of them. A few years ago my folks sold their place and bought a smaller one closer to town."

"Were they rodeo people, too?"

"No. Dad's a mortgage broker and Mom's a real estate agent. They've always ridden, so we had horses growing up."

"How did you start rodeoing?"

"Friends. I got serious in high school. About that and football. I had trouble deciding between the two after graduation."

"What made you pick rodeoing?"

"I won All Around Cowboy at the National High School Finals Rodeo my senior year. I was hooked after that. Luckily, my family's supported me or I wouldn't have made it. Financially or emotionally."

Rodeoing wasn't cheap, and until he'd started winning, Ty, like a lot of competitors, had depended on his family to supplement his income.

"Losing the Iron Grip Ropes sponsorship cost me more than a career opportunity," he continued. "I was counting on the money that came with it to pay back my parents."

"Does your younger sister rodeo?" Adele asked. "You said she wanted to learn to rope."

"She tried barrel racing for a while, but didn't stick with it. My older sister's a single mom with two little girls."

"That must be rough."

"She's doing okay. She has her real estate license and works with our mom. I keep a fifth-wheel trailer at her place and stay there when I'm not traveling. The rent helps. She and my mom have been struggling these last couple years, what with the real estate market being so up and down. Mom's worried about keeping the business afloat. And Dad's job is just crazy. Changing every day."

"I bet."

Ty pushed down on his right stirrup, adjusted his saddle, which had shifted slightly, and said determinedly, "Another reason I don't intend to lose the championship a second time."

"Is your little sister coming out?" Adele asked.

"She'd like to, but probably not. Right now, she's doing an internship with a large animal surgery center."

"She's a vet?"

"Officially, not until next month, when she graduates school." A wave of nostalgia struck Ty, and he made a mental note to call his family tonight.

"Hey, check that out." Adele reined in her mare and pointed to a cluster of trees. Behind the grove, the land sloped down into a small draw. "Is that what I think it is?"

Ty stopped beside her and peered into the trees. He im-

mediately spotted the small face staring at them from between low hanging branches. "One of yours?"

"Has to be. Two head went missing a couple weeks ago,
when they got through a hole in the fence during the night.
I figured they'd gotten lost or…" She grimaced.

"At least one of them has escaped being a meal."

"You game?" Challenge glinted in her green eyes.

"Are you kidding? I'm always game."

They both untied their lassos from their saddles. The calf,
about forty yards away, observed them warily.

All at once Adele shouted, "Go," and the chase was on.

ADELE PRESSED HER LEGS into Bella's flanks. The mare immediately went from a standstill to a full gallop. With Ty
right beside her, they bore down on the lone calf. Because
Bella was smaller and quicker than Hamm, Adele took the
header position. Ty remained a length behind, in the heeler
position. Team roping wasn't her specialty, but she'd done
enough of it through the years to hold her own, even with
someone of Ty's caliber.

Considering they were unaccustomed to roping as a team,
they worked well together, automatically anticipating and
compensating for each other's moves. The calf, spooked into
action, had spun sideways and was hightailing it through the
trees as fast as his stubby legs could carry him. He headed
toward the narrow draw, bawling loudly, then dropped out of
sight beneath the rim. Adele and Ty bent low on their horses'
necks and flew down the side of the draw.

An exuberant "Yee-haw" erupted from her throat before
she even realized it, then "Come on, Bella," when the calf
unexpectedly cut to the right.

Her mare's front hooves hit the ground at the base of the
draw like a ton of bricks. Adele hung on, the resulting jar to
her system acting like a shot of adrenaline. A quick glance

over her shoulder assured her Ty was having no trouble keeping up. Pure unabashed joy lit his face. Her own jaw hurt from smiling so hard.

Chunks of dirt exploded from beneath their horses' hooves as they gained ground on the tiring calf. In the next few seconds, they closed the distance to mere feet. Sensing the moment was right, they reached for their lassos. Adele threw hers at the calf's head a heartbeat ahead of Ty. He aimed his for the animal's rear feet. Her lasso landed where it should, around the horns. Ty's didn't, falling instead to the ground.

The calf jumped and twisted, shaking his head and fighting to break free. Adele reined Bella to a stop and backed her up to bring the line taut. Ty collected his rope and wound it into a coil, a sour expression on his face. He obviously didn't like missing his throws.

Giving their heavily breathing horses a rest, they dismounted. By then, the calf stood quietly, nostrils flaring and flanks heaving, resigned to the fact that his wandering days were at an end.

"Don't look so miserable, buddy." Adele removed her rope, wrapped it around the calf's neck and tied a knot, one designed for safely leading him back home. "We just saved your life. With all the wolves, bears and mountain lions in this area, I can't believe you've survived this long."

Feeling Ty's gaze on her, she looked up, momentarily stuck by what she was doing here with him. She didn't act spontaneously. She certainly didn't tear across the countryside chasing down calves with men she hardly knew. On a bet, for crying out loud.

She didn't normally kiss them, either, but she'd done all those things with Ty, in the same day, no less.

When he didn't say anything, she asked, "What?"

"You look happy."

"That was fun." Okay, she'd confessed, and the ground hadn't opened up to swallow her whole.

"You should do it more often."

"Catch stray calves?" She laughed.

"Have fun. And laugh." His brown eyes bored into hers, studying but not judging. "I'm thinking you don't do either enough."

According to her grandfather, she also didn't date enough. Had she really become that much of a stick-in-the-mud? And when had it happened? Adele didn't like the momentary glimpse of herself through another's eyes.

"Sorry about missing earlier," he said with what might have been embarrassment.

"I doubt that happens much with you."

"No. And I'm not sure why it happened now."

"Mind if I make an observation?"

"That's why I came here."

"Hamm takes aim with his right eye."

"He does?" Ty pushed back his cowboy hat, scratched his head. "I must have watched a half-dozen films of myself on Hamm, and I never noticed."

"You might not if you weren't looking."

He closed his eyes, his brow furrowed in concentration. Adele imagined he was mentally replaying his run, feeling the barely noticeable tug on the reins as Hamm turned his head to the left in order to see better. Realizing he should be loosening the reins and shifting his weight.

"You're right." He opened his eyes and grinned. "You can spot me any day."

Pleasure coursed through her. Satisfaction at helping a student improve—that was her job, after all. But something else. Something having to do entirely with Ty.

"We'd better get this little fellow back home," she said, to cover her sudden rush of emotions. Leading the calf behind her, she mounted Bella and dallied the rope around her saddle horn, glad to be returning home. Ty had an infuriating way of unsettling her.

He also mounted. "Maybe we can finish our tour of the ranch tomorrow."

Of course he would remember.

"We'll see."

Adele clucked to Bella, who obediently began walking out. Ty fell in step beside her, and the calf brought up the rear, not liking the rope, but having no choice in the matter. Soon enough, he settled down.

Their slow climb up and out of the draw wasn't nearly as thrilling as galloping down into it had been.

At the top, Adele pointed to a trail. "This one circles back around to the east pasture."

They slowed their pace to accommodate the calf's exhausted state and recalcitrant nature.

"What made your grandfather pick this place?" As they meandered along, he took in the rolling green landscape and startling blue skies.

"Pop was friends with Garth's grandfather. He told Pop about the vacant land bordering his ranch being for sale. Pop and my grandmother had visited a few times and liked the area. They wound up buying the land sight unseen."

"My mother would never recommend that to a client, but in your grandfather's case, he made a wise decision."

"He and my grandmother lived in a camper for six months while the original ranch house was being constructed. The crew barely finished before the first snow hit. Lucky for Pop, because Grandma might have left him otherwise."

"Can't say I'd have blamed her. It must get pretty cold here in winter."

"Twenty degrees on a warm day. But it's really pretty in a primitive way."

"I'd like to see that."

"There's some good skiing up north."

"I was thinking more along the lines of sitting in front of a roaring fire." Ty's eyes locked with hers. "Snuggled under a blanket."

"Oh." Adele required several seconds and a fair amount of throat clearing to recover. "Pop, um, built the stock barn and the main arena the following spring."

Ty didn't resist her efforts to return the conversation to their earlier topic. Thank goodness.

"When did you start Cowboy College?"

"About seven years ago. We began with the main lodge and the inn building. The cabins came later, a few each year as we grew."

"That was quite a risk you took."

"Pop's the one who took the risk. He invested his life's savings in Cowboy College. And it's paid off."

"You've worked hard." Ty sent her an admiring glance.

Adele waited for the wariness that usually overcame her when a man showed signs of interest. Only it didn't happen, and she couldn't help wondering why. Ty was a poor choice for any romantic entanglements, short-term or long. She should be doubly cautious.

Then it occurred to her that maybe his leaving soon was the reason she felt less on guard. No way would she be stupid enough to let herself fall for him, only to be hurt later. She was too smart for that. Too careful. Knowing she'd keep her heart under lock and key allowed her to let loose a little. Laugh. Chase calves.

Because he was…safe.

She relaxed, her newfound discovery giving her confidence—until he looked at her with a much too endearing expression on his handsome face.

"Do you like to fish?"

"I used to. Pop would take me sometimes when I was young."

"You want to go one day? I hear the fly-fishing's pretty good at Little Twister Creek."

"I, ah…" Feeling safe with Ty—make that *semi*safe—didn't mean she was ready for a date. "We're so busy right now, I really can't afford the time off."

"Well, if you wind up with a free morning or afternoon, let me know. The invitation's always open."

For just a moment, she indulged her imagination and pictured the two of them whiling away a lazy afternoon on the banks of Little Twister Creek. It could be—here was that word again—*fun*.

The discussion changed to roping and the upcoming Buffalo Bill Cody Stampede Rodeo. Ty gave his opinion on who he considered his toughest competition, which included her neighbor, Garth Maitland.

"Will you come watch?" he asked.

"I wouldn't miss it. We usually take a group of students along, too."

They reached the first gate, and once again, Adele opened it without dismounting. When she went to close it, Ty stopped her.

"Can I try?"

"Sure." She backed Bella up to give him and Hamm room. When he succeeded in closing the gate with no problem, Adele tipped her head appreciatively. "Nicely done."

"We're learning to work together, too."

The calf abruptly let out a noisy bawl.

"Guess he's glad to be home." She started forward. This time the animal followed willingly, in a hurry to be reunited with his pals crowding together at the fence in order to get a look at him.

"He's not the only eager one." Ty had to hold Hamm back from running a race to the barn.

They rode first to the calf pen and dropped off their charge in the care of the assistant stock manager, then walked their horses to the barns. When they reached the place where they would separate—he was going to the main barn, she to the smaller one—they stopped as if on cue.

"Thanks for the tour," he said, with that sexy half smile she'd seen countless times in magazines, on cable television and the big screen at rodeos. Only this time, the smile was directed at her. "I know I kind of tricked you into it."

"Kind of?"

"But if we hadn't gone, we wouldn't have found the calf, and you wouldn't have shown me how Hamm takes aim."

Or had such a good time team roping, she thought.

"I might have shown you. Eventually," she said with a grin, and quickly escaped to the quiet seclusion of the barn, where she could give her wildly beating heart a chance to slow.

Who was she fooling, thinking Ty Boudeau was safe? He was as dangerous as they came, especially to someone like her, a country girl with little experience around men like him.

Just as Adele was latching the door to Bella's stall, a woman's voice sounded from behind her.

"That's one fine looking cowboy."

Her mother, of course, would notice, having made fine looking cowboys the focus of her entire adult life. Still, Adele couldn't disagree.

"I suppose."

"He likes you." Lani accompanied Adele to the tack room in the center of the barn, where she hung the mare's bridle on a peg. "You like him, too."

"He's a student, Mom." Adele bristled, the remark hitting too close to home. "And a guest of the ranch. That's all."

She walked away, well aware that her reaction was over the top. But hell would freeze over before she'd discuss Ty with her mother.

"Wait," Lani called after her, struggling a little to catch up, her breathing shallow and raspy.

Smoking and hard living did that to a person.

Only now that Adele thought about it, she hadn't seen her mother with a cigarette or a drink since she'd arrived. Knowing her, she'd probably gotten better at hiding her vices.

"You have every right to be mad at me," Lani said.

The admission was the last thing Adele had expected to issue from her mother's lips. Ever. It brought her to a standstill.

"I have to get to the office," she said, fighting an unwelcome rush of emotion. "Some new guests are arriving this afternoon."

"I'd really like to talk to you."

Adele inched away. "Not now."

"You can't keep avoiding me."

"Why not, Mom?" She spun around. "You avoided me for years."

"I guess I deserve that."

Whatever else Lani intended to say was cut short by Stick barreling down the barn aisle toward them, his shirttail flying and his freckled face flushed beet-red from exertion.

"Adele, Adele! Come quick."

"What's wrong?" she asked, alarmed by the sight of him.

"It's Pop," he said, holding his sides. "He fell. And he's hurt bad."

Chapter Six

Adele reached her grandfather first, ahead of Stick and her mother. He lay flat on his back on the muddy ground near the water trough. Ty, of all people, was kneeling beside him. Where had he come from and how did he get there ahead of her?

"Pop, are you okay?" Breathless from running, Adele bent at the waist and braced her hands on her thighs.

"I'll live," he muttered, his chest rising and falling.

"You're lucky you didn't crack your head open on the trough."

Pop groaned when Ty lifted him to a sitting position.

"Careful," she warned. "He may have broken something." She thought of Pop's hip, the one that was always giving him trouble.

"Quit being such a mother hen."

She ignored her grandfather's comment and came closer, intent on verifying for herself his claim of being uninjured. "What happened?"

"That damn spigot's been leaking for days. Figured I'd fix it." His face twisted into a painful grimace when Ty stood and hauled him to his feet. Putting out a hand in protest, Pop said, "Give me a minute, would you?" in a strained voice.

"Sorry." Ty relaxed his grip but didn't let go.

Good thing, because Pop swayed unsteadily.

"Maybe we shouldn't have moved him just yet." Adele hovered, the mud her grandfather had slipped in pulling at her boots and sucking her in. It also covered her grandfather from head to toe, probably soaking through his clothes.

Several more guests and the assistant barn manager had come over to investigate, crowding around them. Their anxious chatter and proximity grated on Adele's already frayed nerves.

"Can everyone step back, please. He needs room."

"Don't mind her," Pop told Ty. "The least little thing sets her in a tizzy."

"This is hardly the least little thing," she retorted hotly. "You're hurt."

"I'm fine."

"Can you walk?"

"I'm getting to it."

Distressed by the sight of her grandfather's ashen complexion and his attempts to dismiss what could be a serious injury, she confronted Stick. "Why didn't you help him when he fell?"

"Ty got there first. Pop didn't want to tell you, but Ty—"

"You weren't going to tell me?" Adele demanded of her grandfather.

He shot her an isn't-it-obvious-why look. "Don't know what all the fuss is about. I just had the wind knocked out of me."

"And now you can hardly stand, much less walk."

"The hell I can't walk." He shook off Ty's hold.

Adele watched, biting her lower lip. To her relief, Pop didn't topple, but neither did he attempt to take a step. She sent Ty a worried glance behind her grandfather's back.

He nodded reassuringly, letting her know he wasn't moving from Pop's side.

The seconds dragged by. Finally, Pop attempted a step—

and his knees went right out from under him. Ty easily caught him when he pitched forward. Thank goodness.

Adele panicked at the sight of her grandfather's pale face. "I think we should call 911."

"You'll do no such thing."

"You need to see a doctor. You could have broken a rib or sprained an ankle."

He made a sound of disgust.

"She has a point," Ty said.

"That's enough out of the both of you."

"I have an idea." Adele turned to Stick. "Find Mike Scolari and bring him here. His cabin number is fourteen. If he's not there, go to the office and have Gayle pull up his reservation record. His cell phone will be listed under guest information."

"Mike? The husband of Sandy, who talks nonstop?" Ty asked.

"Yes." Adele nodded, her attention remaining on her grandfather.

"What can he do?"

"Mike's a doctor."

"You're kidding!"

"I don't need a doctor," Pop groused.

"Yes, you do," Adele insisted. To Stick, she said, "Hurry."

"Take one step and you're fired."

Stick's gaze traveled between Adele and her grandfather. "Sorry, Pop," he said, and dashed off to do her bidding.

Smart kid.

"What's the matter with you?" she asked Ty, who continued to gape at her.

"I just can't believe Mike's a doctor."

"Because his wife talks a lot?"

"Because roping is a dangerous sport. I can't believe he'd risk injuring his hands."

"Mike's a pediatrician."

Wrong thing to say.

Pop exploded. "I ain't letting no kiddie doctor examine me."

"Then I'm taking you to the emergency room."

"The hell you are."

"Pop, please." She couldn't help the sob that infected her voice.

To her amazement, he conceded. "All right, all right."

"Mom." Adele reached into her jeans pocket and fished out her keys. "Can you pull my truck around?"

"Of course, sweetie." Lani hurried off. A few minutes later, she returned in the truck.

After arranging a horse blanket on the front seat to protect it from all the mud, Ty helped Pop climb in. It was a struggle for both of them.

"Thank you, Ty," Adele said softly when they were done.

"I'll ride with you, just in case he needs help getting out."

She didn't want him along, but knowing her grandfather, he'd be more cooperative with Ty than her. "Okay."

He opened the rear passenger door and climbed in.

"I'll come, too," Lani said, and before Adele could stop her, she'd hopped in the rear driver's-side seat.

"Great." Adele's next thought vanished with the ringing of her cell phone. She recognized the number and quickly flipped the phone open. "Stick, did you find Mike?"

"Sure did."

"Meet us at Pop's house." She slid in behind the steering wheel and reached for her seat belt. "We're on our way."

POP'S HOUSE BORE LITTLE resemblance to the modest structure he'd built over forty-five years earlier. Along with a room added on the back for Adele when she was eight, he'd constructed a new master bedroom suite and completely remodeled the downstairs, including the kitchen. Soon after his wife's death, however, he'd moved back into their old bedroom, and as far as Adele knew, no one had slept in the master bedroom since.

"Down the hall," she instructed Ty as soon as they entered the house. "Second door on the right."

"The family-room couch will do just fine," Pop grumbled.

"You need to lie down."

"What I need is a less bossy granddaughter."

Ty, his strong arm supporting Pop, changed direction, away from the hall and toward the family room.

"Hey!" Adele chased after them. "Ty," she pleaded when neither of them listened.

"It's his house," he said gently. "He has a right to go where he wants."

"I knew there was something I liked about you." Pop grunted as Ty lowered him onto the leather couch. "You ain't afraid of her."

"Are you kidding?" Ty bent close to Pop's ear and whispered loudly, "I'm counting on you to protect me."

Pop laughed, and Adele breathed a sigh of relief. Maybe he wasn't badly hurt, after all.

Stick showed up with Mike Scolari. Adele wanted to stay with Pop during the examination, but he'd have none of it.

"Can't you give an old man some privacy?" he complained.

She and Ty joined her mother and Stick in the kitchen.

"A glass of water, anyone?" Lani asked.

She flitted around Pop's kitchen, making herself comfortable—which rankled Adele.

"No, thanks," she mumbled.

"I'll take one, if you don't mind." Stick accepted the tall glass Lani prepared for him, and guzzled it down.

"Your grandfather will be fine." Ty joined Adele at the

table. The same table she had sat at whenever her mother dropped her off at Seven Cedars to stay. She'd been four the first time, and her feet hadn't touched the floor.

Seeing Lani standing by the sink unleashed an onslaught of memories Adele had been all too happy to shove to the back of her mind. For a moment, she became that little girl again, crying her heart out as she watched Lani's beat-up Mercury pull away from Pop's house and drive away.

Her mother had returned weeks—or was it months?— later. But she'd left Adele with her grandparents again the next year. Then again six months later. The pattern had been repeated with increasing frequency until Adele was fourteen. That summer, Lani and Pop got into a huge fight like never before, and Lani hadn't come back. From then on, the only time Adele saw her mother was during the holidays, when she flew out to wherever Lani was currently living, and only because her grandparents had insisted. Those visits stopped when Adele turned eighteen. After that, Adele saw Lani only when their paths happened to cross at some rodeo.

Looking back, she realized she hadn't visited her father any more than she had her mom. Her trips to Texas, at least, weren't strained, and peppered with petty outbursts. Her father had tried to include Adele in his life, which was more than she could say about Lani.

Mike entered the room, disrupting her thoughts. "You can see your grandfather now."

She stood, vaguely aware that Ty did, too. "How is he?"

"Tough as nails."

"Will he be all right?"

"I'm sure he's strained his back, though he won't admit it hurts."

Adele sighed.

"I gave him ibuprofen, triple the regular dose, told him

to soak in a hot bath for an hour and to take it easy over the next couple of days."

She wondered how in the world she would manage that.

"I doubt anything's broken," Mike continued, "but I'd advise a trip to his regular doctor."

"Yeah." Yet another challenge to test her.

"I also offered him a lollipop, like I do my regular patients. He refused that, too."

"Are you making a joke?"

Mike chuckled and put a hand on Adele's shoulder. "He'll recover. Falls aren't uncommon with the elderly. Luckily, the ground was soft, and he didn't hit the water trough on his way down."

Elderly? Pop had always seemed ageless.

"If he has a bad night or appears worse in the morning, don't hesitate to call me."

Adele nodded. "Stick, take Dr. Scolari, Mr. Boudeau and my mother back to their cabins, please."

"How 'bout I stay?" Ty offered in a soft voice. "Pop may need some help."

He might, even if it was just to undress for bed or get that hot soak in the tub. God knew Pop wouldn't accept Adele's assistance with those things.

"Okay."

"I want to stay, too, baby."

Her mother's show of concern was about two decades too late. "Don't you have to be at work?" Adele asked.

Lani's mouth compressed into a tight line, the reminder of her place at the ranch clearly stinging.

Adele didn't care. Pop was her top priority at the moment, and her mother wasn't anyone he wanted around.

More than that, *she* didn't want her mother around.

"Come on." Ty took Lani's elbow and gave her his most disarming smile. "I'll walk you to the truck."

She relented. Lani was always a sucker when it came to good-looking men.

Stick and Mike said their goodbyes, then followed Ty and Lani out the door. Adele didn't wait. She crossed the threshold into the family room before the kitchen door was closed.

Pop sat propped in a corner of the leather couch, his head tilted back, his eyes closed. She approached quietly, not wanting to disturb his sleep.

Only he wasn't sleeping, just resting, and he opened his eyes the instant she neared.

"I feel like a fool."

"You?" she chided, and perched gingerly on the opposite end of the couch to avoid causing his back discomfort. "A fool?"

"I suppose you think it was stupid of me to try and fix the spigot with all that mud."

"To be honest, I wouldn't have given it a second thought."

"I lost my balance, is all."

"Could've happened to anyone." She reached across the couch.

For several seconds he stared at her outstretched hand, then clasped it in his. Adele felt the world lift from her shoulders.

"Pop, can I ask you a question?"

"Sure."

"Why'd you agree to let Mom stay? And to give her a job?"

He raised his bushy silver eyebrows. "I told you, I think she's ready to make amends."

"I know. But when she left that summer I was fourteen, you told her to never come back."

"That's not entirely right."

His statement shocked Adele. "I was there. I heard the two of you fighting."

"You didn't hear everything." He expelled a long breath, readjusted his position and winced.

From pain or regret?

"What did I miss?"

His gaze turned inward. When he spoke, it was as if he was talking to Lani on that long-ago day. "I said 'if you ever come back, it had better be because you're ready to be a real mother to your daughter.'"

Adele remained quiet, not trusting her voice.

"The way I figure it," Pop continued, "if she finally got the nerve to face me, maybe she's finally ready to be that real mother to you."

If only Adele agreed with him.

TY OPENED POP'S BACK DOOR and stepped out onto the porch. In the distance, the sun was making another spectacular exit, sinking behind the mountains in a blaze of vivid reds and golds. What would it look like in winter, with snow covering those mountains and blanketing the land? Adele's earlier description tempted him to find out.

He wasn't usually one to notice nature's bounties, being too busy most of the time. It was different here at Seven Cedars. His frantic pace slowed enough for him to appreciate sunsets, and the smell of damp earth after a sudden shower, and the taste of freshly ground coffee enjoyed over a leisurely breakfast.

"How's he doing?" Adele rose from the rocker she'd been occupying.

He hadn't seen her sitting there, and tried to hide his delight. "Complaining up a storm."

"Complaining's good. It's when he doesn't that I really worry."

Ty held out the bottle of beer he'd carried with him. "Want a sip? Pop said to help myself."

"I don't usually drink beer." She took the bottle anyway and returned to her rocker.

Pulling up one of the empty stools, he sat beside her, the aged rattan seat creaking beneath his weight.

"Is he in bed?" Adele took a long swallow of Ty's beer.

He studied her every move. "Watching TV. Said no one had helped him take a bath since he was three, and he'd be damned before someone else does again."

"I'm sorry he was so uncooperative." She returned Ty's beer to him.

"No problem." He paused, studying the bottle in his hand, intensely aware of where her lips had been seconds before. Savoring the sense of anticipation for a tiny while longer, he finally put the bottle to his mouth and drained a third of its contents. "You really should call his doctor tomorrow."

Adele stopped rocking. "Is something wrong?"

"This isn't the first time he's fallen. He accidentally mentioned it during one of his grumblings. I thought you should know."

Frowning, she rubbed her forehead.

"Someone with his severe arthritis is bound to fall now and then," Ty said.

"I know. I just wish he wasn't so stubborn about getting hip replacement surgery."

"He wants to see you taken care of first."

Adele shot Ty a sideways look. "Did he tell you that?"

"He didn't have to. I can see it plain as day."

"This is ridiculous." Her voice cracked when she spoke. "I'm worried about him, he's worried about me. What a pair we are."

"You okay?" Ty touched the back of her hand. Just a quick, gentle brush of his fingertips

Laying her head back, she stared at the sky. "I know it

has nothing to do with you, but ever since you arrived, my life's been turned upside down."

He didn't ask about Lani and how much she'd contributed to Adele's topsy-turvy state. "I understand. It was like that for me last December when my horse was injured. I felt like I'd lost control of my life, and nothing I did seemed to help."

"What happened to your old horse?"

"I gave him to a buddy of mine for his teenage girls."

"So, he's not permanently crippled?"

"No. But he can't be used for anything except easy riding, which makes him a perfect family horse."

Ty held out his beer, offering her another sip. She declined with a shake of her head.

Too bad.

"What made you decide to turn Seven Cedars into a guest ranch?" he asked.

She relaxed, maybe for the first time that day. "I became serious about roping in college. Entering local jackpots was a way for me to make extra money, especially during the summers."

"You won a lot?"

"Yeah, I did." The hint of a smile touched her lips. "I would talk to the other competitors about where they were getting their training. A lot of them wished they had access to a more intensive program, one with equipment like professional ropers."

"And Cowboy College was born."

"Pop came up with the name." Her expression softened. "I was so nervous when I suggested the idea to him. I'd spent two months putting a business plan together, with the help of one of my instructors. But Pop, he was behind me one hundred percent from the beginning."

"Sounds like he's always been there for you."

"Always." She stood. "I think I'll go check on him. If he'll let me."

"I should get going." Ty also stood. "I've got an early class, and my teacher is a stickler for starting on time."

Her eyes warmed. "I really appreciate all you did for Pop."

"If you need anything, just call. I don't mind coming back."

"Thanks."

"Let me give you my cell number."

"I already have it."

He extended his hand. "Let me plug it into your phone. Save you a trip to the main lodge to look it up."

"I have it," she repeated in a quiet voice.

Pleasure shot through Ty as the implications of her statement sunk in.

"I'll be right back." She cut past him and went inside, but not before he caught sight of her pink-tinged cheeks.

He waited for her in the kitchen. She returned shortly, brandishing a key ring.

"I'll drive you back to your cabin."

They took Pop's old pickup. Ty wished the ride would last longer than it did. Too soon, their evening together ended.

"I hope I'm not one of those things that has turned your life upside down," he said, referring to her earlier remark.

Their gazes held.

"You are," she murmured.

He was surprised she admitted even that much. "I'm sorry. That wasn't my intention."

"Don't be." She shifted the truck from Neutral to Reverse. "I'm not entirely sure I didn't need a good shaking up."

He considered her remark long after she'd left, hoping it meant what he thought it did.

Chapter Seven

Ty watched as a truck and horse trailer bearing the Maitland Ranch logo rolled past the open area in front of the barns. Maintaining a steady speed of five miles an hour, it continued to the pasture designated for visitor parking. The distance was too great for Ty to identify the driver of the truck, but his gut told him it was Garth Maitland, and that the two of them were in for a rematch today.

Friendship aside, this time Ty intended to win. Garth also wouldn't have it any other way.

On the second Saturday of every month, Cowboy College hosted a roping jackpot competition. Unlike professional rodeos, jackpots were open to anyone, regardless of gender. Participants paid an entry fee and competed against other individuals ranked the same as them. At the end of the competition, the pot was divided among the top three competitors in each group. The more participants, the bigger the pot—and the tougher the competition.

Ty couldn't wait to put into practice everything he'd learned since coming to Wyoming, and have his best time ever on Hamm.

"What are you standing there for?" Pop hobbled toward Ty. "That horse of yours won't saddle himself."

"You're right." Ty started off toward the barn, then slowed when he realized Pop was tagging along. "How you feeling?"

"The next person to ask me that is going to feel the sole of my boot in their arse when I kick them off this place."

"Better, then?"

"I slipped in the dang mud. Not like I fell off the roof."

The fall might have been minor, but not the aftereffects. Pop's arthritis had flared, confining him to the couch for several days. He'd finally gotten up and around yesterday, refusing to miss the monthly jackpot.

"Looks like we got a decent turnout," Ty commented.

"Right decent."

They entered the barn, the shade offering immediate relief from the midafternoon sun beating down. The spectators filling the bleachers were already cooling themselves with whatever they could convert into a makeshift fan, and guzzling cold drinks from the snack bar, run by the local Boy Scout troop.

"Garth Maitland's here," Pop said.

"I saw."

"He'll be riding his new horse. One he's never roped on before."

Ty opened Hamm's stall door. The big sorrel was raring to go and pawed the ground relentlessly while Ty snapped on the halter. "Garth's horse any good?"

"So I'm told."

Adrenaline built in Ty while he saddled Hamm. He ignored it, focusing all his mental energies on the upcoming jackpot. He'd learned long ago that the way to win was to treat every competition, big or small, local or National, like a World Championship.

"You're busy." Pop clapped Ty on the back. "How 'bout I catch up with you later."

Ty had momentarily forgotten he wasn't alone. "Any good advice before you go?" he asked, mounting Hamm.

Pop rolled the toothpick he was always chewing on from

one side of his mouth to the other. "Forget about Garth. The only person you need to be concentrating on is yourself."

Ty nodded. He was right.

"You can beat him."

"Thanks for the vote of confidence."

Pop chuckled. "Well, a piece of humble pie wouldn't hurt Garth Maitland none."

Ty couldn't agree more.

At a slight pressure of his legs, Hamm trotted briskly from the barn. "See you at the winner's table," Ty called over his shoulder.

Outside, he made straight for the warm-up arena. From the nearby bleachers, the crowd cheered as the first group finished. Participants in the second group were lining up behind the boxes, while wranglers readied the calves.

Hamm, picking up on Ty's mood, shook his head and snorted, his front feet dancing.

"He's ready to go."

Ty looked up and smiled. He hadn't seen much of Adele since the night at Pop's house. "We both are." He pulled on the reins, slowing down so she could fall in step beside him.

"Where's Bella?" he asked, indicating the unfamiliar bay gelding she was riding.

"With her owner. He's giving her a go today."

"I'd like to see that."

"You will," she answered smoothly. "He's competing against you."

Realization dawned on Ty, and he smiled at his own gullibility. "You've been training her for Garth."

"Worried?"

"Not at all."

"You sound pretty sure of yourself."

Did he? The truth was his ego hadn't fully recovered from his loss to Garth last December. If he lost again today, he didn't want Adele knowing he'd failed despite having a newly acquired weapon in his arsenal.

"Care to make a wager?" he asked.

"Shouldn't you be talking to Garth?"

"I'm not interested in having dinner with him."

"Dinner!"

The idea had been a spontaneous one, but the more Ty thought about it, the more he liked it. "If I win, you take me to dinner."

"And if you lose?"

"I take you to dinner."

She pondered the wager. "That sounds more like a win-win situation for you."

It could be for both of them. "You want to raise the stakes?"

"Change them."

And here he thought she was going to turn him down. "To what?"

"You win, I go to dinner with you."

"Take me," he corrected.

"Okay, take you."

"And if I lose to Garth?"

Her eyes glinted with michief. "You teach the beginners' class for one week."

Ty's hand must have jerked on the reins, for Hamm suddenly slowed and bobbed his head. He didn't like being restrained.

"You kidding?"

"Not in the least." She smirked, obviously having fun with this.

"Why? Are you taking a vacation?"

"No. I just think the students would benefit, learning from a professional."

"The bet seems a little lopsided."

"Only if you're afraid of losing."

That got him, which was probably what she'd intended. "You're on. Make sure you have plenty available on your credit-card limit, because I have expensive tastes," he said, and broke into a slow trot.

Her laughter followed him as he circled the arena.

At the gate, Ty came face-to-face with Garth Maitland riding the paint mare. Both men nodded. Garth wore a wide, confident grin. Ty didn't let it faze him.

"Good luck, pal."

"Same to you."

This, Ty thought as he continued on, was going to be an interesting jackpot…for many reasons. And he had never been more ready.

ADELE DIDN'T STAND on the fence railing behind the box with the other ropers. She'd be welcome; that wasn't the reason. Mostly, she didn't want Ty to see how nervous she was, waiting for him and Garth to finish their runs. To avoid any potential embarrassment to herself, she waited—make that hid—in the announcer's booth. While old Larry Fisher provided color commentary, his wife, along with the help of their oldest granddaughter, monitored the electronic time-keepers and kept the scores. If they were curious about Adele's presence in the booth, they didn't say.

Each contestant was allowed three turns. Their scores were then added together and averaged. The person with the highest average was the winner. After two rounds, Garth led, with Ty coming in a close second. Chase, a newcomer, wasn't far behind in third place. It remained anybody's game.

She still wasn't sure she wanted Ty to win or lose. Beating Garth would do Ty good and restore some of his lost confidence. On the other hand, Adele had worked hard training

Bella, and the horse was performing well. A win for Garth could potentially bring her new clients.

There was also the matter of her bet with Ty. Having dinner with him would be a mistake. Mind-boggling kissing and long, lingering glances aside, he was leaving soon. Regardless of how attracted she was to him, and she was seriously attracted, she wasn't about to engage in a temporary fling. Her mother had done enough of that for both of them.

Try as she might, however, Adele couldn't put the idea of dinner with Ty from her mind. Joe from Phoenix, as Pop had pointed out recently, was Adele's last serious romance. Sadly, it hadn't ended well. For either of them. Mainly because she wouldn't leave Seven Cedars.

Nothing had changed since then. She was as rooted at the ranch as always.

Anticipation at the final outcome of the jackpot had her standing on her toes to see better. Garth rode into the box and positioned Bella. Chase had taken his run moments before, and currently held the first place position. Dismounting, he hopped onto the arena fence alongside his buddies to wait out the rest of the competition.

Down in the arena, the gate to the chute flew open, releasing the calf. Garth followed in hot pursuit. Bella performed flawlessly. Even so, Adele tensed. Seconds later, it was all over. Prompted by his wife, Larry called out Garth's time, which was quickly added to his other two times to determine his final standing.

"That run, ladies and gentlemen," Larry said, his voice blaring from the speaker, "will put this here young man in first place."

Adele hadn't doubted the outcome. The question was, could Garth maintain it?

"Our last contestant for the day is Ty Boudeau." The crowd applauded. "Come on, folks," Larry coaxed, "don't be stingy. This cowboy needs more encouragement than that if he's going to take home the prize money." The audience broke into cheers.

Adele chewed on her bottom lip, studying Ty's every move as he lined up his horse in the box.

Why had she agreed to such a stupid bet?

Larry's wife swiveled around in her chair. "You doing okay, honey?" she asked Adele.

"Yeah, fine."

"You sure? 'Cause you've been fidgeting something awful."

Had she? Adele willed herself to relax.

Her efforts were wasted. A moment later, the calf sprang from the chute. Hamm went from zero to sixty in one second flat. Ty raised his arm high and threw his rope. It sailed through the air like an arrow, straight and true.

Her hands balled into tight fists, Adele watched Ty jump from Hamm's back and hit the ground at a dead run. In the next instant, he'd roped the calf and was throwing his arms up in the air even as he climbed to his feet.

She knew without looking that his time was a good one. Better than his first two runs. A glance at the digital display confirmed it, as did Larry's announcement.

"Ladies and gentlemen, weren't that a pretty run? Give it up for Mr. Ty Boudeau. Your winner today."

Happiness for Ty swelled inside Adele. This competition might be nothing more than a two-bit local jackpot, but he'd needed the win. To prove he still had what it took. To prove he'd picked the right horse when he bought Hamm. To prove coming to Cowboy College was the right decision.

Larry turned away from the microphone. "Adele, tell Pop when he's got a second—"

"I'll get him for you."

She used the excuse to flee the announcer's booth. Only

it wasn't Pop she went looking for when she reached the bottom of the stairs.

Ty wasn't hard to locate. A group of people, mostly fellow students and wranglers he'd come to be friends with, surrounded him and Hamm, offering their congratulations, shaking his hand and giving him hugs. Adele held back, a sudden and acute bout of shyness cementing her feet to the ground.

Slowly, the group thinned. Before the last person had departed, a lone cowboy approached. Garth Maitland. Adele was relieved to see he was wearing his usual grin.

"Good run, Boudeau." Garth extended his hand.

Ty shook it. "You, too."

"It'll be better at the Buffalo Bill Rodeo."

"I'm counting on it."

"Why don't you come by my place this week? Check out the facilities."

"I'd like that."

"Bring Adele with you."

Ty glanced over, caught her gaze and winked, giving her reason to think he'd known all along she was standing there. "I will."

Humph! What made him so convinced she'd go?

Because she wanted to, and he'd probably seen as much in her eyes.

"Give me a call," Garth told Ty, then turned in Adele's direction. Touching his fingers to his hat, he said, "See you later, Dellie."

Great. He'd known she was there all along, too.

Eventually, the last of Ty's fans left. The bleachers had emptied out and the Boy Scouts were packing up the snack bar. Only Ty and Adele remained. She stood there, still unsure what to do or say. He didn't seem to share her problem.

Tugging on Hamm's reins, he closed the distance separating them, a happy smile stretching across his face.

"I'll start tomorrow, if you want."

"Start what?" she asked.

"Teaching the beginners' class."

"Why? You won."

"Yeah, but I'd like to, anyway. I've been working with Mike, giving him some pointers, and enjoying it."

"Really?"

"Took me by surprise, too."

"Seriously, Ty. You're not under any obligation. And you're here to work on your own skills."

He wasn't taking her to dinner. The stab of disappointment cutting through her was far stronger than she would have liked it to be.

"I owe you that much."

"For what?"

"Figuring out that Hamm takes aim with his right eye." Ty scratched behind his ear, the boyish gesture charming Adele. "The thing is, I was scared. Thinking somehow I'd lost it. Roping came so easy for me on my other horse. I took that for granted. The harder I tried with Hamm, the more I screwed up. Overcompensating, I suppose. Whatever was going wrong, I kept getting more and more tangled up in it. Coming here, focusing on the fundamentals, well, it's cleared my head and put me back on track."

Adele could see the admission hadn't come easy for Ty, and she valued it that much more.

"I'm glad." She returned his smile with a tentative one of her own.

In every direction, wranglers were hard at it, moving the calves to their regular pens, feeding the stock and cleaning up the arena. On the other side of the bleachers, Pop and Larry conversed. Too late, Adele remembered she hadn't in-

ormed her grandfather that the announcer wanted to speak
o him.

"So, how's seven-thirty?" Ty asked, distracting her. "Does
hat give you enough time to change and get ready?"

"For what?"

"Dinner tonight."

"But I thought…you said you'd teach the beginners' class."

"That's a favor." He eased closer. And though he didn't
ouch her, Adele swore the bare skin on her forearms tingled
as if stroked. "I still won."

Yes, he had.

"I intend to collect my dinner date," he added.

She could decline. Ty had coerced her into the bet, and she
doubted he'd insist on holding her to it if she flatly refused.

"Seven-thirty will be fine," she answered in a low voice.
"I'll meet you in front of the main lodge."

Ty shook his head, his eyes glinting. "Nothing doing. This
is a date. I'll pick you up at your place."

"All…right." She swallowed. "See you then."

"I'm looking forward to it."

So, Adele realized, was she. More than she should.

Chapter Eight

Flowers.

Adele accepted the bouquet—fresh picked and tied with a ribbon—from Ty's outstretched hand, her movements tentative.

"Thank you."

As she cradled them to her chest, she tried to recall when a man had last given her flowers. The only incident to come to mind was a pink carnation corsage at her senior prom.

That long ago?

"Come in," she said, and stepped back to admit him, hoping he didn't notice the tiny catch in her voice.

He glanced around her smallish but, she liked to think, comfy living room. "Nice."

"Let me put these in water." The excuse was a good one and got her the minute she needed to compose herself.

Why didn't men give her flowers? Was it their unromantic nature? Her hesitancy to commit to a serious relationship? Maybe she was too much of a tomboy, and men assumed she didn't like flowers.

Except for Ty.

Her heart melted a little as she pulled a glass jar from the kitchen cupboard, filled it with water and arranged the flowers. Smiling to herself, she set them in the center of the table, then moved them to the breakfast bar, where she could see them first thing in the morning when she stumbled in from the bedroom.

"I'd have brought you roses, but there's no florist in Markton."

At the sound of Ty's voice behind her, she momentarily froze. "These are lovely," she said, covering her reaction.

The flowers were perfect, in fact.

Repositioning a daisy that wasn't out of place to begin with, she swallowed and turned to face him.

He looked good, doing justice to his jeans and Western dress shirt, which hugged his broad shoulders. The only place to eat a sit-down dinner in Markton was the Spotted Horse Saloon, and cowboy wear was practically required to get in the door. She'd picked her newest pair of jeans, her most flattering shirt, and left her usually bound hair loose to frame her face. Ty seemed to appreciate her changed appearance, given he'd yet to take his eyes off her.

"You ready?" She hesitated, feeling on unfamiliar territory. Entertaining men in her small apartment behind the main lodge wasn't something she did. "Or would you like a cold drink first?"

Cold drink! She mentally kicked herself for sounding like a waitress.

"We should probably get a move on." Ty flashed her a disarming smile. "We've got eight-o'clock reservations."

"Reservations?"

"It's Saturday night. I figured the place would be packed after the jackpot, and I wanted to make sure we got a table."

Ty was going out of his way to make their date special.

And it *was* a date, despite starting out as a bet. Her tingling insides confirmed it.

"Let me grab my purse."

Outside, Ty opened the passenger door of his truck for her and supported her elbow as she climbed in. Adele was about to protest that she climbed in and out of trucks all day long and didn't need help. At the last second, she shut her mouth and just enjoyed his chivalrous treatment.

Fifteen minutes later, they reached the Spotted Horse Saloon. Adele expected the place to be crowded, and she wasn't disappointed. It took them as long to find a parking spot and walk to the front entrance as to drive there.

"We have a reservation," Ty told the young hostess. "For Boudeau."

"Right this way, please."

Piped in country and western music accompanied them to a dark booth tucked in the corner. The band was scheduled to take the stage soon, and by nine o'clock the place would be hopping.

Ty stood and waited while Adele slid into the booth. He sat beside her—close—and the hostess passed them menus.

"Enjoy your meal."

Ty squinted at the menu, not easy to read in the dim light. "Are the specials any good?"

"Actually, most everything is." The cowboy-type fare at the Spotted Horse was simple but tasty. "I like the grilled chicken, and the fish and chips aren't bad."

Their dinner progressed comfortably, and the mood, much to Adele's relief, was definitely casual, with conversation centering mostly on Cowboy College and the students.

"We'll be taking a group of whoever wants to go to the Buffalo Bill Stampede Rodeo," she mentioned, while buttering a roll. "Pop, of course, wouldn't miss it."

"I'm already entered. Tie-down roping and team roping."

"Who's your partner for team roping?"

"A buddy of mine. Louis Garcia."

"I've heard of him. He's good."

She thought she might have detected a bit of tension in the lines around Ty's mouth. Was he nervous about competing?

It was hard to tell over the mounting noise, a combination of the lively crowd and the band warming up on the stage. Adele recognized several ranch guests among the saloon patrons, as well as locals and out-of-town jackpot contestants. From where they sat, she could see almost as many people packed into the bar area.

"I don't think you ever told me what you do when you're not rodeoing." She fully expected him to answer horse trainer or wrangler or stock breeder. Those professions went hand in hand with rodeoing. She didn't see him following in his parents' footsteps by going into real estate.

"I apprentice at a saddle shop."

"Seriously?" She imagined a small, independently owned shop like the ones she'd visited before. "I don't remember ever reading that about you."

"You've read up on me?" A twinkle lit his eyes.

"I subscribe to horse and rodeo magazines. You're in them." She didn't mention the online searches she'd conducted before he'd arrived in Markton, afraid—make that *convinced*—it would go to his head.

"You're in them, too."

She felt his gaze on her and cleared her throat. "So, you build saddles?" she asked, as casually as if asking if he built bookcases in his spare time.

"A few. Mine, for one. Pop has a couple of old Charlie's."

"He does?" She stopped chewing. Pop owned a lot of custom-built saddles. But Ty had used only one, and she'd recognized the maker immediately. Could it be? "What's the name of the shop?"

"Kingston Saddlery."

"As in Charles Kingston?" She almost choked on her chicken. "You're kidding!"

Ty broke into an amused grin. "Not at all."

There wasn't a serious horse enthusiast alive who hadn't

heard of Kingston Saddlery, and many wanted to own what was considered to be one of the finest custom built saddles available.

"That's where you work?"

"Yep. When I'm not rodeoing."

"And you make saddles. Actually *make* them?"

He laughed. "I actually make them. Though I'm still considered an apprentice. If you ask old Charlie, he's not sure I'll ever amount to anything else."

"How come you never said anything?"

"It's not a secret. Just something I don't publicize. Old Charlie's shop is one of the few places I can go and just be myself." His voice dropped. "So's Seven Cedars."

"Wow." Adele shook her head dumbly, still absorbing Ty's remarkable news.

"Is it so hard to believe I'm learning a trade?" He turned his head and eyed her with a mixture of humor and curiosity.

"Well, saddle construction does take a lot of…" She scrunched her mouth to one side.

"Skill? Craftsmanship? Ingenuity?"

"I was going to say patience."

That earned her another laugh.

"And meticulous attention to detail. I suppose you also have to be good with your hands."

"You have no idea."

Too late, she realized her mistake. He immediately sobered, and the comfortable mood that had prevailed up till now vanished.

Oh, brother. She'd stepped right into that.

"Much as I like rodeoing, chances are I won't be doing it forever," Ty said philosophically around a bite of fish. "I may need a backup career."

Adele breathed easier at the change of subject.

"Besides, I'd like to be on road less, some day. Put down roots. Get married and have a couple of kids."

So much for breathing easier.

"I know a lot of guys—and women, too—who leave their families for months at a time, but I couldn't do it. Raising kids is hard enough for two people. It's got to be darn near impossible for one." He paused, suddenly catching himself. "I'm sorry, I wasn't criticizing. Your dad and mom—"

"It's okay. I agree with you." Adele tried to maintain a light tone. "I wouldn't want to be married to someone who was on the road for months at a time, either." And she wouldn't, not after seeing what that lifestyle had done to her parents' marriage. To her.

"When I do finally have kids," Ty continued, his gaze meeting hers, "I want to be there every moment. From the first visit to the baby doctor to the day they graduate and leave home."

Adele couldn't look away if she tried.

Fortunately, the band chose that moment to begin the first set. Despite being good, the music was loud, and limited conversation. Ty made up for it by sending her smoldering glances between bites. Adele polished off the last of her meal in a rush. This thing happening between them, whatever it was, couldn't go anywhere, and she needed to put a halt to it once and for all.

She was just setting her fork down and hoping they'd be leaving soon when the band launched into a slow number, one of George Strait's more popular hits.

"Let's dance," Ty abruptly said.

"I...ah..."

Her senior prom was the last time a man had given her flowers. It was also the last time she'd danced to such a slow song.

He stood and tilted his head toward the band. "Come on. I won't bite. Not on a first date, anyway."

Was he joking?

Walking ahead of him, Adele tried to convince herself she wasn't making a huge mistake. Just look what had happened the last time Ty had held her in his arms.

"Relax," he said into her ear, and pressed his palm against the center of her back.

She tried. It wasn't easy. The man smelled too darn sexy for his own good.

"Afraid I'm a little more comfortable on a horse than the dance floor," she confessed.

"It's not all that different than riding. You just have to find the rhythm and settle in."

He couldn't be more wrong. Dancing was entirely different than riding.

On horseback, she was in complete control. Wrapped in Ty's arms, she was a stick being carried along by a rushing, storm-swollen river.

But after an awkward minute, she did indeed find the rhythm, and stopped inhaling sharply every time their bodies gently collided, either from a misstep on her part or another couple bumping into them. No sooner did the tension start to ebb than the song ended.

"Wait," Ty told her when she began to pull away.

"The song's over," she murmured. The realization that she rather enjoyed staying right where she was made her nervous all over again.

"They'll play another one."

And the band did, this one also slow. Had Ty known?

Without any prompting on his part, she slipped back into his embrace, her earlier suspicions that they were headed for trouble solidifying into absolute certainty. He felt good. Strong and sure of himself. And those hands he'd bragged about were holding her as if he had no intention of ever letting her go.

As the song played on, she discovered that following his steps wasn't all that hard. When he lowered his head to brush his temple against hers, she didn't retreat or tell him to stop. Stranger still, when his hand moved from the center to the small of her back, she turned her head and rested her cheek on his chest as if she'd done it a thousand times before.

Maybe her lack of finesse on the dance floor had less to do with talent and more to do with not having the right partner.

As they moved to the seductive beat, Ty's heart rate slowly increased. She could sense the pounding more than she could hear it over the loud music. When her fingers walked gingerly from his shoulder to the back of his neck, his heart rate accelerated even more.

People were looking at them, Adele noticed through slitted eyes and a dreamy haze that had begun to surround her. Not that she could blame them. As Pop had pointed out recently, she hardly dated, much less glided across a crowded dance floor in the arms of an incredibly attractive rodeo star. One who also worked for the best custom saddle and leather shop in the Southwest.

She was still trying to wrap her brain around that piece of news when Ty suddenly swung her in a half circle in order to avoid colliding with Mike and Sandy.

"Whew!" It took Adele a moment to regain her balance.

"Sorry," Mike called over the music before he and his wife were swallowed by the other dancers.

"You okay?" Ty asked.

Adele looked up at him, and her own heart began racing. At close range and in the dim light of the honky-tonk, his brown eyes were dark as ebony. They studied her with the intensity of a man with an agenda. An agenda that involved the two of them alone in a secluded place, those talented hands of his discovering the curve of her hips and the texture of her skin.

Adele averted her gaze. She had little experience with the kind of supercharged sexual currents running between her and Ty.

He let go of her hand and, tucking a finger beneath her chin, lifted her face to his. Dancing became impossible, so they stopped, staring into each other's eyes right there in the middle of the dance floor. The people moving beside them were just blurs to Adele, who only had eyes for Ty.

Leaning down until their foreheads touched, he said, "I want to take you home. Right now."

She withdrew slightly, his remark swiftly bringing her back to her senses.

"I—I don't… I can't…"

He wanted her. And she returned the feelings. But she wasn't ready for *that*. Not yet.

He looked stricken. "I wouldn't take advantage of you, Adele." He blew out a breath and, giving her a gentle tug, pulled her back into his arms. "God, I screwed that up." They started dancing again. "I want to kiss you." He caught her gaze once more. "You can't imagine how much." His mouth curved up in an apologetic smile. "I just didn't want to do it here, and figured if I took you home, I'd have my chance."

"I see," she muttered softly.

"This keeps getting worse and worse. I should just shut up."

"No. It's all right." Adele gathered her courage and made a leap she never had before with a man. "Because I want you to kiss me."

"You do?" Ty's grin widened.

She nodded, and said, "Let's get out of here," just as the music stopped.

Unfortunately, several people were close enough to hear her. Including Mike and Sandy, who both smiled knowingly.

"Good idea." Mike waggled his eyebrows and flashed Sandy a look that left no question as to his own intentions.

Adele groaned inwardly. She rigorously strived to keep her private life just that. Tonight, however, she'd broken that rule.

"You've got an early morning tomorrow," Ty said loudly enough for everyone to hear. "And Pop's waiting for you." With a gentlemanly touch to her back, he guided her off the dance floor.

"Thank you," she said, when they reached their booth. Ty had done his best to make it clear he and Adele weren't spending the night together. She liked him for that. More than liked him.

"I'd say I was sorry, except I'm not going to get in the habit of apologizing, or thinking I should apologize, every time I kiss you."

Something about his tone caused a tingle to skip lightly up her spine. Almost like the gliding of fingertips. *His* fingertips.

"You say that as if we're going to kiss a lot."

"A man can hope."

The dinner tab had been placed on their table while they were dancing. Adele reached for it, but Ty beat her to the punch.

"Hey, I'm supposed to pay."

"I'll get it."

"We had a bet."

"You can pay next time."

"Who says there's going to be a next time?"

"There is if you owe me dinner."

"You're impossible!"

Ty removed his wallet and place several bills inside the

folder containing the dinner tab. His gaze held hers as he replaced it on the table. "Don't think this gets you out of kissing me tonight."

"It never crossed my mind," she said softly, reeling from more of those sexual currents.

Despite her earlier vow to keep her personal life private, she didn't object when Ty clasped her hand in his. Together, they wove through the throng of boisterous patrons.

With each step, she tried convincing herself not to get involved with Ty. His return to the rodeo circuit loomed ahead. Unless she could be satisfied with seeing him a few days here and a few days there, engaging in a romantic relationship could only end with her being hurt.

No amount of warning, however, lessened the anticipation building inside her at the prospect of their next kiss. How could she refuse him? Especially when she might not have another chance?

To reach the front entrance, they had to pass the bar area. Typical for a Saturday night, people stood two and three deep. If a big burly man hadn't chosen that exact moment to back away from the bar, Adele might have left without ever having spotted her mother parked on a stool near the end.

The sight of Lani hefting a beer wasn't enough to stop Adele in her tracks. She'd seen her mother in bars before. It was the man she sat next to, with her head bent close to his in what was clearly an intimate conversation, that left Adele chilled.

Henry Parkman, owner of the feed store.

Married Henry Parkman. And until this moment, Adele had thought him happily married.

His wedded state, however, didn't seem to make a difference to Lani. She flashed her white teeth at him before tipping her head back and laughing uproariously.

Adele's mother had always gone after men; that was nothing new. Somewhere along the line she'd apparently moved to married men. Adele felt sick to her stomach.

Every thought fled her head save one: getting the hell out of the Spotted Horse. Legs shaking, she sidestepped Ty and brushed past another couple in her haste to reach the entrance, her escape fueled by an incessant roaring in her ears.

"YOU DON'T HAVE to get out," Adele said when Ty opened his truck door and pocketed his keys.

"I'd like to walk you to your door, if you don't mind."

He assumed the good-night kiss they'd teased about at the Spotted Horse—the one that had sent his pulse skyrocketing—wouldn't materialize. That didn't stop him from wanting to see her safely inside.

Adele's mood had plummeted the moment she saw her mother with Henry Parkman, the owner of the feed store. And understandably so. Ty had remained silent on the subject during the short ride home, commenting on the weather and upcoming rodeo, and not pressuring her when she didn't respond. It had been obvious from the day he first saw Lani in the barn with Pop that any discussion of Adele's mother was off-limits.

From somewhere nearby, one of the ranch's many dogs barked. Ty sat behind the steering wheel, absently tapping a foot.

When Adele didn't immediately exit the truck, he waited another moment, then shut his door. She continued sitting in the passenger seat, staring into the darkness at a row of sprawling cottonwood trees, standing like a black wall against a silver sky.

Strange behavior for someone who'd been in an all-fired hurry to get home not twenty minutes earlier.

Okay, maybe she did want to talk. Or not be alone. When she still didn't move or speak, he hunkered down in his seat, pushed back his cowboy hat and scratched his forehead. The intricate workings of a woman's mind had often eluded Ty, and he'd long ago developed a system to use in situations like this one. When in doubt, wait and say nothing.

"I'm sorry," Adele finally muttered.

"For what?"

"I know this isn't how you expected the evening to end."

"Don't sweat it."

"From the day my mom arrived, I've been trying to figure out why she showed up. I should have guessed it was to find a new man. She doesn't go long without one. I just hadn't realized she'd lowered her already low standards and was including married men in her pickings." Hurt and disappointment roughened Adele's voice.

Ty decided to go out on a limb. "Don't take this wrong, but are you sure your mother was going after Henry Parkman?"

Adele turned her head to gawk at Ty with disbelief. "You saw the two of them at the bar."

"I did." He scratched his forehead again. "Can't say there was much going on between them other than talking and laughing."

"If she'd been sitting any closer to him, she'd have been in his lap."

"The place was pretty crowded. Hard not to sit close to someone with people crammed in all around you."

"Why are you defending her?"

"I'm not defending her. Only saying I didn't see anything more than two people having a friendly conversation."

"Yeah. *Real* friendly. That's how it always starts with her."

Ty let the remark pass, returning to his original plan to say nothing. Women were talkers, he reminded himself, and men were fixers. She probably didn't want his advice, just a sounding board on which to vent her frustrations. At least, that was what his sisters used to tell him when he opened his mouth once too often with unsolicited advice.

Several more moments passed with Adele sitting silently. Ty leaned back, content to be patient, and determined to be what she needed, even if he couldn't figure out exactly what that was.

"You have a perfect family," she murmured, staring out the window again.

"I wouldn't call them perfect."

"Your mom and dad are still married after, what, thirty years?"

"Something like that."

"They not only raised three kids, they both have successful careers. I'd call that pretty perfect."

"They've had their share of rough patches." Some of them a direct result of Ty and a few rather rebellious teen years.

"My parents divorced when I was three." She heaved a sigh. "I don't really know why. My dad refused to talk about it, and the reasons my mom gave always sounded a bit…manufactured." Adele turned toward Ty. "Do people really grow apart?" Without waiting for him to answer, she resumed gazing out the window. "I think she just got tired of him." Adele's voice hitched. "Like she got tired of me."

"That's not true."

"How would you know?"

"All right, I don't." That's what he got for trying to say the right thing. Back to plan one: be quiet and listen.

"She left me here every chance she got. Every time she found a new man to latch on to. What kind of mom does that to her own kid?"

"Maybe she was trying to protect you."

"From what?" Adele asked, her expression incredulous. Ty ground his teeth, cursing his inability to shut up.

"From *what?*" she repeated when he didn't respond.

He was probably going to regret it later, but answered her anyway. "From the lifestyle she was living. From the men she was with. From the constant liquor and partying and living on the road in a motor home or in a hotel room. I can't imagine any mother wanting to expose her child to that."

"Then why didn't she just stay home and get a regular job? Why did she dump me off at my father's or grandparents' every chance she got?"

"You should be asking your mother these questions."

Clearly, he'd blundered, for Adele sprang into action, wrenching open her door and jumping out.

Ty went after her, but she'd gotten a solid head start on him. He caught a break when she fumbled with her keys at the front door.

"Adele, I'm sorry." He came up beside her. "I shouldn't have said that." Dang it all, she was crying. "Oh, sweetheart." He placed a comforting hand on her shoulder.

She went into his arms so fast he momentarily lost his footing.

"I hate being one of those pathetic people with mommy issues," she said, her face buried in the front of his shirt.

"There's a reason Lani came here." Ty put an arm securely around Adele. When she didn't retreat, he tugged her closer.

"That's what Pop says, too," she muttered. "He thinks I should give her a chance to explain."

"Your grandfather's a smart man."

"Not about everything. He overdoes it and falls."

"Well, that's true."

Ty forced himself to concentrate. It was hard holding Adele—feeling her body fitted snugly against his—and not responding. He ached to taste her lips, glide his palms along her supple curves. When his hand inadvertently slipped off her shoulder and down her back, he quickly pulled it away.

"You're right about me talking to my mom," Adele said,

her head nestled in the crook of Ty's neck as if it belonged there. "It's just that we've never been close, and talking about anything serious…" She gave a small laugh. "We don't."

"When's the last time you tried?"

"I don't even remember. How sad is that?"

She sounded so forlorn, he couldn't resist, and placed a tender kiss on the top of her head.

Big mistake.

"Ty." She immediately pushed away from him.

"My fault, I got carried away."

"It's not that. I do…want to kiss you again." She settled her palms on his chest. "Just not when I'm all weak and weepy and an emotional mess. Been there, done that, and once was enough."

He brushed aside a stray lock of her hair. "I'm willing to wait."

Using the key still clutched in her hand, she opened her front door. "Thanks for dinner. I really did have a nice time."

"Nice enough to do it again?"

"You're leaving soon."

"Which doesn't give us time to waste."

In response, she stood on tiptoe and kissed his cheek. He expected her to immediately retreat, but again she lingered, her lips soft on his skin. If she'd wanted to torture him, she couldn't have devised a more effective method.

"Good night, Ty," she whispered.

Unable to control himself, he dipped his head and inhaled the incredible scent of her. Sweet and flowery, like peach blossoms.

"Good night, Adele."

Difficult as it was, he stepped back. Giving her one last look, he touched his fingers to the brim of his hat and returned to his truck.

On the drive to his cabin, he remembered she hadn't given

him an answer about going on another date. He wasn't worried. She'd mentioned wanting to kiss him again.

And Ty had every intention of taking her at her word.

Chapter Nine

Adele sat at the folding picnic table outside the camper she and Pop were sharing during their long weekend at the Buffalo Bill Cody Rodeo. Cheers from the crowd carried across the parking lot to the open field where they and a hundred or so other people had constructed a makeshift RV park. Though it was normally reserved for contestants, Pop and Adele stayed there because of his long-standing involvement in rodeos and his previous championships.

Once a member of the rodeo community, always a member.

Pop opened the door of the camper and climbed down the steps. While Adele had been woolgathering and listening to the distant cheers, he'd been inside taking a short, midafternoon nap.

"Aren't you going to mosey over and watch Ty compete?"

"I will soon." She knew from the schedule on the table that Ty's event wasn't starting for another twenty-five minutes.

"Have you seen him today?"

"Earlier. After the team roping."

As Pop sat down across from her, the lightweight picnic table seesawed, ceasing to move only when he did. "I bet he's mad at himself. A new partner and a new horse are a difficult combination."

Ty had partnered with an old friend for the event. They'd done passably well on Saturday, but bombed the final round today, making several avoidable mistakes.

"Don't tell that to Ty."

Pop chuckled. "I bet he's a nervous wreck about now."

"And doing a poor job of hiding it, from what Mike and Sandy tell me." Some of the students attending the rodeo had reported back to her, too.

"He'd better get ahold of himself if he wants to do well in tie-down roping."

"He will. He's a pro, and committed."

"I figured you'd be down there offering him moral support."

Adele ignored her grandfather's penetrating gaze. This was hardly the first hint he'd dropped that she and Ty had a romantic thing going.

They didn't. In fact, they'd spoken only in passing the last two weeks. He'd been busy teaching the beginners' class, practicing for the rodeo at every opportunity, and fussing over Hamm as if the horse were a newborn baby. She'd given Ty his space so as not to distract him.

Or so she told herself.

In truth, he'd asked some hard questions the night of their date—she'd stopped thinking of it as anything else—and seeing him only reminded her that she had no answers for the questions, and probably never would. Not without talking to her mother, as Ty and Pop had both suggested.

Except Adele could hardly bring herself to say hi to her mom, not after seeing her with Henry Parkman, and avoided her at all costs.

"Pop, why did my parents get divorced?"

His brows shot up. "Where in blue blazes did that come from?"

"I've been wondering about it ever since Mom showed up."

Lani hadn't accompanied the small group of students to the rodeo. Initially, Adele had been relieved; her mother wouldn't be attempting to attach herself to a new man. Then Adele panicked. What if Lani was staying home in order to be with Henry Parkman?

Adele rubbed her eyes and sighed. Ty was wrong. That conversation in the bar hadn't been casual. Adele had seen her mother in action too often not to know when she had her game on.

"What did your folks tell you?" Pop asked.

"Dad never talked about it."

"That doesn't surprise me. Warren was always one to keep his hurt to himself."

"Why did Mom leave him? Was he such a bad husband?" Adele had always suspected it was the other way around— that her mother was a bad wife.

"She did move out, but you couldn't fault her. Not really." Pop massaged the knuckles of one hand, then the other, a sign his arthritis was acting up. "They were young when they got married. And Warren was on the road a lot. I don't think rodeo life is good for a marriage."

Adele couldn't agree more. It was yet another strike against Ty, despite her attraction to him.

"Add a baby, plus a drinking problem on top of that, and it's a lot for two inexperienced kids to handle."

Adele frowned. "Mom's always liked to party, I know, but I don't remember her drinking *that* much. Not while I was around."

"She didn't. Warren's the one with the drinking problem."

"What?" Adele almost slipped from her seat. "Dad doesn't drink. Not a drop."

"He used to. Like a fish. That's what put an end to his

rodeo career. One too many drinks, way too many losses. A shame, too, because he had real talent."

"I…I can't believe it."

Sorrow shone in Pop's eyes. "Warren went on a binge to beat all binges about a year after he and your mom separated. Crashed his truck into a billboard pillar and damn near killed himself."

"Where?"

"On the highway twenty miles outside of Markton."

"I don't remember any accident."

"Your mom took you to Cheyenne, where she had some friends. After the accident, she brought you to the ranch, but didn't tell you about your dad being all banged up. You were just a tyke, and she thought seeing your father in such bad shape would give you nightmares. He recovered and has been on the straight and narrow ever since."

Adele sat back, her head swimming. All these years, she'd assumed her father left Wyoming and ran off to Texas to escape her mother. Or, as a small part of her heart had feared, because he hadn't wanted her. In reality, he'd done so in order to turn his life around.

"Why didn't he tell me?"

"It's hard for some folks to admit their mistakes. Especially to their kids. It's one of the reasons he didn't fight your mother for joint custody of you, much as I wanted him to. He found a good woman who keeps him in line. Reminders of his past, well, they seem to tempt him too much. He falls into old habits."

"I'm not a child anymore," Adele said with a trace of bitterness. "Yet he still refuses to include me in his life."

"That goes both ways."

Pierced by guilt, she averted her glance.

"Someone's got to take the first step," Pop urged.

Hadn't Ty said almost the same thing about her mother?

Adele rubbed her temples, which were throbbing now from her taking in so much at once. Had she been wrong all these years about *both* her parents? The possibility sobered her.

"None of us likes the idea of being a disappointment to our children." Pop's expression softened. "Take it from me."

"You've never disappointed Dad. Or me."

"I did. When I let the ranch practically go to ruin after your grandmother passed."

"That was understandable."

"So is what happened to your parents."

Adele said nothing.

"Could be why your mother came back. Hoping to set things right with you."

She stared at the rodeo grounds across the parking lot. People and vehicles poured in and out, as they had all weekend long. Even at a distance, the tourists were easy to spot, with their shorts, T-shirts, sneakers and souvenirs. Children walked beside their parents, balloons bobbing at the end of strings.

"It took a lot of courage for Lani to show up," Pop said gently. "She had to know you'd still be mad at her."

"I thought you didn't like my mother."

"That's not true. I despised what she did to you, carting you off to some new place on a whim, leaving you on your father's doorstep or mine whenever the mood struck. But then, I knew she was unhappy and that Warren had caused a lot of it. I also remember her the way she was when your dad and she first met. Your mother was the prettiest, sweetest little gal."

No one, as far as Adele knew, had ever described her mother as pretty or sweet. She must have been, however. Pop didn't usually hand out compliments where Lani was concerned.

"Why are you telling me all this now? Why not before?"

"I wasn't altogether sure you'd listen."

Adele *was* listening. Understanding, however, was a different matter. "We're a miserable lot, when you think about it."

"Doesn't have to be that way. Which is why I let Lani stay." Pop reached across the table and patted Adele's hand. "It's not too late for you and your mother to mend some of those bridges."

"I don't know," Adele said wistfully. "I don't think I can, not while she's up to her old tricks."

"What tricks?"

"I saw her at the Spotted Horse last week with Henry Parkman."

The toothpick Pop had been rolling from side to side in his mouth stilled. "Are you sure?"

"Of course I'm sure."

"They were together?"

"Sitting at the bar, big as life."

"I can't believe that. Henry and Carmella have been together over twenty years."

"I know."

"He's devoted to her."

"When Mom goes after a man, she's hard to resist." Adele could still see Lani smiling up into Henry's face, hear her boisterous laughter. "I'm worried that's why she didn't come to the rodeo, so she could be with Henry without the rest of us around."

"Except he's here."

"He is?" Adele's eyes went wide.

"Him and Carmella both. The feed store's one of the sponsors."

"I haven't seen them all weekend." Though she had noticed the store's colorful banner hanging in the main arena.

"Well, they're here. You've probably been too busy with the students and Ty."

Adele wanted to object. She'd been so certain her mother had returned to her old ways.

"What did you see Henry and Lani doing at the Spotted Horse?" Pop asked.

"Sitting close. Talking. Laughing and smiling at each other."

"That all?"

"Don't say it like it's nothing." Adele scowled. "Mom was flirting with him, and he didn't seem to mind."

"Flirting is a far cry from having an affair."

"It's still wrong."

"Are you sure it wasn't the other way around? Henry could've been flirting with your mother."

Adele started to answer, then clamped her mouth shut.

Two people had now told her she may have been jumping to a wrong conclusion. As much as she hated to admit it, the possibility was looking more and more likely. Were her feelings for Lani so negative and slanted that she was quick to assume the worst?

Doubts came rushing in. Adele had been comfortable for years living with her anger at both her parents. Just because the time for change might be at hand didn't mean she was eager to embrace it.

A cheer went up in the stands. It was followed by the announcer's voice, telling the audience to stay seated for the final round of tie-down roping, due to start after a ten-minute break.

"We'd better get a move on." Pop rose from his seat, causing the small picnic table to seesaw again.

Adele also stood. Her grandfather could move only so fast, and they had a fair distance to cover—which gave her plenty of opportunity to think...and reconsider.

DURING THE WALK to the main arena, Adele pulled herself together, only half listening to Pop's chatter and half noticing the endless stream of people, participants and horses. Tantalizing aromas from the concession stands and brightly painted signs atop vendor booths vied for their attention. She practiced smiling, wanting to present a relaxed demeanor to the students sitting in the section of bleacher seats they'd reserved. Pop would head on down to the chutes and boxes to watch the tie-down roping and give last-minute advice to the participants he'd mentored through the years.

The first competitor had just finished his run by the time Adele climbed the bleacher stairs, saying hi to the students and hoping they didn't notice her distracted state. Luckily, their gazes were centered elsewhere.

She sat in the only available seat, which happened to be next to Mike and Sandy. They were leaving Cowboy College the next day, and Adele would be sad to see them go. They'd been two of the ranch's more enjoyable and memorable guests.

"I was pleased to hear about Pop," Mike said, leaning forward to converse with Adele around his wife.

"What about him?" She automatically searched for Ty, finally spotting him behind the chutes and boxes. He sat astride Hamm, waiting his turn and watching the competition from that vantage point.

"The report from his orthopedic surgeon."

Adele squinted curiously at Mike. "What report?"

"When he saw his doctor last week." Understanding and then embarrassment flashed across his face. "You don't know."

"What did the doctor say?"

Mike shook his head. "I'm sorry. I can't tell you."

"But he's not your patient."

"Even so." He looked miserable because of his blunder. "I thought Pop had discussed the report with you."

"Well, he didn't." At the moment, she wasn't sure who to be more agitated with, Pop or Mike.

"Ask him," Mike urged.

"Tell me this much. Do I have anything to be worried about?" Anything *more*. Between Ty's event and the revelations about her parents, she'd reached her stress limit for the day.

Mike broke into a grin, and repeated, "Ask him. But in the meantime, feel free to sleep easy tonight."

That much was a relief.

"Next up," the announcer called, his voice blaring from the speakers, "is a young man all the way from Missouri."

Young was right. He didn't look any older than nineteen. At twenty-seven, Ty was one of the older competitors. He was also one of the more experienced, and that counted in his favor.

When Adele glanced back over at the box, she noticed he was gone. She didn't think much about it, assuming he was warming up Hamm. But when Ty didn't reappear a few minutes later, she started to worry. His turn was fast approaching.

Great, yet another thing to weigh on her mind. She'd be glad when this weekend was over and she could go home, retreat to a quiet place and think things through. Maybe talk to her mother.

Maybe.

The sudden ringing of her cell phone took her by surprise. She tried but couldn't read the display in the bright sunlight. Giving up, she answered the call.

"Hello."

"Come meet me by the stock pens."

She recognized Ty's voice immediately, and a jolt shot through her. "What's wrong?"

"Just come. I need a favor." He sounded anxious.

Various scenarios played in her head. A problem with Hamm or an equipment malfunction. A last minute strategy powwow. Something significant, or else why would Ty call her so close to his run?

"Be right there," she told him, already on her feet and squeezing past people on her way to the aisle.

TY STOOD EXACTLY where he said he'd be waiting, holding Hamm's reins. From a distance, everything looked fine. His equipment was intact, the horse appeared calm and uninjured, and Ty's features were composed, reflecting determination and—this was a good sign—confidence.

Adele wove in and out of the throng of people, hurrying to get to him as fast as she could. She didn't question her sense of urgency or why her heart was suddenly turning somersaults. The last forty-five minutes had delivered one emotional bombshell after another. The entire week, really. No wonder her nerves were a tangled mess and her anxiety level through the roof.

Anxiety? Or excitement?

No denying it. The small thrill winding through her as she drew close to Ty had more to do with attraction than trepidation. Much more.

At last she broke free from the crowd. Feeling like a fish escaping through a hole in a fisherman's net, she slowed down, covering the remaining thirty feet separating her and Ty at a walk. Until that moment, he'd been staring at the arena, his head cocked slightly to one side as he listened to the announcer's evaluation of the last contestant's run—a good one, according to the score. Ty would have to give everything he had and then some if he intended to win.

He must have sensed her approach, for he suddenly turned. When their gazes connected, his eyes lit up, then turned dark and smoldering. The small thrill became a rushing river of awareness. All at once, Adele knew why Ty had called her to meet him, and what he wanted. She didn't hesitate going to him.

Dropping the reins, he came forward. Luckily, Hamm was placid by nature outside the arena, because another horse might have spooked when Adele flung herself into Ty's open arms.

"I've been waiting two weeks for this," he said as his mouth came down on hers.

Only two weeks? It felt to Adele as if she'd been waiting forever. For this kiss. This moment. This man.

Forgetting all the obstacles facing them and the fact that he was leaving soon, *very* soon, forgetting the crowd, which had dissolved into a soundless blur, she returned Ty's kiss with a passion matching his. Instinct told her he needed this connection to her, physical and emotional, in order to compete. Every bit as much as he needed the lariat tied to his saddle.

The sense of contentment stealing over her told her she needed it, too. Perhaps even more than he did, for all at once her world stopped rocking wildly and righted itself.

Offering no resistance to his bold advances, she molded her body to his, relishing the sensation of his hands firmly pressed into her back, his hard muscled length as he anchored her to him, and his tongue as it swept into her mouth.

She could only imagine the number of open stares they were garnering, but she didn't care. Every harsh breath he drew, every groan issuing from deep in his chest told her neither did he.

A loud, bawdy whoop penetrated her foggy brain, returning her to reality.

"Hey, Boudeau! Hate to break up the party but you're up soon. Better get a move on."

Ty broke off their kiss, his reluctance showing in his eyes. "I want to see you tonight."

"Another date?" she asked, still holding on to him.

"Okay."

The way he said "okay" gave her reason to think he'd had something else in mind.

So did she.

"All right."

He grinned.

"On one condition."

"What's that?" He bent as if to nuzzle her neck. Her next words stopped him.

"You take first in tie-down roping."

He lifted his head. "You think I can't?"

"Not at all. But if you want to see me tonight, you'd better be bringing that belt buckle with you."

"Be ready at seven." Letting go of her, he gathered the reins and mounted Hamm in one fluid motion. "And wear something sexy."

With that, he trotted off to the area behind the box.

Ignoring the snickering and gawking, Adele ran back to the bleachers and her seat.

She couldn't help feeling that Ty winning this event was more important than him getting back on track, and more significant than going on another date with him.

It seemed to Adele as if her whole life was suddenly poised to change.

Chapter Ten

"Boudeau, you're up next!"

Ty nudged Hamm into place behind the box. The horse responded with the tiniest of cues, already in the zone and ready to go. Ty wished he could say the same for himself. Kissing Adele had affected his concentration—among other things.

That hadn't been his plan. Not intentionally. He'd only wanted to talk to her. Why, he wasn't sure now. Only that two weeks without close interaction had been too long. The need to see her, even briefly, before he went into the arena had been so powerful, he hadn't thought his actions through, simply punched in her number.

And she'd come. Just like that. Without requiring an explanation.

When he'd seen her hurrying toward him, eager anticipation brightening her expression, the part of his brain not a slave to logic had taken over, and he'd kissed her. *Really* kissed her. And it had wiped away every memory of every other woman before her.

He couldn't wait for tonight.

Except if he didn't get it together, and fast, there would be no "tonight" with her.

He had to take first place.

For her, but also for himself. Somewhere along the way,

winning at roping and winning over Adele had become intermingled, and he didn't think he could separate the two.

"On deck, Boudeau."

"Sorry," Ty said, realizing his name had been called a second time. He urged Hamm closer to the box.

"You got this in the bag, son."

Ty glanced down to see Pop hobbling over. "That's what I'm hoping."

The older man gave Ty's leg an encouraging pat. "Billy Carpenter broke the barrier."

"Is that so?" Ty had missed Billy's run and the penalty. It must have happened while he and Adele were kissing.

"The only ones left who can possibly beat you are Mitch Benson and Garth Maitland."

"I'm not worried about Benson," Ty said. Lifting his head to see over the crowd, he watched the man in question throw his rope. "He chokes under pressure."

Benson's toss sailed straight and true, but when he went to tie the calf's legs, his hand accidentally slipped, costing him precious seconds. The announcer commiserated and encouraged the audience to give him a round of applause.

"That leaves Garth," Ty said, his jaw tightening.

"He goes last."

"I know."

Taking no chances, Ty checked his equipment with the thoroughness of a heart surgeon preparing for a transplant operation.

"Boudeau!"

He only had to loosen his grip on the reins slightly, and Hamm charged forward into the box, ready to go. As the big animal settled in, Ty knew he'd been right to purchase him. There wasn't a better horse around or a better horse for him. They could win today.

Hell, they could go all the way to the National Finals

Rodeo in December, where participants from all over the world competed.

Pop had followed Ty as far as the fence. One of the cowboys moved aside and made room for the older man, who hoisted himself onto the bottom rail with a grunt.

Ty barely noticed. He was too preoccupied rewinding his lariat into a coil for the third time and hefting it in his hand. He didn't stop until the lariat felt exactly right.

"This probably isn't the time to tell you," Pop said, loudly enough for Ty and everyone else to hear, "but I approve of you courting my granddaughter. If that's your intention."

Caught off guard, Ty looked up. Had Pop seen them kissing? "It is my intention, sir. But I have to bring home a buckle first."

Pop laughed till he choked. "She tell you that?"

"She did. And I think she's serious."

"Then you'd better have the run of your life."

Ty couldn't agree more.

He could feel the eyes of every man standing on or straddling the fence. They knew his history, many of them having seen him lose to Garth last year. They realized today could be, make that *was*, Ty's comeback. He wasn't going to disappoint them.

Or Adele.

"Good luck, Boudeau."

"You got it in the bag, Ty."

He settled deeper into his saddle, ignoring his buddies. They weren't expecting him to reply, anyway, understanding that he was getting himself where he needed to be mentally.

A last tug on his gloves. One more inspection of his lariat and the knot that secured it to his saddle horn. A final stretch of the pigging string before he placed it between his teeth. One more hat adjustment. With each action, he narrowed his concentration until all he saw, all that mattered was his horse, the calf and the wrangler manning the gate to the chute.

"Get ready, boy," he said under his breath, giving Hamm's neck a quick pat.

Long days of honing his skills, learning about himself and his horse, were about to pay off. A burst of confidence exploded inside him, growing stronger as if he'd drunk a magical elixir.

"Go." The single clipped word accompanied a brusque nod of his head.

The gate to the chute opened with a harsh metallic swish. An instant after the calf escaped, Ty and Hamm were in motion, operating on pure adrenaline and instinct. Ty's arm came up in the air at just the right moment. The rope flew from his hand with precision and accuracy, sailing toward the running calf on a perfect gust of air. Even before the lasso reached its target, Ty was swinging his leg over the saddle, leaping off and hitting the ground at a dead run.

Hamm did his job, stepping backward and pulling the rope taut. Ty also did his job, sliding his hand along the rope as he ran forward. The instant the calf was down on its side, he wound the pigging string around its legs and threw his hands in the air to signal he was done.

He didn't need to hear the announcer or glance at the scoreboard to know he'd performed well. He could feel it in the thundering of his heart and the surge of energy racing through him.

Untying the calf, he collected his rope and pigging string, walked over to Hamm and gave the horse's neck another pat. "Thanks, partner."

Hamm bobbed his head up and down, then knocked his nose into Ty's shoulder. It seemed he was also happy with their run. The two of them made for the gate, Ty leading Hamm by the reins.

Applause broke out as Ty's official score appeared on the board. He stared, committing this moment to memory. Seven seconds flat. Good enough to put him in first place.

Ty didn't celebrate. Not yet. Garth Maitland still had to go. And while seven seconds flat was a damn fine time, Garth had beaten it before and could again today.

STICK APPEARED ON the other side of the gate. "That was sure a nice run, Ty."

"Not bad."

"Want me to take Hamm for you?" Stick didn't add, "So you can stay and watch the rest of the competition." He didn't have to.

"Appreciate that."

After the teen left with the horse, Ty climbed onto the fence. He picked a spot away from the other competitors. If Garth beat him, he wanted a few minutes to himself before facing his friends.

But that wasn't going to happen. Not after the great run he'd had today.

The next contestant, a young man from Ecuador, finished at thirteen-point-three seconds. Ty hadn't been worried. The contestant after that had the potential to bump Ty out of the first place standing if he pulled off a miracle. But he didn't. The calf got loose at the last second, disqualifying him.

That left only Garth.

He was riding his regular horse and had been all weekend. The Buffalo Bill Cody Stampede might not be the biggest rodeo on the Turquoise Circuit, but he still wouldn't take a chance on a new horse.

"Folks, this cowboy needs a time of six-point-nine seconds to take over first place." The announcer's voice blared from the speakers overhead. "If anyone can do it, Garth Maitland sure can."

That was no lie.

Ty turned away from the box where Garth was going through his final equipment check, and scanned the crowd. He knew where the students from Cowboy College were sitting, and sought out Adele. At this distance it was impossible to see her face clearly. Even so, he was certain she was looking at him and not Garth.

The sound of the chute opening had Ty snapping his attention back to the box.

He willed Garth to have a good run. Not that Ty didn't want to win. But he wanted a victory because he'd earned it, not because his biggest rival performed poorly.

The calf darted toward the far end of the arena. Every movement Garth and his horse made was straight out of a textbook. Running along the rope his mount held taut, he dropped the calf to the ground and tied its legs.

The crowd roared, their applause and cheers drowning out the announcer.

Ty didn't need to hear. His gut told him the run was a good one. Better than good, it was great. Equal to his own.

But was it better?

"Ladies and gentlemen, bear with us," the announcer's voice declared. "This is close, and the officials need to be one hundred percent sure."

Ty caught sight of Garth as he reached the gate. Their gazes connected, and Garth gave the briefest of nods. Ty returned it, his silent message the same.

Good run, cowboy.

"Hold on to your hats, folks, we have it," the announcer proclaimed. "Garth Maitland's official time is seven-point-three seconds. That makes Ty Boudeau your winner today!" Cheers exploded from the stands. "With Garth Maitland in second place and Ricky Morales in third."

Ty closed his eyes and dropped his head, savoring the moment. He'd won before, plenty of times. But no victory had ever been sweeter or more hard earned. He was, he knew now without a doubt, on his way to the top. This time he wouldn't lose at the National Finals Rodeo. He and Hamm would take home the title of World Champion and a generous sponsorship deal with it.

All at once, he was surrounded. Friends and fellow contestants pulled him off the fence, congratulating him and slapping him on the back.

"Hell of a run, Ty."

"You had me scared there for a minute, buddy, but you pulled it off."

He took it all in, his grin stretched so wide his face hurt.

"I knew you could do it." Pop appeared beside him.

"I couldn't have without your and Adele's help. I owe the both of you." Ty pulled the older man into a hug. More back-slapping followed, for both him and Pop.

"Maybe I should sign up for a week at Cowboy College," a young man said jokingly.

"Maybe you should," Mitch Benson answered, his face serious.

Ty didn't think that was such a bad idea.

The speakers crackled to life again, and the announcer's voice carried across the arena. "The day's not over yet, folks. Stay in your seats, 'cause next up is the event you've been waiting for. Bull riding."

"See you in Sheridan?" Mitch asked.

Ty shook the hand he extended. "I'll be there. And having another run like today."

"I'm counting on it."

Eventually, everyone started clearing away. Some returned to their trailers to pack up, done for the weekend. Others took a place on the fence or in the bleachers to watch the bull riding.

Ty and Pop hadn't gone more than a few steps when Garth appeared in front of them.

"Congratulations," he told Ty.

"You didn't do so bad yourself today."

"First in team roping. I guess I can live with that."

"Enjoy it while it lasts. I plan on entering team roping at Sheridan."

Pop clapped Ty on the shoulder. "I'll catch up with you later, son. Garth, give your family my regards."

After Pop left, Garth asked, "Who's your partner?"

"I'm not sure yet." Louis had informed Ty earlier that he wouldn't be going to Sheridan.

"How 'bout me?"

Ty laughed. "You're not serious."

"As a heart attack. Willie's kids are getting older, and his wife doesn't want him to go on the road anymore."

Ty understood. "Team rope with you?" he repeated, surprised at how much the idea appealed to him.

"Why not?"

Why not indeed.

"I guess we could give it a try. See how we work together."

Garth grinned. "How long until you leave Seven Cedars?"

He'd been planning on leaving mid-week. Now, he wasn't so sure. "Not for a few days."

"Why don't you come by Tuesday morning? We'll give it a go."

"I'll be there."

"Seven o'clock. Main arena."

No sooner did Garth walk away, than Adele appeared. Ty had no idea how long she'd been standing there or what she'd heard. Only that he couldn't be happier to see her, or wait any longer to hold her.

"You won." She smiled shyly.

"I did." He took a step toward her. "Now, about our date—"

"There he is!"

"Whoo, hoo! Ty, you were amazing."

All at once, he was surrounded by Mike and Sandy and the other students from Cowboy College. Enduring more backslapping, handshakes and hugs, he craned his neck to catch sight of Adele. Good. She hadn't left.

"We're having a celebration potluck cookout tonight at Pop's camper." Sandy's eyes pleaded with Ty. "Say you'll be there."

"Well, I…"

"I know you're probably going out with the other contestants." Her face fell. "But please come. Just for a little while."

"Don't pressure the man," Mike admonished.

Just beyond the group, Adele smiled coyly, obviously amused.

Ty pushed back his hat. "I guess I can come for a while."

Sandy threw her arms around him.

"You'll be there, too, won't you?" one of the students asked Adele.

Her gaze, soft and warm and hinting at what the night might bring, landed on Ty.

He drew in a sharp breath.

"I wouldn't miss it for the world," she said.

Neither would he.

ADELE SURVEYED THE AREA beside her grandfather's truck. If not for the absence of a flickering fire and nocturnal creatures calling to each other, the setting for their gathering could have been a cookout in the woods by Little Twister Creek.

Lawn chairs and overturned crates had been set up in a circle around the portable grill, enhancing the simple but hearty meal they all shared and the conversation that flowed easily—most of it centered on Ty. Kerosene lanterns atop folding tables attracted moths, while alternately casting shadows and light on people's faces.

Ty sat at the head of the circle, relishing the moment. Well, he deserved it, thought Adele. It wasn't easy coming back from a crushing defeat like the one he'd endured. She'd been proud of him today, admiring his tenacity and drive.

Then again, there were a number of things she admired about Ty, including the natural camaraderie he had with people, drawing them to him like those lanterns did the insects. He'd known most of the students here tonight only a short time, yet he treated them like old friends, and they him. It was no surprise Iron Grip Ropes had approached him about a sponsorship deal last year. He'd have made a perfect spokesman. If he continued winning, which he would, maybe they'd approach him again.

Building custom-made saddles the quality of Charlie Kingston's was a fine occupation, but Adele couldn't help thinking Ty was better suited to doing something that got him out and about, rather than being stuck in a workroom all day.

Well, she doubted he'd be building saddles full-time for a while. Not until he retired from rodeoing, which, now that he'd discovered the previously missing connection with Hamm, wouldn't be for several years at least.

Adele went around collecting trash and depositing it in a plastic garbage bag. Some of their neighbors had already packed up their trailers and RVs and departed, leaving open spaces in the makeshift gypsy camp. Most were like her and Pop, planning to start out for home at the crack of dawn.

Pop, in his element, stole the spotlight from Ty and regaled the students with stories from back in the day when he'd competed. Everyone, including Ty, listened raptly.

Despite having had an emotional day with highs, lows and moments of downright confusion, Adele felt a sense of satisfaction. This pleasant gathering of friends, guests and people she cared about was the kind she'd envisioned when she and her grandfather first started Cowboy College.

Not that there weren't sacrifices. She had few opportunities to travel and see the country as she longed to, given all the responsibilities she shouldered.

Yet another reason she and Ty were a poor match. He would settle down eventually. In the meantime, however, he'd be going wherever his rodeo career took him, and that would be miles and miles away from Markton, Wyoming.

"Need help with that?" Sandy asked. Their potluck dinner had consisted mostly of leftovers, topped off with ice cream and peach pies someone had purchased earlier at the market down the road.

"I'm fine," Adele said. "You go sit yourself back down."

Sandy paused, her arms crossed, and stared at the group. "I'm going to miss all this."

"We'll miss you, too."

"Tomorrow when we check out, Mike and I are going to make reservations for next summer."

"That's great. We'd love to have you back."

"We want to come at the same time Ty does."

Adele paused in the middle of securing the garbage bag with a twist tie. "I…don't think he's coming back," she said carefully.

"No?" Sandy appeared puzzled. "He said he was."

"When?"

"Just a little bit ago."

"He did?"

Adele must have given herself away, for Sandy laughed richly. "I thought that might make you happy."

"Of course it does. It's our goal for all our guests to return."

"But Ty in particular."

No, what she really wanted was for Ty to stay and not leave.

But he would. Especially after winning the gold buckle today. That was the whole reason he'd come to Cowboy College. To figure out what he'd been doing wrong, fix it, return to the circuit as soon as possible and resume his promising career.

"*You and Mike* in particular," Adele emphasized, trying to cover her slip.

"Hey, we all think it's great that you and Ty hooked up."

We all? As in the entire guest roster? Adele waited for mortification to overcome her—only it didn't. To her shock, she realized she wasn't upset that guests, and no doubt staff, too, knew she and Ty had "hooked up," as Sandy put it.

"We will see you before we leave, won't we?"

Sandy's question roused Adele from her reverie. "Of course. We'll have a goodbye party at lunch."

"What's that about a party?" Mike asked, coming up and giving his wife's waist a squeeze.

"Adele said we're having one at lunch tomorrow."

"Can I come, too?"

At the sound of Ty's voice behind her, Adele went still.

"Of course." Conscious of her audience, she set the bag of trash by the truck door for disposal later. "Everyone's invited."

"Sandy and I were thinking of going to the country and western bar up the road for something stronger than this." Mike held out his plastic bottle of iced tea. "Some of the folks were saying the band's not half-bad. You two want to go?"

"It's not a far walk," Sandy prompted.

"I don't know." Ty sent Adele a questioning look.

Technically, they had a date tonight, payment for him winning his event. If he wanted to go to the bar, she'd gladly accompany him.

The gleam in his dark eyes, coal-black in the lantern light, indicated he was thinking of something more than a few close dances and a searing kiss or two under a star-filled sky.

Was she ready for that and all the complications that went with it?

If not, she had better tell him no right now.

"Be back in a while, Pop," she called out, without looking away from Ty.

"Stay out of trouble, you two," he hollered back, an unmistakable smile in his voice.

Define trouble, Adele thought as Ty fell into step beside her.

Chapter Eleven

Sandy's mile-a-minute chatter hid the fact that Ty and Adele contributed very little to the conversation. Adele couldn't speak for him, but in her case, an acute case of nerves had frozen her vocal cords. Instinct told her whatever happened tonight between them would be entirely up to her. He would respect and honor any decision she made.

If only she was certain what her decision would be.

Correction.

If only she was certain she wouldn't end up being hurt.

Sandy's prattling continued as they reached the outskirts of the makeshift gypsy camp.

"Hold on." Ty stopped in midstep and patted his jeans pocket. "I forgot my wallet in my trailer."

"We'll walk back with you," Mike offered.

"I hate to hold you up."

"You sure?" Sandy asked, her oval face lit by the parking lot lights.

"Go on ahead and find us a table."

They started out, then stopped again. "You coming?" Mike asked Adele.

Her vocal cords had yet to thaw.

"Come on." Sandy linked arms with her husband. "They'll be along in a minute." Dragging him with her, she glanced over her shoulder and chimed, "Take your time, you two."

"My trailer's this way." Ty inclined his head in the direction they'd come.

Adele nodded, swallowed and took a step.

He reached for her hand. When it was clasped firmly in his, walking wasn't nearly so difficult.

"I didn't plan this," he said, his voice low and husky. "I really did forget my wallet."

She believed him. Cowboys didn't usually carry their wallets when they competed, and Ty hadn't returned to his trailer since winning his event.

They saw many familiar faces as they navigated among the campsites. If their joined hands solicited any attention, Adele didn't care. As Sandy had pointed out, everyone at Cowboy College knew about her and Ty's attraction. So what if the rest of the world found out, too?

Suddenly, Adele wasn't indecisive anymore. Her heart, which had been whispering to her softly for weeks, now spoke loud and clear, urging her to seize the moment.

"I'm parked over there."

She followed his gaze. Ty's trailer stood alone, his neighbors having left already. Hamm, along with the other horses, was bedded down in the event stables.

Going straight to the rear wheel well, Ty located a hidden key and unlocked the side door, careful not to let it bang against the wall. At this time of night, the noise would carry half a mile.

"I won't be long," he said, and reached through the open door.

A dim light came on, illuminating the postage-stamp-size living quarters. Placing an old footstool on the ground, he grabbed the side-mounted handhold and easily hefted himself up and inside the trailer.

Adele heard the scrape of a sliding drawer. The scuffle of boots on linoleum flooring. The jingle of keys being dropped on the counter. She also heard the sound of her own boots on the footstool as she copied Ty and clasped the handhold.

He turned, his expression unreadable as he took in the sight of her standing in the trailer doorway. "The place is a little small, but I'd be happy to show you around."

Was he keeping his emotions in check? Making a joke in case he'd misinterpreted the reason she'd so boldly entered his private space? A space that could be even more private if the door was shut. Reaching behind her, she swung it closed. The clicking latch echoed loudly in the suddenly quiet interior.

So did the beating of her soaring heart.

"Adele?"

She hadn't spoken since leaving Pop's campsite, and didn't now.

Crossing the small distance separating them, she reached up and circled his neck with her arms. His eyes, which had tracked her progress, instantly went from unreadable to blazing hot.

"You know this is dangerous," he said in a roughened voice, pulling her close until their bodies were flush and their hips aligned.

Was it? Adele had been thinking it was exciting and daring and incredibly intoxicating. Not dangerous.

She sought his mouth, moaning softly at the first touch of his lips. Moaning again when the kiss became possessive. Heat arrowed though her, igniting every nerve in its path. This, she thought numbly, was only the beginning. There could—and would—be so much more.

Ty pushed away from her, catching her off guard, his chest heaving. "We'd better slow it down some."

Adele made a sound of protest.

"I can't take much more of this and stay sane."

They'd have to risk his sanity, she thought, a smile pulling at her lips. She liked the hard ridge of his erection pressing firmly into the junction of her legs—liked it too much to stop.

Nestling closer, she rubbed her calf along his and twirled her fingers in the soft curls at the back of his neck.

As if in surrender, he leaned against the closet door behind him. "Adele, sweetheart. Please."

Please what? Leave him alone or give in to the desire that had been building practically since the day he arrived at Cowboy College?

She laid her palms flat on his chest. Beneath the fabric of his shirt, his heart beat fast and erratically. How much of it, she wondered, had he given to her? Enough that it would be torture for him to leave her in a few days?

Yes. She didn't require a declaration made on bended knee to know she'd come to mean something special to him. Something he wouldn't find anywhere else, regardless of where his travels took him.

She brought her hands together over the top button of his shirt and quickly unfastened it.

Before she got to the second button, he grasped her wrist, staying her motions. "Are you sure?"

Nodding, she gazed at him, hoping he saw the depths of her feelings for him reflected in her face.

"Say something, Adele. Please."

She put him out of his misery. "Make love to me, Ty."

She expected him to respond with another kiss, one designed to rob her of her ability to think coherently. He didn't. Instead, he tucked her head snugly against his chest and brushed his lips across her hair.

"I want you to know this won't be a casual fling."

Could it be anything else? He was leaving soon.

"I'll be back for you. Count on it."

His earnestness touched her.

"I'll be waiting," she said.

He kissed her then, sweetly, tenderly and with a gentleness she wouldn't have expected from a rugged, brawny cowboy like him.

Quickly, however, the kiss turned scorching. His mouth, unsatisfied with teasing and tormenting just her lips, sought out other sensitive places on her body. Her neck. The delicate skin of her earlobe. The soft hollow at the base of her throat.

Adele's limbs went weak as a needy moan escaped.

All at once Ty was tugging at her shirttail, releasing it from the waistband of her jeans. Then he reached up under the fabric and grasped her waist.

Opening his shirt, she ran her hands down his white cotton T-shirt, enjoying the sensation of downy fabric over the taut planes of his chest. All during their sensual interplay, his lips continued exploring her sensitive regions. That stopped when her fingers brushed against his belt buckle. With a deep groan, he claimed her mouth again, stripping her shirt from her as he did.

The lighting was dim, but Ty still had a clear view of her baby-blue bra. He traced a fingertip along the lacy trim, murmuring, "Nice."

And it was. Adele might be all cowgirl on the outside, but she had an appreciation for delicate underthings.

"You told me to wear something sexy."

Emboldened by his hungry gaze, she peeled his shirt from his shoulders. He took over, shrugging it off and removing his T-shirt. She'd expected him to have a well-honed body, considering how hard he worked at roping, and she wasn't disappointed.

All at once she saw it, a lasso tattoo circling his upper right arm. It fit Ty's personality and brought a smile to her lips. "Nice," she murmured, echoing his earlier remark.

"You don't mind tattoos?"

"I have one, too."

His eyes lit up. "Where?"

She lowered the strap of her bra, revealing a tiny horse's head with flowing mane above her left breast. The same one used in the Cowboy College logo.

Ty's breath caught. Lowering his mouth, he pressed his lips to the tattoo.

Even if Adele had wanted to guard her emotions, she couldn't any longer. Not after this. Not with Ty.

She gasped when he unexpectedly tugged down the front of her bra and cupped her freed breast. Gasped again when he circled the nipple with his tongue.

In a hurry, she grabbed at her own belt.

Ty raised his head. "No rush, sweetheart. We've got all night. Unless you still want to go to the bar with Mike and Sandy."

"Not on your life." She finished unbuckling her belt, then attacked the snap on her jeans.

"Wait." Ty covered her hands with his.

"What?"

Before her insecurities could get the better of her, he said, "I...have protection." He fumbled for the wallet on the counter, opened it and withdrew a condom.

"That's good." Stupid her. She'd been so caught up in making love with Ty, she'd forgotten about being responsible.

"I want you to know..." Again he hesitated. "This has been in my wallet awhile." He tried to grin. "In case you thought otherwise."

There were cowboys on the rodeo circuit notorious for sleeping around. And they had plenty of obliging women at their disposal. Adele believed Ty, however, and not just because he had a reputation for being one of the honorable guys. She believed him because of the genuine worry in his expression.

"I didn't think otherwise," she said. "And for the record, it's been a long while for me, too."

"Glad that's settled," he said, and kissed her again.

With all doubts erased and all barriers eradicated, they were able to revel in the feel of each other's body and the wildly erotic sensations generated by their intimate explorations. The tiny living quarters didn't allow much space for maneuvering. And without stopping to convert the dining table into a sleeping bunk, they had nowhere to lie down.

Ty showed himself to be good at improvising.

Removing the remainder of Adele's clothing, he lifted her onto the table. When she reached for him, he grabbed a pillow from the seat, placed it behind her and lowered her backward.

Starting at the horse's head tattoo, he traveled the length of her body to the V of her legs, leaving moist kisses in his wake. The skill of his mouth was matched only by the skill of his fingers. Both tantalized her unmercifully, and within minutes, she was perched on the pinnacle of release.

He didn't, however, take her over the edge, and she almost cried out in frustration when he straightened. All was forgiven when he unbuckled his jeans and stepped out of them.

She raised up on her elbows, to better see Ty in his slim fitting boxer briefs. Without the least bit of modesty, he removed them, opened the condom package and sheathed himself. Pulse soaring, she sat upright, every nerve alight with anticipation.

Except he didn't move.

"Ty? What's wrong?"

"Nothing." His dark eyes studied her from head to toe. "I just like looking at you."

He certainly knew how to prolong the agony. Or was that pleasure? Definitely pleasure. Her entire body hummed with it.

Unable to wait any longer, she arched her spine and smiled temptingly.

That did it. With an agonized groan, he grasped her legs and anchored her to him.

Adele gasped in surprise, then delight, when he entered her. Wrapping her legs around his middle, she clung to him, wanting an emotional connection with him more than she did a physical one.

Ty held back, she could tell. And as much as she wanted to tumble over the edge, she also wanted their lovemaking to last.

Murmuring sweet, sexy endearments, he bent her backward until she once again lay on the table. Covering her with his body, he kissed her deeply, his hands cupping her breasts.

Adele could wait no longer and climaxed, Ty's name on her lips. He found his own shattering release seconds later.

She clung tightly to him, savoring the aftermath of their shared storm almost as much as she had the storm itself.

Slowly, their breathing returned to normal. What could have been an awkward moment was made comfortable and easy when Ty lifted her off the table and enveloped her in a warm embrace.

"That was amazing," he said, caressing her back with strong strokes. "You're amazing."

Adele turned her face into the side of his neck. She hardly considered herself an accomplished lover. Yet it *had* been amazing with Ty. More than that, it had felt…perfect.

For a moment, she imagined them together always.

Then, too soon, reality returned.

"I suppose we should get to the bar," Adele said, easing away from Ty to look for her clothes. "Mike and Sandy are expecting us."

"Do you really want to go?"

She shook her head. "But I'm not sure I want to stand here all night. Naked, at that."

One corner of his mouth tilted up in a wicked grin. "The table converts to a bed."

She liked that idea.

Laughing together, they hurriedly removed the tabletop and replaced it with a plank, then arranged the cushions into a mattress. Ty pulled a worn sleeping bag from the overhead cupboard, and they cuddled beneath it, his arm draped over her protectively and their fingers linked.

"Come with me to Ogden," he said out of the blue.

"Utah?"

"The Pioneer Days Rodeo starts the third weekend in July."

"That's only two weeks away."

"Plenty of time to pack."

"I'd love to go with you." She rolled over to face him. "More than you know. But I have to work. I can't just up and leave, not on such short notice."

"There's no one to cover for you?"

"It's our busy season."

"Then I'll skip Ogden."

"No, you won't." She pressed a light kiss to his lips. "You're winning again. You have to ride the momentum all the way to Nationals."

"I'm winning because of you."

"You always had the ability. I just helped you realize it."

"I'm coming back to Seven Cedars." He moved suddenly, throwing a leg over her and pinning her to the cushions. His hand boldly roamed her buttocks and thighs. "Don't think I'm not."

She arched into him. "I'll be waiting."

"Promise me."

A vulnerability she hadn't seen before shone in his eyes.

"I promise." The vow came easily.

"I know long-distance relationships are difficult, but we can make this work. There isn't anything I want more."

Hearing his conviction, she almost believed they could succeed where her parents had failed. Ty spent the next hour convincing her, with actions that left no doubt as to his sincerity.

HAMM ENTERED THE horse trailer without his customary balking, as if he couldn't wait to leave Cowboy College and Seven Cedars Ranch.

Adele would have preferred he put up a fight.

She'd been dreading this moment for the last five days, ever since the night she and Ty had spent together in his trailer. Standing off to the side, she watched him shut the trailer door, latch and lock it, then check the lock again just to make sure. Was he really worried that the door would swing open during the drive or simply delaying their final goodbye? He'd already missed his planned 9:00 A.M. departure time by almost an hour.

If anyone had noticed she'd spent the last four nights in Ty's cabin rather than her apartment, they said nothing. Probably because they approved of her and Ty's relationship, albeit for different reasons. Pop had more than once vocalized his desire to see Adele settled, and the employees were, she suspected, glad their boss was enjoying something other than work for a change. Reese had openly expressed her joy during Ty and Garth's first official team roping practice on Tuesday. But then, she was happily engaged to be married, and wanted all her friends to be happy, too.

"You drive careful, you hear?" Cook said. She was among the small crowd that had gathered to see Ty off.

"You're welcome back anytime." Pop's voice had a slight catch in it.

So, Adele thought, did Ty's when he answered. "I'm taking you up on that offer."

The two men started out shaking hands, but Ty pulled Pop into a bear hug. Adele felt her throat close. Five days of mental preparation obviously wasn't enough. She couldn't remember the last time she'd done anything half this hard.

"Stick, I'm counting on you to watch out for Adele and Pop while I'm gone." Ty hooked an arm around the skinny teenager's neck.

"Sure thing."

"You're a good man."

Stick's perpetual goofy grin widened.

Ty spoke to each person there, dispensing handshakes, hugs and pecks on cheeks, including one for Lani. Adele and she were on better terms, thanks in large part to Pop's recent revelations, but Adele continued to be guarded around her, unconvinced her mother had changed her ways.

Watching Lani hug Ty, Adele thought she saw genuine tears well in her mother's eyes, and she was struck with a sentimental pang. The next moment, she dismissed it. Lani knew how to put on an act with the best of them, especially around men.

Tipping his hat in one last farewell to all, Ty went to Adele and took her hand. "Walk me to my truck."

Though she generally shied away from public displays of affection, no way was he leaving without a last, lingering kiss.

Ty was of the same mind, except he carried it one step further. Amid good-natured hoots and hollers, he bent her over his arm and planted a kiss on her mouth to beat all kisses. Adele's toes were still tingling when he released her.

"I'll call you tonight."

She nodded, afraid she might cry if she tried to talk.

He reached for the door handle.

"Wait!"

Throwing her arms around him, she stood on tiptoes and pressed her face into the curve of his neck. "I'll miss you."

"Me, too, sweetheart."

Two minutes later, he was gone, his truck and trailer pulling out of the open area and heading down the long drive that would take him past the main lodge and to the highway beyond.

Adele stood there watching until the last plume of dust had dissipated. During her vigil, the others left, perhaps sensing her need to be alone.

Not yet ready to return to work, she strolled to the small barn. It had been several days since her last visit with Crackers. More than that, the quiet solitude would enable her to fortify her defenses before having to deal with people and the inevitable well-intentioned platitudes or personal questions.

Crackers nickered hello. The filly—Adele had named her Ritz—pushed her nose up, seeking a petting. Naturally curious and playful, Ritz couldn't get enough attention.

It was exactly the balm Adele needed to soothe her aching heart. She'd done her best to resist Ty, and yet she'd fallen for him. Head over heels and faster than she'd ever imagined possible. The three weeks until he returned were going to seem like three decades.

"There you are!"

Adele winced. *Oh, no! Why now?*

"I'm glad I found you." Lani scurried toward her, a big, bright smile on her face.

"Hi, Mom. I was just about to get ready for class." Yes, it was a lie, but Adele felt she'd be forgiven this once.

"There's something I need to tell you." Lani came to a stop, looking chagrined. The expression took several years off her face, transforming her into the attractive woman she'd once been. Adele also noticed her mother had filled out a little recently, the extra weight adding a softness to her previous bone-thin frame. "I've been stalling and stalling, and I just can't anymore."

She's leaving! Adele had been anticipating just such an announcement for weeks.

"I'm moving." Lani's smile reappeared.

"Where to?" Adele didn't add, "this time."

"Right in town. I found an efficiency apartment to rent. It's not much, but will do for a while. I need to get my own place and stop mooching off you and your grandfather."

"Oh." When did her mother start worrying about being a mooch?

"And it's close to the feed store."

Adele's stomach dropped to her knees. She should have guessed Lani wanted her own place nearby in order to carry on her affair with Henry.

"He's a married man, Mom."

"Who?"

"Henry."

"I know that."

"And it doesn't stop you?"

"From what?" Lani shook her head in confusion.

"Sleeping with him," Adele all but spit out.

"Good heavens! Is that what you think?"

"I saw you and him at the Spotted Horse."

Hurt—and disappointment?—glinted in Lani's eyes. "He offered me a job."

"A job?"

"At the feed store. His assistant manager gave notice." Lani sniffed. "I don't take up with married men. And I certainly don't take up with my boss."

"I—I..." Adele was speechless.

"I thought if I got a full-time job and my own place, that maybe you and I could, well, work things out. I've made a ton of mistakes over the years and was just trying to fix a few of them." She sniffed again. "I guess I was wrong."

"Mom." Adele struggled to find the words—any words—to say. "I'm sorry. I jumped to the wrong conclusion."

Lani's face crumpled. "I'm sorry, too. I really did want to do the right thing for once. And when Henry offered me the job, I figured it was a good place to start."

A job and an apartment. One Lani paid for herself. Not an affair. And a chance to repair some of those burned bridges. Small steps in a very right direction.

Part of Adele resisted. Lani had never been much of a mother, disappointing her one too many times for her to be sucked in by the promise of change.

But if she didn't acknowledge her mom's efforts and support them, then perhaps she wasn't much of a daughter, either.

"It is a good place to start. I'm glad for you."

"Really?" Lani's teary eyes shone.

"And...proud."

"Oh, baby." Lani pulled her into a fierce hug. "I'm so proud of you, too. Everything you've done, the ranch, Cowboy College. Much as I tried to screw you up, you still turned out to be this incredible woman. Smart and talented and... oh, that Ty Boudeau is one lucky fellow to have you."

Slowly, very slowly, Adele returned her mother's hug. After a moment, she increased the pressure.

Maybe it was having a wonderful man like Ty in her life. Maybe it was being secure at Seven Cedars and knowing her place in the world. Whatever the reason, Adele felt some of the resentment she'd carried around for over twenty years fade, and her spirits, which had sunk so low when Ty left, gradually lift.

Chapter Twelve

All Ty wanted, all he'd been thinking about for the last eight hours and the last four hundred miles, was seeing Adele. Holding her, kissing her, unraveling that long braid of hers and running his fingers through her silky hair. Seven phone calls, starting this morning and ending just outside of Markton, hadn't slaked his desire to see her. If anything, they'd increased it.

The sight of the main gate leading into Seven Cedars hit Ty like a drink of cool water after a long walk in the hot desert.

He was home.

Wait a minute! When had he started thinking of Seven Cedars as home?

Since he'd left three weeks ago. Not an hour passed when he didn't imagine returning to Adele and everything he'd come to hold dear.

His gaze scanned right and left as his truck bumped along the drive and into the open area in front of the barns. He was early, but had hoped Adele would be waiting for him. They'd agreed during one of those seven phone calls that he would take Hamm to the small corral east of the arena and let him run around a bit before putting him up for the night.

A night Ty intended to spend every moment of, waking and sleeping, with Adele.

Hamm, impatient as always to be free, banged a foot on the trailer door the instant the truck came to a stop. Three minutes later, the big gelding was trotting off steam, tossing his head, and strutting his stuff for the other horses in the nearby pasture.

Ty took out his cell phone, intending to call Adele.

"He looks happy to be out."

He spun at the sound of Pop's voice behind him, and grinned broadly. "He's not the only one."

"Long drive?"

"Too long. My legs are killing me."

"How about I trade you for mine?"

Ty had noticed the older man's limp was more pronounced than before. "Hip bothering you?"

"Some. But not, I hope, for long."

"I heard you finally agreed to the replacement surgery."

Adele had given Ty the news the day after he left. It seemed Pop had postponed telling her so as not to interfere with her and Ty's time together.

"A week from Thursday," Pop said. "I wanted to wait, but that granddaughter of mine is a hard one to resist."

Ty concurred wholeheartedly.

"She's in her office if you're looking for her."

"I don't want to disturb her if she's working."

"I'm thinking she won't mind."

"Hamm needs to—"

"Go on. I'll take care of your horse."

"You sure?"

Pop scowled. "I'm not a cripple yet."

Ty needed no further persuading.

As he walked across the lobby's hardwood floor, he was reminded of his first day at the ranch and of how much had changed during the last seven weeks. He and Hamm were in perfect sync, with three shiny new buckles to show for it.

Two in tie-down roping and one in team roping with Garth. That didn't count the two second-place finishes Ty had taken in steer wrestling. Altogether, the winnings were enough to bankroll him for the next six rodeos, as well as make a small but overdue payment to his parents.

And then there was Adele. He hated being apart from her, but knowing that what he was doing would eventually give them the means for a life together fueled his determination and made the long, lonely days without her bearable.

He hurried his steps, their echo resounding through the empty lobby. She must have heard him, for she appeared in the office doorway just as he was rounding the registration counter.

"You're early," she said, her face alight with excitement.

"I broke enough traffic laws to put me away for years if I'd been caught."

"I'm glad you weren't."

Not caring if anyone walked by and saw them, he clasped her in his arms. The next instant, his mouth was where it had wanted to be for hours. Days. Weeks. And he didn't hurry, despite them having only until the morning before he had to leave again for the next rodeo. This moment was worth savoring.

Except Adele had other ideas.

She didn't merely return his kiss, she took control of it, giving him a hint of what to expect later.

"That's some greeting," he said, his entire body responding to the fire in her eyes and the heat in her touch. "Mind if I leave and come back for another one?"

"Don't worry, cowboy. There's more where that came from."

He laughed, his first real one in weeks. Did she have any idea how good she made him feel? "I've missed you."

Her features abruptly crumbled, and she shielded her face with her hand.

"You're not crying, are you?"

"No." But she was.

Ty escorted her into her office, shutting the door behind them. "What's wrong, sweetheart?"

She wiped her cheek with the back of her hand. "I'm just happy to see you."

He sat down in her desk chair, then pulled her onto his lap. The chair groaned under their combined weight. "I'm happy to see you, too."

She curled into a ball, combing her fingers through his hair while he stroked her back.

"This isn't how I wanted it to be," she murmured. "I had other plans."

"From what I could tell earlier, I like your plans."

She tilted her face up to his, and he kissed her again. This time tenderly. "I don't know what's wrong with me lately. I've been so emotional."

"You have a lot going on. Pop said his surgery's next Thursday."

"Yeah. And while I can't wait for him to have it, I'm not looking forward to it." She outlined some of the details of the procedure and the daunting challenges she and her grandfather faced.

"Pop will do fine. He's not about to let a little thing like hip-replacement surgery get him down."

"You're right. I'm just not sure about me." She nestled closer with a soft sigh. "Are you hungry yet?"

"Yes." Ty lowered his head and nibbled her ear.

She wriggled away. "I meant for food. We can have an early dinner in the dining hall and then…" She ended the sentence with an inviting smile.

"Or we could 'then' first, and have a late dinner."

He'd been joking—sort of. Adele surprised and delighted him by agreeing.

After stopping briefly to check on Hamm, they sneaked off to her apartment. Or tried to. Every few minutes they ran into someone glad to see Ty and wanting to chat. A half hour later they were finally alone, secluded in Adele's bedroom and tearing off each other's clothes.

When Adele would have hurried, Ty restrained her, determined to prolong the enjoyment. Afterward, they lay with their limbs entwined in her antique brass bed, her lavender sheets strewn across their bodies, the last rays of sunlight streaming through the parted curtains of her window.

"I talked to Garth yesterday," he said, his lips brushing the soft tendrils at her temple.

"Mmm?"

"His parents and Reese are flying out to the Steamboat Springs Rodeo this weekend. They've invited you to come along."

She shook her head. "I can't."

The conversation sounded a lot like their previous one. Regardless, Ty continued. "Why not? You'd only be gone three days."

"Pop's having his surgery."

"Next Thursday. You'll be back in plenty of time."

Adele shifted. Only a little, but the two inches felt like two feet.

"There are tests he has to have. Blood work, X-rays, consultations with the doctors. The medical center's a two-hour round trip. He can't drive it alone."

"Stick could go with him."

"But he can't help Pop with all the paperwork. And believe me, between the doctor, hospital and insurance company, there's a mountain of it. On top of that, I have to meet with the barn manager and the head wrangler. Make sure Pop's work is covered while he recuperates."

Ty felt overwhelmed just listening to her, and wished there was more he could do for her.

"I'm sorry." He pulled her against him, not satisfied until those two inches separating them were reduced to a hair's width. "I'm pressuring you, and that's not my intention."

"I really wish I could come."

"Maybe I'll skip Steamboat Springs. Spend a few extra days here."

She immediately sat up and said sternly, "You'll do no such thing."

"I don't have to compete in every rodeo between now and Nationals."

"Have you qualified yet?"

"No, but—"

"Paid back your parents?"

"Not everything."

"Seriously, Ty." She groaned with exasperation. "You know better than anyone that things happen. Unexpected things. You've come too far and worked too hard to risk not qualifying."

She was right, though a part of him wished she wasn't.

"I guess we'll just have to make the most of this visit." He reached under the sheet, seeking and finding the smooth curve of her hip.

Her sigh of contentment turned into a moan of pleasure when he parted her legs.

The ring of her cell phone couldn't have come at a worse time.

"Don't answer it," he murmured, lowering his mouth to her breast.

"That's Pop's ring tone. If I don't pick up, he'll come looking for us."

Ty would have preferred weighing their options. Not Adele. She swung her legs over the side of the bed and rummaged around on the floor for her jeans.

"Yeah, Pop." She listened a moment, then held the phone away from her mouth. "Cook's putting together a little celebration dinner for you."

"Sounds like I can't say no."

"Wise man."

He lay in bed, both pillows stuffed under his head, watching her dress.

"Come on," she urged. "We're going to be late."

"I'd rather stay here with you."

She tugged on his arm. "It's only temporary."

Was it? He and Adele hadn't spoken about the future, not specifically and not beyond Nationals this winter. He suspected that, like him, she was thinking long term.

She'd *better* be thinking long term, Ty amended as he finally rolled out of bed and reached for his clothes. Because he had zero intentions of letting her go. Now or ever.

"THIS WAY." ADELE took two steps. When she heard nothing, she stopped and glanced anxiously over her shoulder. "Easy now."

"I'm all right," Pop snapped. He'd caught one front wheel of his walker on the threshold leading from the garage to the kitchen.

She resisted hurrying to his aid. He was too stubborn to accept her help even if she did. Besides, Stick stood right behind him. The teenager might be skinny, but he was strong, and more than capable of catching her grandfather if he teetered.

The wheel finally gave, hopping over the threshold, and he maneuvered the shiny red walker into the kitchen. His steps were hesitant, measured and stiff, burdened by the compression stockings he was required to wear.

Adele hurt just looking at him.

The doctor, nurses and physical therapist, however, had praised Pop's progress, stating repeatedly that he was doing well for a man his age.

A man his age!

Adele had begun to view her grandfather through different eyes and didn't like what she saw. Though in good health, he was getting older and slowing down. More of the responsibility of running the ranch and Cowboy College would fall to her, and not just during his recovery.

She prayed the next few weeks would go easier than this last one had. Talks with Pop's doctor prior to the surgery hadn't prepared her for the sight of him lying in the hospital bed surrounded by tubes and monitors, a bulky dressing on his hip and his complexion the color of paste. Her emotions, riding so close to the surface of late, had overwhelmed her, causing tears to fall at the least little provocation.

Oddly enough, it had been her mother who was there for Adele the day of the surgery, sitting with her in the family waiting area. Lani also found time to make the long drive and visit Pop twice during his hospital stay, though she remained only briefly because of her work schedule.

It was Ty, however, who had provided the most support for Adele during and after Pop's surgery. He volunteered to fly in for a day or two, but she'd have none of it, insisting he stay and continue to ride his winning streak. She'd have felt differently if Pop's surgery had been life threatening. Ty's phone calls, three a day at least, were enough for now. They gave her a break from the many nerve-racking demands placed on her, and reassured her that what they had together was special and important to him.

That didn't stop her from occasionally wondering if they'd

be able to endure the continued long separations. When Ty mentioned her traveling with him on the circuit, or returning to Santa Fe to visit his parents, she allowed herself to get swept up in his excitement. Then she would look at her grandfather and accept the reality that she'd probably never travel any farther than the medical center in Cody. Not for a while, anyway.

Would Ty wait for her?

She hadn't yet found the courage to ask him.

All at once, a wave of nausea struck her. She sucked in a harsh breath and pressed a hand to her stomach. Just as quickly, the feeling subsided, and she exhaled with relief. The stress was getting to her. She'd been feeling mildly ill off and on since before Pop went in for his surgery. And tired. Some mornings, she barely had the energy to climb out of bed, requiring a second cup of coffee to get her day started. She'd be so glad when Pop got back on his feet.

"Did you remember my prescriptions from the car?" Pop stood in the middle of the kitchen, his chest rising and falling from the exertion. And all he'd done was walk from the car.

"Right here." Adele held up a small white sack.

"What about my overnight bag?"

"I'll get that later. Unless you need it this second."

"Guess not," he grumbled.

He wasn't being intentionally difficult, she knew. His doctor had warned Adele to expect periodic mood swings. In addition to the surgery taking a toll on him, there was the daunting prospect of being mostly housebound for two to four weeks. Pop didn't do modified bed rest and restricted activity well.

"Come on, Pop," Stick said good-naturedly. "I'll help you to bed."

"All right, all right. Don't rush me."

"You want some lunch?" Adele asked.

"Not yet. Maybe later."

Her grandfather going willingly to bed and not hungry? Her worry instantly flared. He must really feel awful.

"I'll take something, if you're offering." Stick grinned sheepishly.

"Coming right up."

While he settled her grandfather in bed, she threw a quick lunch together. The aroma of grilling cheese sandwiches started her stomach roiling again. Piling the one she'd fixed for herself on Stick's plate, she heated up a bowl of canned chicken-noodle soup, hoping that would sit better.

She was just putting the lunch on the table when Ty called her cell phone.

"How's Pop? You two get home okay?"

"A little bit ago." The sexy timbre of his voice warmed her from the inside out. No matter how often he called, she never grew tired of hearing it. Especially late at night.

Stick came down the hall, spied the lunch on the table and fell on it like a typical ravenous teenager.

"How's Pop?" Adele mouthed.

"Sleeping," Stick managed to say between bites.

"Stick's here, helping out," she told Ty.

"That's good. Hey, I was thinking of coming out on Monday for a couple days."

"Aren't you in Missoula?"

"Just pulled into the fairgrounds."

Missoula was a long way from Markton. "When do you compete?"

"I'll be done Sunday afternoon by five. I checked with the airlines and can catch a late flight. A friend of mine's agreed to take care of Hamm for me. Problem is, I wouldn't land until about 10:00 P.M. your time. Is that too late?"

Yellowstone Regional Airport was over a hundred miles

away. Picking up Ty added yet another task to her already extensive list. Then driving him back two days later.

But, oh, she wanted to be with him. Sleep for ten hours straight wrapped in his arms. Okay, she admitted it. Sleep wasn't the only activity she had in mind. After showing him how happy she was to see him, they'd loll around in bed all morning, not rising until the sun was high in the sky.

No, they wouldn't. She'd have to come here and check on Pop. Make sure he was doing okay.

"I—I don't know," she stammered.

"I miss you."

His longing carried across the miles, and her heart melted. "I'll be there at ten sharp waiting for you."

If necessary, she'd hire a nurse for two days. Or see if one of the wranglers' wives was interested in earning a little extra money. Pop might be more receptive to that idea.

"Wear your blue bra," Ty said in a husky drawl.

She laughed and stepped into the family room, away from Stick's prying ears. He didn't need to hear the more private details of her conversation with Ty. Some minutes later, when they disconnected, she rationalized her decision to let him come by telling herself a visit from him would boost Pop's morale.

But it was her own morale that was now soaring in anticipation. So much so that she wolfed down her reheated soup and went back for seconds.

"Call if you need me," Stick said later, on his way out the door.

"I will." Adele hoped she wouldn't have to.

While Pop continued to nap, she tidied the kitchen and emptied the car. The four-door sedan belonged to Garth's parents. They'd been kind enough to lend it to Adele and Pop while he recovered, for which she was enormously grateful.

She couldn't imagine trying to wrestle her grandfather in and out of his tall truck.

When she finished unloading, she went into the old master bedroom and unpacked her few belongings. They'd agreed she would reside with Pop until he could manage on his own. She hadn't brought much with her, figuring on returning to her apartment every day for whatever she needed.

Her grandparents' bedroom had remained virtually untouched for eight years, and Adele found herself studying pictures on the wall and knickknacks on the dresser that were still where her grandmother had placed them.

It would be strange spending the night here, sleeping among the memories.

A knock on the kitchen door had her hurrying down the hall in her stocking feet.

"Coming!" she called, then remembered her grandfather was sleeping.

Whoever had shown up was comfortable enough that they'd used the back door. Probably one of the hands checking on Pop, or someone from the kitchen. Adele had arranged with Cook to have meals delivered during his convalescence.

It was none of those people.

"Hey, baby girl."

"Mom! What are you doing here? I thought you were at work."

ADELE STEPPED BACK so that her mother could come inside, silently chiding the part of her that wished Lani had called first and not just shown up.

"Henry let me off early today." Lani carried a plastic grocery sack bearing the name Bush's General Store, Markton's one and only market. It probably contained a get-well present for Pop. "How are you holding up?"

"Better now that we're home."

"You look tired." Lani studied Adele with a critical and unusually maternal eye.

"Actually, I'm feeling better than I did a while ago."

"Still getting queasy?"

"Sometimes," Adele answered reluctantly. This wasn't the first time Lani had inquired about her health, and she'd begun to regret mentioning her intermittent bouts of nausea. "If you want to visit Pop, you'll have to wait or come back. He's napping."

"I really came to see you." Lani set the sack on the table.

"Something the matter?" Fresh worries immediately sprang to Adele's mind. Was her mother's job at the feed store not working out? Did she want to return to the ranch? And get her old one back?

"No. Not with me, at least." Lani's expression was kind and filled with a concern Adele hadn't seen in years. "You've not been yourself lately."

"I have a lot going on at the moment," she said, a bit testily.

"I know you do. You're tired and irritable and—"

"Stress does that to a person."

"So does pregnancy."

The comment came so far from left field, Adele couldn't immediately absorb it. "I'm...not pregnant."

"Are you sure? You have the symptoms."

"Why would you... That's ridiculous!" She wasn't about to admit to her mother that she and Ty had been intimate, or discuss the type of protection they'd used.

"If you're not pregnant, then it could be something else. Better to know for sure." Lani opened the grocery sack and withdrew a box. "I bought this for you. I figured you wouldn't want to. Not in Markton. One thing I've learned since moving here is that folks *love* to gossip."

Adele stared at the home pregnancy test, not sure what

shocked her the most—her mother having the gall to butt into her personal life, or the possibility that she really was pregnant.

When was her last period?

She'd been too busy with Pop and his surgery to think about it. Now that she did, she realized she was late. By several weeks.

It couldn't be! She and Ty were careful.

But condoms weren't foolproof. And he'd said he'd been carrying that one in his wallet a long time.

Adele had to sit down before her knees buckled. With an unsteady hand, she pulled out a kitchen chair. Her mother was talking, but the words were only partially registering.

"This is one of those twin-pack early pregnancy tests. I didn't know if maybe you wanted to take one test this afternoon and then the second one tomorrow, just to be sure."

"Take the test now?"

"It's pretty simple." Through a fog, Adele watched her mother remove the kit from the package and unfold the instructions. "It's been a while since I've used one of these, but I doubt they've changed much in the last ten years."

Little by little, the enormity of the situation began to sink in. Adele could indeed be pregnant. Or not. Either way, she needed to find out.

"How does it work?" she asked in a weak voice, taking the testing kit from Lani.

While her mother read the instructions out loud, she rolled the wand between her fingers. Then she went to the hall bathroom and completed the test.

She waited the required time, sitting on the closed toilet-seat lid, an undefined ache lodged beneath her breast. Under different circumstances—if she and Ty were married, for instance—this would be a joyous occasion. Except they weren't married. They hadn't even discussed anything beyond dating.

Her mind swirled as question after question formed.

What about Pop and work and the ranch? She was only just beginning to grapple with the likelihood of having to take on additional tasks in the coming months. A child would triple her responsibilities. How would she cope?

Maybe she wouldn't have to. The results might be negative.

She gazed down at the testing wand in her hand, the plus sign clearly visible now. Even so, she squinted, doubting what her eyes saw.

Then it hit her. An emotion that could only be described as elation. It crashed over her in waves, bringing a huge smile to her face.

A baby! She was having a baby.

Adele stepped from the bathroom and into the kitchen, the testing wand extended in front of her.

Lani stood, her face expectant. An affection Adele hadn't felt for her mother in years filled her, and she impulsively opened her arms. Lani rushed to her, returning the hug *and* the affection.

"Well?" she asked when they separated.

Adele showed her the wand, and Lani, too, broke into a radiant smile.

"I'm going to be a grandmother."

Chapter Thirteen

Adele stood in the middle of Pop's kitchen with her mother, dazed and a little in awe at the realization that she was pregnant.

Possibly pregnant, she amended. As the package instructions recommended, she should take the test again tomorrow morning just to be sure.

Except Adele *was* sure. The undefined ache she'd felt earlier had actually been her heart growing bigger with love for the tiny baby she carried. Soon her entire life would change, and in ways she could only imagine.

What about Ty's life? It would change, too. Adele had been so preoccupied with herself, she'd failed to consider him.

How, she wondered, would he react? With happiness? Anger? They'd talked about their respective families many times, but not about starting one of their own. Certainly not this soon. Why would they? While their relationship had moved quickly, the fact was she and Ty had been dating only a couple of months, and half that time he'd been on the road.

She'd *have* to consider him, however, and soon.

But not yet. Not until she'd taken the second test and given herself a few days to reflect on her pregnancy and all the ramifications. There was also Pop and his recovery requiring her full and immediate attention.

Suddenly overwhelmed by everything she was facing, she sat back down at the table. Lani, beaming like a million-dollar lottery winner, joined her.

"How did you know?" Adele asked.

Her mom laughed. "I've been pregnant before. I recognized the symptoms."

That was a long time ago, Adele thought. Had being a mother made such an impression that Lani remembered even the smallest details twenty-eight years later?

"Did you have a lot of morning sickness?"

"With you? Heavens, no. I never felt better. With the…" Lani paused, guilt reflected in her eyes. The moment didn't last. Forcing a smile, she picked up right where she'd left off. "Some women are sick day and night."

The remark her mother had made earlier about home pregnancy tests not changing much in ten years came back to Adele.

"Were you pregnant more than once?"

Lani's eyes closed and her posture sagged. "Me and my big mouth."

"Mom?"

"I never wanted you to find out."

"What happened?"

"After you were born, I got pregnant again. But I lost the baby. A little boy."

"I'm so sorry. How terrible for you."

"It was hard. On your dad, too. Neither of us talked much about it, but soon after that he started drinking heavily."

"Why didn't you tell me?"

Lani patted Adele's hand, the first spontaneously caring gesture she'd made in years. If any barriers had remained between them, they vanished in that moment.

"It wasn't a burden I wanted you to bear."

"What happened ten years ago?"

Lani wiped her misty eyes and shook her head as if chiding herself for once again saying too much. "I got pregnant yet again, if you can believe it. But I guess it wasn't meant to be, because before I could even tell the baby's father, I miscarried." She let out a wistful sigh. "I had nothing but trouble after that. Female trouble. I finally got a hysterectomy this past March."

A hysterectomy? Was that the reason her mother had looked so thin and frail when she'd first arrived at Seven Cedars?

"But enough of that talk. You don't need to be hearing any of it. Not now." She patted Adele's cheek. "You're going to have a beautiful, healthy baby, and I'm going to be a grandmother. You should make an appointment with an obstetrician right away."

"I will." Maybe she could arrange that for next week, when she drove Pop to the medical center for his checkup and physical therapy.

"Not that it's any of my business, but when are you going to tell Ty?"

Adele didn't know how to answer her mother.

If she told him she was pregnant, he might quit rodeoing. No, he *would* quit. He'd probably propose, too, and move to Seven Cedars, believing marrying her to be the right and honorable thing to do.

She couldn't let him. Not that the idea of marrying Ty wasn't appealing…and there was the baby to consider. But what about the championship? He'd lost once before, when it was just within his grasp. Then there were his parents. They could really use the money he owed them. If he won, he could repay them every dime. For a man with Ty's pride, settling his debts was not just important, it was imperative.

Mentally counting backward, Adele determined that she was around six weeks pregnant, give or take. Plenty of time before she had to decide what to do. Before she began showing.

She suddenly remembered he was flying in Sunday evening. How could she see him, look at him, *be* with him, and not think of the baby? Maybe she should call him and postpone his trip, citing Pop as an excuse. Give herself a little more time to come to grips with...everything.

"I don't know when I'll tell him," Adele murmured contemplatively. "I want to see the doctor first. Make sure the baby's okay."

"Oh, honey bun." Lani's features fell. "I've scared you with my stories, and I shouldn't have. Shame on me."

"I'm glad you told me." Adele welcomed the change in subject. "It explains a lot. I've been blaming you, and to a lesser degree, Dad, for things that weren't your fault. I think I have a lot of making up to do with both of you."

"That's sweet of you to say, but the truth is, I was a lousy mother. I hope you won't hold that against me, because I intend to be the best grandmother in the world."

"Good." Adele inhaled deeply. "I'm going to need a lot of help."

They reached across the table and shared another hug, only to be interrupted by a loud banging noise from down the hall.

"Pop!" Adele sprang from her chair.

Lani followed her to his bedroom. They were both aghast to find him sitting up in bed, his lap table on the floor and his walker leaning at a crooked angle.

"What are you doing?" Adele cried.

"Trying to get up. What the hell does it look like?" he barked, his face flushed a deep crimson.

"Are you in pain?" She glanced at the nightstand, where she'd left his medications, then at the clock. His next dose wasn't due for another two hours.

"Hell, yes, I'm in pain. I just had my hip replaced with some damn metal contraption."

"Oh, Pop," she soothed, wishing she could wave her hand and magically erase his suffering.

To her surprise, he let out a choked sob. "Why didn't you tell me you were having a baby?"

He must have heard her and Lani talking in the kitchen!

Before Adele could tell him she'd just found out herself, she was slammed with a wave of intense nausea, and barely reached the hall bathroom in time.

"HEY, BOUDEAU." A man Ty had handily beaten in steer wrestling that morning jogged toward him, tugging the brim of his ball cap down against the pouring rain. "What's the rush?" he hollered.

"Besides this weather?" Ty tossed his overnight bag into the backseat of Garth's pickup truck. It landed atop a plastic crate, rain gear, a laptop case and a well-worn duffel bag.

"A bunch of us are heading to the Chuck Box Bar and Grill," the man said upon reaching Ty. "You and Maitland want to come along?"

"Thanks, but we can't." He slammed the truck door shut, sidestepping a rapidly growing puddle. "I've got a plane to catch in two hours, and thirty miles to drive."

Garth had volunteered to drive him to the airport. Barring any traffic delays due to the rain, or longs lines at airport security, he had just enough time to make his flight.

"Guess I'll see you in Fort Benton."

"That you will."

Lifting the collar of his jacket, the man departed, his hunched form leaping over streams of running water.

Luckily for the participants, the weather had held for most of the rodeo. Saddle bronc riding, the last event of the day, had turned into a mud-flying free-for-all, and the closing ceremony was canceled. Ty hadn't minded. He'd grabbed his winnings and buckle—only one this weekend—and high-tailed it to where he'd parked, meeting the friend who had agreed to drive his truck and trailer to her place in the next town over. Ty had known Nancy and her brother for years, and was confident Hamm couldn't have a better caretaker. When Ty returned from seeing Adele, Nancy would meet him at the airport and give him a lift to her place. From there, he would continue on to Fort Benton.

A lot of trouble and a lot of favors called in, but Ty felt it would be worth everything and more to see Adele.

He'd originally arranged for Nancy to drive him to the airport, but when Garth got wind of Ty's plans, he'd insisted on taking her place. A consolation prize, perhaps, for beating the pants off Ty earlier today.

And speaking of Garth…

Ty checked the time on his cell phone, cupping his hand to protect it from the rain. Where the heck was he? If they didn't head out soon, Ty might miss his plane.

He turned to see Garth running toward him, water exploding in great sheets from his boots as they hit the ground. Ty hated to think how soaked his friend's feet must be getting. Hopefully, he had an extra pair of shoes buried in that pile of stuff in his backseat.

"Sorry I'm late. I needed a pick-me-up for the road." Garth lifted his rain poncho and removed two large travel cups of coffee he'd been carrying. By some miracle, they'd survived the journey intact.

Ty took the one Garth held out to him. "Thanks." He hoped the hot liquid would act like high-octane fuel, combating the sluggishness brought on by two days of intense competition and not enough sleep.

They climbed into the truck and began slowly traversing the muddy lake that had once been the parking area. Deep ruts hampered their progress. Ty had to force himself to keep from checking the time every few minutes. There was nothing he could do about the weather, so he might as well relax.

Yeah, right.

He tried distracting himself by guzzling coffee and listening, at least a little, to Garth ramble on about Reese and their upcoming wedding.

"We finally set a date. Valentine's Day. Reese insisted we wait until after Nationals. You're coming to the wedding, aren't you?"

"You still going to want me there when I take away your title?"

"After this weekend, I wouldn't bet on that."

Both men laughed. Ty wasn't worried. He might not have won every event today, but his scores were good enough to put him one step closer to qualifying for the National Finals Rodeo.

They were about a mile down the road when Ty's cell phone rang. His pulse jumped at seeing Adele's name flashing on the display. In a few hours, they'd be together. He dreaded thinking about the months stretching ahead of them until December. Instead of becoming easier, the separations were harder and harder. When he returned to Markton for Garth's wedding—and he would, win or lose—he planned on staying a full month with Adele. Maybe by then he could convince her to go with him to visit his parents.

"Hey, girl. How you doing?"

"Hanging in there."

Slouching in the seat, he readied himself for a long talk. While he couldn't pinpoint anything specific, she'd sounded odd the last few days. When he questioned her, she'd blamed her grandfather. Ty understood. Taking care of Pop couldn't be easy, though Adele swore he was doing remarkably well.

Ty promised himself she'd get as much rest as possible

during his visit, even if it meant he had to play nursemaid to Pop. As long as he and Adele had their nights together…

"You have no idea how good it is to hear your voice," he said.

Beside him, Garth made a sound of disgust, as if to imply Ty was nothing but a sucker for a pretty woman. The grin he wore, however, said Ty was in good company.

The two them were a pair, and Ty had to chuckle. Like Garth, he'd found the woman of his dreams. Ty also thought he might have found the place where he wanted to settle down for the rest of his life. Much as he loved Santa Fe, Wyoming had a lot more to offer. When he wasn't on the circuit, he could teach roping. Construct saddles in his spare time. Train with Garth. Woo Adele.

Life couldn't get any better. Except maybe with winning the title of World Champion.

"How'd you do today?" Adele asked.

"First in team roping. Second in steer wrestling." He shot Garth a dirty look. "Fourth in tie-down roping."

"Not bad."

"Fort Benton's going to be a whole 'nother story."

"You think," Garth muttered.

Ty ignored him, preferring to concentrate on Adele. "What's the latest on Pop?"

"Improving."

"Your mom?"

"Fine."

Her monosyllabic answers bothered him. "Is everything okay?"

"Great."

"What about Ritz?"

"Getting big."

Just when he was beginning to really worry, she asked, "Have you left for the airport yet?"

"On our way. Should be there in about forty-five minutes." She didn't immediately reply, and he thought they might have lost their connection. "You there?"

"Yeah." Another long pause followed. "Ty, I hate to ask this of you…."

"What's wrong?" Alerted by her tone, he sat bolt upright.

"Is there any chance you can postpone your trip?"

"Postpone? Why?"

Garth glanced over at him questioningly. Ty shrugged, not sure yet what was happening.

"I'm sorry." Adele sounded as if she was on the verge of crying.

"Sweetheart, what happened?"

"Nothing. It's just not a good time. Pop requires so much care—"

"I thought you said he was improving."

"Did I? Well, he is. I mean, the surgery site's healing. The, um, physical therapy isn't progressing at the speed the doctor wants."

"You told me yesterday he was almost ready for a cane."

"He is. He will be. Eventually. The therapists want me to take him in for an extra session this week."

"I'll go with you. Heck, I'll take him. You can stay home and nap. I know you're working your tail off." He wished she'd relinquish even a small amount of her grandfather's care to someone else rather than doing it all herself.

"It's not only Pop. We have…we have new calves arriving tomorrow, which I need to oversee. And the grain shipment's being delivered on Thursday."

"Can't the barn manager handle that?"

"He's, um, sick. The flu."

With sudden certainty, Ty knew Adele was lying. The question was why?

He immediately assumed the worst, and his stomach tightened into a knot. "You don't want to see me?"

"Of course I do!"

Ty sensed Garth's curious gaze on him, but he couldn't be bothered with his friend right now.

"I'm just so overwhelmed." A tiny sob had crept into her voice. "I really do want to see you."

For the first time since she'd called, he felt she truly meant what she said. "I want that, too. Like crazy."

"Next week will be better," she added, suddenly more composed. "Or the week after. By then Pop should be getting around better, and won't be so demanding."

"Is he giving you that much of a hard time?"

"More than you know," she answered tiredly.

Perhaps Ty was reading too much into her request. It could be exactly as she claimed, and she wanted him to come out when her grandfather was more self-sufficient and her own energy not so depleted.

It occurred to him to fly out anyway, regardless of what she said. Every bone in his body longed to do just that.

"Please, Ty," she implored. "I need a little more time."

Desperate as he was to see her, he wouldn't make her life more difficult. "I'll reschedule my flight for next week."

"Or two weeks."

He'd be in Albuquerque then. And his family had talked about coming out to watch him compete. No problem. He'd find a way to make it work. "All right. Two weeks."

"Thank you."

"Hey, Stick called me the other day."

"He did?" She sounded alarmed.

"Said he was trying to get you to hire his cousin."

"Oh, yeah."

"Asked me if I—"

"Ty, I've got to go."

"Is it Pop?"

"Y-yes. He's calling me. Sorry. Bye."

Ty flipped his phone shut and stared out the window at the downpour.

"Everything okay?" Garth asked, taking his eyes momentarily off the road.

"I'm not sure." Ty removed his cowboy hat and flung it on the truck floor with more force than necessary. "Any way you can turn this vehicle around? We need to head back."

"Forget something?"

"Seems I'm not flying out today."

After a quick explanation, Ty called the airlines. Then he phoned Nancy. She expressed sympathy over his canceled trip, and readily agreed to meet him and Garth at the rodeo grounds.

"I appreciate all your help," he told Garth, then picked up his hat, brushed it off and returned it to his head.

"No problem."

After another mile, he said, "You know Adele pretty well, right?"

"Since we were kids."

"Tell me, how is she at handling stress?"

"You kidding? She's a rock. I remember when she and Pop started Cowboy College. Everything they had to go through to get it off the ground. And when her grandmother died, Adele was the one who held Pop together. He'd have drowned in his own grief without her."

Ty frowned.

"Why?"

"She's having a difficult time coping with Pop's hip-replacement surgery. I guess he's being irritable and demanding."

"When isn't he? She's used to that."

Yeah, she was.

"And she's got all kinds of help there," Garth continued. "Built-in food service, housekeeping and drivers if she needs them. There's not an employee on the ranch who wouldn't pitch in if she asked them."

That was what Ty thought, too. "So why is she acting the way she is?"

Garth mulled the question over. "You really want my opinion?"

"I wouldn't ask if I didn't."

"There's something else going on," he said, confirming Ty's suspicions. "Something she's not telling you."

POP HOBBLED INTO Adele's office without knocking, awkwardly closing the door behind him. During the three and a half weeks since his surgery, he'd graduated from the walker to a cane, and was getting around quite well.

Enough that he'd decided two days ago he was ready to resume his previous responsibilities. Adele would have none of it, convinced he'd trip on something and injure his brand-new hip. Stick had been assigned to drive Pop wherever he wanted to go in the golf cart, and to keep an eye on him. Fortunately for Adele's nerves, Pop tired easily and had yet to do more than chat with the barn manager, watch a few classes and check out the new grain shipment.

He also made trips to her office to inquire about the running of the ranch.

She bore those visits as patiently as possible.

Except when he asked about the baby. Other than to respond that she was feeling well despite continued morning sickness, she clammed up. Pop gave new meaning to the word *relentless* and was constantly pushing her to do what he thought was right, namely tell Ty about the baby and, as Pop put it, make an honest woman out of her.

She refused to argue, as determined as her grandfather

to handle the situation her own way. Which, at the moment, was to do and say nothing.

"Hey, Pop. What brings you here?" She smiled brightly, already knowing the answer and bracing herself for a string of questions about reservations, food orders and class schedules.

"What time is Ty arriving?" He bent and grabbed her visitor's chair, pulling it away from the wall.

Adele automatically leaped up to help him.

"Sit your fanny down," he grumped. "I can manage. Don't need you hovering every second of the day." And he did manage. Just fine.

Was it true? Did she hover?

Probably.

She sat poised on the edge of her seat until Pop leaned his cane against her file cabinet, exhaling lustily as he did.

"We had two new reservations," she said, facing her computer and moving her mouse. "At this rate—"

"When is Ty getting in?" he repeated.

"After lunch sometime," Adele answered, hoping her tone gave no indication how nervous she was about his visit.

"Where's he staying?"

"Room nine's vacant."

"It's a little small for him."

"Better than his horse trailer."

At the mention of Ty's trailer, Adele was inundated with memories of when they'd made love in his tiny living quarters. Consulting the calendar after her trip to the obstetrician's office, she felt certain that was the night she'd gotten pregnant.

"If you need to rent the room out, he can bunk in my house."

"I don't need to rent it out."

She didn't mention that Ty would probably stay with her.

"You going to tell him about the baby?" Pop had asked the question no less than two dozen times.

Her answer was always the same. "Eventually."

"Eventually over the next two days or eventually sometime before the kid's born?"

"I'll tell him when the moment's right."

He grumbled an expletive under his breath. "You can't hide this forever."

"No. But I can for a while."

"Dellie," Pop warned.

She opened her mouth to object, then promptly closed it at the sight of his watery eyes. Struck by a rush of tender emotions, she got up and went to him, stooping over to give him a loving hug.

"I can't believe I'm going to be a great-grandfather," he mumbled. "Your grandmother would be overjoyed. God, I wish she was here."

"Me, too." Adele swallowed a sob.

"I know you think I'm being a crotchety old busybody."

"Did I say that?"

"I only want what's best for you and the baby. And that's a father. A father *and* a husband."

Adele returned to her desk chair. "You need to let me and Ty work this out between us."

"Don't know why you're taking so long," Pop complained, back to his former grumpy self.

She didn't mind. He put on a gruff front, but deep down he was a sentimental slob.

"I need time, Pop. This is a big deal. Life altering. For both of us."

"Are you afraid he's going to leave you high and dry?"

"No. Just the opposite, in fact."

"As it should be. He has a responsibility." Her grandfather's voice rose.

Adele glanced worriedly at the office door, then shushed him. "But not one he asked for or planned on so soon in our relationship," she said in a subdued voice.

"He's a good man, Dellie. He'll take care of you and the baby."

"I know. But an unplanned pregnancy isn't an automatic reason to rush into marriage. There are other things to consider. Other people."

"Just because your folks were lousy parents, don't assume you and Ty will be, too."

Her grandfather's words sliced into her, opening wounds she thought were finally closed.

"That's not it."

"Are you sure?"

"Yes," she replied. Only she wasn't. Not entirely.

Already she loved the baby with every breath she drew, and wanted more than anything for him or her to have a better childhood than she'd had. Two parents, Adele knew, was no guarantee for happiness.

Her cell phone abruptly rang. "It's Ty," she told her grandfather, after checking the screen, and answered with a forced but chipper, "Hello."

"I'm pulling in the drive."

"Already!"

"I couldn't wait to see you."

His enthusiasm was catching. "I can't wait to see you, either."

"Where are you?"

"My office."

"Meet me out front in two minutes."

Adele was instantly on her feet. "You coming?" she asked Pop, after disconnecting.

"Naw. You go on. I'll meet up with him later."

"Promise me you won't say anything about the baby until I've talked to him."

Pop grumbled his assent.

She was out the door and halfway across the lobby when she remembered she hadn't made sure he could rise from the chair without assistance. Starting back, she halted when he appeared in her office doorway.

"Get going." He shooed her away. "I'm fine."

Standing on the front porch, she watched Ty's truck approach, toy-size at first, then growing larger as it neared.

He had come home to Seven Cedars. And *her*.

All at once, happiness bubbled up inside her, vanquishing her earlier doubts and insecurities. Whatever obstacles they faced, and there were a lot of them, they'd find a solution. Together. The sight of his grinning face, full of gladness and affection, further convinced her that nothing was impossible.

She ran down the steps and into his arms the instant he climbed out of his truck.

"I have some great news!"

"So do I," he said, giving her a smacking kiss on the lips.

She laughed, giddy with delight. "You go first."

"Big Sky Trailers has offered me a sponsorship contract with a bonus if I win at Nationals."

"They did?"

"It's only a one-year contract to start, but they're talking magazine ads and even cable TV spots if all goes well."

"That's...wonderful."

"I'll have to go to Texas for the month of January. That's where their headquarters is located."

Adele's heart went from beating wildly to skipping painfully. So much for springing her announcement on him.

"Can you believe it?" He lifted her off her feet, swung her in a circle and gave her another kiss. "Hey, I missed breakfast this morning and I'm starving. Any chance the dining hall's still open? We can talk about why you've been avoiding me over lunch."

Chapter Fourteen

Pop had joined Adele and Ty for lunch. With his mouth set in a grim line, he sat listening to Ty expound on the details of the Big Sky Trailers sponsorship contract, which were exciting to say the least.

Exciting for Ty.

"If I win at Nationals, they want to feature me and Hamm in their advertising campaign." He seemed to have forgotten all about her news. Perhaps that was for the best. "Even more incentive for me to win," he said with single-minded determination.

Ty was well on the way to getting everything he wanted. Not at all like when he'd first come to Cowboy College... what? Nearly three months ago.

Adele was partially responsible for the transformation. Little had she known at the time that helping him fix his problems with Hamm and launch a career comeback would return to hurt her.

Little had she known she'd fall in love with him.

She pressed a hand to her breast, trying to soothe the ragged pain beneath it. Given the chance to do it all over again, she'd change nothing. Not loving him and certainly not having his baby.

"Of course, I'll be here for Garth and Reese's wedding," he continued, finishing the last of his steak sandwich.

Pop hadn't ordered any food, and Adele only picked at her shrimp salad. Ty didn't appear to notice their lack of appetites.

"That's good," she said, mentally calculating which stage she'd be in her pregnancy come Valentine's Day. No hiding it then. Even if she tried, someone was bound to say something.

"Why don't you come with me to Texas?" He reached under the table and rested a hand on her knee, his eyes alight with boyish charm. "You can visit your dad. Big Sky's headquarters is only a couple hours from where he lives."

When Adele didn't immediately respond, Pop made a disgruntled sound, which Ty misinterpreted.

"Sorry, Pop. I should've talked to you first about stealing her away."

"Not my decision," he muttered crustily.

It was on the tip of Adele's tongue to explain her grandfather's dour mood, only she couldn't think of anything to say without mentioning the baby. Instead, she asked Ty, "Is this what you want? The sponsorship contract?"

He gave her a surprised look. "It's a great opportunity. And not just because of the money."

She nodded. No argument there. "I thought you wanted to build saddles."

"Charlie's shop will be there when I'm ready."

Adele couldn't help but wonder if he planned to include her in his long-term goals. He'd made no mention of the future other than her accompanying him to Texas in January.

Wasn't she just as guilty of making plans without him?

Not the same, she told herself. She *was* thinking of him.

Ty would quit competing and give up a lucrative sponsorship the moment he learned about the baby. It wasn't fair, not when he'd worked so hard and so long to achieve his dream. Neither was it fair to make his parents wait additional months, perhaps years, for the money he owed them.

Especially when they could really use it and had already been exceedingly patient.

She could see why the Big Sky's marketing people had approached Ty. Not only was his meteoric return to roping catching the attention of fans, he was a great spokesperson, possessing good looks, talent and a natural charm. Not to mention a gorgeous and athletic horse. Some ropers competed their whole lives and had little to show for it. Ty could, if all went well, build an impressive career from this one sponsorship offer.

She wouldn't be the one to take it from him.

"We don't have to decide anything right this second," she said cheerfully, attempting to smooth out the awkward pause.

Her smile must have appeared as fake as it felt, for Ty stopped eating, set his fork down and turned to her.

"I haven't signed the contract yet. I can always change my mind."

"It's a great offer. You'd be a fool not to take it."

Pop's closed hand came down a little too hard on the table.

Ty's gaze darted to him, then back to Adele. "Yes, but I don't want to be away from you."

"We'll talk more tonight," she told him, her fake smile still firmly in place.

Pop grumbled angrily and, leaning heavily on his cane, rose from the table. Without a word, he limped away.

"I guess I upset him."

"It's not you." Adele also stood, and patted Ty's shoulder. "I'll be right back."

He stopped her by snaring her wrist. "Are we okay? Are *you* okay?"

She didn't answer him. "Give me a few minutes alone with Pop, will you?"

His eyes followed her as she hurried out of the dining hall. She could only guess what he was thinking.

Spying Pop outside, she called to him. "Wait."

He halted, but one glance at his fierce expression had her wishing she'd let him go on ahead without her.

"You need to tell him about the baby," he barked when she was within earshot.

"Not so loud." She tugged on his arm imploringly. "You know what will happen if I do. He'll stay here and give up the Big Sky sponsorship contract. Quit team roping with Garth. Probably propose to me."

"As he should!"

"What makes you think I want to marry him?"

Pop gaped at her. "Why the hell not?"

Adele grimaced and moved in front of him, as if that would stop his voice from carrying to the guests nearby. "He already lost one championship and one career opportunity. I don't want to be the reason he loses a second one. I certainly don't want to be the reason his mother loses her real estate business."

"We could lend him the—"

"Do you think for one second Ty would take money from us?"

"He might. If you two were married."

"No, he won't. He has too much pride. Just like he'll quit competing if I tell him about the baby. He'd want any child of his to have two parents at home. Like he did. Like I didn't."

Pop grumbled.

"I can't risk Ty coming to resent me for taking everything away from him. And he will, even if he doesn't mean to. Worse, he might come to resent our child."

"Dellie."

She hugged her grandfather, hating the frailty in his frame, which hadn't been there before. "The best day of my life was when I came here to live permanently." The best day until she'd learned she was pregnant. "I want my child to grow up with everything you and Grandma gave me. A good home, security, wide-open spaces and the best horses in the state to ride." She wiped her damp cheeks.

"I can't take the place of a father."

"You did for me."

"I still think you should tell Ty." Though Pop continued insisting, much of the fight had gone out of him.

"I will someday, but not right now."

He ruffled her hair as he had when she was young. "I love you, Dellie."

"I love you, too, Grandpa."

He chuckled, though it was filled with sadness. "You haven't called me Grandpa since you were fourteen."

"Maybe I should start again."

"Whatever excuse you're going to give Ty, you'd better think fast." Pop tilted his head toward the lobby door. "Because here he comes."

Adele's pulse spiked at the sight of Ty striding in her direction, looking every bit like a man who wouldn't settle until he knew what the heck was going on.

ADELE DIDN'T HAVE a destination in mind when she and Ty started walking. After a few minutes, she noticed their feet were taking them to the corral where Stick had placed Hamm while they had lunch with Pop. Probably because the corral was away from the ranch hands and guests, and gave them a modicum of privacy.

"What's wrong?" Ty demanded when they neared the fence. Given how poorly he was concealing his frustration, she was impressed he'd waited. "And this time, Adele, I want an answer. No more sidestepping."

Having little experience in breaking up with men, she decided quick and clean was the best approach.

Easier on you, too, a small voice inside her whispered.

True. But why prolong the agony?

Sticking to her hastily concocted plan, she blurted, "I've recently realized I'm not cut out for a long-distance relationship."

Ty visibly jerked and his eyes widened, but when he spoke, his words were measured, as if he was weighing each one. "It's only been a couple of months."

Good point. And if not for the baby, she'd be willing to give their arrangement a considerably longer trial period.

"I don't need any more time. This isn't working out for me."

"I'd have come two weeks ago. You're the one who told me not to."

"Pop just had surgery."

"And I respected your wishes. Now, all of a sudden, you tell me it's not working out, and act as if it's my fault, when you're the one pushing me away."

He was absolutely right.

Nonetheless, Adele continued, afraid her courage would desert her. "You have every right to be angry at me."

"I'm not angry, I'm confused."

She could see it clouding his eyes, along with the hurt she was inflicting.

Damn. She'd been in such a hurry, she hadn't considered he might put up a fight. She was, however, committed to finish what she'd begun. They would both come away from this bruised and possibly a little embittered, but everyone would be better off in the long run.

"The reason my parents' marriage fell apart was because Dad only stayed home a few months of the year."

"Is that what you want?" Ty asked. "For us to get married?"

It was her turn to jerk. "No!"

"Why not?"

She drew a shallow breath. Anything deeper was impossible, not with the huge knot of pain pressing against her ribs. "Seven Cedars is my home, and Cowboy College is my business. I'm not leaving either of them. Asking you to give up your home and your dream isn't right, either."

"I don't get it." He rubbed the back of his neck, his jaw working furiously. "Why can't we continue the way we are?"

"Because my heart shatters every time you leave and every time you hang up the phone after calling me." That much, at least, was completely true.

"And you think the answer is to break up with me?"

Adele involuntarily crossed her arms over her middle. "Yes."

"Have you met somebody else?"

"Of course not!"

He shook his head, his brows forming a deep V. "This makes no sense."

Hamm must have sensed the seriousness of their mood. Rather than trot in circles as usual, he stood solemnly in the center of the corral, head lowered, tail swishing, his breath stirring up small dust clouds.

"I'm sorry," Adele murmured.

"Just like that? You break up with me out of the blue, tell me you're sorry, and I'm supposed to be okay with it?" Ty might not have been angry before, but he definitely was now.

"Please try and see this from my side."

"How much does this have to do with the sponsorship offer from Big Sky?"

He'd finally put two and two together.

"Some," she admitted.

"Because I'll be gone the month of January?"

"Nationals isn't until late December. Add January, when you'll be in Texas, and you're asking me to wait half a year."

"We'd see each other every few weeks."

"For a day or two."

"I have a break over the holidays."

"What about next year?"

"Who says I'll compete next year?"

"You know you will. You told me you wanted to compete until you physically couldn't anymore."

"I…" He hesitated and shifted awkwardly.

Was this the moment she'd been hoping for? When he'd tell her he loved her? She chewed her bottom lip, waiting… and waiting.

"I…care about you. A lot. I'm not ready for this to end."

If he only knew how much she wasn't ready for this to end, either.

She could always tell him she'd had a change of heart. They would kiss, make up and pretend this morning had never happened.

Except what would that accomplish other than delaying the inevitable? Unless she was prepared to tell him about the baby, be the reason he quit competing, forfeited the championship, postponed paying back his parents, she had to let him go. Now.

"I'm being selfish, I know that," she said. "The idea of ending up like my mother… I won't let that happen to me."

"I'm not your father."

"No, but you'll be gone as much as he was."

"I just don't understand why you can't come with me sometimes. I'm not asking you to leave the ranch for weeks on end."

"You saw Pop. He can't get through a day without taking a nap. How's he going to run this place by himself, even for a weekend? We're also smack-dab in the middle of our busy season."

"Those are excuses." He narrowed his eyes, as if trying to

read more into what she said. "If you really wanted to take a few vacation days, you could."

"They're valid excuses." Adele refused to wilt under his penetrating stare. "I can't turn my back on my family and my business. A lot of people depend on me."

"So do I."

He depended on her? For what? Help with his horse? A place to crash between competitions? Disappointment sliced through her.

"I wish things were different."

"You're not giving me a choice." His anger had returned, lending his voice a steely edge.

"And what choice would that be? Have me wait for you for what could be years? Give up my life here, my home and my business? Leave my ailing grandfather? That's asking a lot."

Her words were harsh, as she'd intended. In response, his expression closed, like a door slamming shut.

She clenched her hands into fists and held them at her sides. It was the only way to prevent herself from going to him.

"Can we sleep on it? Talk again in the morning?"

His request was utterly reasonable. Except Adele knew if their breakup wasn't a swift one, she ran the risk of reconsidering and relenting. Or allowing Pop to sway her, as he would surely try to do if Ty stayed on the ranch. Even overnight.

"It won't make any difference."

She swore he flinched.

In that moment, Adele hated herself.

"If you ever—"

"I have to go."

Turning on her heel, she walked the entire distance to her apartment, without once stopping or looking back. Thankfully, Ty didn't follow her, saving her from having to test her willpower.

Oh, God, what must he think of her?

How could she have been so cruel?

In the solitude of her bedroom, she cried until a bout of nausea sent her running to the bathroom. A while later, Pop called to check on her and to let her know Ty had loaded Hamm and pulled out about thirty minutes earlier, telling no one where he was going.

Adele suspected he needed a friend about now and might head over to see Garth.

"Are you sure you didn't make a mistake, Dellie?" Pop asked.

She might have been able to lie to Ty, but her grandfather was a different story. "No, I'm not sure at all."

"When he finds out, and he will eventually, he's going to be mad."

She could deal with that. What she couldn't deal with was Ty hating her. And he very well could after what she'd done to him.

Chapter Fifteen

"What's with you, bro? You suck today."

Ty's little sister, Dana, couldn't be more right. In the three weeks since Adele had given him his walking papers, he could hardly put his boots on the correct feet, much less rope. He wasn't just back to where he'd been after Nationals last year, he was worse. Worse than worse. He couldn't rope a calf if it climbed up in the saddle with him. Even Hamm snorted in disgust whenever Ty approached.

Dana circled the big gelding, studying him intently. "I don't see a thing wrong with him," she said, shaking her head contemplatively. "He's in great shape."

"I was afraid of that."

Dana had met up with Ty the evening before. He was in St. George for the Lions Dixie Roundup Rodeo. She'd traveled to a town twenty miles over the hill for a job interview with a prestigious equine hospital. Though he knew her side trip to St. George was a thinly disguised attempt to check up on him at the request of their parents, he was still glad to see her. Last night, over a couple of beers, she'd offered to examine Hamm, on the slim chance Ty's recent string of losses was due to an injury or illness.

As he'd expected, he had no one to blame but himself.

"What are you going to do?" Dana asked.

"About what?"

She ticked off the items on her fingers. "Competing tomorrow. Big Sky's offer. Adele."

"Nothing."

"Not a good answer."

"Keep trudging along."

She made a face. "Excuse my language, but you need to get your shit together."

He did. His standings were slipping. Fast. At this rate, he wouldn't qualify for Nationals. Big Sky's people had started getting a little antsy. If Ty didn't win or place in the top three soon, they might pull out of their contract, citing the clause that gave them the right to do so if he didn't perform at a certain level.

So much for paying his parents back in one lump sum.

His folks would cut him some slack. Continue being patient.

Ty, however, was fast losing all patience with himself. This wasn't how it was supposed to be.

"Have you talked to Adele since she kicked you to the curb?"

Ty winced. "Do you have to be so blunt?"

"Yes. Everyone's been walking on eggshells around you, afraid of saying the wrong thing because you might have a meltdown or cry or something. I say you need a good shaking up."

They were in the barn at the rodeo fairgrounds, standing in Hamm's stall. Leaving it, they latched the door behind them and headed down the aisle. Ty had competed yesterday in both team and tie-down roping, doing badly in the former, his lasso missing the calf by a good foot. Garth didn't say much afterward, taking the disqualification in stride. Ty half wished his partner would blow up at him. Maybe then he wouldn't feel so guilty.

Amazingly, he hadn't done quite so terribly in tie-down roping, currently holding sixth place. A position that landed him in the final round later today.

Big Sky Trailers, however, wasn't interested in a spokesman who came in sixth.

"The answer is no, I haven't spoken to Adele, and I'm not going to."

"Why not?" Dana pressed. "You're nuts about her."

"I won't beg."

He would, actually, if he thought it would do any good. Hell, he'd get down on his knees. But Adele's cold tone during their last meeting still haunted him, and he doubted she'd softened her stance since then.

"Who said anything about begging?" Dana sent him a conspiratorial smile. "I had sweet-talking in mind. And flowers."

Wildflowers. That's what he had given Adele before, and she'd liked them very much.

Ty pushed the memory away to a dark corner in his mind.

While Dana continued to yap about the pros and cons of various tokens of affection, they cut behind the main arena, bypassing the food and vendor booths and hordes of people milling about. By nine o'clock tonight, the rodeo would be over and the grounds resembling a ghost town.

Much the way Ty's insides felt.

He'd replayed his last conversation with Adele repeatedly in his head, unable to shake the feeling she hadn't been entirely honest with him. Try as he might, he could detect nothing specific in her words or actions, except one. When he'd said he depended on her, she had instantly withdrawn, emotionally and physically.

What a fool he'd been. Given a second chance, he would have hauled her into his arms, told her he loved her and kidnapped her to his trailer so they could relive their first night together.

Because he did love her. Ty realized that now. Much too late, unfortunately.

"Markton's a four-hour drive from here," Dana was saying. "You could head over tonight after the rodeo."

"I can't."

"I'll come with you," she added, as if she hadn't heard him.

His temper flared. "Butt out, sis."

They stopped and faced each other, Dana with her hands on her hips, Ty with his teeth grinding together.

"Well, you need to do something. Cowboy College fixed you before. Maybe it can again."

Cowboy College? Or Adele?

He'd gone to Seven Cedars looking for that missing magical element that would turn Hamm and his good partnership to an unstoppable one. And he'd found it.

Not in the minor discoveries he'd made, such as how Hamm moved or which eye he took aim with. Ty had found it with Adele. Her belief in him and his desire to make her proud of him were what had inspired him to push himself harder than he ever had before.

"You're right," he told his sister, his anger dissolving. Not that he ever stayed angry at Dana long. "Cowboy College did fix me."

She grinned. "So, what are we waiting for? Let's go."

"If I do, I'd have to be willing to give up rodeoing, Nationals and the Big Sky sponsorship contract. For good. Adele doesn't want a man who's on the road all the time. That's why she kicked me to the curb in the first place."

Dana's expression turned serious. "Are you willing to do that?"

It was, he realized, the million-dollar question.

ADELE DROVE STRAIGHT from Pop's house to the main lodge and parked in front, leaving her truck sitting at a crooked angle. She'd been looking for her grandfather all over the ranch for the better part of an hour, with no luck. He hadn't shown up for class after breakfast, and according to everyone she asked, no one had seen hide nor hair of him all morning. Her mild concern over his abrupt disappearance was quickly blossoming into outright worry.

Where could he be?

Climbing the steps to the main lodge, she called his cell phone for the tenth time, angrily pressing the disconnect button when it went straight to his voice mail.

Did his battery die, or had he shut off his phone?

Not for the first time she wondered how much his disappearance had to do with their argument last night. Ever since Ty left Pop had been nagging her to tell him about the baby. Try as she might, she couldn't blame her grandfather. He was old-fashioned and set in his ways, and believed a man should be responsible for his children.

As Ty did.

Her throat ached at the thought of him. Not an hour passed that she didn't miss him and second-guess her decision to send him packing. It was crazy how completely he'd become a part of her life in just a few months.

Then again, with the baby she was carrying, he'd be a part of her life always. Even if he didn't know it.

Pushing thoughts of Ty to the back of her mind as she crossed the lobby, she concentrated on Pop. Wherever he was, he must have his truck. It wasn't in his garage or in his usual parking space at the barn.

After peeking in her office—a long shot, but she tried anyway—she went down the hall to the kitchen. If she didn't find him there, she was going into town and would scour it end to end. That failing, she was calling the sheriff. They probably wouldn't do anything, not until Pop had been missing twenty-four hours. Hopefully, they would put the word out to look for him and his vehicle. Especially when she explained about his bad arthritis and recent hip-replacement surgery.

All at once, she had a brainstorm. The Maitlands would help her search for Pop. She pulled out her cell phone to call Garth, only to pause. They were at the rodeo in St. George. Garth had mentioned the other day he and his family were all going.

Ty was there, too.

Returning her cell phone to her pocket, she pushed open the door to the kitchen and entered. The staff was busy preparing for lunch, and she didn't want to get in the way.

"Sorry to bother you," she called out. Heads turned in response. "Has anyone seen Pop?"

"Not since breakfast." Confirming nods accompanied the dishwasher's reply.

"Okay." Adele's spirits plummeted even as her worry escalated to new heights. "If anyone does see or hear from him, tell him to call me right away."

As she was leaving, she ran into Cook coming out of the walk-in freezer.

"What are you doing here, girl?" With her generous girth and perpetually red complexion, Cook resembled an overgrown cherub.

"Trying to find Pop."

"Well, he's not here." The woman chuckled.

"I know."

"He went to St. George. Left about a half hour ago."

"What?" Adele's jaw quite literally dropped. "You're kidding."

Cook looked perplexed, then alarmed. "Didn't he tell you?"

"No." Adele was torn between relief and irritation. Relief won out.

"He asked me to pack him a lunch. Said he'd be home by dinnertime."

"What was he thinking? He can't drive that far. Not at his age and with his hip."

"I'm sorry, Adele. I had no idea he didn't tell you."

This wasn't Cook's fault. Adele tried to remain calm, knowing she'd have more luck stopping a moving freight train than Pop when he set his mind on something.

And Adele was fairly certain she knew what that something was.

He had gone to track down Ty and tell him about the baby.

Dammit. He had no right.

"I'm going after him," she told Cook, calculating how much of a head start her grandfather had on her. Luckily, he always drove five to ten miles under the speed limit. "I'll let you know when I find him."

Once in her truck, Adele made a series of phone calls. First to the barn manager, instructing him to have Stick cover the day's classes. Next, she called Garth and, getting his voice mail, left a message for him to keep an eye out for Pop at the rodeo. Lastly, she contacted the sheriff's office, just in case Pop had an accident or his truck broke down on the highway.

She considered calling Ty, then chickened out. He'd want to know why Pop was coming to see him, and Adele wasn't ready to explain.

In town, she stopped at the gas station to fill up. Just as she was returning the nozzle to the pump, her mother pulled up in her pint-size economy car and rolled down the window.

"Hey, Dellie. I was just on my way to see you. I know it's probably a little early for this, but I brought some nursery—"

"I can't talk now. Pop took off without telling me. He's on his way to St. George to find Ty. I'm going after him."

Lani didn't hesitate. "I'll come with you."

Until very recently, Adele would have refused to let her mother accompany her anywhere.

Not today.

"Park your car over there, and let's go."

TY AND DANA WOULD HAVE made better time getting Hamm to the warm-up arena if not for being waylaid by Mike and Sandy.

"What are you guys doing here?" Ty greeted his friends and former fellow students warmly.

"Mike surprised me with tickets," Sandy gushed.

Ty introduced Dana, and the four of them chatted amiably. Well, Dana did most of the chatting. Ty's mind was occupied elsewhere.

Funny how knowing what to do gave a man a sense of peace. As soon as he finished his event this afternoon, he'd load up and hit the road again.

Garth meandered over while they were talking, leading his own horse.

"You on your way to warm up?" he asked Ty, after saying hello to Mike, Sandy and Dana.

Ty started to answer, then was distracted by the sight of Pop emerging from the crowd and coming toward him. Ty's first thought was that Pop's limp had significantly lessened. The hip-replacement surgery was obviously a success.

"Hey, Pop." He smiled, ridiculously pleased to see the older man. "What are you doing here?"

At his greeting, everyone in their group turned, matching smiles on their faces.

Ignoring them, Pop came straight at Ty, his wizened features fixed in a purposeful scowl, his stride deliberate. "I need to have a word with you, young man."

A word? Young man?

"Sure." Ty handed Hamm's reins to Dana and stepped forward. "Is something the matter?"

"This is for taking advantage of my little girl."

Before Ty could respond, Pop's fist connected with his jaw in a lightning fast right hook worthy of a man one-third his age.

Ty's head snapped to the side. Pain radiated through his entire face, neck and shoulders, and he stumbled backward from the force of the blow.

Sandy let out a little scream.

Ty shook his head, dazed and more than a little confused. It didn't occur to him to retaliate.

"And this is for leaving her in a fix."

Pop's left fist plowed into Ty's stomach, knocking the wind clean out of him and sending him sprawling to the ground, flat on his rear.

"Stop him," Dana cried.

"Hey, that's enough."

Ty heard Garth and his sister over the dense ringing in his ears, and had a vague impression of Garth scuffling with Pop and pulling him away. Thank God. Pop might be seventy-seven and suffering from debilitating arthritis, but he still packed a mean punch.

"What do you mean, I left her in a fix?" he sputtered, his knees bent and his throbbing head cradled in his hands. Fortunately, the ringing in his ears had started to subside.

"Dellie's pregnant."

"She is?" Squinting, he looked up at Pop, an action that sent fresh waves of pain pulsing through him.

"You're going to be a father."

"I am?" The blows he'd taken must have dulled his thinking, for nothing made sense.

"You all right?"

Mike's face appeared, and Ty had the impression of hands tenderly and expertly probing him all over for injuries. He was also aware of a growing audience.

"I don't know," he slurred, trying not to move his sore mouth.

"Sandy." Mike pulled a handkerchief from his back pocket. "Put some ice from your drink in this." She did and Mike pressed the ice pack to Ty's jaw, while Dana hovered nearby.

Garth knelt down beside Ty, his face splitting in a wide grin. "Congratulations, pal."

"She never said anything." Ty looked around for Pop. "I swear, if she had, I wouldn't have left her."

Suddenly, Garth, Dana, Mike and Sandy all stood and stepped away. Ty's vision had cleared enough for him to see Adele emerging from the crowd and running toward him, her mother and a security guard not far behind.

"What happened? Ty, are you okay?"

Adele took Garth's place, kneeling beside Ty. Mike went to talk to the security guard.

"Did you fall?" she asked, her touch more tender and more welcome than Mike's.

"Your grandfather slugged me. Twice."

"Pop!" Adele turned and sent her grandfather an infuriated glare. "I apologize for him," she said, returning her attention to Ty.

"How come you didn't tell me you're pregnant?"

"I—I…because I was afraid you'd quit rodeoing."

"Hell, yes, I will."

"You can't."

"I'm not leaving my—"

"You will not lose the championship again. You hear me? Too much is riding on it."

The side of his mouth that didn't ache pulled up in a smile. "Kind of bossy, aren't you?"

"I was wrong, Ty." She lowered her gaze. "I should have told you about the baby."

"Yes, you should have."

"It's just that you've worked so hard to get to this point, and you deserve to win."

"You deserve to have the father of your baby there with you when you need him." The fog around him had lifted. In fact, his head was clearer than it had been in weeks.

"What are you—"

"Shut up." Cupping her face in his hands, he drew her to him for a kiss that would have lasted longer if his mouth didn't hurt so much. "Help me up," he demanded when they broke apart.

"Are you sure you should? You could have broken something."

He beckoned to Garth to give him a boost. "I'm not going to propose to you sitting on my ass in the dirt."

"Propose!" Adele gasped. "We need to talk first."

"Plenty of time for that later." Pop sidled over to them.

"This is what you wanted." Adele stared at him accusingly.

"Damn straight," he said with undisguised satisfaction.

Sandy didn't hide her tears as she squeezed Mike's arm. "Isn't this romantic?"

Ty wasn't sure how getting the tar beaten out of him was romantic.

"Wait until Mom and Dad hear!" Dana exclaimed with glee, and whipped out her cell phone, taking pictures to commemorate the moment.

Adele rose along with Ty as Garth pulled him to his feet.

He wobbled only for as long as it took him to put an arm around her and nestle her against him.

"I know there's a lot we need to figure out." Everything that had happened during his last visit to Seven Cedars suddenly made sense. And now that he understood her concerns, he would do everything in his power to lay them to rest. "We'll do it one day, one problem at a time."

"I don't want you marrying me because you feel obligated."

"I'm not. I love you, Adele. And I should have told you that weeks ago." He could see a trace of uncertainty in her expression. "Would it help you to know I was planning on driving to Seven Cedars tonight after the rodeo?"

"You were?"

"And when I got there, I was going to demand you give us a second chance."

"Oh, Ty. I love you, too."

"I'm glad you said that." He tugged her closer, threading his fingers in her hair. "So, how 'bout a September wedding?"

"Not so fast, cowboy." She leaned back, appraising him critically. "There's a little matter of the World tie-down roping and team roping championships."

"I thought we agreed—"

"We did no such thing. You're going to finish out the season. The baby will wait until then."

"What if I can't?" He felt his grin expand.

"You can come home every couple of weeks. And I'll fly out to see you. Once. Maybe twice." She was grinning, too. "If you win the championship, and only if you win, then I'll consider marrying you."

Her challenge was like the one she'd issued him at the Cowboy College jackpot. Then, it had been a dinner date at stake. Today, it was the rest of their lives.

"You think I can't?"

"I know you can't unless you qualify," she answered smugly.

Ty accepted his fallen hat from Garth, slapped it against his leg to knock off the dust and put in back on his head. "Seems I have an event to win."

"You sure you're up to it?" Mike asked with doctorly concern.

"I am." Ty only had eyes for Adele. "And when I do win, then we'll talk about *my* list of requirements."

She raised her brows in surprise. "Such as?"

"If I'm going to retire after Nationals, we make some changes at Cowboy College. I want to expand the program to include professional ropers. With three experts in residence, we can attract an entirely new clientele."

"And one on the way," Lani added. "With genes like theirs, how could the kid not be a roper?"

"I like it." Pop smiled approvingly and draped an arm around Lani.

"Me, too." Adele stood on tiptoes to give Ty's cheek a tender kiss.

"Hate to break up the party, buddy," Garth said, "but we'd better get a move on." He swung up into the saddle.

"No taking it easy on me just because I'm injured and newly engaged," Ty warned his friend.

"I wouldn't dream of it."

Much as Ty hated to, he left Adele to join Garth in the warm-up arena.

An hour later, the announcer's voice blared from the speakers, proclaiming Ty the tie-down roping winner. Amid the applause and cheers that followed, he shouted the news that Ty had set an arena record with his last run.

Ty hardly heard the man. He was too busy kissing his wife-to-be and the mother of his child, and planning their future, one that included the realization of all their dreams, a display cabinet full of gold belt buckles and a three-generation legacy to pass on to their children.

* * * * *

THE ACCIDENTAL SHERIFF

To Pamela, best friend.
Thank you for all the body parts you've lent me through the years. An ear to bend when I've just got to vent, a hand to hold when I'm afraid, a shoulder to cry on when I'm sad, a foot planted firmly in my rear end when I need a good kick, an elbow in the ribs to keep me lined out, your thumbs up when I've done a good job, your fresh pair of eyes for critiquing my chapters, and your big, sweet, generous heart that you've given me time and again. I love you.

Chapter One

The Marley Brothers Band was loud, but not so loud their music covered the sickening sound of squealing tires, spitting gravel and—here was the bad part—crunching metal.

Carolina Sweetwater whirled around and gasped. The left rear fender of her brand-new PT Cruiser was crushed beneath the front end of a giant, jet-black Hummer.

That wasn't all.

"Briana, are you all right?" she hollered, and hurried toward the two vehicles, mindless of her three-inch spike heels and the yards of taffeta swirling around her ankles.

The Hummer lurched, hissed and then backed slowly away from her car. She reached the Cruiser's driver's-side door at the same moment her niece stepped out.

"Aunt Carolina, I'm so sorry."

"It's all right." Weak with relief, she hugged the shaking teenager and glanced over her shoulder. The occupants of the Hummer were also climbing out and, like her niece, appeared to be unharmed.

"I looked both ways, but I swear I didn't see them."

"What matters most is no one was hurt." Now that Carolina had a chance to catch her breath and assess the situation, she realized the only serious casualty of the minor parking lot collision was her car. The SUV had suffered nothing more than a small scratch or two.

"Are you okay, young lady?" The driver of the SUV, Major Linc Harrison of the U.S. Army, and his wife, whose name momentarily escaped Carolina, approached. He wore a scowl. Her expression was considerably kinder.

"I'm fine," Briana sniffed.

"How about you?" Carolina asked. "Are either of you injured?"

"In that?" The major's wife rolled her eyes at the Hummer. "Hardly."

The major took out his cell phone and punched in a number. "I'm calling nine-one-one."

"Is that necessary?" Carolina tried not to let his precision-cut steel-gray hair and crisp dress uniform, the left side of which was completely covered with medals and ribbons and little colored bars, intimidate her. "Can't we just exchange insurance information and phone numbers? My niece and I would really like to get back to the wedding."

His reply was to lift the phone to his ear and glower at her.

"Dad's going to be really mad, isn't he?"

"He won't be happy." Carolina put an arm around her niece and drew her several feet away to the edge of the parking lot. "This is your second accident since you started driving."

Technically, Briana wasn't Carolina's niece. Her father and Carolina were cousins, which made her and Briana third cousins or cousins once removed or… Calling each other aunt and niece was just a whole lot simpler.

"I'm dead," Briana whimpered.

"You're not dead. Grounded for sure. And you can forget about driving for a while. Like until college."

The teenager burst into fresh tears.

"Come on. I was joking," Carolina said, rubbing Briana's back. "Don't worry. I'll handle your dad. This is partly my fault anyway. I'm the one who let you drive my car." The beautiful, shiny, cobalt-blue convertible she'd bought last month to celebrate her thirty-third birthday.

"Because I asked you if I could."

"And I said yes. Hence, shared responsibility."

In hindsight, Carolina should have driven the five minutes to her cabin and gotten those spare camera batteries herself. Instead, she'd caved when Briana had pleaded with her to run the errand.

The Marley Brothers Band finished their number. After a round of applause, they turned the microphone over to Carolina's older sister Vi. Like the music, every word Vi spoke carried clearly from the lawn in front of the dining hall, over the roof of the main lodge and across the parking lot to where Carolina, her niece, the major and his wife stood. Thanks to the rolling hills, sprawling oaks and towering pines surrounding the main buildings, acoustics at Bear Creek Ranch were great.

"Ladies and gentlemen, friends and family," Vi announced, "please clear the dance floor for the bride and her father."

Carolina cringed. She was going to miss the entire dance—her sister Corrine's glowing face, her father's beaming smile and the besotted expression the groom would be wearing when he cut in to sweep his new wife away from his father-in-law.

Damn! Her throat closed and, for the hundredth time that week, she willed herself to keep it together.

Something about her little sister's wedding had her walking an emotional tightrope. If she didn't know better, she'd think she was envious. Not because of Corrine's new husband, but because of her obvious bliss at being married.

Now, wasn't that a surprise? Who would have guessed avoid-commitment-at-all-costs Carolina Sweetwater harbored a secret longing to find that one right guy she could spend the rest of her life with?

What had triggered the recent change in her thinking? The wedding? Her birthday? Her bid for better, meatier assignments at work being shot down? The five-year anniversary of her broken engagement? Definitely the last one. For too long she'd mourned a man who wasn't worth it.

Carolina needed to get serious if she wanted the kind of contentment two of her sisters had found. A contentment that included a wonderful man, a satisfying career and one day maybe children.

Problem was, the selection of available bachelors between her family's guest resort in the Matazal Mountains of northern Arizona and the nearby small town of Payson was pretty slim. Carolina had already dated most of them in an attempt to convince herself her ex-fiancé hadn't permanently broken her heart.

"We're really screwed, aren't we?"

Carolina didn't reprimand her niece. In certain circumstances, the term was appropriate, and this definitely counted as one of them. "We'll be fine. I have ample insurance."

"I think the major's mean," Briana said.

"Not so much mean as by the book."

Bear Creek Ranch had never hosted a U.S. Army major before. He was her sister Corrine's former commanding officer and had traveled all the way from Fort Bragg in North Carolina to attend the wedding.

"His wife seems nice," Carolina observed.

As if sensing they were being talked about, the couple strode over. "How much longer do you think this will take?" the major groused, checking his watch. A Rolex. "It's almost six, and we should have been on the road by now."

"Hard to say." Carolina was proud of her well-modulated voice. She had her part-time job as morning traffic director at KPKD to thank for that. "The ranch is outside Payson's town limits. Which means we have to wait for the county sheriff or one of his deputies. A nonemergency like this could take hours."

The major grunted.

"How about we let my niece go back to the wedding. There's no reason she has to miss out on everything."

He vetoed Carolina's suggestion with an ogre-ish "No. Your niece is in serious trouble, Ms. Sweetwater."

Well, Briana came by it honestly.

Carolina's own free spirit had landed her in hot water on a regular basis since preschool, when she dumped an entire container of fish food into the classroom aquarium and then lied about it. Sometime in grade school she stopped lying, but not landing in hot water. Take today, for example. If there was any way her cousin Jake could manage it, he'd ground *her* along with his daughter.

At the distant rumble of an approaching vehicle, everyone turned in unison. A marked patrol car traveled the long dirt road leading into the ranch and then swung into the parking lot. Carolina craned her neck to catch a glimpse of the driver. Old Sheriff Herberger had a soft spot when it came to her family, who donated regularly to the department's various outreach programs.

Luck, unfortunately, wasn't on her side. It was the much younger, not so kindly Deputy Sheriff Neil Lovitt who stepped from the parked car.

"My, my," the major's wife said, an appreciative hitch in her voice.

Carolina silently seconded the sentiment.

The major's uniform might have sharper pleats and more medals pinned to it, but Deputy Sheriff Lovitt did his own khaki shirt and slacks pretty darn proud. Adjusting his straw cowboy hat and sunglasses, he made his way toward them, his gait casual yet confident, a small notebook in his hand.

"Good afternoon, folks," he said upon reaching them. Almost two years in this neck of the woods hadn't softened his New York accent one iota.

"Hi." Carolina was the only one who smiled.

Why she bothered, she had no clue. He'd never responded to any of her attempts at friendliness. That included the double date they'd once gone on—ironically, not with each other. Carolina's date worked with Deputy Sheriff Lovitt, which was how they'd wound up going to the community fair together. She'd been far more interested in the deputy than…Mark, was it? Or Alfonso. She wasn't sure. Her attention had been riveted on the department's newest addition.

He hadn't reciprocated her interest, and as far as she could tell, nothing had changed in the time since that disastrous double date.

His loss, Carolina decided.

It was a shame, though. Of all the available prospects in the area, he was the most attractive.

"So, what happened here?" he inquired, his gaze encompassing everyone present.

Briana and the major launched into simultaneous explanations, raising their voices to be heard over each other.

"Enough." Deputy Sheriff Lovitt held up a hand. "You first." He pointed at Briana and put pen to paper, readying to take notes.

The major harrumphed his displeasure.

"I was backing out and…and he…" Briana's nerve seemed to desert her.

"Go on," the deputy sheriff said, his tone encouraging.

"I…he…" She fidgeted.

The major began tapping a very polished boot, staring hard at the cluster of trees on the other side of the parking lot.

"I was being real careful, I swear." Once she started, she couldn't stop. "I checked the rearview mirror and the side mirrors. I didn't even have my foot on the gas pedal. Next thing I knew, this gigantic SUV came from out of nowhere."

"You hit me, young lady," the major boomed.

"That's not true. It was the other way around."

"I was heading toward the exit and you backed out right in front of me." His loud bark caused Briana to wilt.

Carolina fought the urge to step in front of her niece and shield her.

"I had the right-of-way, Officer." The major's already broad chest seemed to swell.

"Deputy."

"Of course," he grumbled. "Excuse me."

"May I see both of your licenses, registrations and proof of insurance, please?"

Carolina went to her car, mourning the damage once again as she passed the bumper. Fetching the necessary paperwork from the glove compartment, she returned to the group, her three-inch heels catching in the uneven asphalt.

Neil removed his sunglasses, dropped them in his shirt pocket and monitored her every move with unconcealed interest.

When had she started thinking of Deputy Sheriff Lovitt by his first name?

Since he couldn't take his to-die-for chocolate-brown eyes off her.

Carolina experienced a small thrill of awareness when she handed him the paper.

"The Chrysler's yours, Ms. Sweetwater?" He said her name without looking down at the registration, which indicated he remembered her from their double date.

She didn't know whether to be flattered or worried.

"Yes."

"Brand-new, I see."

"Fresh off the lot."

"I hope you have a low deductible on your insurance."

"Not low enough." She was already kicking herself for trying to save a few dollars.

Neil skimmed through the major's documents before turning to Briana. "Where's your license?"

"I...ah..."

Carolina had a sinking feeling in the pit of her stomach.

"Miss?" Neil's patience was obviously running low.

"It's a wedding." Briana's shoulders folded in on themselves. "I didn't bring my purse with me."

"Does she need her license?" Carolina jumped to Briana's defense, if only to wipe the satisfied grin off the major's face. "This is private property."

The look Neil shot her could have seared every petal off the wildflowers growing by the road.

Carolina responded by standing taller, which brought his mouth into her direct line of vision. She couldn't help staring at it. After a moment, the corners of his lips, which were really quite nice, started to turn up. Just a little. Hardly noticeable.

Gotcha.

The thought had hardly formed in her head when Jake came charging down the fieldstone walkway toward them. He was accompanied by her uncle and Will, her sister Vi's husband.

"Oh, goodie, here comes the cavalry," she mumbled under her breath, and waited for all hell to break loose.

CAROLINA SWEETWATER TURNED away to face her family. Neil avoided staring at her backside, which was every bit as attractive as her front, a fact that hadn't gone unnoticed when she went to her car to fetch her registration. Her lime-green bridesmaid dress was—well, words couldn't describe it. But Carolina carried the dress off with the poise of a supermodel.

A different time, different circumstances...

"What's going on here?" Jake Tucker, manager of Bear Creek Ranch resort, commanded everyone's attention. "Briana, are you all right?"

"Everyone's fine." Carolina glided to the center of the men, a tropical flower surrounded by penguin suits. Several stray tendrils had escaped the rhinestone clasp holding her hair in place. They lay on her bare neck, the dark brunette color standing out against her lightly tanned skin.

Neil forced his gaze down to his citation book.

"There was a slight fender bender," she said, her voice calm.

He listened to that same voice every morning on KPKD.

"You wrecked your new car?" Jake's voice was anything *but* calm.

"No." Briana visibly braced herself. "I did."

"Your daughter ran into me." The major stepped forward.

Jake closed his eyes and blew out a long breath.

"Please don't be mad."

He shot his daughter a foreboding look. "At the moment, it's hard not to be."

Neil almost felt sorry for her. Almost. He could see his own five-year-old daughter Zoey as a teenager, trembling from head to toe, waiting for the ax to fall. Unfortunately, Briana had been driving without a license and, from what he could determine, had caused the accident. And while it had occurred on private property, the ranch parking lot was accessible to the public.

The choice of whether or not to issue her a citation was Neil's.

Jake listened to an account of the accident and, despite his obvious anger, did an admirable job of maintaining his cool with both his daughter and Carolina. Not that Neil figured she took any guff from her cousin. Or anyone else, for that matter.

"Can my wife and I leave now?" the major asked when Neil was finished taking statements and collecting contact information.

"You folks drive careful," he warned them. "Traffic can be congested this time of day."

"Thank you again for coming to the wedding." Jake shook the major's hand. "I know Corrine really appreciates it."

"I wish we could have stayed longer," the major's wife gushed. "You have a beautiful place."

Neil agreed. The spectacular scenery and quiet country living were the main reasons he'd picked the Payson area in which to settle down. Other than the occasional drunken brawl and dispute between neighbors, not much happened here in the way of crime. Quite a change from Manhattan's Upper West Side, where he'd spent ten years on the force—the last one in a daze, struggling to cope in the wake of his wife's death.

Four years had dulled the pain but not the guilt.

He shouldn't have listened to her, shouldn't have done his duty. Maybe then, she'd still be alive.

Neil retrieved his sunglasses from his breast pocket and put them back on.

"If you need anything, you have my number." The major and his wife returned to their rented SUV after saying goodbye.

"Look, I know the accident was Briana's fault." Carolina moved to stand beside Neil. "But is there any way you can cut her some slack?"

"What are you suggesting, Ms. Sweetwater?"

"A warning?"

"Carolina," Jake interrupted, his tone clearly telling her to butt out.

In truth, Neil *was* inclined to cut Briana a little slack, but not because of her father or Carolina. His instincts told him Briana was a good kid, if not a good driver. And as scared as she was at this moment, she'd definitely exercise more caution in the future.

"You committed two violations." He ignored everyone else and addressed Briana. "The first was failure to yield the right-of-way, and the second was driving without a valid license."

She nodded resignedly.

"Today—and only today—I'm going to let you off with a warning."

"No way!" Her jaw dropped, and her eyes bugged.

"If I'm called out again to an accident in which you're involved, rest assured I'll throw the book at you."

"I promise. I'll be really, really careful from now on. I'll check both ways three times and never go over thirty miles an hour."

"Just practice reasonable caution." Neil made a few more notes, then wrote up Briana's warning. "That's all I ask."

He received three thank-yous. Briana's was relieved, Jake's appreciative and Carolina's accompanied by a flirty smile.

Oh, boy.

Neil wasn't a recluse. He dated once in a while, but not seriously and not with the intention of remarrying. He liked it that way. From what he'd heard around town about Carolina Sweetwater, she subscribed to a similar philosophy. It should be a perfect match.

But he had no interest in finding that out.

What Neil saw when he looked at her was a woman he wouldn't mind getting to know a whole lot better. And when he linked her name and the idea of remarrying, his stomach didn't turn to stone. For those two reasons, he diligently maintained a safe distance from her. His job was dangerous. It had cost him his wife and his child her mother. He refused to put another person he cared about in danger, the way he had Lynne. Avoiding serious involvements seemed the easiest solution.

"Is that all?" Briana returned his citation book after signing the warning. She was doing her best to gnaw her bottom lip in half.

"For now." He tried to sound stern. Inside, he was chuckling. "Good day, everyone." Touching his fingers to the brim of his hat, he took his leave. "I trust I won't see any inebriated wedding guests on the road this evening."

"Absolutely not," Jake assured him.

Neil's exit was delayed by a soft, feminine hand on his arm.

Carolina's.

"Would you like a piece of cake for the road? And maybe one for your daughter? I could pull a few strings and arrange for an icing rose to be on it."

She smelled nice, the scent light and floral. He remembered it from the night they'd double-dated, when he realized his interest in her was more than casual and not at all appropriate for someone his coworker was taking out.

"Thank you, ma'am, but no." She had yet to remove her hand, and Neil could feel a slight warming where her fingers pressed into his skin.

"Okay," she said smoothly. "I guess I'll see you around, then."

Maintaining that safe distance was a lot harder when she was standing three inches away and touching him. Neil slipped up.

"I'm looking forward to it, Carolina."

"Me, too."

He returned to his car before committing a second blunder, taking her floral scent with him. The last thing he saw before pulling out of the ranch parking lot was Carolina climbing the stone walkway, the setting sun gleaming off her lime-green dress. It was a sight he wouldn't forget.

He had no sooner reached the highway when a call came in on his radio.

"Hey, Neil, you're needed back here on the double. We have a ten-twenty-four." Miss Emily was one of four dispatchers and his favorite. Perhaps because she reminded him a little of his grandmother.

"What's wrong?"

"It's a ten-thirty-five."

Miss Emily wasn't much for protocol and had been with the department too long to frazzle easily. Which was why her urgency and use of official codes concerned Neil. "Be there in twenty," he told her.

"Make it sooner."

Neil accelerated. In the eighteen months he'd been on the job, not once had he been called back to the station for an emergency, much less a confidential one. He couldn't imagine what was wrong.

The Gila County Sheriff's Station was located off the Beeline Highway, which ran through Payson. Weekend recreationists were visiting the town in record numbers, triple-digit degrees in Phoenix driving them north to the much cooler parts of the state. Growing increasingly frustrated at the constant slowdowns, Neil switched on his flashers. Traffic magically parted, and he sped the remaining distance to the station.

After parking at the rear of the building, he entered through the side door. The central room was vacant, which was almost unheard-of. Voices carried from down the hallway, loud and panicked. Neil headed in that direction. Nearly a dozen individuals were crammed in the sheriff's office, among them three other deputies, only one of whom was in uniform.

Neil scanned their worried faces. One person was noticeably missing. "Where's Sheriff Herberger?"

"That's just it." The county commissioner came out from behind the sheriff's desk to meet Neil. "He's at the Payson Regional Medical Center."

"Is he all right?"

"We hope so. He's had a heart attack."

"How bad?"

"Right now, he's stable. The doctors will know more later tonight after they run additional tests. But they say it's likely he'll require bypass surgery."

That explained the worried faces.

"What do we do?"

"The first order of business is to appoint an acting sheriff." County Commissioner Daniels placed a firm hand on Neil's shoulder. "That, my friend, is you."

"Me?"

"The City Council members and I are all in agreement. There's no one better suited to fill in for the sheriff than you."

"Excuse me, sir, but there are other deputies with more years in the department than me." Two of them were standing a few feet away and glaring at Neil.

"None with your experience in law enforcement."

"If it's all right with you—"

"Enough, Neil. We've made our decision. Congratulations." The county commissioner tightened his grip.

Neil had the uneasy sensation of being trapped.

"We've arranged for you to do an interview with KPKD," the man continued. "Tomorrow morning, nine a.m. sharp."

"So soon?"

"The people of this county need to know everything's status quo and that they have someone competent to rely on during Sheriff Herberger's recovery."

What they had, thought Neil, was an acting sheriff who didn't want the job.

Chapter Two

Carolina arrived at work twenty minutes early, as was her habit. She liked getting a jump on the day, though lately she felt there wasn't much for her to get a jump on. While grabbing a cup of coffee in the staff lounge, she contemplated various program ideas and tried to formulate a new approach with her boss. Being shot down seven times in a row had only increased her determination to take on a greater, more respected role than that of morning traffic director.

Step one in her life-redirecting plan.

Cup in hand, she headed toward the cluster of cubicles, one of which she shared with her counterpart, the evening traffic director. A friendly voice stopped her.

"Morning, Carolina."

"Hey, Adrian."

The techie—Carolina wasn't sure of his exact title because he did a little of everything—fell in step beside her.

"How was the wedding?"

"Wonderful. Perfect. The happy couple are leaving today for a ten-day cruise of the Caribbean."

"I heard you smashed your new car."

"My niece did, actually. It's not too bad." At least that was what she kept telling herself. "I have an appointment at the body shop after work."

"Hey, listen." Adrian turned suddenly shy. "My brother

scored a couple extra tickets to the jazz concert at the casino October sixteenth. You want to go?"

Carolina flashed him a wide smile, hoping it would help ease the letdown. "Sorry, Adrian, I can't."

"Other plans?"

"Yeah." Her plans didn't involve a date but rather step two of her life-redirecting plan.

As recently as last week, she might have accepted Adrian's invitation, despite the six-year age difference. Carolina wasn't bound by convention and had dated men both younger and decades older than her.

Today, however, marked a change in policy. Henceforth, she refused to go out with anyone who didn't genuinely appeal to her—which made Neil Lovitt the only candidate.

Until yesterday she'd considered him a lost cause. But then he'd smiled at her and told her he was looking forward to seeing her again. Carolina recognized interest when she saw it. Whether Deputy Sheriff Lovitt would act on it was another thing.

Not that she was planning to wait and see. Carolina had every intention of eliciting another smile from him and finding out how far it would lead.

Her boss, the news director, poked his head around his cubicle. "Carolina. Good, you're here. I need to see you." His head promptly disappeared.

"Catch you later, Adrian."

"Sure." He lumbered off, eyes glued to the carpet, the bounce gone from his gait.

For an instant, she regretted her actions. Maybe later she'd offer to bring him back some lunch. That should help restore his good mood and reestablish that their relationship was strictly platonic.

"What's up, Ward?" She sat on the visitor chair squeezed

into a narrow space between her boss's desk and the cubicle wall.

"I need you to pull double duty today. Melanie called in sick."

"Oh, okay." Carolina periodically covered for deejays. While the position was considered senior to hers, she didn't think it was anywhere near as enjoyable or challenging as the one she had in her sights—roving announcer. No being shut in a control room four hours at a stretch for her.

"We have an important interview this morning. You're going to sit in with Rowdy."

Rowdy Rodgers was the station's popular morning show host. He'd been lured away from one of Phoenix's big five in an attempt to boost KPKD's ratings and steal the number-one slot from their closest competitor.

"No problem." Carolina perked up. Coanchoring an interview with Rowdy wasn't exactly the meaty assignment she longed for, but it was a darn sight better than reading traffic reports. "Who's the guest?"

"The new acting sheriff for Gila County." Ward stared at his computer monitor while he talked, clicking his mouse and scrolling through Web pages. "We have an exclusive, so this is huge stuff."

"What happened to Sheriff Herberger?"

"He had a heart attack."

"No!"

"Yes. I want you to head over to the hospital the moment he's allowed to have visitors and interview him."

Carolina barely noticed she'd gotten her first big break. "Will he be all right?"

"That's the latest. He's having surgery today."

She made a mental note to call her cousin Jake. The family would want to send flowers.

"Who's taking his place?" she asked.

"Neil Lovitt."

"Really!"

"He's here now. They're prepping him."

Carolina suppressed the small thrill that coursed through her at the prospect of seeing Neil again so soon.

"I'll get right over there." She stood. "Thanks for the opportunity, Ward."

"Let Rowdy handle the interview. All I need from you is backup." Her boss looked up from his monitor. "Don't get carried away."

She raised two fingers in a pledge. "Scout's honor."

"Yeah, right."

His sarcastic tone wasn't lost on her, and she left his cubicle wearing a grin.

NEIL LOOKED SO uncomfortable and out of place, Carolina had to bite the inside of her cheek to keep from laughing. She doubted he could sit any straighter or clench his jaw any tighter.

Without making a sound, she slid into the chair beside Rowdy. He was currently pitching a local restaurant owned by the station's newest sponsor. Without missing a beat, he pushed a sheet of paper across the table toward her. She quickly scanned the questions they would ask Neil—make that, Rowdy would ask Neil—and soundlessly set the paper down. Then she sent Neil her warmest smile.

He didn't respond. In fact, he was so focused on the microphone in front of him, he hardly acknowledged her. A line of perspiration dotted his brow, and his left hand was balled into a tight fist. Funny, she'd always thought of him as oozing confidence. It was odd seeing him so nervous.

Rowdy announced Sheriff Herberger's illness and Neil's appointment as acting sheriff, doing it all with his usual just-this-side-of-silly style.

Carolina utilized the twenty or so seconds left to study Neil and abruptly changed her mind. He wasn't nervous but rather…angry? No, uncomfortable and unhappy. And she got the feeling it wasn't because of the interview.

"Welcome to KPKD, Deputy Sheriff Lovitt. Or, should I call you *Sheriff* Lovitt now?" Rowdy opened the interview with the ease of a well-practiced professional.

"Thank you for having me."

Carolina noticed Neil didn't answer Rowdy's question.

"First off, how's Sheriff Herberger doing?" The deejay motioned for Neil to move closer and speak directly into the microphone. "I know everyone out there is concerned."

"He's doing well at the moment. His surgery is scheduled for this morning."

They went on to discuss the sheriff's prognosis. Neil's responses were clipped and to the point, demonstrating none of the skills required to make it as an on-air personality.

"Do you have any plans for the position over the next couple months?" Rowdy switched topics, a trick deejays used to keep listeners' attention.

"No."

"None at all?" Rowdy chuckled.

Neil remained stubbornly silent.

"Come on, Sheriff. This is your big chance. You could maybe wipe a few laws off the books, or how 'bout relax the dress code? Those uniforms have got to be itchy."

"I don't have that kind of authority."

"It was a joke, Sheriff."

Neil didn't so much as blink.

Rowdy shot Carolina an I'm-dying-here look.

She ignored the sheet of paper with its questions and asked one of her own. "Sheriff Lovitt, I understand you served with the NYPD for ten years. Can you tell us a little about that experience?"

His knee suddenly jerked. Coincidence, or had her question triggered the involuntary response? She decided to find out.

"I'm sure our listeners would enjoy hearing about your work in New York and how it differs from Payson. Is it anything like the show, *NYPD Blue?* And what brought you here, practically to the other side of the country?"

Another knee jerk.

She'd definitely stumbled on to something.

"The crime rate is higher in New York," he finally said.

Since Rowdy didn't seem to mind, Carolina continued with the interview. "What exactly was your position?"

"Homicide detective."

"Thank goodness we don't have much need for that here," Rowdy interjected.

"Yes."

Neil's carefully guarded control was puzzling, and Carolina liked puzzles.

"Did you ever have to shoot anybody in the line of duty?"

"Yes." The muscle in his jaw flexed.

"Often?"

"No. Just once."

Rowdy wiped imaginary sweat off his brows. "Whew! That's good to know." He signaled Carolina that he was taking back the interview.

She resigned herself to sitting quietly.

Ward's head and shoulders abruptly appeared on the other side of the glass. Because of her position, she was the only one who could see him. He pressed a sheet of notepaper to the glass. On it was written "Ask him if he's ever been shot at." When she raised her eyebrows, Ward shook his head and rolled his hand in a hurry-up gesture.

Strange, but Carolina wasn't in a position to question her boss.

"Has anyone ever shot at *you?*" she interjected during the next pause.

Neil's knee jerked again, hitting the underside of the table.

Several seconds of dead air space followed, which wasn't a good thing in radio.

Rowdy gave her an annoyed look and jumped in. "Sorry, folks. Slight technical difficulty. I think we're good now."

He pointed a finger at Carolina then placed it on his lips. She hitched a thumb at the window, mouthed *Ward* and shrugged one shoulder. Neil stared curiously at them, obviously not understanding the byplay.

"How does your daughter, Zoey, like Payson?" Rowdy read from the list of questions. "She's five, right?"

"Yes. Six next month."

"Is she in school?"

He nodded.

"The folks can't see you, Sheriff," Rowdy joked. "You have to actually talk."

"Yes, she's in school."

Ward held up another paper instructing Carolina to ask the question about being shot at again. Rowdy didn't give her a chance.

"How does she feel about her dad being appointed acting sheriff?"

"She hasn't said," Neil replied.

Ward wiggled the paper.

Carolina threw up her hands, indicating she was helpless. They'd moved on to a new topic. It made no sense going back to the old one.

All at once, Neil swung around.

Ward immediately yanked the paper down. Carolina wasn't sure if Neil had seen it or not. When he turned back around, his gaze locked with hers.

Yeah, he'd seen it all right. There was no mistaking the anger blazing in his eyes.

Rowdy conducted the rest of the interview, which lasted another two minutes, keeping it light and mildly informative—which was a credit to his talent, considering Neil didn't make it easy for the deejay.

After the interview, they went right into a song.

"Good luck, Sheriff." Rowdy shook Neil's hand. "Appreciate you dropping by today."

"No problem." Neil didn't hide his desire to get out of there as fast as possible.

Carolina tried to detain him outside the door. "I'll be interviewing Sheriff Herberger later this week. Any chance I can do a follow-up interview with you?"

"Afraid not." He inclined his head. "Have a nice day, Ms. Sweetwater."

No sexy slight curving of his lips, no murmuring her first name.

She watched him walk away, thinking she'd liked him a whole lot better yesterday.

Ward materialized from nowhere and barked in her ear, "My office, fifteen minutes!"

Good. She had a few things to discuss with him, too. Like what the heck he'd been doing waving those papers at her?

"WELL?" WARD ASKED.

Carolina once again occupied the visitor chair in her boss's office, squished between his desk and the cubicle wall.

"It's compelling reading, but so what?" She handed him back the pages he'd printed out, copies of articles that had originally appeared in the *New York Times*.

"This is news."

"Actually, *old* news. And not necessarily relevant."

"The people of this county are entitled to know about

their new acting sheriff. The man responsible for their safety and well being."

"Know what? That his wife died tragically, the victim of a stray bullet?" Even as she said it, Carolina suffered a stab of pain. How truly awful that must have been for Neil. Not to mention his poor daughter.

"A bullet that was fired by the man he was attempting to apprehend," Ward said. "That raises some serious concerns in my mind about whether or not he acted appropriately. Whether he's the right man for the job of acting sheriff."

"According to the article, he was investigated by Internal Affairs and found innocent of any wrongdoing."

"The story is newsworthy, and it's our job to present it."

"When did KPKD get into the investigative reporting game? We're not a twenty-four-hour news station. People tune in to us to be entertained. 'Information is a perk delivered in small doses,'" she added, quoting him from a departmental meeting the previous month.

"Management wants us to raise the quality of our news segments in order to compete."

"By exploiting Neil Lovitt's personal tragedy?"

"By informing the public of a situation that concerns them."

"Surely he passed a rigorous background check when he was hired as deputy sheriff. If there had been anything irregular or questionable, he wouldn't have been hired."

"People lie."

Neil didn't strike Carolina as the lying type. "Why didn't you bring this up with me before the interview?"

"I just happened to do an Internet search on him."

She couldn't help gaping at Ward. "And you happened to do this *during* the interview, not before?"

"It was an afterthought. A good one."

"I still don't understand what any of this has to do with

me." While she didn't agree with Ward, he was the news director and decided what stories were read on air.

"I'm putting you in charge of the story."

"Me!"

"You have the experience."

"I'm no reporter."

"Your degree's in journalism, right?"

"Yes, but—"

"And you interned for two years at *The Arizona Republic*."

"I wrote obits and two-paragraph fillers on spelling-bee champions or Eagle Scouts. This kind of stuff is way out of my league." Not that she'd do it even if she was qualified.

"I thought you wanted more responsibility."

"I do, but not at the sake of Neil's reputation." Had it been anyone else, Carolina would have jumped at the opportunity. She liked Neil, and investigating him felt a little like betraying a friend.

"Fine." Ward rocked back in his chair. "Then I'll give someone else the Sheriff Herberger interview."

Her mouth fell open. "That's blackmail."

"That's reassigning. And my prerogative as news director."

"Why me?" Her indignation was turning into anger. She didn't like being manipulated.

"Because Neil Lovitt likes you."

"Hardly."

"He does, and he's more likely to let his guard down with someone he likes."

Manipulating her *and* Neil. "What if we—"

He cut her short with a raised hand. "I've made my decision. It's your story. End of discussion."

She refrained from saying more. For the moment.

"Get moving," he told her. "You're on again in four minutes."

Carolina went to her own cubicle around the corner and familiarized herself with the latest traffic update. Her heart, however, wasn't in it. As expected, there were no changes from earlier. Traffic was slow and go in the center of town, and an RV with engine trouble was creating delays on the highway just outside of town.

Glancing at her watch, she noted the time and jumped from her chair, shoving it just a little too hard. The loud screech caused two heads to pop up over the cubicle walls.

"Sorry."

She hurried down the hall, waging a silent war with herself. Ward didn't make idle threats. If she refused this assignment, he might fire her, claiming insubordination. He'd done it before.

How could he not see there was nothing more than a sad, heart-wrenching story in the death of Neil's wife? Then again, Neil *had* responded oddly several times during the interview and didn't appear happy about his temporary promotion.

Could there really be more going on with him than immediately apparent?

Her old journalistic itch unwillingly returned.

Damn Ward. He was probably counting on that.

NEIL'S FIRST DAY as acting sheriff wasn't going well, not that he'd expected anything different after the interview with Rowdy and Carolina. Fortunately, his shift was almost over.

Lifting the phone to his ear, he pushed a button on the dial pad. A generic female voice told him, "You have forty-six new messages. Press number sign to—"

He disconnected before the voice could finish.

When he'd first arrived at the station after leaving KPKD,

he'd listened to the two dozen messages already waiting for him and taken another dozen calls before issuing instructions that all nonemergencies be sent directly to his voice mail. The congratulations were nice, if tedious. Even the complaints and angry rants didn't bother him.

It was the threat to resign or else that got to him, turning his blood to ice and releasing a flood of unwelcome memories.

Neil had no idea if the anonymous caller was serious—the threat wasn't specific, only saying he'd regret accepting the position of acting sheriff, but he'd refused to take any chances and immediately reported the incident.

He pushed another button on his phone. "Mary, can you come in here, please."

"Yes, sir."

Mary Twohorses, Sheriff Herberger's—and now Neil's—secretary, padded into his office, amazingly light on her feet for a woman of such generous proportions. She'd started with the sheriff's department back when two small rooms served as headquarters and typewriters were used in place of computers. "Can I help you with something?"

"Go through my voice messages from today, please. Delete the unimportant ones and make note of the calls I need to return."

"Of course."

"There are a lot of them."

"No problem."

She wore the same patient smile she always did. Nothing ruffled Mary Twohorses's feathers, for which Neil was glad. It had taken him less than an hour on the job this morning to realize he'd be lost without her.

"Thank you." He opened the top right drawer and retrieved his few personal possessions.

"Are you leaving for the day?" she asked.

"Yeah. I have to pick up my daughter from after-school day care." He pocketed his cell phone and keys. "Is R.J. here yet?"

"Just arrived."

"Good."

Mary followed Neil down the hall as far as her office. She would normally have gone home already but was staying late to help with the transition. In the central room, Neil met up with R.J., his lead deputy and the one in charge tonight, and quickly briefed him before leaving by way of the rear door.

The ride to the elementary school his daughter attended didn't take long. He swung into the main parking lot and joined the long line of vehicles already there. A few minutes later, Zoey, along with a crowd of about twenty-five children, burst through the double glass doors. They were closely monitored by a trio of energetic day-care workers. Zoey was released only when Neil stepped out of the patrol car and came around to the passenger side.

She skipped over to him, clutching a packet of papers as if they were constructed of spun gold while dragging her Hello Kitty backpack on the ground. The hair her babysitter, Carmen, had so carefully arranged that morning hung down into her face. Her T-shirt was rumpled and stained with what Neil guessed was finger paint, and her sneaker laces were untied.

He ignored her disarray. To him, his daughter looked adorable.

"Daddy, Daddy!" She delicately peeled the papers away from her chest and waved them at Neil. "Look."

"How about a hug first?" He bent down to her level.

She obliged his request. When he would have held her a moment longer, she pulled away. "You have to read this."

As if he could. The papers were upside down and moving from side to side. He did manage to recognize the Kinder

Kids logo, the after-school activity club to which Zoey belonged. He assumed the papers were information about another field trip to the movies or the museum.

"Okay. When we get home."

"No, now. Pretty please," she added, her small china-doll face filled with excitement and anticipation. "It's really important."

"I have to drive." Her profound disappointment tugged at him while he buckled her into the passenger seat, walked around the car and climbed in behind the steering wheel. "Why don't you tell me what it says," he suggested and turned the key.

Her blue eyes, so much like her mother's, lit up. "They're giving riding lessons. Every Saturday. Can I go?"

"I need to know more before I say yes." Cost wasn't the issue. Neither was transporting Zoey, though it could be complicated while his schedule remained up in the air.

His daughter's safety was his biggest concern. The anonymous caller hadn't mentioned Zoey but until Neil found out if the threat he'd received today was real or a prank, he wasn't about to let her go anywhere except to school without him.

"You promised," Zoey complained. "You said when we moved here I could learn to ride a horse."

She was right. He had, in fact, made several promises in an effort to ease their relocation from New York to Arizona. Ones he'd since come to reconsider. She'd begged him for a pony. He had appeased her with an offer of riding lessons. But that was before he saw how big horses were and how tiny and vulnerable his daughter looked sitting on top of them.

"I've taken you riding. Twice." He joined the line of exiting vehicles loaded with their cargos of children.

"A pony ride at the fair doesn't count."

"What about that time at Carmen's cousin's house? You had fun."

"Which is why I want to go again."

She sounded too adult to be just five-going-on-six. Old enough, he supposed, to take riding lessons. The after-school program wouldn't be offering them to students unless there was minimal risk, right?

Why didn't she want a kitten or to be a ballerina like other little girls?

"I'll go over the paperwork when we get home. See how much the lessons cost, what time they are and how long they last." If they were only an hour, he would stay and watch Zoey. *Closely.* "Wintergreen Stables isn't too far from home."

"That's not where they're having them." Zoey studied the papers, her brow furrowed and her mouth pursed. Despite her efforts, Neil doubted she could read more than a couple dozen words. "Miss Meyers said Bear Creek Ranch."

"Huh. Really?"

Well, that threw a whole new light on the subject. After the interview this morning, Neil wasn't sure he wanted to cross paths with Carolina again. Not until Sheriff Herberger returned to work. She'd asked too many personal questions. Questions Neil hadn't wanted to answer.

On the other hand, what were the chances she'd be at the ranch when he was there with Zoey? Probably nil. Certainly not enough for him to break a promise he'd made to his daughter.

"I'm not saying yes, mind you," Neil told Zoey. "But if everything works out, you can take lessons. For a while, anyway. Then we'll see how it goes."

"Thank you, Daddy." She leaned across the seat as far as her seat belt would allow and hugged his arm. "I love you."

"Love you, too, kiddo."

Neil hoped he didn't regret his decision. Carolina's probing questions weren't his main reason for avoiding her.

It was the temptation she presented and what could happen if he gave in to it.

The threatening call had served to remind him of the dangers associated with his job and his commitment to keep the people he cared about safe. Something he'd failed to do with his late wife.

Protecting Zoey might prove difficult, but protecting Carolina was another story. He just had to stay the hell away from her.

Chapter Three

Carolina stood at the foot of Sheriff Herberger's hospital bed and listened to him answer Rowdy's questions. An earbud attached to a tiny portable transmitter allowed her to hear both ends of the interview, though the echo effect was disorienting.

A firm grip on the bed rail and a tapping right foot allowed her to vent a little of the frustration building inside her.

Ward hadn't been completely forthright with her the other day, which made his strong-arming her into doing an investigative piece on Neil all the more unconscionable. Carolina wasn't interviewing Sheriff Herberger as much as babysitting him, a task one of the techies like Adrian could have easily handled. The questions she'd been given for the sheriff were actually being asked by Rowdy. Her job was limited to going over the list with Sheriff Herberger before the interview and coaching him with his responses if necessary.

Right. The sheriff might have undergone major surgery two days ago, but twenty-six years as an elected official had honed his public-speaking skills, enabling him to carry off a simple radio interview with ease.

Carolina watched him and wavered between telling Ward off when she got back to the station or being a good girl and just shutting up. This could be a test, she reasoned. If she pitched a fit, Ward could use her reaction to shoot down her next bid for a better assignment...and the next, and the next.

If they turned out like the one she was doing on Neil, maybe she should consider changing careers.

A few tentative forays into researching the death of his wife had produced little more than what Ward had already learned and nothing that implicated Neil. Carolina hoped additional digging would provide the same. Then she'd go to Ward and tell him she couldn't find dirt because there wasn't any.

She tried not to think about the—in her opinion, non-existent—possibility that Neil had acted irresponsibly and caused his wife's death.

Sheriff Herberger caught her eye. She smiled encouragingly, giving him a silent thumbs-up. For someone who'd just had a heart attack followed by a triple bypass, he looked good.

Then again, the man was made of granite, as his record proved. He'd seen a lot of change in the past quarter century and endured his share of difficulties, both professional and personal. He'd stood strong for what he believed in, even when those beliefs weren't popular, and was a staunch advocate for the rights of the people who'd elected him.

He was also a longtime friend of the Tuckers, especially Carolina's uncle, who'd managed the ranch before her cousin Jake took over. From tales her uncle told, he and the sheriff had run around together as teenagers and young Otis Herberger had tangled once or twice with the law before deciding to switch sides.

"Well, thanks for having me today, Rowdy," he said into the phone.

"We're glad to hear you're doing well."

While the sheriff and Rowdy were wrapping up the interview, Carolina's thoughts drifted to the station and what she'd say to Ward when she got back. It took a moment for her brain to register that Neil's name had been mentioned.

"I'd be back on the job tomorrow if those dang doctors would let me," Sheriff Herberger continued. "In the meantime, I'm sure Deputy Sheriff Lovitt will do a bang-up job, no pun intended."

The sheriff and Rowdy both laughed.

"He's kind of a serious guy, isn't he?" Rowdy asked.

"When it comes to work, yes. But off duty, he can relax and kick back with the best of them." Sheriff Herberger glanced at Carolina and winked.

She felt her cheeks warm. Did he know about the double date she and Neil had shared last year? Touching a finger to her earbud, she smiled back while trying to appear preoccupied with the broadcast.

The sheriff and Rowdy exchanged a few final comments, then said goodbye. Carolina went over to the sheriff and helped him hang up the phone, which was on the nightstand and beyond his reach.

"How'd I do?"

"You were great." She patted his arm, the one without tubes and monitors attached to it. "A real pro."

"I hate this." His smile dissolved. "I've never been sick a day in my life. And now…" He laid his head back on the pillow and closed his eyes. In that moment, he looked his age and then some. "Three months' mandatory leave of absence. I don't know if I'll be able to hold up without going crazy."

The door cracked open, and a nurse peeked in. Carolina waved to her, and she entered, brandishing yet another floral arrangement. "I didn't want to interrupt if you were still doing the interview." She went over to the dresser.

"No problem, we're done."

The nurse moved two arrangements to make room for the new one.

"It's starting to look like a damn funeral parlor in here," the sheriff grumbled.

"You should be glad it's not a funeral parlor," Carolina said.

"You're right." He laughed again. "Be sure to tell your family thank you for the flowers they sent."

"I will."

The nurse left. Carolina would give anything to do the same, but figured she might not have another opportunity to be alone with the sheriff for a long time. Besides, if Ward asked, she could tell him with complete honesty she was working on the story about Neil.

"We did a little research on Deputy Sheriff Lovitt before his interview the other day."

"Is that so?"

"To help us with questions." She winced at the bald-faced lie. Fortunately, the sheriff didn't appear to notice. "I read about his wife's death."

Sheriff Herberger shook his head sympathetically. "A truly terrible accident."

"I saw that he was investigated by Internal Affairs."

"Standard procedure. Nothing more. Neil acted properly and in the line of duty. There were also more than twenty civilians who witnessed the incident."

"Is it normal for an off-duty police officer to go after a suspect?" Carolina hated to admit it but she was becoming curious, from a strictly personal standpoint. "Especially out in the open like that with lots of people in the area?"

"Protecting the public doesn't stop just because a law enforcement officer clocks out. He had a responsibility."

"I suppose you're right."

"Neil's a good cop." The sheriff yawned. "He'll be a great acting sheriff."

"Of course." She gathered the rest of her things. "You're tired. I'll leave and let you rest."

His thick salt-and-pepper eyebrows came together in a pronounced V. "Is there some reason for your curiosity about Neil?"

"I'd like to know that, too."

Carolina whirled at the familiar voice. The slight embarrassment she'd felt earlier with Sheriff Herberger was nothing compared to now.

Neil stood in the doorway. On second thought, *filled* the doorway was a better description. There were two inches of empty space between his shoulders and the doorjamb. She involuntarily swallowed.

"Neil!" Sheriff Herberger instantly perked up. "Did you hear the interview?"

"No, sorry. I was in the E.R."

"Someone hurt?" The sheriff became instantly alert, all signs of drowsiness gone.

"A hiker took a fall near Windy Canyon. Nothing serious but we brought him in just to be on the safe side." He shot Carolina a piercing look.

She straightened her spine, not about to let him see his unexpected arrival had unnerved her. "Good morning, Sheriff Lovitt. Sheriff Herberger and I were just chatting about you."

"So I heard." He didn't move except for his eyes, which tracked her as she slid away from the head of the bed. "If you have any questions about me, I'd rather you ask me directly and not trouble other people."

"Good idea." Sheriff Herberger's weary face broke into a grin, and he shooed them out of the room. "It's about lunchtime. I hear the cafeteria makes a decent cheeseburger, not that my doctor will let me have one."

"I really need to get back to the station." Carolina made

the excuse, thinking she was saving Neil an awkward situation.

He took her completely aback when he said, "Lunch sounds great," and stepped aside to let her pass. "My treat."

THE CAFETERIA WAS CROWDED and noisy. Not exactly the best place for a personal discussion. But, then, was there ever a good place to lay open old wounds?

One good thing, Neil thought as he bit into his club sandwich, the food was decent. He'd wolfed down most of it, which meant he couldn't put off talking with Carolina much longer.

He still wasn't sure how much he'd tell her. Generally, he didn't care what other people thought of him. The months of living beneath a microscope after Lynne's death had thickened his skin. But of everyone he'd met in Payson, Carolina was the one person besides Sheriff Herberger that he wanted to know the truth and not some distorted version of it. Why her opinion of him counted, he wasn't sure, but it did.

She ate her tuna salad, patiently waiting for him to start. He liked that about her. He'd found most people in the media to be pushy and high energy. Carolina had an appealing calm about her, though he sensed she wasn't a softie by any means.

Amazing that some lucky guy hadn't swept her off her feet and slipped a ring on her finger. She must have had her share of offers.

Neil polished off the last of his sandwich with some milk.

"You going to eat all of those?" Carolina asked, eyeing his French fries.

"Help yourself."

She did—to three large ones, dunking them in the leftover pool of ketchup on his plate before popping them into her mouth. It was something his daughter, Zoey, would do.

He chuckled.

"What?"

"You."

"I gave up fries a while back. Too many carbs." Carolina smiled coyly. "Sometimes my willpower gives out."

He started to answer, then stopped, realizing she'd asked for the fries more to put him at ease than to satisfy any food craving. It was enough to break the ice.

"His name was John Leity," Neil began without preamble. "A normal-sounding name, a normal-looking guy. If you were standing behind him in line at the grocery store, you wouldn't think him guilty of anything more serious than an unpaid parking ticket. We called him the Delivery Man because that was his method of entry. No one was afraid of his face when they saw it through a peephole."

"He was a serial killer."

"Suspected of raping and killing seven women, slitting their throats and leaving them to bleed out on their apartment floors."

Carolina gasped softly and placed her folded hands in her lap.

"There was also sufficient DNA evidence to tie him to a string of other, lesser crimes." Neil absently rubbed his thumb up and down his glass of milk, removing the condensation. "We'd been searching for him for six months. He always managed to remain one step ahead of us."

Neil paused. It had been years since he'd told anyone the entire story. Emotions long buried rushed to the surface, and he needed a moment to rein them in.

"Lynne and I were having a late brunch at a neighborhood outdoor deli. They had the best lox and bagel in the city, and she liked to go there on my days off." The memory struck a gentle chord in his heart. "Zoey was asleep in her stroller, which was parked beside our table. Lynne and I were talking, I don't even remember about what, when I suddenly looked up and saw the Delivery Man at the news-stand across the street." He involuntarily tensed, much like he had that day. "I didn't believe it at first. His regular territory was forty blocks away."

"What did you do?"

He'd gone after the guy. Carolina knew that. He decided to tell her what she didn't know, what very few people outside the NYPD did.

"I told Lynne what was going on and pulled out my cell phone. I wanted to call in his location before he got too far away. She grabbed the phone and told me to go after him."

"That was very brave of her."

"It was." The background din of the busy cafeteria faded into nothingness as Neil relived that horrific day. "You'd have thought with all the violent crimes she dealt with in her own work, she'd have been afraid. For Zoey, if not for herself. But Lynne understood the importance of catching that bastard before he killed another girl."

"What did she do for a living?"

"She was a crime scene investigations analyst. She took an extended leave of absence when she was pregnant. I wish now she'd gone back to work. We might not have been at the deli that day."

"I don't remember reading anywhere she was a cop."

"The media somehow always forgot to mention it. Painting me as the irresponsible cop husband willing to endanger his wife and child sold newspapers and raised TV ratings." Anger and bitterness roughened his voice, and he cleared his throat. "It was bad enough I lost Lynne. Worse that I played a direct part in her death and would have to live with the guilt and grief. But the media went out of its way to make my life a living hell."

"I'm so sorry."

A lot of people had spoken those words to him. Few with as much sincerity.

"A group of *concerned citizens* thought I should be fired for being remiss in my duty. The really screwy thing is, according to protocol, I would have been remiss in my duty if I hadn't gone after the guy."

Neil forced himself to relax and breathe deeply. The air in the cafeteria had become stifling. When he could talk again, he said, "I was almost on him when he spotted me. I figured he'd run, especially when I pulled my gun. Hell, who wouldn't run?"

"But he didn't?"

"Turned and hit me like a three-hundred-pound defensive tackle. People scattered like a bomb had exploded. I went down hard on the concrete but got a hold of his pant leg. He shook me loose and cut back across the street instead of disappearing into the crowd."

"Toward the deli?"

He could hear the horror in Carolina's voice. It wasn't unlike the horror gripping his chest, freezing his heart. The kind he experienced every time he recalled what happened next.

"I ran after him. He fired two shots at me. I…didn't realize he had a gun—he'd always used a knife on the girls— though I'm not sure it would have made a difference. I was operating on pure adrenaline by then. The second bullet grazed my scalp. I returned fire. And didn't miss." Neil concentrated on the condiments clustered in the middle of their table, sensing Carolina's gaze on him, feeling her compassion. "The same bullet that winged me hit the building and ricocheted off…into Lynne's neck. A quarter inch to the left, and it would have missed the artery. She was dead before the ambulance arrived. Loss of blood. Like all his victims."

"Oh, Neil." Carolina laid a warm hand over his.

He didn't flinch or withdraw, his usual reaction. Instead, he absorbed the sympathy she offered, letting it fill some of the hollow places inside him.

"I was suspended until the investigation was complete, basically for my protection. And Zoey's. After I was cleared to return to work, the department was flooded with letters and phone calls, demanding I be fired. I saved them the trouble and resigned ten months later."

"What did you do after that?"

"Went and got Zoey from her grandparents. I was a mess when Lynne died. Physically and emotionally. I thought I couldn't take care of Zoey and that she'd be safer away from me and the city. Lynne's parents live in upstate New York and adore Zoey. They were happy to have her."

"Giving her up must have been really hard for you."

"It was. I managed because it was temporary." He paused a moment before making his most important point. "I don't want Zoey growing up hearing the details of her mother's death and my part in it. I'll do whatever's necessary to prevent it." He ground out the last sentence.

"She doesn't know how Lynne died?"

"Only that it was an accidental shooting."

"It's not my place to ask, but do you think that's wise?"

"She's too young to understand."

"She won't always be young."

"I won't have Zoey hate me because she blames me for her mother's death."

"You weren't the one who fired the gun that killed Lynne. The Delivery Man did."

"Because I went after him."

"Zoey loves you. She won't hold you responsible."

"Maybe. Maybe not. I'm not taking any chances."

"She may find out on her own one day. It won't be hard. You're all over the Internet. Are you ready for that?"

Carolina had just voiced Neil's biggest fear. "You're right about what you said earlier. It's not your place to ask."

"I apologize."

"Zoey is everything to me. More important than my career. She's the reason I quit the force, took a year off and rented an apartment in the same town as my in-laws so that Zoey and I could be close to them. When I stopped seeing Lynne's blood covering the sidewalk every night in my dreams, I figured I was ready to go back to work. It took me another six months to find the job I was looking for."

"Deputy sheriff?" Carolina removed her hand from his.

Neil wished she hadn't. Her fingers had felt nice resting on his. "For a while I considered getting out of law enforcement altogether or going into a related field, like security. Then I'd remember Lynne and her commitment. She believed with all her heart we were making the world a better place. Me by catching criminals and her by processing the evidence that helped put them behind bars. I decided to stay in law enforcement to honor her."

"She would be proud of you."

"I couldn't stay in the city. Zoey's safety is my main concern." He thought of the threatening phone call from the other day. Fortunately, there had been no more. "Rural law enforcement seemed like a good fit. Gila County has its share of trouble, but not like New York. I swore I would never put myself or my family in jeopardy again."

"Is that why you don't want to be acting Sheriff?"

Leave it to Carolina to figure him out.

"One thing I've learned, the higher profile the position, the greater the danger. There are too many wackos out there, and they tend to target those in charge."

"I see now why you didn't like being interviewed."

"My relationship with the media isn't a good one."

"After what you've been through, no one could expect

differently." She glanced away, then back at him. "I suppose I should explain myself."

"Not if you don't want to."

"I owe you that much after everything you've told me." She sighed. "You won't like it. I sure don't."

"Try me."

"I've been assigned to do a story on you."

"I see," he said flatly.

"My boss inferred that if I don't do the story, my job could be on the line."

Even though he'd already decided not to pursue a relationship with Carolina, he'd stupidly hoped her interest in him was personal. Well, this definitely clinched it. Steering clear of her would be much simpler from now on. If he weren't sitting down, he'd give himself a swift kick in the rear. He pushed back his chair, well aware he was about to be rude but not caring. "I guess I've just given you everything you need for your story." He was surprised at how much it angered him that Carolina was the one about to bring his world crashing down around him.

"No, Neil." She reached over the small table for his arm, gripping it tightly. "You've just given me every reason to tell my boss exactly where he can shove this assignment."

"You'd give up your job for me?"

"I have my integrity."

Her eyes shone with sincerity and her voice rang with conviction.

So why did Neil feel he still couldn't trust her?

Chapter Four

"Are you crazy!" Rachel looked stunned.

"I don't usually agree with Rachel," Vi said, "but seriously, kiddo, have you thought this through?"

"It so happens I have."

Carolina took her older sisters' criticism in stride. She'd expected nothing less than shock and outrage from her family when she'd informed them of the run-in with her boss after lunch with Neil. The only one of them who might have understood her reasons was Corrine. She, however, was still cruising the Caribbean with her new husband and wouldn't be back for several more days.

"What if you lose your job?" Vi asked.

She was the oldest of the four sisters and the first to make their mother's fondest wish come true by giving her a grandchild. A girl. No surprise there, the Tucker-Sweetwater clan was overrun with members of the fairer sex. Even their cousin Jake, the lone male in their generation, had produced four daughters. With Carolina and Rachel still single and Vi having trouble getting pregnant a second time, all hopes were now pinned on Corrine to break the trend.

"I won't lose my job." Carolina tried to convey a confidence she was far from feeling. Ward had made his displeasure at her defiance abundantly clear. She was still smarting from his verbal reprimand. "If he was going to fire me, he'd have done it already."

"Maybe not. He could be waiting." Jake stepped out onto the redwood deck, carrying a plastic pitcher of fruit punch and a bag of potato chips. He'd invited his cousins over for a lazy Saturday afternoon of hanging out in his backyard and enjoying the spectacular mountain views. The girls had insisted on playing in the hot tub. Briana was recruited to supervise them in exchange for getting a day shaved off her punishment. She'd been grounded a month for the parking lot fender bender.

"Waiting for what?" Carolina sipped her iced tea. She'd contemplated asking for a beer but was afraid it might look as if she was drowning her sorrows.

"You to quit," Jake said.

"Why would I quit?"

Jake set the fruit punch and chips down on a picnic table beside the hot tub. His three oldest daughters, along with Vi's rambunctious preschooler, scrambled from the hot tub in a noisy, chaotic frenzy. Leaving a trail of puddles and wet footprints in their wake, they pounced on the snack as if they hadn't eaten in days. The only one missing was Jake's youngest. A year old, she was much too little to swim in the hot tub with her sisters and cousin. She and her mother had gone into town for some shopping, leaving Jake in charge of keeping the masses entertained.

"Here. Put these on before you catch cold." Vi jumped up from her chaise longue and handed the girls towels, making sure to wrap up her daughter snugly.

"This isn't Denver, Vi," Rachel admonished. "It's, what, seventy-two?"

Jake tipped his chair back and studied the thermometer mounted beside the door. "More like seventy-eight."

"How quickly they forget." Rachel laughed. "Fall in Arizona is like summer everywhere else."

Carolina's relief that the subject had veered from her current work dilemma didn't last. Jake refused to let it go.

"Your boss might try and force you to quit," he said, shooting her a quelling look, "by making your job a living hell."

"Don't swear in front of the girls," Vi hissed.

"Sorry."

"I doubt Ward would pressure me like that. It would be considered harassment, and the station has a no-harassment policy." Carolina leaned forward and reached for a chip, promising herself she'd have just one. A half dozen magically jumped into her open hand.

"Not necessarily," Jake answered. "Depends on how he went about it."

"What would be the benefit of me quitting versus firing me?"

"He wouldn't have to give you severance pay, for starters. And you probably couldn't collect unemployment."

"Humph. I'm not sure even Ward's that devious. He's more of an explode one minute and forget about it the next kind of manager." More potato chips appeared in Carolina's hand and made their way to her mouth. "That's why I think if he hasn't fired me by now, he won't. Of course, I can forget about any more special assignments or promotions." The last chip lodged in her throat as that dismal reality sank in, and she coughed to clear it.

"I think you should quit," Vi said hotly. "You have way too much talent for that dinky station."

Big sisters. Hate them one minute, love them the next.

"What would I do for a job? The other stations in town aren't hiring or I'd have heard."

"We're shorthanded in the office."

Jake's suggestion earned him a disgruntled groan. "Work for you? No, thank you. Helping Mom is enough." Like most of the family members, Carolina split herself between the ranch and an outside job. In her case, she assisted her mother, Millie, who was in charge of their many and frequently elaborate weddings. "Besides, I like working at the station. Most of the time," she added. "I'm not ready to throw in the towel yet."

"Just in case, I think you should give Howard a call," Jake said.

Carolina frowned at the mention of the family's attorney.

"What all did this new acting sheriff say that would make you go against your boss?" Vi asked.

Carolina reminded herself that her sister had moved away from Bear Creek Ranch almost ten years ago, and although she returned regularly to visit, she hadn't met Neil yet.

"You wouldn't ask that question if you saw him." Rachel's radiant grin spoke volumes.

"Oh."

"Yeah," Carolina concurred with a sigh.

"What?" Jake looked from one to the other, his expression befuddled. "Is this some sort of female code?"

"Neil Lovitt is hot," Rachel translated for him.

"Seriously hot," Briana chimed in, plopping down on the end of Carolina's chaise longue. Her younger sisters, evidently reenergized from their snack, had returned to the hot tub, their little cousin in tow. "For, you know, an older guy and everything."

"Old?" Jake recoiled. "What does that make me?"

Briana rolled her eyes and turned her attention back to Carolina. "I don't blame you for refusing to do the story. He's really nice and doesn't deserve to have his reputation trashed."

"He is nice." Carolina smiled. "And not just because he

cut you some slack with that ticket." The things Neil had told her about his late wife's death and raising his daughter alone had deeply affected her. She hadn't been able to stop thinking about him since their conversation.

"Is that your only reason?" Jake asked.

"Absolutely." Carolina instantly put up her guard. She and Jake weren't merely related, they were good friends. He knew her as well as, if not better than, her sisters. "He's a nice guy, as Briana says, with a sad past. What other reason do I need?"

"You forgot to mention hot." Rachel, still grinning, rubbed sunscreen onto her bare arms.

Jake's gaze narrowed on Carolina. "I know for a fact there are a lot of nice, *hot* people with sad pasts that you wouldn't risk your job for."

She didn't answer him—which was a mistake because it became immediately obvious that everybody present over the age of ten suspected there was more to her motives for defending Neil than she'd admitted. Close families definitely had their drawbacks.

"Be careful," Jake warned. "No reason to screw up your life for some guy you hardly know."

"Language, please." Vi glowered at Jake. Again.

Carolina pondered Jake's point while he and her sister debated whether or not Vi's daughter had already heard the words he'd used at preschool.

Neil wasn't "some guy" as far as Carolina was concerned. She definitely experienced a connection with him, of the zing-clear-to-her-toes caliber. The connection could, she feared, be one-sided. He hadn't exactly bubbled over with joy in the hospital cafeteria when she'd promised him she would defy her boss and not do the story on him. If anything, he'd appeared hesitant to believe her and had required considerable convincing on her part.

Carolina liked to think of herself as a good-hearted person, but Jake was right. She wouldn't lay her job on the line for just anyone. It prompted her to wonder exactly how strong her attraction to Neil was and what, if anything, she should do about it.

"Let me see how Ward acts on Monday," she said, speaking over Jake and Vi's silly argument. "He might not mention the story again. Depending on how it goes, I may call Howard."

"Good." Her declaration appeared to satisfy Jake. "I'll be right back," he said when the trill of a phone sounded through the partially open door. "Briana, watch the girls, please."

Rachel waited until Jake was inside to pin Carolina down. "So, you going to ask him out?"

"No!"

"Why not? You want to go out with him."

"She may *want* to go out with him—" Vi sent her sister a superior look reminiscent of when they were teens "—but that doesn't mean she prefers to do the asking."

Briana, who hadn't returned to the hot tub, vacillated between watching the younger girls and observing the adult goings-on with starstruck fascination.

"You know me." Carolina lifted one shoulder in a casual shrug. "If a man appeals to me, I have no qualms about making the first move."

"That's true," Vi agreed, "if you don't like him all that much. If you do, then you suddenly go from laughing in the face of convention to strictly traditional."

Carolina winced. "I do not."

"Come on, sis. When's the last time you hesitated about taking the initiative?"

She could pinpoint the day exactly. It had been on her disastrous double date with Neil. She'd hoped he would pick up on her attraction to him and respond in kind. Luckily, she hadn't shared the details of that night with her sisters. Or not luckily, she thought, after hearing Vi's next remark.

"It was Lonnie, right?"

Not that Carolina was having fun in the first place, but why did her sister have to bring up the dreaded ex-fiancé?

"I'm sure there's been someone else I've hesitated to ask out since him." There *had* to be. Carolina racked her brain and came up blank. Uh-oh. Her sisters were right. She really did like Neil. Damn!

"I think one of the girls got water up her nose," she said, but her plan for distracting the four unwavering stares fixed on her failed. "I can't concentrate with all this pressure."

"See?" Vi sat back in her chair. "Told you."

"Aunt Carolina's crushing," Briana said in a singsong tone.

"I'm not crushing on Neil." Carolina was afraid it might be far worse. Like total and complete infatuation.

"So, prove us wrong and ask him out."

Jake's timing couldn't have been better. She'd never felt so glad to see him come through a door.

"Hey, you're—" she began to say, but the disturbed look on his face stopped her midsentence. "What's wrong?"

"That was Gary on the phone," Jake said, referring to their manager of guest amenities. He started picking up damp towels and hanging them on the railing to dry. "Come on, girls, we have to go inside. Party's over."

"Aw, Dad," his daughters chorused.

"Sorry. Something important came up."

Sensing his urgency, Carolina rose and began to help. "What did he say?"

Gary had been an employee for over thirty years and knew the operation of the ranch better than anyone except the immediate family. For him to phone Jake at home signaled a serious problem.

"Little José was on the north ridge this morning where it butts up against federal land, checking the high trails before the weather turns." Clearing trails of debris was a task the ranch hands regularly performed every March and October. "He found something. Gary drove out there this afternoon to verify it in case Little José was wrong. He wasn't."

"Jeez, Jake." Rachel jumped up and also started helping. "You talk like he discovered a dead body."

"No, not that."

"Thank goodness."

"It was evidence of illegal mining."

"Look for a numbered marker around the next bend."

"Gotcha."

Neil downshifted into a lower gear and floored the gas. The Jeep bounced and banged over rocks and rain washes with every foot of rugged mountain terrain they covered. Veering sharply to the right, he narrowly avoided a sprawling ponderosa. As it was, a low-hanging branch scraped across the Jeep's canvas top. The noise was momentarily deafening.

"Take it easy, will you?" Neil's deputy, R.J., flopped around in the front passenger seat. Clutching the grab bar, he jammed the soles of both feet into the floorboard. "I'd like to get there with all my bones intact, if you don't mind."

Neil shifted again as they crested the top of a small hill. The trail they'd taken was minimally maintained, narrow and designed for horses or ATVs, not full-size vehicles. The fact he and R.J. had made it this far was a testament to the Jeep's sturdiness and, Neil liked to think, his ability as a driver.

He'd discovered a passion for off-road driving soon after moving to Payson, never having encountered anything like it in New York City or the outskirts of Schenectady, where he'd grown up. The sheriff's department's standard issue Jeep didn't compare to his own tricked-out, four-wheel-drive pickup, but he still pushed the older vehicle for everything it had, relishing the rush of adrenaline surging through him.

Challenging himself with an almost unnavigable trail had the added benefit of keeping troublesome thoughts at bay—like Carolina and her promise not to do the story on him. He still didn't know whether he could believe her or not. And her warning that his daughter would learn the part he'd played in her mother's death was disrupting his sleep, dulling his appetite and affecting his mood. He'd have to be more careful in the future. Just this morning at breakfast Zoey had asked him if anything was wrong. He hated lying to her, but what choice did he have?

"Are you on a suicide mission or what?" R.J. swore as the GPS device he'd been holding went flying.

"This is nothing," Neil answered. And it was.

"Says you."

"Hang on!" He cranked the steering wheel hard to the left.

Thankfully, the old Jeep didn't let him down. Its tires hugged the ground, sending dirt and small rocks spraying in every direction. The sense of power revived Neil, and he wished he could control everything in his life with the same ease he did the Jeep.

"Damn it to hell," R.J. complained when his cowboy hat collided with the sun visor, shoving the brim down over his eyes. He pushed it back up and blinked. "Slow down, for Pete's sake. We're not in a race."

Neil let up on the gas only when they reached the top of the next small hill. At the bottom a pair of pickup trucks and three ATVs were parked, reminding him that the reason for their wilderness adventure was business, not pleasure.

He pulled up alongside the closest truck and cut the engine. Two men—one young, one older, neither of whom he recognized—were removing kerosene lanterns from a crate in the bed of the truck and lighting them. Good thing. The sun was quickly disappearing beneath the distant mountaintops, and any minute now they would be swallowed by darkness and surrounded by cold.

Across the gully, seven more people had gathered together on a slope that looked no different than the half-dozen others in the immediate area—except for the crude, gaping hole in the side, four feet high by three feet wide. Neil was no authority, but even he realized the hole was not a product of Mother Nature.

He and R.J. exited the Jeep. Opening the rear compartment, they grabbed their jackets, a pair of flashlights, a toolbox and a roll of yellow crime-scene tape before parting ways. Neil joined the two men lighting lanterns while R.J. battled trees and a dense thicket to reach the group of people standing in front of the hole. Most of them had their backs to Neil. Even so, he recognized Jake Tucker's unmistakable stance.

"Evening." Neil addressed the men beside the truck.

The older of the two glanced at the badge on Neil's shirt and extended his hand. "Howdy, Sheriff. I'm Gary Forester, and this is Little José. He's the fellow who found the shaft."

Neil reached inside his jacket and removed a notebook. "Can you tell me more about that?"

"I was riding the trail, looking for areas that needed clearing."

"Where's your horse now?" Neil scribbled as Little José talked.

"We trailered him back to the ranch so I didn't have to ride in the dark."

"How did you happen to notice the mine shaft?" Out of the corner of his eye, Neil observed R.J. attempting to remove the people from the slope and the crime scene. He was being met with some resistance, from Jake in particular.

"I *didn't* notice it," Little José said. "Not at first. What I found was this." He lifted one of the lanterns, illuminating the truck's lowered tailgate where a long, cylindrical piece of iron lay. "It was right there in the middle of the trail."

Neil fished a handkerchief from his back pocket. "Who else besides you has touched this?" he asked.

"Just Gary."

Careful not to smudge any possible fingerprints and incur the wrath of the CSI team, Neil used the handkerchief to lift the object. His hand dipped slightly at the unexpected weight.

"It's a chisel," Little José informed him.

"And finding this prompted you to go looking for a mine shaft?" Neil set the chisel back down on the truck's tailgate.

"Not the chisel so much as the footprints and tire tracks."

"Where?"

"Everywhere." Little José indicated the ground near them and up the slope.

Neil took in all the people and vehicles and groaned inwardly. Any trace of those footprints and tire tracks was probably eradicated by now. Why hadn't Jake called Neil first before storming out here and bringing three-fourths of his family with him.

The three-fourths, he promptly realized with another glance at the slope, that included Carolina.

His scribbling momentarily faltered.

"This is private property," Gary interjected. "No one comes up here who doesn't work for the ranch."

"What about neighboring ranchers?"

"They have no reason. And the fences are diligently maintained. We can't afford to have our guests coming in contact with stray cattle."

"You rent out ATVs, right? Could any of the guests have come up here?"

Concentrating required all Neil's effort. Carolina's pale yellow jeans and green trench coat made her hard to ignore.

"These trails are too dangerous and off-limits," Gary said.

"Not everyone obeys the rules."

"I suppose." Gary adjusted the knob on one of the lanterns. The flame caught, then glowed brightly. Up at the mine shaft, flashlight beams zigzagged over the ground and on the rock walls.

"So, after you found the chisel and noticed the footprints and tire tracks, you went searching for the mine shaft?"

"I didn't know what I was looking for at first," Little José explained, "only that someone had been here. I followed the tracks up the hill. Once I got close enough, I could see the hole hidden behind a pile of brush. They didn't do a very good job camouflaging it."

"Or they were in a hurry because you surprised them," Neil suggested. "What did you do after you found the shaft?"

"I radioed the ranch. Reported my location and what I'd found."

"I drove straight out here as soon as he told me," Gary said. "Then I called Mr. Tucker. He told me to contact you."

R.J. had done his job. He'd rounded up the family and was bringing them down the hill.

Jake stopped briefly at a white truck then made straight for Neil. "Sheriff Lovitt."

"Mr. Tucker. Do you have any idea who might have done this?"

"None at all." He didn't hide his anger well. "But whoever they were, they had access to some fairly sophisticated equipment."

"Why do you say that?"

"Marks on the rocks. They might be using hand tools now,

but the shaft was originally excavated with a high-powered drill. The experts will be able to tell us more."

"Experts?"

"I've contacted the Arizona Geological Society. Asked them to send out a crew."

"Call them back." Neil wrote furiously in his notebook. "Tell them to wait until someone from CSI contacts them and gives them the go-ahead to proceed. In fact, no one is to go within a mile of this mine shaft without permission. Is that clear?"

Jake nodded curtly, not liking being put off but complying. "I wonder how much gold they've found so far, if any." The question seemed to be directed at himself rather than Neil.

"Maybe the crew from the Geological Society can tell you once they've examined the mine." Neil wrote down a reminder to have someone research places in the state that purchased or processed unrefined ore.

Jake raked his fingers through his hair, his expression showing shock and disbelief.

Neil had seen the same look on countless victims during his career. "Did you have any idea there was gold on your property?"

"No."

"Yes." Carolina stepped forward, hugging her arms to ward off the increasing chill.

Even if Neil wanted to, he couldn't ignore her any longer. Whenever she got within visual range of him, everyone and everything else disappeared. It had been that way from their first encounter.

"Those are just local legends." Jake sounded irritable.

She lifted her chin. "I disagree."

Neil almost smiled. Was there no one who intimidated her? He was instantly reminded of their conversation in the hospital cafeteria, and his fledgling trust in her increased a tiny fraction. He could see her having no reservations whatsoever about defying her boss. And since nothing had surfaced about him or his late wife on the radio, in the newspapers or around town, it appeared she'd kept her promise.

For now anyway.

"What legends?" he asked.

"These mountains were heavily prospected about the time of the Civil War and until the late 1880s," she explained. "Nobody ever struck it rich, but enough gold was found to generate rumors of a mother lode. It's not unreasonable," she added when Jake heaved a tired sigh. "Remember that strike they found outside of Payson twenty…twenty-two years ago?"

"Not really. I was away at college."

She huffed. "Well, I do."

"How much gold did they find?" Neil asked.

"Quite a bit. In the tens, if not hundreds of thousands of dollars."

In today's market, that amount could easily be doubled.

"Have you had the area tested?" Neil asked Jake.

He shook his head. "Gold fever had long since died by the time our grandparents bought the land and built the ranch. Not that our grandfather believed the rumors."

"But Grandma Ida did," Carolina said.

"That's true." The young woman interrupting them looked too much like Carolina to be anyone other than her sister. "She took us once to the Rim County Museum when we were kids. They had this old treasure map on display. A family in town had donated it after finding it among their deceased father's belongings. Grandma showed us where the ranch was on the map and laughed, saying she should get Grandpa to dig for gold."

Neil's glance traveled up the slope to the mine shaft,

nearly obscure now in the dark. "I'd say someone else believed the legends, too."

"Or they have the map," Carolina said.

He turned to face her. "Is it still on display at the museum?"

"I have no clue. I haven't visited in years."

Neil underlined the words *map* and *museum* in his notebook.

"You can't seriously believe there's a connection," Jake said.

"People are illegally mining for gold on your property, Mr. Tucker." Neil felt compelled to point out the obvious. "No one would undertake such an operation without being reasonably confident it's going to pay off."

His observation was followed by a round of silence. He used the lull to finish up his notes.

"Hey, Jake," Carolina's sister said, her voice bright with excitement. "We could be rich. Did you ever think about that?"

Chapter Five

While the Tucker and Sweetwater family members mulled over the ramifications of what a potential gold strike might mean to them, Neil went with R.J. to inspect the mine shaft, a process that required a good half hour. When they were done, he radioed the station. The evening dispatcher took down the information he gave her, assuring him she'd contact CSI the moment she hung up. As there was no evidence of a homicide, he didn't expect the investigators to make an appearance until morning, when they had sufficient light to see. In the interim, Neil and R.J. would secure the crime scene to the best of their ability.

"You willing to stay overnight?" Neil asked R.J. "I don't want to take a chance whoever did this comes back." Neil would have volunteered, but Carmen had midterms this week and couldn't babysit Zoey past ten o'clock.

R.J. shrugged. He was a home boy, born and raised in the Payson area. "Won't be the first time I've spent the night in the mountains on the lookout for bad guys."

Neil was grateful the young deputy didn't appear to hold any grudges. He'd been with the department longer than Neil and might have resented not being appointed acting sheriff. The same couldn't be said for all the deputies, and their not-so-subdued grumbling had reached Neil's ears.

He would have to address the problem eventually before it

escalated. Perhaps Sheriff Herberger might have some advice for him. Neil wasn't egotistical or career hungry and had no qualms about asking for help when he needed it.

"I'll send Willie to break you around dawn," he told R.J.

"Be sure he brings a thermos of coffee."

"He doesn't drink it."

"But I do." R.J. grinned.

"You want a doughnut with that?"

"Doughnuts are for city cops. Out here, we have burritos with our coffee. Ernesto's opens early. He can stop there."

"I hope you're carrying a roll of antacids."

"Sissy."

One by one, the family members left, none of them willingly. Neil understood. If his property had been violated, he'd want to stay and protect it, too.

He was shutting the back of the Jeep when his personal cell phone abruptly rang. Unhooking it from his belt, he flipped open the phone and verified the caller ID. His heart rate increased when "unknown" flashed on the small screen. Only very few people had this number—Zoey, her babysitter Carmen, the elementary school, his parents and his late wife's parents.

Had Carmen changed carriers again? He put the phone to his ear. "Sheriff Lovitt."

There was no answer. Only the dull, crackling sound of an open line.

"Hello, Sheriff Lovitt," he repeated, then more firmly, "Who's there?" He was immediately reminded of the threatening phone call from the other day.

A series of beeps sounded, and the line went dead.

He snapped the phone shut. Quickly changing his mind, he dialed his house.

"Everything's fine," Carmen told him when he'd asked about Zoey. "She's watching TV. You want to talk to her?"

"In a minute. Has anyone called the house tonight?"

"Yeah, right before you. Like thirty seconds. I thought when the phone rang again it was them calling back."

"Who was it?"

"They hung up."

"What did the caller ID say?"

"Unavailable. I know I'm not supposed to answer when that happens but I forgot."

"Just be more careful next time." Neil's free hand closed into a fist. Two blocked calls within a minute, one to his private cell and one to his home. He didn't believe it was a coincidence and decided to have Mary Twohorses check his phone records in the morning. "I'll be home in an hour. If they call again, ask for their name and get in touch with me right away."

"Sure." Carmen's tone reflected the nervous anxiety he'd no doubt instilled in her with his brusque questions. "Here's Zoey."

"What's up, kiddo?"

"Daddy, when are you coming home?"

"Not till after you're asleep, I'm afraid."

"Again?"

"Sorry." Zoey's disappointment was no greater than his. Reading her a bedtime story was a ritual they both looked forward to every night. Unfortunately, Zoey would have to get used to him not being there. For a while, at least. Until Sheriff Herberger returned to work. "But I'll come in and kiss you good night."

"Promise?"

"Cross my heart."

She went on to tell him all about the Disney DVD Carmen had brought with her, and for a moment, Neil's world was perfectly right, devoid of unknown callers, dissension among his deputies and fear that his daughter would learn the truth about her mother's death and blame him.

Carolina came over shortly after he'd disconnected, giving him reason to suspect she'd been waiting for him to finish. The cool evening breeze had left her hair in an attractive disarray that he found very appealing. Then again, was there anything about her that didn't appeal to him? She attempted to brush a wayward strand from her eyes, only to have it fall back into place.

He was instantly and unwillingly charmed.

"Hi," she said.

He could sense her trepidation and resisted reassuring her with a friendly comeback. For one, he was on duty, investigating a crime. For another, she was a distraction he could and *should* avoid. Lastly, he still wasn't comfortable with where he stood with her. If the story about his wife broke locally, his career could be in danger. But Neil cared far more about Zoey and the potential emotional impact on her.

On *them*.

If she wound up hating him… He refused to consider the possibility.

"Good evening, Ms. Sweetwater."

"Oh, we're back to that."

"Can I help you with something?"

The lanterns had been extinguished in preparation of everyone leaving. Only a three-quarter moon remained to illuminate the site. Shadows played across her face, adding a hint of mystery to a woman who already mystified him on many levels.

"I was thinking…" Her voice trailed off.

"Yes."

"I'd be happy to take you to the museum and show you the map. If they still have it, that is. If not, I might be able to locate the original owners. I'm sure my mother and uncle remember them."

"Thank you. I appreciate the offer. But I'll have to decline."

"You aren't going to check it out?" She drew back in surprise.

"Yes. But we have procedures. One of my deputies or an officer from the Payson Police Department will likely be following up on leads. Not me."

"The Payson Police?"

"Local agencies work together when crimes cross jurisdictions."

"I see." She wavered.

He wondered why she didn't leave. "Do you have something else on your mind?"

"The stories about prospecting in these parts are really interesting." A hint of annoyance infected her voice. "Despite what Jake says, they may have a bearing on our illegal mining problem. We could meet, and I could tell you the stories in detail. At, um, the station, of course. Not for a meal or anything. Unless you wanted to eat," she ended in a rush.

Neil paused. "Are you asking me out, Ms. Sweetwater?"

She evidently found her courage and answered strongly and confidently, "Yes, I am."

For a brief second, he contemplated saying yes. The idea of going on a date with Carolina, just the two of them, was appealing. But he couldn't accept for many reasons, most of which wouldn't make sense to her.

"I'm honored. Really, I am."

"That sounds like a no." She swallowed, the only visible sign that his rejection had hurt her.

"Sorry."

A horn beeped. "Be right there," she hollered over her

shoulder. To Neil, she said, "Is it because of my job? I told you, I refused the assignment."

"Carolina..."

"I like it better when you use my first name."

She smiled, and his resolve weakened, not that it was ever strong where she was concerned.

"The problem is your job, but also mine."

"Yours? How so?"

"It's complicated."

"Try me."

He was tempted. Good judgment, however, prevailed. "It won't make any difference."

"How do you know?" She stepped forward. No more than a matter of inches, yet it was enough to change their positions—or was it the atmosphere?—from casual to intimate. "Look, there's something between us, don't bother denying it."

He didn't. They'd both have to be blind or naive not to notice the sparks that went off like tiny rockets every time they were together. "Trust me, you're better off with someone else." He started toward the door of the Jeep.

The horn beeped again. Carolina's sister was growing impatient.

"Wait, Neil." She spun around and cupped her hands to her mouth. "Go on without me. Sheriff Lovitt is taking me home."

"Carolina." This time, his voice was stern.

"You have to drive right past my cabin to leave the ranch. Well, practically." She didn't wait for him to answer and dashed around the Jeep to the passenger side.

Neil opened his door. She was already in and buckling her seat belt. The one remaining vehicle with her sister had left and was bumping up the nearby slope. If he didn't take Carolina home, R.J. would have to when Willie relieved him.

Recognizing defeat when it stared him in the face, Neil climbed in behind the steering wheel, hoping he wasn't making a huge mistake.

"Take the left fork," Carolina said.

Neil shot her a sidelong glance. "That's not the way we came." Neither, he was sure, was it the way the other vehicles had gone.

"I know a shortcut. The trail's a little rough, though. If you're worried—"

"I'm not." He downshifted.

"I didn't think so."

He couldn't see her face in the Jeep's dark interior, but he felt relatively certain she was smiling.

"Careful, the next slope drops off sharply." She tightened her hold on the grab bar and gave an excited "Whee" when they exploded down the other side.

Great. One more thing to like about Carolina Sweetwater. His deputy R.J. could take a few lessons from her when it came to the art of off-road driving.

The noise, the bouncing and the level of concentration required to steer the Jeep hindered any meaningful conversation until they reached the outskirts of a maintenance yard and the main dirt road that led through the ranch. They continued driving, guided by lights peeking out from between the trees, evidence that many of the guests were still awake in their cabins.

"How much farther?" he asked.

"About a quarter mile. Keep going."

Hiking and ATV trails veered off in various directions. Carved wooden signs tacked to trees proclaimed the various trail names. Cute names, like Bear Tracks and Fox Cub and Juniper Berry. One name stood out.

"Did I read that right? Carolina May?"

She nodded. "Grandpa Walter named a trail for each of us grandkids."

A stone monument stood at the base of the next trail. They were going too fast for Neil to read the entire rectangular brass sign.

"Hailey…?"

"Hailey Beatrice Trail. For my cousin, Jake's sister. She died in a horse riding accident almost four years ago."

"I'm sorry."

"Thanks. She was a great person. We all really miss her. Jake especially. They were close, and he took her death pretty hard."

Neil sometimes forgot that he wasn't the only person to ever suffer the loss of a loved one.

"There." Carolina pointed ahead. "Go right."

If not for her, he would have missed the turnoff. The lack of lights, denser foliage and narrowing of the road indicated this part of the ranch was less traveled.

"We're here."

Neil slowed the Jeep and parked.

The one-story structure, set slightly back from the road, had the appearance of a home rather than a guest cabin. Flowers lined the stone walkway leading to a porch complete with a swing on one end and a pair of wicker rockers on the other. A white picket fence straight out of *Little House on the Prairie* surrounded the property, and a rooster weather vane sat atop the peaked roof. Along the side of the yard was what appeared to be a vegetable garden.

At first, the quaint country charm of the place seemed in contrast to Carolina's sophistication. But on closer inspection, Neil decided she fit right in. He could easily picture her planting tomatoes in the garden or curled up on the porch swing, a book in one hand and a glass of lemonade in the other.

It was also the kind of place where he could picture himself, sitting next to her on the swing, her bare feet in his lap, the two of them lolling away a lazy Saturday afternoon.

An unexpected noise penetrated Neil's thoughts. "Is that a dog barking?"

"My sister's French bulldog. Actually, it's her husband's. The dog came with him as part of the deal. I'm babysitting while they're on their honeymoon."

"Should you let her out?"

"Give her a second. I had a doggie door installed, and she's still getting used to it."

Carolina had no sooner spoken than a compact black bullet traveling close to the ground came tearing out from behind the house. The dog stopped at the gate and proceeded to raise the alarm, letting everyone within hearing distance know an intruder had invaded the premises.

Carolina rolled down her window. "Quiet, Belle, it's me."

The dog immediately went from barking to scratching at the gate before plunking her behind down to wait.

"Is she okay there?"

"The gate's latched, she can't get out. Besides, she enjoys being outside. Give her a minute, and she'll find a hole to dig or a cricket to chase."

On cue, Belle trotted off, her nose glued to the ground.

"Zoey wants a dog." Neil had no idea why he said that.

"They're a lot of responsibility. I haven't had one since I left home for college, and I'd forgotten how much work's involved."

"But you like the dog." He could tell from her voice.

"Yeah, I do. If I weren't so busy, I'd get one of my own."

"I try that same argument about being too busy on Zoey, but she doesn't understand."

"Kids are tough to fool."

"She also wants a horse."

"I did, too, at her age."

"But you had a place to keep one."

"True."

"She's going to start riding lessons next week. Here, in fact. Her school's offering an afternoon program."

"I know. This is something new for the ranch. We've had such good luck partnering with the Horizon Adult Day Care Center, the family decided to try a similar program with the elementary school."

"She's excited. I'm not sure how but she twisted my arm and convinced me to buy her a pair of pink cowboy boots." He leaned back in his seat. Being with Carolina was effortless. He'd felt that way about her since their double date.

Being with her, however, was also tempting, and Neil knew he should leave before his impulses won out and he did something stupid.

Except he didn't leave.

"Would you like to come in for a minute?" Carolina tilted her head at an engaging angle.

"Thanks, but I can't. I need to get home. Zoey's babysitter has to leave by ten." The excuse was a weak one, given it wasn't quite eight-thirty.

"Please. It's important."

"I don't—"

"This isn't easy for me."

It wasn't for him, either. The desire to touch her was powerful—link fingers, nuzzle cheeks, inhale the scent of her windblown hair. He didn't care what so long as there was intimate contact.

"We really should talk."

"One of my deputies will contact you."

"Not about the illegal mining."

"Okay."

No, not okay. Neil wasn't sure he wanted to pick up where

they'd left off at the mine site when he'd rejected her dinner invitation. Sitting with her in the dark, close enough that he could feel the seat shift every time she moved, he might not have the willpower to say no if she asked him out again. His imagination drifted to the porch swing, the two of them sitting with her long, bare legs draped across his lap.

Wait, wasn't that feet? When did she go from wearing jeans to shorts?

He fumbled for the keys.

"I went out on a limb, suggesting we meet for dinner," she began softly. "I think that entitles me to know the real reason you turned me down."

"I told you. It's my job."

"Is there a conflict of interest because I'm the victim and you're heading up the investigation?"

"There could be."

"The investigation won't last forever."

"No." With any luck, the culprits had left a piece or two of incriminating evidence behind in their haste to leave when Little José surprised them.

"And besides," Carolina continued smoothly, "we're both adults and more than capable of separating our work from our personal lives."

"Maybe *you* are." Even that small admission was more than Neil had intended.

"I'm flattered," she said, a smile in her voice.

He scrubbed his face, the bristles of his five-o'clock shadow scratching his palms. This was going from bad to worse, and the only way he could see to prevent disaster was to level with her. But that would require he let down his guard.

Neil hadn't done that with anyone since Lynne. Not even with Zoey, and she was the center of his universe.

"I guess that's my cue to go," Carolina said with a hint

of disappointment. Unbuckling her seat belt, she reached for the door handle.

His hand covered the small space separating them and gently took hold of her arm. He had no idea what he'd done until he felt the cool fabric of her coat sleeve beneath his fingers.

"What?" She turned. Her gaze darted to his hand before connecting with his.

Insane for sure, but his grip on her tightened.

"What?" she repeated more softly.

Neil had always been a man of action, not words. That the right thing to say should fail him now was no great surprise.

"Stay." He swallowed, took a breath. "Please." He had to explain. Make her understand.

She remained rigid. "Give me one good reason. You've already hurt me once. I can't handle a second time."

He nodded and let go of her arm.

But before she'd moved so much as an inch, he raised his hand to her cheek and cradled it tenderly.

"How about this for a reason?" he said, and drew her toward him.

CAROLINA RESISTED NEIL'S advances, and he let her. After all, she was right. He'd hurt her.

Besides, he was still buckled in and unable to maneuver more than a few inches. If they were going to finish what he'd started, it was entirely up to her.

"You're infuriating," she told him.

No argument there.

"And you don't play fair."

"Guilty as charged." To prove her point, he traced the outline of her ear with his index finger.

She gave the tiniest, softest of moans.

It was probably just as well the seat belt restrained him. No telling what he'd do otherwise.

"Sometimes you can be a real jerk."

Ouch! That was harsh. His finger stilled. He'd obviously underestimated her anger and should let her go. But not before he apologized.

"Carolina—"

She leaned across the seat divider, cradled his face in her hands and brought his mouth to within inches of hers. "But mostly, you're incredibly sexy, and I'd never forgive myself if I didn't take advantage of the moment."

For several long seconds, nothing happened. Neil remained perfectly motionless, suspended midway between heaven and hell, afraid she'd start kissing him, afraid she wouldn't and that he'd miss out on what was promising to be one of the best experiences of his life.

Finally, thank God, she ended his torture—or was that began it?—by sliding closer and melting into him.

Neil's arms went around her, settling into place as if they belonged there. What started out as a hesitant exploration quickly built into an explosion of supernova proportions they were both at a loss to contain. She tasted exquisite, felt incredible and wreaked the kind of havoc on his senses that could send him hurtling toward the edge in a matter of minutes.

He knew he should put a stop to her while enough of his brain function remained for him to think straight.

In the next instant, she angled her head, slipped her hand inside his jacket and laid her palm over his pounding heart.

After that, thinking ceased altogether. There was only Carolina. How could he have gone so long without this? Her mouth tantalized his, her scent enveloped him, her heat invaded every inch of him. He must have been crazy.

No, he *was* crazy.

Leading her on was wrong. Unfair. Unkind. He had to… had to…

He clasped her by the shoulders to gently ease her from him. She must have misread his intentions for she deepened their kiss, taking him to a place he hadn't been for years.

Four years, to be exact.

Neil had dated and kissed women since coming to Payson. Pecks, mostly. On the cheek or sometimes the lips. But not like this mind-blowing, can't-get-enough-of-her kiss that pushed his resolve to its very limits.

She saved him from a total loss of control by pulling back. "Well, so much for my sister's theory," she said, and slid back into her seat.

"What theory?" His heart continued to hammer, and perspiration lined his brow. He wiped the dampness away with the back of his hand and might have unsnapped the buttons of his jacket except for fear he'd be sending her the wrong signal.

"She had the nerve to suggest I only ask out guys I'm not interested in." Obviously made of stronger stuff than him, she showed no evidence of waging an emotional war with herself.

"You were trying to prove them right?"

"Yes," she purred.

"Okay." The dig gave him a much needed reality check. It also served to remind him just how vulnerable he was where she was concerned. "I guess after all the things I said to you earlier, I deserved that."

"You goon." She laughed and rolled toward him, wrapping a shapely leg around his. "Don't you get it?" Clutching the front of his jacket, she lifted her face to his for a quick kiss that was nonetheless reeling. "I'm interested in you, Sheriff Lovitt, and have been from the moment we met."

All his silent reasoning in the past five minutes hadn't sobered him as much as what she'd just said.

The dog, bored with being left to her own devices, appeared at the gate and resumed whining.

Carolina groaned. "She's worse than having a mother who flashes the porch light. I really should go and feed her before she dumps over the garbage can. I didn't know anything so little could get into so much trouble." She sifted her fingers through the hair at Neil's temples. "Come inside with me. Never mind," she said, before he could answer. "I forgot Zoey's babysitter has to leave."

He'd disappointed her again. And once started, he couldn't stop himself from doing it over and over.

"It wouldn't make any difference."

She stilled. "Because?"

"I can't go inside with you. Can't go to dinner with you. Can't be alone with you."

"I see." She visibly stiffened.

"Before you storm off," he said, "please listen to me." He exhaled slowly. "I care about you."

"Really?" The tilt of her head implied he had a strange way of showing it.

"I do. Much more than I should." Here was the part where he could use a coach to help him choose what to say. "Lynne's dead because of me."

"It was an accident."

"Call it whatever you like, my lack of judgment triggered a chain of events that ended with her dying. Afterward, I promised myself I wouldn't put the people close to me in danger. It's the reason I sent Zoey to live with her grandparents. It's the reason I took a job in a small town when I couldn't stand being separated from her."

"How is shutting yourself off from a relationship with me going to protect me?"

He blinked away an image of Lynne in a pool of blood. "If we're not together, you're less likely to wind up in the path of a killer's bullet."

"There are no killers lurking in the shadows, Neil," she said, her voice gentler.

"There could be."

"This is Gila County. Hardly anything bad ever happens here. You said so yourself."

"Ten years ago Sheriff Herberger's house was torched by the brother of a man he'd arrested."

"That's one incident. And if I remember correctly, no one was home at the time."

"One incident is all it takes."

"You're willing to risk Zoey's life."

"Yes, and I live in constant fear for her safety. It's gotten worse since I was appointed acting sheriff. I'm suddenly more visible. More people know who I am. Who my daughter is." He laid his head against the seat back and closed his eyes. "Zoey's my only child, and I'm her only parent. I tried giving her up. My life wasn't just incomplete without her, it was unbearable."

"But you can give me up." Disappointment more than anger tinged her voice.

"Today I can." He turned to look at her. In the semidarkness, her features were soft and sweet and achingly lovely. "What scares me is that if we keep seeing each other, keep doing what we just did, I won't be able to give you up. Ever."

"It's hard to tell, but did I hear a compliment in there somewhere?"

"You did."

She studied him, her gaze critical. "Are you sure you're not overreacting just a little?"

"Not everyone in Payson supported the county commissioner's decision to appoint me acting sheriff."

Her eyes widened. "Has something happened?"

"I received a minor threat the day of the interview, and someone's been calling my home and private cell phone and hanging up. The same type of thing happened after Lynne died."

"Pranks?"

"Not all of them." A chill coursed through him. "Twice I was accosted outside my home. The perpetrators got away."

"What about Zoey?"

"Fortunately, she was at her grandparents' then. I'll do whatever's necessary to safeguard her until Sheriff Herberger's well and I can go back to being just a deputy."

Or back to hiding in a hole, as Neil referred to it during those rare moments when he was honest with himself.

"What about us? Can we…keep doing what we just did when Otis is well?"

He didn't respond immediately.

Her laugh this time was bitter. "Boy, I just keep setting myself up, don't I?"

"I can protect Zoey better than I can you. She's five and has to do what I tell her to."

"And I don't," Carolina stated.

"You *won't.* You're very much your own person. I like and admire that about you, but it makes protecting you damn near impossible."

A range of emotions flickered across her face. Neil began to think he was finally getting through to her.

"I don't believe you, Sheriff Lovitt, and I'm getting tired of your excuses."

Wrong again.

"Carolina."

She wrenched the handle beside her, flung open the door and stepped outside. "Sounds to me like you're trying to protect yourself. Not Zoey and certainly not me."

"Even if you're right, which you're not, it won't change anything. I have a duty and a responsibility."

She sniffed. "I need a man who isn't afraid to get involved."

"I understand."

"I think you'll regret this one day." She slammed the door shut and walked away.

He didn't have to wait that long. He was already regretting it.

Chapter Six

"Don't think just because your family's guest ranch is one of our sponsors you can pick and choose your assignments."

"That's not it, Ward." Carolina sat with her hands on the table in front of her, trying not to twist the tennis bracelet on her left wrist. She'd returned the diamond engagement ring Lonnie had given her but kept the bracelet he'd surprised her with their first Christmas together.

Not all her experiences with her ex-fiancé were bad. Just the final ones.

After the other day, when she'd informed Ward she'd rather not do the story on Neil, her boss had blown up, but promptly cooled down. Then today, he'd called her into the small conference room, demanding she accept the assignment on Neil. His annoyance came across like an afterthought, as if he were following a protocol he didn't fully support.

But even with the lack of intensity, his reproof still caused her extreme discomfort. For an awkward moment, she was that little girl who'd dumped the entire container of fish food into the aquarium. Apparently she hadn't matured much since then.

"I'm sorry to disappoint you, Ward, but I can't help feeling a negatively slanted exposé on Neil would hurt him and his daughter unnecessarily. Not to mention adversely affect the people of this county and their safety."

"How so?"

"Targeting Neil, creating problems for him, could distract him and compromise his ability to perform his job."

He crooked an eyebrow at her. "That's a stretch."

"Not a big one. We don't know how he'll react. Cops have that adrenaline thing going."

Talk about a stretch. Neil was the epitome of cool. Except when he'd kissed her. He'd been hot enough to blister the Jeep's leather seats.

"Are you willing to risk your job for him?"

Ward's question gave her a start. Vi had asked Carolina the same thing, and she'd believed then her boss wouldn't threaten her with unemployment.

Wrong again.

"Yes," she said, gulping.

Reporters had ethics, right? Like Woodward and Bernstein. They'd gone to jail to protect their source.

Comparing herself to journalistic legends didn't take the sting out of potentially losing her job.

"I'm not going to fire you, Carolina," Ward said evenly.

Whew! That was a relief. She tried not to go limp or burst into tears.

"But there will be repercussions."

"I understand." She'd prepared herself for a formal written warning.

"You can forget about any more roving assignments for the foreseeable future."

While not entirely out of the blue, the announcement still hit her hard. Step two of her life-redirecting plan was to advance her career. This was a huge setback.

"And you'll be put on probation for ninety days."

Correction, a brick wall.

"Isn't that a little extreme?" she choked out.

"Not for insubordination. Read your employee manual."

She didn't reply. How could she with a giant, painful lump lodged in her throat?

What would Neil say if he knew all she was going through for him? Would he change his mind about dating her?

Doubtful.

If she didn't like him so much and sympathize with his position, she'd resent him.

"I'm sorry, Carolina," Ward said.

"Me, too." She nodded.

"If it were up to me alone, I'd let you off with just a verbal warning."

Because he did sound genuinely sorry, she risked her fragile state and looked at him. His face showed a strain she hadn't previously noticed.

"Are you okay?" she found herself asking.

"Fine. Why?"

"You just seem…a little distracted."

He busied himself with her personnel file, which lay open in front of him.

"You're not usually so nice," she blurted.

"Nice?" He glowered at her. "I just put you on probation for ninety days."

That was more like it.

"Is there anything else?" she asked.

"No." He didn't glance up.

She started to rise from the conference table. Being confident she'd done the right thing was some solace but not enough. She really had her heart set on being a roving announcer. It was hard seeing her dream put on indefinite hold.

Unless…

Inspiration was a beautiful thing.

She sat back down.

Ward lifted his head and appraised her curiously. "Forget something?"

"Did you hear about the illegal mining operation they found on the ranch this weekend?"

"No." His expression quickly went from surprise to interest.

"It was in yesterday's paper."

"Erica and I were in Tempe over the weekend, visiting Len. We didn't get back until late last night."

Their eighteen-year-old was a promising freshman quarterback, attending Arizona State University on a full athletic scholarship. Ward couldn't be prouder. Neither could his wife, who tooted her stepson's horn as loudly as his father did.

"What happened?" He pushed Carolina's personnel file aside.

"One of our hands was riding the trail and found a mine shaft. Turns out, someone's been excavating for gold on our property."

"No fooling!" Ward listened attentively as Carolina filled him in on the details. "What are you going to do?"

"Nothing at the moment. We're stalled until the authorities complete their investigation. That could take weeks or even months."

"Do they have any idea who's behind it?"

"Not so far."

"I'm amazed. Really. There hasn't been any significant gold discovered in this area for decades. It's quite a story."

"That's kind of my point." She readied herself for the pitch she was about to make. "You said yourself you wanted to raise the quality of our newscasts. Well, here's our chance."

"Explain." His pen beat a rhythmic tap on the tabletop.

"This story has far-reaching ramifications. It's not just a matter of a crime being committed. Apparently, there's gold in our hills. It could impact the entire town, if not the county."

His eyes flickered.

Bingo, she thought with a smile. "Gold fever. Imagine the scores of new listeners we can win over by covering this story. We could run daily updates. Include local lore and stories from the mine strike twenty years ago." She reminded herself to check with the museum about the map.

"What strike was that?"

"Up by Quail Butte. Southeast of town." She frequently forgot Ward wasn't a native of Payson. "I'll copy the old newspaper clippings for you."

"If I agree to let you cover the story, will your family give the station exclusive rights?"

"No one will be allowed on the ranch unless they work for KPKD."

"And no interviews except to us?"

"Absolutely."

"What do you want in exchange?"

"We can negotiate."

"Free advertising for the ranch?"

"That's a start."

He stared at her. "You want to be in charge of the story."

"Yes."

"I did just tell you to forget about any future roving assignment."

"There is that."

"I can put someone else on the story."

"Then I can't guarantee KPKD exclusive rights. Besides, I'm the best candidate."

"Are you?" He sat back, evaluating her.

"It makes perfect sense." Riding the momentum she'd already started, Carolina ticked off the reasons on her fingertips. "The illegal mining is on my family's ranch. I grew up in Payson and am familiar with the town's history. I have previous journalism experience and a connection with the local law enforcement."

"Sheriff Lovitt," Ward said.

"Actually," she said, swallowing to clear her voice, "I was referring to Sheriff Herberger. He and my uncle are old friends."

After the fiasco with Neil Saturday night, any "connection" she'd had with him was severed. Every time she recalled asking him out, she cringed with embarrassment. When she thought of their kiss, her cheeks flamed. And remembering his final rejection made her want to kick the closest piece of furniture or break down and cry.

So far, the love-life portion of her redirecting plan was one big fat disaster. She'd move past Neil and focus her attention elsewhere, except no one else remotely interested her.

Not to the degree he did and not after the other night.

Neil had amazing kissing skills. Angels-singing, earth-moving, heart-going-pitter-patter kind of kissing skills.

Stop thinking about him, Carolina silently scolded herself.

Hadn't he been crystal clear about not wanting to get involved with her? She might consider his so-called promise to himself stupid, but he was committed to it, and she wasn't desperate enough to grovel.

"Sheriff Lovitt would be a better connection," Ward said, "and he likes you."

Yeah, for all the good it had done her.

"Sheriff Lovitt is very much by the book," she said, "and he's already refused to cooperate. I doubt I can get much information from him."

"Use your feminine wiles."

"He's immune."

"You know?"

"I've tested the waters. He's not biting."

"It's Sheriff Lovitt or no deal," Ward said decisively.

"What?" Carolina sat up as if poked with a sharp stick.

"You can be in charge of the story but only on the condition that you cultivate your connection with Sheriff Lovitt."

"Why? Sheriff Herberger is—"

"He's on medical leave. Not actively involved in the investigation."

Oh, dear. This wasn't what she'd planned.

"You want the assignment or not?"

"Yes. I do."

"Excellent." Ward smiled as he stood. "I'll tell the station's legal counsel to draw up the contract."

"My family will have to review it first," Carolina mumbled. She was still in a bit of a daze. "I don't have the authority to sign without their consent."

"Fine. In the meantime, you can move your stuff into Frank's old cubicle."

"Really?"

Her own cubicle. One she didn't have to share with the evening traffic director. Her spirits immediately rose, only to plummet as she remembered the tradeoff—working closely with Neil.

Not a problem. She could, she assured herself, be a professional.

And just who did she think she was kidding?

"WHAT ARE YOU doing here? I thought you had a meeting with your boss this afternoon."

Jake's surprise was legitimate. Carolina seldom visited the ranch's riding stables. Hailey, Jake's sister, had been the serious rider in the family, a position his oldest daughter, Briana, now held. Most afternoons, the teenager was either practicing her barrel racing, working with her high school equestrian drill team or giving riding lessons to the special-needs individuals from the Horizon Adult Day Care Center.

"I got off a little early," Carolina said.

"Really? Why?"

"That's sort of what I wanted to talk to you about."

She had caught Jake just as he was coming out of the barn office. He was probably consulting with Gary Forester about ranch business. While the family met and voted on major issues, day-to-day operations were Jake's responsibility.

"I had an interesting meeting with my boss this morning. Told him in no uncertain terms that I wasn't comfortable doing the story on Neil." They both began walking toward Jake's truck, which was parked in front of the main corral.

"How did that go?"

"Not as bad as I anticipated."

"Excellent!"

They reached the truck and, by unspoken agreement, leaned their backs against the sidewall to carry on their conversation.

"Yeah, I guess."

"You don't sound too happy."

"I thought Ward would be tougher on me." She flipped up the collar of her coat to ward off the breeze. In a matter of days, their Indian summer had ended and the weather had turned chilly.

"And you're disappointed?"

"No, confused. He's been acting a little weird lately—not like himself. He gets mad over the most minor incidents then turns around the next day and blows off something that would normally send him through the roof."

"Count yourself lucky you got off as easily as you did."

"There's a little more to the story."

"And a little more to your visit here, I'm betting."

Carolina grinned sheepishly.

Of all his Sweetwater cousins, she was closest to Jake. Maybe because she was most like his late sister Hailey. Not in looks or horsemanship but in personality. Hailey had also liked to defy convention. Carolina hoped the soft spot Jake held for her would sway him into going along with her plan.

"What do you need?" he asked.

"Why do you automatically assume I need something?"

"Carolina." His tone was reproachful.

He definitely knew her too well.

"All right, here's the thing. I've tentatively agreed for the family to give KPKD exclusive rights to the illegal mining story in exchange for me being put in charge of it."

"I see."

As she explained the details of the tentative deal she'd struck with Ward, Carolina observed Briana from the corner of her eye. The teenager led a group of about a dozen very young children from the barn into a small corral. At first, Carolina assumed the children were offspring of guests at the ranch. As they came closer, she saw they all wore identical lime-green ball caps and name tags on the front of their jackets. Bells went off in Carolina's head. These children were participants in the after-school riding program.

Which meant one of those squirming and squealing munchkins was Neil's daughter.

"Do you think the family will have a problem with it?" she asked Jake after she'd told him everything.

"I'm not sure we should talk to anybody about the mining. Not until we know more, which could be a while."

"We wouldn't be providing details of the crime itself as much as the effects of the illegal mining from the victims' standpoint."

"Won't talking to the media hinder the investigation?"

"Or help it. Whoever's behind the mining is probably local or has local connections," she said, quoting the newspaper report. "The more people are made aware of what's going on, the more likely someone will report suspicious activity to the Silent Witness Hotline."

"Yes, but—"

"And people have a right to know what's happening in their community." Carolina liked the sound of that and would use the same argument on Neil when she attempted to enlist his aid.

"The free advertising with KPKD's sister stations across the southwest is good," Jake reluctantly concurred. "Will your boss let us choose when commercials for the ranch air? Three o'clock in the morning won't reach our targeted market."

"We'll simply make that a condition of our agreement."

Jake continued to weigh the pros and cons with her for several minutes. Carolina half listened, the noise and commotion in the corral diverting her attention to her niece and the class she was conducting. She tried to pick out which one of the eight girls was Zoey. From this distance, and with their identical ball caps, it was impossible.

"I think a family meeting is in order," Jake announced.

"I figured you'd say that. We have to decide right away. I told Ward I'd have an answer for him by Wednesday."

"That's cutting it close."

"The illegal mining is breaking news. We have to act quickly."

"I'll call you later. Let you know what time's convenient for everyone tomorrow."

She pushed off his truck and gave him a brief hug before heading to her car. After a week in the body shop, it looked as good as new. The fender bender might never have happened.

Instead of getting into her car and driving away, Carolina meandered over to the corral. Briana was using Big Ben, the very old, very gentle mule that belonged to the Horizon Adult Day Care center, to introduce the children to equine basics.

On closer inspection, it wasn't so difficult to pick out Zoey. At least, Carolina was fairly certain the girl with the bright pink cowboy boots and saucy ponytail poking through the hole in the back of her ball cap was Zoey.

A young woman who didn't look much older than Briana wore the same ball cap as the children, identifying her as part of the after-school program. If she was supposed to be in charge, Carolina had her doubts. The woman was clearly terrified of large animals, even one as gentle as Big Ben. She visibly trembled as she brought the students up in pairs to pet the mule. Luckily, Briana's experience extended beyond horses to children. She was a babysitter extraordinaire and a wrangler on trail rides.

Zoey was in absolute awe of Big Ben, and he seemed equally enamored of her, lowering his head and nuzzling the hand she extended.

"Very good," Briana said. "Did you all see how she kept her hand flat so Big Ben wouldn't nip her?"

Beaming at the praise, the little girl returned to the group.

Carolina continued to watch the children from her place at the corral fence, debating whether she should stay or go. If she remained much longer, she'd risk running into Neil when he came to pick up Zoey. Unless he sent his daughter's babysitter, in which case, Carolina would miss him. She wasn't certain which scenario she preferred.

If KPKD and her family came to an agreement, she'd be given the illegal mining story, and have no choice but to solicit Neil's cooperation. Given that they hadn't exactly parted under the best of circumstances the last time they were together, the prospect of seeing him again triggered a bout of nerves. Better to wait another day to conduct what could be a delicate conversation with him.

Having made up her mind, Carolina started to leave.

"Who wants to sit on Big Ben?" Briana asked.

"Me, me!" Small hands flew like crazy into the air.

Except for one.

"Teacher, teacher, I have to go to the baf-room."

"Can you wait?" the young woman asked. "We're almost done."

"I gotta go now." The little girl jumped up and down to emphasize her need.

"Me, too." This time it was Zoey.

"Sorry. You're going to have to wait. I can't leave the other kids alone. It's against the rules."

"But this is a 'mergency," the first little girl pleaded, her face contorted.

The young woman glanced around, visibly flustered. "I guess we can break for a little while so all of us can go."

A chorus of voices rose in protest.

"Hey, Aunt Carolina," Briana called out. "Have you got a minute?"

Carolina halted. "Uh…sure."

"Can you take these kids to the restroom?"

"I don't know," the teacher said uncertainly, tugging on the strings of her hoodie.

"Don't worry. She's my aunt and one of the owners."

Carolina changed direction and walked toward the gate. "Taking riding students to the restroom just happens to be on my list of duties."

"Okay," the young woman relented.

Good thing. She'd probably have a riot on her hands otherwise. The remaining students were arguing over which one would be the first to sit on Big Ben. Briana handled them with the kind of patience that kept her phone ringing off the hook with babysitting requests.

The two pint-size cowgirls met Carolina at the gate.

"Come on, follow me," she said, directing them to the barn where the public restrooms were located.

They beat the crowd by a few minutes. A group of guests were just returning from a trail ride. Their horses, all of them old pros, trotted into the open area in front of the barn, eager to be home. Carolina listened to the guests' excited banter as she held open the restroom door so the first girl could go in.

Which left her standing outside the door and alone with Neil's daughter.

She was sure the girl was Zoey. Besides the pink boots, she had Neil's serious expression and the same dimple in her chin.

"Hi, I'm Carolina. What's your name?"

"Zoey."

All doubts were put to rest.

"I hear you like horses."

The girl peered up at her, intrigued. "How do you know that?"

"I'm a friend of your father's."

"Oh." Zoey scratched the toe of her boot in the dirt.

"Do you like school?"

"It's okay."

Was Zoey normally shy or just around strangers?

"I work at the radio station. I interviewed your dad last week. Did you hear it? He mentioned you."

"No, I wanted to listen but Daddy said I had to go to school."

"That's too bad. If you want, and your dad says it's okay, I can get you a copy of the interview and you can listen to it at home."

"Really?" A smile blossomed on Zoey's face.

"Sure."

Without warning, a banging noise sounded from inside the restroom.

Carolina knocked on the door. "Are you all right in there?"

"Yes," came a muffled reply.

She waited, and when no other noise followed, shrugged off the incident. "I like your boots."

"Thanks." Zoey bent and brushed away some dirt from the top of one.

Their conversation was stilted and probably wouldn't be occurring at all if Carolina wasn't trying so hard. She considered herself good with little girls, thanks to having so many nieces. She wondered if Zoey's shyness was a result of being an only child, having no mother, or just her personality.

Come to think of it, her father wasn't much for casual chitchat, either.

When he chose to, however, he could make up for any lack of words with action.

The restroom door abruptly banged open, and the other little girl emerged. She started to race back to the corral.

"Hey, wait! Don't go."

"She never listens," Zoey said with very adultlike exasperation.

Carolina was torn between chasing after the little girl or remaining with Zoey. In the next instant, the dilemma was solved when the child reached the corral gate and the supervisor signaled Carolina.

"Okay, your turn," she told Zoey, who stepped into the restroom with all the enthusiasm of Dorothy entering the witch's castle.

After giving the interior a thorough once-over, she turned around and shut the door—only to come charging out three seconds later, squealing and hopping from foot to foot.

"There's a tarantula in there!"

"Are you sure?" Carolina was flabbergasted. The huge spiders were indigenous to the area but reclusive, normally choosing to avoid people. "Where?" She poked her head inside the restroom.

"In the corner. Behind the toilet." Zoey's voice quaked.

Carolina bent cautiously to have a look. Despite their size, scary appearance and bad reputation, tarantulas were relatively harmless. That didn't mean she was in the mood for a close encounter with one.

"I don't see it."

Zoey tiptoed up beside Carolina and pointed. "There. On that silver thingie."

The valve? Carolina squinted. A spider with a body no bigger than a pinhead clung to a small iridescent web.

"That's not a tarantula."

"You sure?" Zoey squeaked.

"Positive. Tarantulas are this big." Carolina demonstrated with her hands. "That spider's only this big." She pinched her thumb and index finger together.

"My daddy says I should be careful of spiders."

"And he's right. You don't always know which ones are dangerous. But this one isn't."

"I don't have to go to the bathroom anymore."

"You want me to get rid of the spider?"

"Don't kill it!"

"I won't, I promise. I'll just ask it to leave."

"You can do that?"

"Watch me." Carolina waved her hand in front of the spider. It immediately scurried off, disappearing into a crack in the wall. "See. All safe."

"What if it comes back?"

"It won't. Not till you're gone. I promise."

Zoey looked skeptical but need apparently won out. She went back into the restroom, leaving the door open a tiny crack. A few minutes later, she came out, still wary. By then, several people from the trail ride had joined them.

"Did the spider come back?" Carolina asked.

"No."

The bottom of Zoey's pant leg had become caught in her boot.

"Here." Pulling her aside so the others in line could get by, Carolina stooped and straightened it. "Can't have you looking like a greenhorn."

"What's that?"

"Someone who doesn't know anything about horses."

"But I don't know anything about horses."

Zoey was so earnest, Carolina had to laugh. "But you will soon." They started walking back to the corral.

"Daddy!"

Before Carolina had a chance to react, Zoey sped off. Neil stood by the corral fence. What Carolina saw next strummed her heartstrings like nothing else had in a long, long time.

Neil, wearing an expression of pure joy, scooped his daughter into his arms and hugged her as if it had been months rather than hours since they'd last seen each other.

Zoey was one lucky little girl to be the recipient of such obvious love.

"Hey, pumpkin pie. How are you?" He set her down and held her away from him so he could look at her.

"I'm going to ride a horse. Wanna watch me?"

"You bet."

She skipped off, then came to a sudden stop. "There was a big, scary spider in the bathroom. Carolina asked it to leave and it did." With that, she was gone.

Neil turned to Carolina. "Hi."

She knew it was his daughter that had put the besotted smile on his face but she basked in its radiance anyway, forgetting for a moment the awkwardness and injured feelings of their last parting.

"Hi yourself." She walked over to join him. They both

leaned their arms on the corral railing to watch Zoey with Big Ben.

"You asked a spider to leave?" Neil appeared skeptical.

"It's a long story and not nearly as exciting as Zoey made it sound."

"That's a strange-looking horse."

"He's a mule. The differences are lost on young children."

"I think they're lost on me, too."

"Half horse, half donkey."

"I'm not going to ask how that works. I don't think I want to know."

"I'm sure Zoey will tell you after Briana explains it."

"I can't wait."

Zoey finally got her turn to sit on Big Ben. Neil and Carolina both shouted encouragement and clapped when she was lifted off. Cars pulled into the open area, parents arriving to collect their children. Guests from the trail ride continued to mill around the stables, watching the hands unsaddle the horses and put them up for the night. The place had turned into a hive of activity.

"I should probably get going," Carolina said.

"I'm sorry about the other night."

Neil's comment was out of the blue. She waited a moment to gather her thoughts before responding.

"Apology accepted."

"To be clear, I'm not sorry about kissing you."

Neither was she.

"I wish I'd handled things better. Not hurt you." His hand involuntarily opened and closed around the railing. "I'd like us to be friends."

She let that trite platitude pass for the moment. "Good. Because I may need your help in the near future."

"With the investigation?"

"Sort of. My boss is putting me in charge of a new story. If we can work out the details."

"What story?"

"The illegal mining operation." She drew on her courage, which was in shorter supply than usual these days. "And you're my connection in the law enforcement agency."

Carolina was pretty certain she'd struck Neil dumb, but then he answered her, just not the way she expected.

"I accept."

Her jaw dropped. "You'll do it?"

"No. I accept your dinner invitation."

"I'm...confused."

"You're right. We need to talk. Is Thursday okay? I'll pick you up at your place. About six okay?"

He didn't wait for her reply, merely strode off to get Zoey.

Chapter Seven

At Neil's knock, the dog—he couldn't remember its name—started barking. Carolina promptly opened her front door, and her smile flickered for only the briefest of seconds.

"You brought Zoey!"

"I hope you don't mind."

"Of course not."

"You have a dog." Zoey squealed and knelt down on the porch floor to welcome into her lap what had to be one of the ugliest dogs he'd ever seen. "What's his name?"

"*Her* name is Belle. And I'm just babysitting. Until tomorrow. After that, she's going back home to my sister's house."

"She's so cute," Zoey cooed between dog kisses.

That was a matter of opinion. With a short, squat body, a severe underbite and round bat ears, the dog wouldn't win any beauty contests. Zoey, however, didn't appear to notice.

"I want a dog."

"Me, too," Carolina said.

"Daddy says we're too busy."

Belle flopped down and rolled onto her back. Zoey got the hint and began to scratch the dog's pudgy belly.

"Maybe you can come with me to the animal shelter and help me pick out my new dog."

"Really?" Zoey beamed.

"Are you serious?" Neil didn't beam.

"I'm sorry," Carolina said, meeting his gaze. "I should have cleared it with you first before asking her."

"No, I meant, are you serious about getting a dog?"

"Yeah. I'm tired of living alone."

Her quick laugh didn't cover the trace of loneliness he detected in her voice. For a moment, Neil was taken aback. Carolina had impressed him as being completely satisfied with her single life. Was he wrong?

"I heard the dog pound is overcrowded and having an adoption drive all month long," Carolina said.

"Can I go with her, Daddy? Please." Zoey stood and took Carolina's hand.

They presented a formidable front.

He studied the two of them for a moment, unable to speak. Zoey had formed relationships with women in her young life besides her grandmothers: preschool teachers, mothers of friends, the very nice lady next door. But she'd been relatively shy with them at first, requiring a long period of adjustment before she'd trusted them enough to initiate physical contact. She'd met Carolina briefly at the ranch and was already holding her hand.

On second thought, Carolina had had much the same effect on him. They hadn't been fifteen minutes into their double date when he wanted to trade places with the guy across the table from him.

"I shouldn't have mentioned getting a dog," she said apologetically.

Neil reached out and smoothed Zoey's flyaway hair. "Sure. You can go."

Zoey dropped to her knees again to hug Belle. "Did you hear that? You're getting a new brother or sister."

"That was sweet of you." Carolina smiled at Neil.

He promptly remembered what he planned to tell her tonight and wondered if she'd have the same opinion of him afterward. Probably not.

"Let me grab my jacket, and I'll be ready to go." She retreated, appearing a moment later with the same green trench coat she'd worn the night he'd been called out to investigate the illegal mining operation. The same night they'd kissed. He could still feel the coolness of the fabric beneath his fingers...and the soft heat of her lips on his mouth.

He tugged at his shirt collar. Bringing Zoey tonight wasn't an afterthought. He'd known he would need a buffer, that being alone with Carolina would test his willpower to its limits.

"Come on, sweetie," he said to Zoey when Carolina stepped outside onto the porch. "The dog has to stay here."

They literally had to pry Zoey and Belle apart. Neither wanted to be separated. Once the dog was safely behind the closed front door, Carolina grabbed hold of both Neil's and Zoey's arms.

"Hurry." She dragged them along with her. "We only have about thirty seconds before she escapes through the doggie door."

They made it in the nick of time. Belle barked goodbye at the gate.

"Where are we going?" Carolina asked when they were in the car and pulling away from her cabin.

Zoey pressed her face to the rear passenger-side window and waved at Belle. The dog stood with her front feet on the gate, a forlorn expression on her cute-ugly face.

Seems Zoey was as quick to make friends with the dog as she was with Carolina.

"Pickle's Pizza," Neil answered her question, naming a kid-oriented pizza parlor with arcade games and rides. He thought Carolina might cringe at the suggestion.

She didn't.

"I love that place!"

Figured.

Even on a Thursday night, the restaurant was packed with families and children. That was what Neil wanted. More buffers to help him remain focused and not let his thoughts drift to other things. Like how sexy Carolina looked in black jeans. Or the way the dangly gold earrings she wore kept drawing his eyes to her face and the lovely curve of her lower lip. He'd tasted that lip and traced the outline of it with his tongue—

Zoey let out an excited squeal. She'd spotted two of her friends from school at one of the games. Rather than ask Neil to go with her, it was Carolina she coerced into playing skee ball when he handed over a fistful of game tokens.

"Do you mind?" Carolina asked.

"Have at it." He sat by himself to order their pizza.

All around him, children ran, screamed, laughed, played, bickered, cried and made messes. Most of the adults sat at their tables, attempting to converse or enjoy their meal. A few of the heartier ones like Carolina joined the fray, monitoring the younger children or playing games.

He watched her and Zoey, the two of them enjoying themselves, and wondered again why his daughter had taken so quickly to Carolina. Even Carmen, whom Zoey adored, had required a "warming up" period that lasted several days.

Was it his fault? Had he sheltered Zoey so much he'd inadvertently instilled in her a wariness of new people? That wariness could protect her from harm, but too much, and she could become socially isolated.

Maybe her instincts were right on target, and she sensed that Carolina was someone she could trust, someone who wouldn't hurt her.

He could learn a thing or two from his daughter, he supposed. His trust in Carolina was still tentative, though growing with each passing day.

And now she wanted his help with her story on the illegal mining. No doubt he owed her a favor for keeping his past under wraps and for being so kind to Zoey. Refusing her request would be hard.

It was also necessary.

Neil had worked diligently and sacrificed much to get his and Zoey's lives where they were today. Quiet, safe, normal, secure. Not just physically but also mentally and emotionally. Carolina threatened to disrupt their perfectly ordered lives.

She could give him reason to care for her, had done it already if he were completely honest with himself. And the idea of loving again, of gambling with another person's life and possibly losing her, terrified him.

NEIL'S HEAD SHOT UP when Carolina appeared in his line of vision. Before he could issue an invitation, she sat down beside him at the picnic-style table. "I don't think I've ever seen you out of uniform."

"I'm off duty."

"New York Yankees fan, huh?" Her glance strayed to his T-shirt and lingered.

"Where's Zoey?" he promptly asked, needing his buffer.

"With a friend at the miniature basketball game."

"Did she wear you out?"

"Are you kidding?"

"Is that a yes?"

Carolina let her shoulders sag and blew out a breath. "A little."

"You lasted a lot longer than I would have."

"Practice. I come here often with my nieces." She gave him a thorough and considerably longer once-over. "I like it."

"The pizza place?"

She shook her head. "You look good in civilian drag."

So did she. Damn good.

"Not so tough," she added with a grin.

"Don't be fooled by the clothes."

"You forget, I've seen you with Zoey. You have a marshmallow for a heart."

"Only for her."

"No one else?" Carolina asked coyly.

Was she a mind reader, too? He wanted to say something witty back to her but his speech center had temporarily shut down.

She laughed and blithely moved on to a new subject, effectively reducing his confidence around women to that of a high school freshman.

"I'm beat. How do you keep up with Zoey all day?"

"I can't. That's why I hired Carmen."

"Smart man."

Casual bantering came easily to Carolina. It would be equally easy to respond to her. Neil needed to shore up his defenses—and fast—if he was to stay on track during the evening ahead.

"Did your family agree to give the radio station exclusive rights to the illegal mining story?" he asked.

She hesitated, then, in typical Carolina fashion, forged ahead. "Yes, they did."

"And did your boss award you the story?"

"Yes, he did."

Neil didn't realize until that moment how much he'd been hoping for a different answer.

"You aren't going to help me," she said flatly.

There went his plan for letting her down slowly. "No."

Before he could elaborate, the pizza arrived. Neither of them dug in. Neil scanned the crowd for Zoey. Finally finding her, he summoned her over to the table by holding up a paper plate with a slice of pizza on it. While he and Carolina waited for his daughter, she dished up two more slices, giving one to him.

For Zoey's sake, Neil wolfed down his pizza. She was already asking too many questions about his restlessness and diminished appetite. The last thing he wanted was for her to pick up on the tension between him and Carolina, who was making a much better show of eating than he was. He figured it was her way of demonstrating to him that his refusal to cooperate with her request didn't bother her.

"What kind of dog are you going to get?" Zoey asked Carolina around a large piece of crust that was almost more than she could handle.

"I haven't decided. Probably one that was a stray or abandoned and really needs a home."

Carolina and Zoey went on to discuss the merits and drawbacks of various breeds, big versus small, fluffy versus short-haired, purebred versus mixed, cute versus—well, they were all cute according to Zoey.

Neil began to reconsider his plan to wait to get a pet. If his daughter was occupied with a dog, she'd pay less attention to him and the stress that was affecting his mood. Then, when Otis returned to work, Neil's life could resume its quiet routine.

Except for Carolina.

"Can I go play now?" Zoey asked when she was done eating. Pizza sauce was smeared all over her face.

He picked up a napkin and started to wipe her chin.

"Daddy." She grabbed the napkin from him and scrubbed at the sauce. "I'm not a baby."

"Sorry. I forget sometimes."

She fled the table with only half the sauce removed but all of his heart.

"She's adorable," Carolina told him. "You're a very lucky father."

"I am." The time had come to be honest. "I had a reason for bringing her with us tonight."

"Oh?"

"I wanted you to see firsthand how important she is to me."

"I never doubted for one second she wasn't."

"I admit, I'm overprotective of her. It comes with the job and being a single parent." Neil pushed aside the aluminum tray with its three slices of uneaten pizza. "Also the circumstances of Lynne's death."

"You're going to have to let Zoey go eventually."

"Spoken like someone who doesn't have any children."

Carolina didn't appear offended by his blunt remark. "You're right. It's not my place to judge or criticize."

"And you're right, too. I will have to let her go one day. But not yet."

"I don't wish to be unkind, but are you sure that isn't your guilt talking?"

"It probably is." Admitting a potential flaw in his thinking changed nothing.

She placed the leftover pizza in a take-out box the server had left on the table for them. "I don't see what any of this has to do with refusing to cooperate with me on the story about the illegal mining. I thought you'd be happy I was given a new assignment."

"The illegal mining operation is no backyard recreation project. You can bet whoever's behind the digging is serious, has resources and is dangerous." The CSI team's preliminary investigation had confirmed Neil's initial findings. "They don't want to be exposed. They don't want to be caught. And there's no telling what action they'll take to prevent either of those things from happening. You could find yourself an unintentional target, caught in the middle or…hurt."

He imagined worse but refrained from saying it.

"People are entitled to know what's going on in their community," she proclaimed passionately.

He'd heard that line before and was immune. "I don't care about the people in this community."

She gave a soft, mirthless chuckle. "That's a strange attitude for the man charged with serving and protecting them."

"Not like I care about you."

That shut her up. For about ten seconds.

"How much?"

She had to ask.

"Too much."

"Then why won't you help me? This assignment is important to me. It's the career break I've been waiting for."

"Because your safety and well-being are more important to me than your job."

"You're overreacting," she insisted. "I'm not in danger."

"You are, just by virtue of being one of the ranch owners. Investigating the illegal mining will triple the risk. I can't, I *won't*, elevate your exposure by helping you with the story."

"I think you're letting Lynne's death affect your judgment."

"Hell, yes, I am."

"We're not dealing with a serial killer here."

He could almost feel the gun in his hand, hear the Delivery Man's shot as it ricocheted off the brick building outside the deli. "That doesn't make the individuals behind the digging any less ruthless."

"Now that the mine's been discovered, I'm sure they've left town. Why would they stick around?"

"Because they live here."

She sat up. "I know that's what the papers are saying, but do you really think so?"

"Yes. There are two aspects to every operation, brains and money. The money may not be local but the brains are. How else would they know where to dig?"

"Which is even more reason for me to do the story. We have criminals operating and residing among us."

Rather than dissuade her, his argument had fired her up.

"Wrong. If these people know the area, it stands to reason they know you and your family. You're not the only one who could be in jeopardy. What if something were to happen to Briana or one of your other nieces?"

His remark appeared to take at least some of the wind from her sails. "What if I promise to be careful?" she asked.

"It's not that simple."

"Fine." She wiped her hands on a paper napkin and tossed it aside. "I'll just find another connection in the department—or the Payson Police or the Arizona Geological Society."

"Don't be so stubborn."

"Don't be so controlling."

"I'm trying to protect you."

"Right. Because you care about me. Which, let's face it, is irrelevant because you refuse to get involved with me."

"If I did get involved with you, would you turn down the story?" He knew he'd messed up the instant the words left his mouth.

She drew herself up. "Thank you very much, but I don't need to negotiate for a man in my life."

"Sorry." How often was he going to apologize to her? "That came out wrong."

"I'm leaving now." She lifted a leg over the picnic table bench. "Don't worry, I can catch a ride back to the ranch."

"I'll drive you home." Neil also untangled himself from

the table, with much less grace than Carolina, and went on the hunt for Zoey. When he found her with some of the boys at the air hockey table, he called her name. She didn't look happy at having to leave her friends.

Swell. Now both his dinner companions were angry at him.

He helped Carolina on with her coat, then Zoey. Neither of them appreciated his efforts.

"Do we have to go?" Zoey complained.

"It's a school night."

"My fault, sweetie." Carolina took hold of Zoey's hand. "I have an early curfew. But I promise to make it up to you."

"How?"

Carolina scrunched her mouth to one side, deliberating. "We could go for ice cream after we finish dog shopping."

"Dog shopping?" Zoey giggled.

They walked ahead of Neil toward the exit, intentionally or unintentionally excluding him.

Frankly, he didn't know how he felt. Part of him was pleased to see his daughter bonding with Carolina. Zoey needed a strong female role model in her life. The other part of him resented the intrusion. He was used to having his daughter to himself. That she should so easily respond to someone other than him left him mildly jealous and, he was reluctant to admit, a tad insecure.

Reality hit him square in the heart.

Like it or not, whatever safeguards he took, his daughter was going to meet and develop meaningful relationships with people outside their small family, including some future young man. Neil could accept that, as long as Zoey loved him and included him in her life. And waited. Fifteen, twenty years ought to do it.

What about him? Was he willing to wait fifteen or twenty

years until Zoey was grown and out of the house to have a serious relationship?

Carolina was too vibrant and attractive, not to mention impatient, to hang on for that long on the off chance he'd wise up. Especially when he offered little in return.

Lately, he'd found himself wondering how Lynne would have felt about the prospect of another woman filling her shoes. They'd only discussed how she and Zoey would continue on if anything happened to Neil, a much more likely possibility considering their jobs. Knowing the depths of her love for him and Zoey, he guessed she'd want them to cherish her memory and their years together, but to find someone else who made them happy.

None of that, however, lessened the guilt he suffered over her death or the fear that history would repeat itself with someone else.

With Carolina.

An older couple and two youngsters who looked like grandchildren entered the restaurant at the same time Neil was exiting. He recalled the couple from a vandalism he'd responded to the previous month at their house.

"How are you?" He nodded pleasantly.

They gave him an odd look and a murmured, "Hello."

Neil thought it was a bit strange, but people's reaction to law enforcement officials was often reserved and uncomfortable, even when they had no reason to be nervous.

Carolina and Zoey were already outside, and he quickened his pace in order to catch up with them. Turned out there was no need. They were waiting for him by the newspaper box, chatting up a storm.

In the next instant, that changed. Carolina grabbed Zoey's arm and yanked her away, saying in a falsely bright voice something about finding the car.

Neil's instinct kicked in, and he closed the distance between them in a hurry. "What's wrong?"

Carolina's cheeks had lost all their color. *I'm sorry,* she mouthed, and her eyes darted to the newspaper dispenser.

A stack of the evening edition faced out.

Neil read the headline. A sensation akin to being kicked in the stomach almost brought him to his knees—Acting Sheriff Lovitt Investigated In Late Wife's Death.

Chapter Eight

"Neil!" Sheriff Herberger boomed, ushering Neil inside. "Good to see you."

"Hi, Otis. Hope I'm not bothering you. When I called earlier, your wife said you wouldn't mind the company."

"Are you kidding? A week at home and I'm already going nuts. Driving Patty nuts, too," he said, referring to his wife. "It's going to be a long leave of absence for both of us."

Neil removed his hat, hung it on a nearby coatrack and followed the sheriff into a cozy front room. Despite the older man's obvious good spirits, his step lacked its usual spring, evidence that the recent heart surgery had taken a toll on him.

"Can I get you a cup of coffee or cold drink?"

"Coffee's fine." Neil took a seat in the chair facing the window. The entranceway to the living room was on his left. Old cop habits died hard, he thought as he sank into the soft cushions. The chair's location allowed him to see the room from all angles as well as the street outside.

"Cream and sugar, right?" Otis asked.

"If you have it."

"I'll warn you, the coffee's decaf. Patty won't let me drink anything else."

"Decaf's fine."

Neil would have appreciated the extra kick to his system.

He'd spent half the night tossing and turning or pacing the floor, trying to get that damned newspaper headline out of his mind. The second he'd seen it, he'd been hurled back in time four years ago to a similar headline in another newspaper. That one had nearly destroyed what little had been left of his life.

"Sit tight, I'll be right back," Otis said, leaving Neil alone.

The decision to visit the sheriff had come to him about two in the morning during one of his numerous trips to the kitchen. It would probably be an exercise in futility, but he wasn't one to sit around doing nothing. He needed to find out who had leaked the story about Lynne to the newspaper and why. The sheriff might be able to help. If nothing else, he was someone Neil could confide in without having to hold back or watch what he said. That alone would be a relief.

While he waited for Otis, he removed his jacket and studied the room. It was packed with enough antiques, old photographs and personal memorabilia for three houses. This wasn't Neil's first visit to the Herberger home since moving to Payson. On those occasions, Otis had recounted the house's long and colorful history as one of the oldest residential dwellings in town.

The house had belonged to his wife Patty's family. Her great-grandfather, a renowned bootlegger and swindler, had settled in the area—some claimed escaped there—from Iowa during the 1910s when prohibition was in effect. The family's lawlessness had ended with him. Future generations went on to become some of the town's most upstanding citizens.

"Here you go." The sheriff returned, bearing two mugs of steaming coffee.

Neil stood, realizing he should have offered to carry the coffee himself. The older man's face was flushed from the mild exertion.

"I'm assuming this isn't a social call," he remarked once they were both seated. "What's on your mind?"

Neil cut to the chase. "Did you happen to see last evening's paper?"

"No. I usually try to read it after dinner but the doctor has me taking a short walk instead, and once I get home from that, I can't stay awake if my life depended on it."

"Here." Neil reached inside the jacket lying across his lap and removed a folded section of the paper. Leaning forward, he passed it to Otis.

Removing a pair of reading glasses from his shirt pocket, the older man snapped open the newspaper. "Well, I'll be damned," he said, then proceeded to read in earnest. When he was done, he handed the paper back to Neil, his features reflecting his disgust.

"You didn't know they were going to run this?"

"Hell, no!"

"Sorry if I offended you," Neil said. "You're well connected in town. I thought someone might have mentioned it to you."

"I've been existing in a cocoon since the surgery. I think folks are afraid of upsetting me and giving me another heart attack."

"I probably shouldn't have come by."

"No, no. I'm glad you did. I'm not an invalid." He shook his head. "But back to this," he said dismally. "Finding out about you isn't hard. Anyone with access to a computer and the Internet could pull up information."

"Do you have any idea who'd want to do that and why?"

"Have you made any enemies since coming here?"

"There are a few individuals who don't like me."

"It goes with the territory."

"Some of them are on the county payroll."

His bushy eyebrows shot up. "Just what in the Sam Hill is going on?"

"A couple of the deputies aren't happy about my appointment." Neil filled the sheriff in on the grumblings he'd heard and the string of dead phone calls.

"Do any of them dislike you enough to try and damage your reputation?" he asked when Neil was done.

"I'm not sure. You know them better than me. What do you think?"

"I can see one or two of them getting their noses out of joint. Hank especially. He's been with the department almost as long as me. But to go so far as to employ petty scare tactics and launch a smear campaign?" He jerked his thumb at the newspaper in Neil's hand. "I don't know. Strikes me as kind of underhanded, and Hank's more of the in-your-face type."

Neil agreed. "If you hear from him or any of the guys, let me know."

"Count on it."

"And if you have any advice on how to handle things, I'm willing to listen."

Their visit continued with Otis giving Neil the benefit of his vast experience. He, in turn, brought Otis up-to-date on what had been happening at the station and in the community. Besides the illegal mining at Bear Creek Ranch, there wasn't much. Their conversation centered mostly on the current status of the investigation. Neil could almost feel Otis's desire to get back to work, and he sympathized. Men like him didn't cotton well to inactivity.

"What about Carolina Sweetwater?" Neil asked.

"What about her?"

"You're friends with her family. Would she have leaked information about me to the newspaper?"

"I don't see why she would."

Neil wasn't about to explain the complexities of his relationship with Carolina to the sheriff. "Last week, her boss at the station ordered her to do a story on me."

"Why?"

"It was right after my appointment. He apparently considered me newsworthy."

The sheriff scratched behind his ear. "I don't recall hearing anything on the radio."

"Carolina refused to do the story."

"You don't say?"

"My question is," Neil said, "do you think she would have leaked the story to the newspaper?"

"I think a better question is, why would she do it now? What would she have to gain? If she wanted to expose your past, she'd have agreed to do it for KPKD."

Neil had come to the same conclusion last night when he'd been sitting in his dark kitchen, unable to sleep.

"Carolina may be a bit of a flirt," Otis said, "and date a lot of men, but don't let that fool you. She's as solid as they come. Honest as the day is long."

Neil didn't know her like the sheriff, but he tended to agree.

"Shame about her and that ex-fiancé of hers. The company he worked for shipped him to Mexico City for a two-year assignment. She wanted to go with him but her parents pressured her into staying. Mainly because the family trust doesn't allow for owners to live outside the U.S."

Though tempted, Neil refrained from asking any further questions. The sheriff might become curious as to the reason for Neil's interest, and he wasn't ready to explain.

Fortunately for him, the sheriff was in the mood to talk. "Rather than wait two years for her, the bum dumped her. Broke her heart."

Neil couldn't imagine any man in his right mind dumping Carolina.

Then again, hadn't he, in a roundabout way?

No, there was a difference between refusing to enter into a relationship and breaking one off. Especially an engagement.

"That's too bad." Neil purposefully kept his response neutral.

"It changed her, but then, I suppose those things do. Patty thinks that's why Carolina dates so much. She's trying to forget how much the SOB hurt her." The sheriff scoffed. "But after five years, you'd think she'd have gotten over him."

Neil knew firsthand some things were just too painful to ever get over.

"Another cup of coffee?"

"Wish I could. I have to hit the road."

Otis walked Neil to the door and clapped him on the shoulder. "Stop by anytime."

"Rest up."

"That's all I do." He rubbed his protruding belly. "And eat rabbit food. That damn doctor put me on a diet, too. There's no end to his torture."

Back in his cruiser, Neil turned on the radio and adjusted the volume to low. Since he was the last one to drive the vehicle, the radio was already set to KPKD. At the end of the commercial, Carolina's voice came on. She was giving her final traffic report for the morning.

Neil turned up the volume and listened. How any woman could sound sexy reading a list of current traffic conditions, he didn't know. But Carolina did. Was every man in listening range thinking the same thing as Neil? For a moment, he pictured a townful of men in their cars or at their desks, all of them fantasizing about kissing Carolina.

Neil didn't have to fantasize; he could simply remember. And it was killing him.

When she finished, Rowdy Rodgers bantered with her for a few seconds before promising to see her on Monday.

She and Neil had hardly spoken last night on the drive to her home from the pizza parlor. He'd been too shocked to talk. A hundred possibilities had swirled around in his head, and a hundred new worries and fears constricted his chest. All he'd known was that he needed to rush Zoey home and, if possible, get his hands on every copy of the newspaper before people read them.

He'd only succeeded on the first count.

Carolina had sensed he didn't want to talk about the headlines in front of Zoey and occupied his daughter by asking her about dogs and school and horseback riding and favorite flavors of ice cream.

Was it a clever ploy? Despite what Otis had said about her honesty, Neil needed to speak to her in person about the leak.

At the next intersection, he went straight instead of turning right. The radio station and Carolina were one short mile down the road. When he arrived in the parking lot, he immediately spotted her blue PT Cruiser. She was still at work.

He sat in his vehicle for several minutes, debating whether to go inside or wait for her to come out. By the time the third person walked past, looking at him nervously, Neil made up his mind and went in.

"I'm here to see Carolina Sweetwater," he told the receptionist behind the large and cluttered front desk.

She almost broke three long, glittery fingernails in her haste to buzz Carolina.

"Is there somewhere we can talk?"

"My cubicle's this way."

"In private."

Carolina suppressed the small frisson of worry coursing through her. She had no idea what to make of Neil's unexpected appearance. Obviously, it had something to do with the article that had appeared in last night's paper and the follow-up one this morning. But since she hadn't tipped off the reporter, a fact she'd stressed as strongly as possible during their brief moment alone at her front door, there had to be another reason behind his visit.

His sole response to her claim of innocence had been a tight-lipped nod, which could be interpreted multiple ways. He didn't believe her, or he believed her but was angry at whoever had leaked the story. He believed her but didn't want to discuss the matter with Zoey nearby, which could account for his visit this morning. *He didn't believe her.*

It was hard not to come back to that.

"Management is using the conference room for a meeting," she said, conscious of Marcie the receptionist's avid interest. "The only other semiprivate rooms are the break room, which is like Grand Central Station, or the supply room."

The idea of being shut in a crowded, messy supply room with Neil struck Carolina as terribly sitcom cliché. It also thrilled her. She might be mad enough at him to spit nails, but that didn't change her attraction to him or her desire to repeat the searing kiss they'd shared.

Under different circumstances, of course. Not when he was standing across from her, glaring from beneath the brim of his cowboy hat.

She imagined him in the dress blues of the NYPD. The khaki uniform of the Gila County Sheriff's Office suited him just fine but so would the other. No denying it, those shoulders of his would do justice to any jacket.

"Is there someplace else we can talk?" he asked.

"Afraid not."

Adrian, the techie who'd invited Carolina on a date a few weeks ago, cruised by with the office manager. Both cast not-so-discreet glances at Neil. Clearly they'd read the newspaper article or heard about it.

Neil ignored them, though the muscle in his jaw twitched, showing Carolina he wasn't immune. "Are you off work yet?"

"Normally, I would be," she said. "But I'm working late on the illegal mining story."

That went over like a lead balloon.

"Can you leave?" His request came out like an order.

She resisted rolling her eyes and said to Marcie, "Let Ward know I'm going out for lunch."

"You got it!"

Carolina could just picture the station's phone system lighting up like a Christmas tree as the entire staff buzzed about her leaving with Neil.

They headed down the street rather than toward the parking lot.

"How about Ernesto's?" he asked, putting on his sunglasses.

"For what?"

"Lunch."

"That was just an excuse I gave Marcie."

"So, you're not hungry?"

"Are you?"

From behind the dark lenses, he gave her a look she could only guess at. "Let's walk. There's a little park on the corner."

"Fine."

Carolina was acutely aware of the attention they garnered from pedestrians and occupants in passing cars. Even those people who didn't recognize Neil were probably wondering why a woman was strolling along the street with a uniformed lawman.

The park brought back memories. It wasn't far from the

Rim County Museum, and Carolina's grandmother had often brought her and her sisters here on their visits to town.

"How's this?" Neil indicated a vacant bench beneath an oak tree, its leaves deep in the throes of changing color.

"Can we sit over there in the sun?" She tugged on the sleeves of her sweater. "I forgot my coat."

"Take mine." He removed his leather jacket and, before she could protest, draped it over her shoulders.

Warmth from his body instantly engulfed her.

He took her elbow and led her to the bench.

"Won't you be cold?" she asked, her voice ridiculously high-pitched.

"I'm from New York. Our summers are colder than this."

"Did you grow up in the city?"

"No. Schenectady."

Because the bench was small, they sat close together. Above them, birds flitted from branch to branch, occasionally swooping to the ground to peck for food.

If Carolina and Neil were dating or lovers, the setting would have been perfect. He'd probably slip an arm around her, and she'd rest her head in the crook of his neck. Their hands would reach across their laps, fingers entwining—

"I didn't move to New York until I enrolled in police academy."

The vision, which was sheer madness anyway, disappeared in a small poof.

"Is that where you met Lynne?"

"No. It was much later."

"Were you on a case together?"

"I didn't bring you here to discuss Lynne," he said more gently than she would have expected.

"I know. I'm stalling." She toyed with the hem of his jacket. "How bad is the backlash from the articles?"

"Bad." He didn't elaborate. "And it will only get worse."

"Maybe not."

"Trust me. I've done this before."

"I didn't leak the story to the newspaper. I swear it."

"I believe you."

"You do?" His revelation pleased her.

"You have no reason. If anything, you'd have done the story for the station."

"Well…" She flashed him a guilty grimace. "I could have done it out of revenge when you refused to cooperate with me."

"You're not that type."

This revelation also pleased her. Whatever differences they had, he trusted her. At least when it came to keeping her promises. "How's Zoey taking it? Or haven't you told her yet?"

"I haven't, and I'm not going to."

"Are you sure that's wise? What if she hears about it from one of the kids at school?"

"Kindergarten kids aren't interested in me." He tapped the toe of one boot rhythmically on the concrete sidewalk.

"They might be, if the daughter of the sheriff is in their class. Their parents certainly are."

"I'm *not* telling her."

Common sense told Carolina to drop the subject, but she ignored it.

"You said the other night that you cared about me. Well, I care about you, too. So, I want you to listen to me." She touched a hand to her heart. "Because what I say comes from here. Think seriously about telling Zoey."

"I have."

"Think harder. If you don't tell her and she finds out from someone else, she may feel betrayed and angry."

"She'll feel that way and a lot more if I tell her."

The misery in his voice tore at Carolina. "Maybe not. If

you tell her first, you'll have the chance to explain. Prepare her for when she does hear it. There are professional counselors who can advise you if you're not sure what to say."

"She won't understand."

"Don't underestimate her, Neil. She's a pretty incredible kid. She gets it from her dad."

He removed his sunglasses and stared straight ahead, seeing something Carolina couldn't. "I can't take the chance she'll hate me."

For the first time, she realized just how truly scared he was of losing his daughter's affection. Reaching for his hand was an unconscious act. He didn't withdraw when her fingers encountered his.

"Who do you love more than anybody else?" he asked, his voice low and empty of emotion.

"My family. My parents and sisters. And my cousin Jake. He's the older brother I never had."

"You said his sister died in a riding accident. What if you were the one responsible for that accident, and he had no idea. Would you want him to know?"

"He'd have the right."

"What if him knowing would destroy your relationship?"

It was on the tip of her tongue to insist Jake would understand and forgive her. Then she remembered what it had been like four years ago, when he'd wrongly blamed his former brother-in-law for Hailey's death. There had been no understanding and forgiveness in him then. Only later did he gain a new perspective.

"It might take a while, but he'd make peace with me eventually."

"What if he didn't? What if he couldn't stop blaming you for robbing him of the person he loved most?"

That had almost happened. Jake changed only when his

anger at his former brother-in-law hurt one of his oldest and dearest friends.

"I'd have to tell him," Carolina said. "I don't think I could live with the guilt."

"You'd tell him just to make your life easier?"

"Not at all! It's…it's…" Would she? "No, I'd be taking responsibility for my actions."

"Believe me. I take full responsibility for what happened to Lynne." Neil's features hardened. "And I can live with the guilt. For the rest of my life if I have to. So long as I don't lose Zoey."

Carolina could see there was no budging Neil, so she changed tactics. "I can do some digging if you want. Try and find out who leaked the story about you to the newspaper."

"Forget it."

"Don't you want to know?"

"Yes, but I don't want you involved."

First the illegal mining and now this. He really was carrying the overprotective act too far. "What harm is there in asking a few questions?"

"More than you know."

She suddenly got it. "You think the person who's calling your home and cell phones is the same person who sicced the newspaper on you."

"I doubt it's a coincidence."

He had a point. Maybe the situation was more serious than she'd realized. "Have you reported the phone calls to…?" Who did the sheriff call when he was the victim of a crime?

"I have." His tone implied he expected few results. "And there's nothing I can do about the articles unless something libelous is printed about me."

Regardless of what he said, she was going to contact her sources at the newspaper, two men she'd dated briefly on different occasions, and see what they had to say.

"I'd better get back to the station." She attempted to withdraw her hand from his.

He held fast. "I'm sorry."

"For what?"

"Everything. Mostly for taking advantage of you that night in front of your house and then telling you we couldn't be together."

"You didn't take advantage of me. I seem to recall it was the other way around."

"I made the first move." His thumb kneaded the inside of her palm. "You're hard to resist, Carolina Sweetwater."

"You appear to be managing well enough."

He turned his gaze directly on her. "I'm not."

Her heart fluttered.

The blue sky overhead, the birds in the tree, the soft breeze playing tag with her hair added to the moment. Kissing him would be a big mistake but she longed to do it anyway.

"Where do we go from here, Neil?" The question left her lips on a whisper.

"I'm not sure."

Her cell phone rang, disrupting the moment. She removed it from her trousers pocket. "Hello."

"Hi. Am I speaking to Carolina Sweetwater?"

"Yes."

"This is Kyle Dunstan, the assistant curator at the Rim County Museum," a cultured male voice said. "I have good news for you. We've located the map you were inquiring about."

"That's wonderful." She felt Neil's eyes on her. "From what you said, I didn't think you would."

"It's in my office if you want to take a look."

"Can I come now?" She glanced at the building across the street. "I'm in the area."

340 The Accidental Sheriff

He chuckled. "I'll page the front desk. Give them a heads-up."

"Thank you." She disconnected. "The museum found the map," she told Neil. "I'm heading over."

"So am I."

She couldn't stop him, and if she tried, he might get an injunction or whatever it was called against her. Better to let him accompany her and "cultivate their connection" as Ward had put it. If she stuck close to Neil, she might learn something useful for her story, the first installment of which was due tomorrow.

"Okay, Sheriff Lovitt." She jumped up from the bench. "Let's go."

While she phoned the station to let them know of her change in plans, he radioed the sheriff's department.

"Don't think this means we're working together," he said when they were both done.

"Of course not."

But as they entered the museum and met with the assistant curator, it felt like just that to Carolina.

Chapter Nine

"Counting the gold strike twenty years ago up on Quail Butte," Mr. Dunstan explained, "there have been a total of three significant mining operations in a three-mile radius." He drew an invisible circle on the map with his finger.

Carolina and Neil stood beside the assistant curator, one on each side. The overhead light illuminated even the smallest detail on the map. It also burned into the top of her head and the back of her neck. Another minute of the intense heat and she'd break out in a sweat. Holding Neil's heavy jacket didn't help. She shifted it to her other arm, afraid to lay anything down in the cluttered office in case she damaged an artifact.

"Here's the illegal mining operation." She tapped the map near the center of the area Mr. Dunstan had indicated.

"More like here." Neil's finger lighted a few inches from hers.

"Perhaps they've located the mother lode." Mr. Dunstan's brows lifted. "Wouldn't that be something?"

"Mother lode?" Carolina sputtered the question a scant second ahead of Neil.

"All three mines played out relatively quickly. According to the assayer's records, old newspaper stories and the journal of a particularly colorful young man from Iowa, there were rumors of a mother lode running through the ridge. No one's ever found it." Mr. Dunstan paused for effect. "Not yet."

Carolina immediately conjured up a dozen what-ifs. The most significant one: what if Jake's experts from the Arizona Geological Society reported they'd found gold?

In the meantime, she had a great kicking-off point for her story.

"Do you think whoever's behind the illegal mining operation knows about the mother lode?" Mr. Dunstan asked.

The firm set of Neil's mouth led her to believe he was already considering the possibility.

"Wow" was all Carolina could say.

"Would you like to read the journal?" Mr. Dunstan asked. "It's very interesting and gives an insightful account of life in our budding metropolis during the late 1800s."

"I'll have one of my investigators contact you and make arrangements to pick up the journal and the map," Neil said.

"I'd like to read the journal, too," Carolina said.

"It may be evidence." He glared at her over the assistant curator's head. "Along with the map."

"Not a problem." Mr. Dunstan appeared unaware of any friction between his guests. "I can't release the originals, of course. But I have copies of each. Excuse me a moment, and I'll instruct my secretary to get them for you." He left the room, his rubber-soled shoes falling softly on the hardwood floors.

Neil's boots thumped as he walked to the window then back again to stand beside her.

"I told you, I don't want you involved," he said in a harsh whisper.

"I already am."

"You don't have to do the story on the mining." He inched closer.

She used his jacket as a shield. "Yes, I do."

"No job is important enough to put your safety on the line."

"This isn't just about my job. Someone has stolen from my family and vandalized our property."

"*Attempted* to steal."

"The distinction is a tiny one."

"I understand wanting to help your family."

"I should think so. It's what dictates your entire life. Your every decision. Your relationship with every person you know."

He retreated a step and drew himself up.

"I'm sorry," she said softly. "That was uncalled-for."

"Have you considered what might happen if word spreads about a potential gold strike on your family's ranch?"

"A boom in reservations?" Her tone was more flippant than necessary, but then his had been annoyingly condescending.

"It's possible. But you might also get trespassers, either curiosity seekers or undesirables itching to help themselves to some of your gold. Unless the mine shaft is secured 24/7, trust me, there will be break-ins."

"He's right." Mr. Dunstan returned, carrying a pair of large manila envelopes and two maps rolled into tubes and fastened with rubber bands. "Especially if there is a mother lode. You'll notice there are quite a few instances in the journal of fights over claims. If you haven't already, you might want to check with your attorney."

"I will." Carolina hadn't thought of that.

"He or she can also verify who owns the mineral rights on your land. According to some of the old deeds we have here, the rights didn't always transfer."

Carolina's knees went a little weak.

She needed to call Jake right away. Their grandparents had purchased the ranch over fifty years ago. Who even

knew anymore what the original deed said and what rights
Grandpa Walter and Grandma Ida had kept or given up?

NEIL SAT AT his desk and studied the copy of the map the assistant curator had given him. If it held any secrets or clues,
they were hidden to him.

Mary Twohorses entered his office. The distraction wasn't
a welcome one.

"Here's the latest report of your phone records," she said.

He didn't ask if she'd read it already. She had. Nothing
much at the station slipped past her.

"Anything of value?"

"No. The numbers, there's two of them, are from pirated
cell phones."

Neil raised his eyebrows. The person behind the prank
calls was going to a lot of trouble to hide his identity.

"And the duration of the calls is too short for the phone
company to pinpoint the location."

"It wouldn't do any good anyway. You can bet the user is
busy now obtaining another pirated one."

The question was why? Since taking over as acting sheriff, Neil had done nothing that wasn't routine.

Mary sat down in the chair across from his desk, automatically swinging her long braid over her shoulder to lie in
her lap. From old pictures hanging in the break room, she'd
been wearing her hair in the same style since the day she
started with the department. The only difference was the
amount of gray interspersed in the braid.

"What's up?" Neil asked. Mary rarely sat down and only
if she had something important to say.

"I know you have to leave soon to pick up Zoey from day
care, but I thought you should see this first."

She laid the evening edition of the paper on the desk in
front of him, open to the editorial page. There were six let-

ters to the editor, all of them about Neil. He picked up the paper and sat back in his chair. His blood pressure rose with each letter he read.

Neil was the first to admit he had plenty of faults. Being a bad cop, however, wasn't one of them, and having the authors of the letters imply as much angered him to no end. Two of the letters even suggested Neil's appointment be reversed. Not that he'd wanted to be acting sheriff. But there was a huge difference between voluntarily stepping down and being forced to step down.

His gut screamed that there was more going on here. His head, however, cautioned him to proceed slowly. The media onslaught and prank calls were not unlike what he'd gone through during his Internal Affairs investigation after Lynne's death, and he might be overreacting.

Why hadn't this come out when he was first hired on as deputy sheriff?

Because whoever was behind the smear campaign hadn't considered him a threat until now.

He tossed the paper onto his desk.

As much as he hated involving Carolina, maybe he should take her up on her offer and have her check with her sources at the paper. It would also give him a reason to talk to her again. Not that he wanted to start anything, he just wanted to hear her voice. If anyone had asked him last month what part of a woman he found the sexiest, a dozen other attributes would have popped into his head. Since the day he'd responded to the fender bender involving Carolina's niece, a slightly husky, sultrily sexy voice had jumped to the top of the list.

Hearing her on the radio every morning no longer satisfied his craving.

"The last letter isn't so bad," Mary said.

Neil skimmed it. "The person doesn't defend me as much as sympathize with me for losing my wife."

"Sheriff Herberger's contacted the editor and requested they cease publishing letters about you. The paper has a history of supporting him and the department."

"I wish he hadn't. People are entitled to express their opinions." Even if they were ill informed and their opinions half-baked. "It's one of the rights we, as law enforcement officers, protect and defend."

"The editor offered to interview you and run the article on the front page."

"Forget it." No more interviews. The first one with KPKD had caused him enough trouble.

"You might think it through a little more before turning them down."

"It doesn't matter what I say. They'll slant the article the way they choose in order to sell papers." He'd been down this road before. The one interview he'd given after Lynne died had been a fiasco. The reporter took everything he'd said and either quoted it out of context or twisted it to make Neil sound like he'd cared more about the glory of bringing down a notorious serial killer than the lives of his wife and child.

"Your decision." Mary folded her hands neatly in her lap. "It's just that I've worked for this department a long time, under three different sheriffs, including you. In my experience, ignoring problems has never solved them."

"I'm the acting sheriff. This is a temporary job."

"It could be permanent. Otis will retire eventually."

Neil laughed. "I won't run for the position."

"Why not? You'd be good at it."

Because being sheriff would put him and Zoey in the spotlight and elevate the risk to their safety.

"What else?" he asked when Mary still didn't leave.

"Hank's in the break room."

"Okay." The deputy sheriff's shift was due to start soon.

"He's talking to the men about you."

"I take it he's not singing my praises."

"You might want to hear for yourself." Mary's message was clear enough.

Whether he wanted the job of acting sheriff or not, he had it. Neil didn't shirk his responsibilities, and he sure as hell wouldn't let any of his men get away with talking trash about him.

"See you in the morning."

"Have a nice evening." Taking the hint, she stood, a smile on her lips. Mary showing any emotion was a rare sight. He found his own smile lingering after she left.

The break room resembled an efficiency apartment, minus the bed. A kitchenette and dining set occupied one half of the room, a couch, recliner, bookcase and TV the other. Lockers lined the wide hall leading to the room, large enough for each man to stow his personal belongings.

The setup was a far cry from the station where Neil had served back in New York. But as a place to gripe and air disputes, there was no difference. Hank wasn't happy with Neil and anyone within earshot was hearing about it.

"I figured he was hiding something from the start. Now we know."

"Bull crap. You figured squat."

Neil waited by the lockers, listening to Hank bellyache and R.J. jump to his defense.

"Ask Willie if you don't believe me."

"You don't like Neil because he beat your scores."

It was true. Until Neil came to Payson, Hank had held the marksmanship record for the department.

"He got lucky is all," Hank argued.

"Three times? That ain't luck, pal."

"Yeah? Well, I didn't kill my wife."

Neil almost doubled over. Four years, countless accusations, and he still reacted as if slugged in the gut.

"Neither did he." R.J.'s voice took on an edge. "And I'd stop spouting my head off if I were you. Like it or not, he's our boss."

"Not for long," Hank grumbled.

"Is there a problem in here?" Neil stepped out around the lockers.

"Not at all, Sheriff. Me and R.J. was just shooting the breeze before shift starts."

Neil sent Hank a look that the other man would have to be dense not to understand. "Well, if you have anything important to discuss, why don't you do it with me later? Away from the station."

"I'll do that," Hank said evenly.

"I'm looking forward to it," Neil replied.

"Hey, did someone call a meeting or what?" Willie entered the break room. Like Neil, he was heading off duty.

"Waiting on you," Neil said. He briefed R.J. and Hank, letting Willie provide input, then left to pick up Zoey from day care.

As usual, the line of vehicles outside the school stretched to the end of the parking lot. The encounter with Hank had put Neil a few minutes behind schedule, and he had to wait longer than usual. Zoey, never patient to begin with, would be giving the monitor in charge a run for her money.

Instead, his daughter was sitting on the low cement wall surrounding the flagpole and got up only when he pulled alongside the curb. Her backpack dragging on the sidewalk, she trudged toward him, eyes glued to the ground in front of her.

A knot of concern formed in the pit of Neil's stomach. Something had happened. Another fight with her best friend?

An unsatisfactory mark on her progress report? Tomorrow's riding lesson canceled?

Her problems might pale in comparison to the ones Neil had dealt with all day at work, but to her, they were important and therefore to him, too. By the time she opened the cruiser door and crawled in, he was more than ready to listen.

"What's wrong, pumpkin pie? You seem sad."

"Nothing," she mumbled unconvincingly.

He pulled ahead to the exit and turned right. "You sure?" No reply.

In fact, she said nothing until they were a few blocks from home. He was just beginning to think she might be sick and that he should take her temperature as soon as they got inside when she said, "Some of the kids at school were talking today."

Neil's foot hit the brake and the cruiser came to a stop.

Zoey turned her small face to him and asked in a tiny voice, "Did you shoot my mommy?"

His heart stopped, then started again with a painful thud.

"No, sweetie, I didn't." When had the talk gone from him being responsible for Lynne's death to actually pulling the trigger? "I told you, your mommy died in an accident. A terrible accident."

He pulled to the side of the road before someone rear-ended them. Carolina had warned him of this happening. He should have listened to her.

Zoey's eyes had taken on a distant look, and Neil was suddenly terrified. Did she think he was lying? He reached over, unbuckled her seat belt and pulled her close to him.

"Don't listen to what those kids are saying. They're just being mean."

"Why, Daddy?" She buried her face in his jacket sleeve.

Neil stroked her hair, struggling to come up with a good explanation that his sweet little daughter could understand.

"You know Sheriff Herberger's sick and that Daddy's taking his place until he's well again, right?"

She nodded.

"Not everybody is happy about that."

"Why?"

"They don't think I should have gotten the job."

"Why?"

"Because we haven't lived here very long. Not like the other deputies. Some people don't want a stranger as acting sheriff. They think if they say bad things about me, I'll quit."

"We're not strangers."

"No, we're not. And I'm a good acting sheriff. They'll see that and stop saying lies about me." Or once Otis was back on the job, Neil would no longer be the focus of attention.

"Tell me again about my mommy."

Neil continued to stroke Zoey's hair. She'd been so young when her mother died. She didn't remember Lynne at all. Photographs and stories were his daughter's only connection. He made sure she had plenty of both.

Ignoring passing traffic, Neil recounted for at least the hundredth time how he and Lynne met and how happy they'd been when she was born. When he was done, her mood was greatly improved.

"Would you like to go to Dairy Queen for supper?" he offered on impulse. The leftover fried chicken he'd been planning on serving could wait until tomorrow.

"Yes!"

One of her school friends was at the restaurant. The girl must not have participated in the day's cruel taunting because Zoey was overjoyed to see her. While they played, Neil took out his cell phone and made a call.

"Hello," Carolina answered, a bit warily. "I didn't realize I gave you my number."

"You didn't. I have resources."

"Of course."

He thought he heard a trace of amusement in her voice and was glad. Now wasn't the time to offend her.

"What can I do for you?" she asked.

"I changed my mind."

"Again? That seems to be a trend with you and me."

He didn't comment. She was right, and he was already having trouble keeping his emotions in check.

"I'd like to take you up on your previous offer," he said.

"Which one?"

"To call the newspaper and see if you can find out who's behind the articles on me."

"I already did."

He should have guessed as much. Before he could ask her what she'd found, Zoey came running back to their booth. Her friend's family was leaving.

"I can't talk now," he told Carolina. "Is there any chance you can swing by my house before you head home?"

"Sure, but I won't be leaving for another thirty minutes."

"That's fine." He winked at Zoey and indicated for her to finish up her hot dog. "Let me give you my address."

"No need. I have it."

"You do?"

"I have resources, too, Sheriff Lovitt."

That shouldn't have surprised him.

"ANOTHER GREAT STORY, Carolina!"

"The phones haven't stopped ringing since yesterday!"

Carolina walked down the hall at the station, accepting accolades from her coworkers. Inside, she was tingling with happiness. Her twice-daily reports on the illegal mining operation couldn't be going any better and were generating high ratings.

"Nice job this afternoon, Carolina."

"Thanks, Ward."

"What's on tap for tomorrow?"

"I'm still playing with a particular angle." If everything went well, Neil would give her something new when she saw him shortly. His call had taken her aback, and she wondered what had prompted his change of heart. Perhaps the newspaper articles were getting to him after all.

She frowned, recalling the letters to the editor in yesterday's evening edition. The accusations made were cruel and untrue. She began mentally composing a letter in response.

"See you in the morning," Ward said.

"Bright and early."

She had barely reached the parking lot when Jake called. "What did Howard have to say?" she asked.

Her cousin had contacted the family attorney the moment Carolina advised him of the assistant curator's comments regarding previous claim disputes and mineral rights.

"He's still researching it," Jake answered. "The deed is old and the language unclear. He's contacted a colleague to review the deed. We're supposed to hear back by the first of the week."

"I was afraid of that."

How ironic would it be if the mother lode were on their property and they had no right to it?

"We've had some other news, too. Good and bad."

"Tell me." Carolina switched to her Bluetooth so she could talk on the phone and drive.

"The police called this afternoon. The CSI team is done. I've already contacted the Arizona Geological Society. Their crew will be out first thing tomorrow."

"That is good news." For the family—they'd finally get some answers about how much, if any, gold was in the mine—and for her report tomorrow.

"Unfortunately, the police have nothing further to say on who's behind the illegal mining."

"I'll try and get something out of Neil when I see him shortly."

"You're going out with him?"

"No. Stopping by his house."

"Carolina."

Why did everyone say her name that way, with an unspoken warning tagged on the end?

"It's not what you think. I have information regarding the articles the newspaper has been running on him."

"And you get information from him in return for your reports?"

"Exactly. Purely professional."

Jake's laugh deteriorated into a choking fit.

"Seriously."

"If you say so."

Carolina tried her best to work up a good mad at her cousin. It wasn't easy when she knew deep down he was at least half-right. "We're done discussing this."

"I've got a call on the other line. Hang on."

She drove toward Neil's, pretending the butterflies in her stomach had nothing to do with seeing him and everything to do with her mounting excitement over obtaining information on the illegal mining.

Jake came back on the line. "That was your boss's secretary. The station wants another interview with me tomorrow morning."

"So soon? You just gave them one yesterday."

"It appears they've already heard about the police releasing the crime scene to us."

"That was fast."

"Your boss must have a direct line to the police chief."

"I guess." She turned onto Neil's street. "Hey, I'm almost here. I'll call you later."

"Be careful," Jake said.

"Neil's the acting sheriff. I think I'm pretty safe with him."

"That's not what I was referring to."

"Oh?"

"Don't fall too hard for him, Carolina. He's a good guy but maybe not the one for you."

"I'm not falling for him at all."

Correction, she *was* falling for him, but holding herself in check. So far, anyway.

Clicking off from Jake, she pulled into Neil's driveway. The one-story ranch house had lush landscaping and a spacious front yard filled with a swing set, bicycle and discarded roller skates.

The sun, which had been dropping by degrees during her drive over, was about ready to slip beneath the horizon when she rang the front doorbell.

A moment later, Neil flung open the door.

"Hi, I'm—"

Without any warning, he hauled her into his arms.

Chapter Ten

Carolina wasn't sure what to expect from Neil. A wild, passionate kiss that went on and on? Throwing her over his shoulder and carting her off to the bedroom? Knocking her to the floor a microsecond before a thug lunged at them from behind the bushes?

What she got was a hug.

Not the kind of hug you give someone you haven't seen in ages, but the kind you desperately need when life throws you a curve.

"What's wrong?" she asked, her hands sliding up to circle his shoulders. The hug might not be romantic, but she could still enjoy the sensation of his body conforming ever so nicely with hers.

"Zoey asked me today if I shot her mother."

"Oh, Neil." Her heart ached for him.

"You were right. Some of the kids at school were taunting her."

Carolina pulled back and gazed into his dark brown eyes, brimming with hurt and confusion. "I so hate that I was."

He nodded. "Me, too."

"What did you do?"

"I told her there were people in town who weren't happy I'd been appointed acting sheriff and they were getting back at me by saying bad things about me."

"Did she believe you?"

"I think so. It's more or less true."

"I'm not sure."

He stepped away and stared down at her. "What did you find out?"

Three seconds apart and already she was longing for his touch again.

"Not a whole lot. My contacts were less than cooperative."

"Let's sit down." He motioned for her to follow him into the kitchen.

"Where's Zoey?" Carolina didn't think he'd want his daughter to hear their conversation.

"At her friend's house across the street. You want anything?"

"A glass of water if you have it."

He got one for each of them while she made herself comfortable at the cozy dining table.

Neil's house was reasonably tidy, the clutter typical of a rambunctious five-year-old and single dad. Although homey and decorative accents were missing, the house felt warm. Carolina's house, which had plenty of homey decor and no clutter suddenly seemed empty in comparison.

"Here you go." He set the glasses of ice water on the table.

"You gonna be all right?" she asked.

He almost smiled. "Why? Do I look that bad?"

"Actually, you do."

His uncharacteristically distracted appearance concerned her. Neil was a rock. The person everyone leaned on in a crisis. Then again, it was easier to be strong for others, and this crisis hit at the very heart of his family.

He made a disgruntled sound and ran his fingers through his hair. It didn't improve his appearance. A small tuft stood up in the center of his head. Carolina found it—and him—

endearing. There was something very appealing about a strong, capable man showing his vulnerability.

"Here. Let me." She got up and went to him. "You're making it worse." She smoothed the errant tuft and couldn't resist combing her fingers through the hair at his forehead and temples. "There. Much better."

His gaze locked with hers and intensified. "Thanks."

"You're welcome." Carolina started to move toward her chair but didn't get far. When had he taken hold of her wrist?

Without saying a word, Neil lifted her hand to his cheek and trapped her fingers against his warm skin. The innocent gesture sent a spiral of desire curling through her.

He must have sensed her response for his eyes went smoky.

Her heart raced in anticipation. What now?

In the next instant, Neil let her hand drop and closed his eyes.

Okay, nothing was going to happen. Probably wise, considering.

Carolina continued to stand there for an awkward moment then, with a forced laugh, returned to her chair. "I think you're fit to be seen in public now."

He scowled. So much for showing his vulnerable side. Was he irritated at her or himself?

Since the highly charged moment had obviously passed, Carolina got down to business. The sooner she told him what she'd learned, the sooner she could leave and nurse her injured pride.

"I wasn't able to find out exactly who tipped off the newspaper about your IA investigation after Lynne's death."

He gave a curt nod.

"There's more."

"What?"

"It might be nothing. I could be trying to connect two unrelated dots."

His scowl deepened. "Tell me."

"My contact hinted that the editor of the newspaper decided not to run anything on you after receiving the tip. That he'd researched you and decided the story wasn't relevant."

"What changed his mind?"

"My contact wouldn't say, only alluded to pressure being applied."

"What are the dots you're trying to connect?"

"My contact mentioned that my boss, Ward, and the editor have been talking a lot lately."

"Are they friends?"

"Acquaintances. They're both in the news business and belong to the same professional organizations. But I'd say they're more rivals than friends. Definitely not prone to talking."

Neil appeared to digest the information.

"I wouldn't give it a second thought," Carolina said, "except Ward's been acting strange lately."

"How so?"

"Just not himself. Cutting employees slack when he'd normally bite their heads off, then making a huge deal over nothing." She didn't mention her recent reprimand.

Neil tapped the knuckles of his closed fist on the tabletop. "I agree. I'm not sure there's a connection. But what you said does seem to confirm someone's attempting to target me."

"Do you know why?"

"No." He glanced at her again, his expression devoid of emotion. "And as far as I can tell, I haven't done anything to be a threat to anyone."

"Not yet. This could be a diversion tactic. Insurance against something you might do."

"Perhaps." He sat back in his chair. "I tend to think one of my deputies is carrying a grudge."

"That does make sense."

"I have a few leads I'm going to check out tomorrow."

"Anything I can help with?"

"Thanks. You've done enough already."

"If you change your mind, let me know."

The back door banged open and Zoey bounded into the kitchen. Her face lit up. "Hi, Carolina." She didn't act surprised to encounter an unexpected visitor.

"Hey, kiddo."

"Ms. Sweetwater," Neil corrected.

"Carolina's fine," she said, and winked at the little girl. "We already decided. Zoey can call me Carolina, and I can call her greenhorn."

Zoey giggled hysterically.

Neil rose from the table and pulled her to his side for a brief hug. "What are you doing home? You're not supposed to cross the street without calling me first."

"Casey's mom walked me."

"Okay." He bent and kissed the top of her head. "But next time, call."

"Yes, Daddy." She tried to send Carolina a return wink, only she had trouble keeping one eye open and the other shut.

Carolina was completely enamored.

Neil was blessed to have a daughter like Zoey. No wonder he went to such lengths to protect her. In his place, Carolina would do the same.

Though the idea of lingering appealed to her, she couldn't. "I'd better go."

"When are we going puppy shopping?" Zoey asked.

"Soon. Another week or two." When she was done with the series on the illegal mining. Even if the culprits weren't found, there was only so long she'd be able to ride the tide of excitement. After that, interest would wane. "I'll have some time off work then to spend with the dog."

"Don't forget we're going for ice cream."

"I won't. Oh, wait!" Carolina reached into her purse and pulled out a CD. "Speaking of promises. Here's a copy of your dad's interview." She gave the CD to Zoey. "Your dad said he didn't mind."

"Thank you!"

"Do you have a CD player?"

"Yes, yes," Zoey exclaimed. "Can I listen to it now, Daddy?"

"How about we both listen to it after dinner?"

Zoey stuck out her lower lip but made no further protest.

"Why don't you finish your homework while I walk Ms. Sweetwater to her car."

"Goodbye." Zoey threw her arms around Carolina with such force she almost lost her balance.

"Bye, kiddo." She fought back a wave of unexpected emotion. "I'll call you soon about the dog shopping."

Outside, Neil's expression was unreadable again. Did he not approve of his daughter's budding friendship with her?

"If I'm overstepping my bounds with Zoey, let me know."

"You're not. I'm glad you two are hitting it off."

Okay, apparently something else was bothering him.

"I know I'm probably talking to a brick wall," she said, "but try not to be too upset about the newspaper articles. There might be a mild furor now but it'll pass soon."

No answer to that. Carolina decided to give up.

"Thank you."

He speaks!

"For what?"

"Your help. Being so nice to Zoey. Not pestering me for information on the illegal mining operation."

"Now that you mention it…"

He glowered at her.

"Just one tiny tidbit."

He sighed, long and loud. "Fine. I guess I owe you that. The CSI team was able to lift a number of boot impressions from the site."

"Really!"

"They estimate three men are involved."

"You're not telling me everything." She could read as much in his face.

"That's all you get."

It was enough. "Does the newspaper have this information?"

"Nope. You'll scoop everyone."

"Yes!"

Ward would be delighted. Carolina couldn't help it and threw herself at Neil. He caught her, his arms automatically circling her.

"Whoa!"

"Thank you, Neil. Thank you, thank you."

They both went instantly still as the intimacy of their positions became apparent.

When Carolina would have retreated, Neil held on to her.

"I thought you said this kind of stuff was a mistake," she whispered.

"It is." He lowered his head to nuzzle her cheek and ear.

Shivers danced up her spine. "Then why?"

"Because I can't resist you."

No man had ever said anything so sexy, so disarming, so exciting.

She didn't wait for him to kiss her. Standing on her tiptoes, she raised her lips to his. The resulting explosion was immediate and enough to shake her to her very core. It wasn't, however, enough to jar her loose from his embrace.

She clung to his jacket, taking all of him in, letting him fill her senses and stir her arousal.

Wanting more—*much* more—she parted her lips. His tongue swept in and tangled with hers, sending more shivers dancing up her spine. He tasted cool and clean, like the ice water they'd been drinking. The rest of him was anything but cool. He teased and coaxed her with unspoken promises of just how good it could be between them if she gave him the chance to show her.

Their kiss went on and on, which was perfectly fine with Carolina. At some point, his hand slipped inside her coat to capture her waist, eliciting a soft sigh from her. Then his hand moved upward. Higher still. His thumb made a single sweep across the tip of her breast before his palm closed over her.

Wow!

The jolt had both of them springing apart. Not that Carolina objected. His driveway just wasn't the place. That was made more evident when they discovered the neighbor—Zoey's friend's mother?—watching them from across the street.

Fortunately, darkness had settled, so the woman's visibility was limited.

"Howdy, Sheriff Lovitt!" she called, her voice containing a mischievous lilt. "Nice evening."

He groaned.

"Look on the bright side." Carolina escaped his embrace and opened her car door. "At least people have something else to write about you in their letters to the editor."

"Not funny," he grumbled.

She shut the door after getting in and rolled down her window. "That depends."

He braced his hands on the open window and leaned down. "You're dangerous."

"I know."

"Not the way you think."

"I know that, too."

"Be careful."

"Nothing's going to happen to me."

"I don't want to lose you, too."

Carolina was touched.

For a moment, he looked as if he might say more. Instead, he shook his head, straightened and tapped the open window. "See you later."

"Count on it, Sheriff Lovitt." Her voice contained its own mischievous lilt.

CAROLINA EASED THROUGH the door of the control booth and shut it behind her. On the other side of the glass, the engineer gave her a thumbs-up. The gesture might have brought a smile to her face if she wasn't already grinning from ear to ear. Her report this morning had gone well, another rocking installment in her series. But that wasn't the only reason for her happiness.

It was Neil.

Three days has passed since their kiss in his driveway and still she couldn't stop thinking about it. She was getting to him, she could tell. At this rate, she'd break down his defenses in no time. Then what would happen? She could hardly wait to find out.

She passed Ward's cubicle on the way to hers. Her *own* cubicle, she reminded herself. A ridiculously small thing, but the space symbolized her recent success…and she loved it!

"Morning, Ward," she said, peering over the wall.

"Good segment."

"Thanks." Her impossibly huge smile grew.

Sitting at her desk, she automatically pressed a button on her phone. Immediately, KPKD's current broadcast played through the speaker. She kept one ear tuned to the broadcast while she booted up her computer. Reading viewer emails after her report was the highlight of her day.

As she worked, her Mail Received icon flashed every few minutes. Carolina skimmed the incoming letters. She'd read them more thoroughly later. She was on the seventh one when something on the newscast caught her off guard. Turning away from her computer screen, she listened more intently.

"What the…?" Her blood went cold, then hot. Leaping from her chair, she marched into Ward's cubicle. "You liar!"

His eyebrows came together in a frown.

Carolina was instantly aware she shouldn't take such a severe tone with her boss.

She changed her approach. "You promised."

"Promised what?" he said sternly.

"The story on Neil—Sheriff Lovitt," she amended, re-alizing her mistake. "Leonard's reading it now." Poor Neil. He'd be crushed. Disappointed. Angry. And he'd think she was responsible.

"I made no such promise."

"Yes, you did. I'm doing the series on the illegal min—"

He didn't let her finish. "I agreed to put you in charge of the illegal mining story, but I never agreed not to run the story on Sheriff Lovitt."

Pleading with Ward was pointless. Leonard had already read the story. The damage was done.

"There's nothing more to discuss." Ward added insult to injury by turning his back to her.

Carolina reined in her emotions. Letting loose, blurting out what she really thought would get her fired. While she might feel vindicated, the fact was she could get to the bottom of what was going on with Ward and be of more help to Neil if she stayed.

"Why?" she asked. "Can you at least tell me that?"

"It's relevant news and, as you well know, we're attempting to raise the level of our newscasts."

"Bullshit," she muttered under her breath.

His eyes narrowed. "I beg your pardon?"

So much for reining in her emotions.

"Nothing." She spun on her heels and returned to her cubicle. Ward had been unpredictable lately. Dealing with him was a wasted effort.

At her desk, she opened a drawer and grabbed a tissue from a box she kept there, allowing herself a few quiet tears. A popular country-and-western song played through the speaker on her phone. The lyrics barely registered with Carolina. All that mattered to her was that the horrible newscast had ended.

Would Ward repeat it during the afternoon segment? Please, God, no.

She considered phoning Neil. If he hadn't heard the newscast, surely someone else had alerted him. What could she tell him other than that she wasn't the one behind the story? No, better to wait and contact him when she had more information.

Lately, the station owners had been pressuring all the department heads to step up their efforts to expand their listening audience. Ward could be under the gun himself, which would explain why he'd changed his mind about doing the story on Neil.

What she really needed to do was start work on her report for tomorrow. The draft was due on Ward's desk by one today. But try as she might, she couldn't focus. Neil totally consumed her thoughts.

Wait a minute!

What if she made him and the good job his department

was doing with the illegal mining investigation the focus of her report?

Yes! It wasn't much, but any positive media exposure would help offset the bad.

She returned to her computer, intending to exit out of her email program. Instead, she opened the next message by mistake and automatically skimmed it.

The email contained a single line and wasn't signed. With each word she read, blood drained from her face.

Stop your reports on the illegal mining or you and your family will be sorry.

Her phone rang. The shrill buzzing caused her to jerk reflexively. Without thinking, she reached for the receiver. Heart hammering, her eyes still riveted to the computer screen, she placed the phone to her ear and muttered weakly, "Hello."

A crackling pause ensued, then a sharp click as her caller disconnected.

Chapter Eleven

Neil flew past the receptionist's desk at KPKD without stopping. "Where's Carolina Sweetwater?"

"Conference room. Second door on your right."

He couldn't remember thirty feet ever taking so long to cover. The doorknob stuck and he nearly yanked it off in his haste to open the door.

Carolina sat at the long table, a man Neil assumed to be her boss beside her. She looked small, shaken and pale. Relief washed over him only to collide head-on with anger. She didn't rattle easily. Whoever had done this to her, put that stricken expression on her face, would pay. He'd see to it.

"You're here." She pushed away from the table.

He was on duty, responding to an emergency, and someone else was in the room with them. Neil didn't care. He went to her and took her trembling body in his arms.

"Are you all right?"

"I'm fine."

He needed to know for certain and touched her cheek with one hand. Her skin was cool. Everything about her was cool. And vulnerable.

He vowed again to find the bastards responsible.

"I'm sorry to bother you," she said, leaning her face into his hand.

"I'm glad you called." He released her. Reluctantly. "Are the police still here?"

"They left about ten minutes ago," her boss answered.

Neil cursed the long drive. He'd been thirty miles outside of town at the deserted Remington place when Carolina had called, her voice breathless and sounding on the verge of tears. He'd instructed her to hang up immediately and dial 911. The homeless individuals reportedly holed up in the dilapidated barn could wait. Carolina had been threatened.

The past rushed up to meet the present. The situations weren't the same but his emotions were, especially the ones that left him angry and feeling helpless. He'd failed to protect Carolina, just like he'd failed Lynne.

"Did the officer give you his name?"

"*She* left this card," her boss said, and stood.

Neil accepted the card and read the officer's name and badge number. He'd crossed paths with the woman before and knew her to be competent and thorough. That much was good.

"Thank you." He handed the card back to Carolina's boss.

"Do you need a copy?" he asked.

"No."

The atmosphere in the room suddenly became awkward. "I'll get back to work." Carolina's boss patted her arm. "Take tomorrow off, why don't you."

"I'll be fine."

"Really. In fact, take the rest of the week off."

Neil sensed her stiffen.

"You're removing me from the illegal mining story?" Her voice hitched.

"Under the circumstances, I think it would be wise."

"No, Ward. Please."

"You were threatened, Carolina."

"It was an email. People in the media get hate emails all the time."

"We'll talk later, when you're not upset." He turned and left.

Neil couldn't say he liked her boss, especially after this morning's news bite on him. But the man was being smart. Carolina needed to be removed from the story for her own safety.

"I suppose you agree with him." She was doing her best to appear tough.

Neil didn't buy her act. "Come on. I'll drive you home."

"I can drive myself."

"Not while I'm here."

She stuck out her lower lip, reminding him of Zoey. He could see why they got along so well. Both were determined to test his patience on a daily basis.

"I'm driving you home. If you refuse, I'll cuff you and take you against your will."

"Why, Sheriff Lovitt," she said with exaggerated silkiness, "I had no clue you were so kinky."

"There's a lot you don't know about me."

That shut her up, and she went willingly with him.

While Carolina gathered her things from her cubicle, he waited in the reception area and called the Payson PD, leaving a message for the officer who'd been at the station. He ignored the receptionist, whose eyes bored into the back of his head. Let her, Carolina's boss and anyone else at the station think what they did about him. Neil had nothing to be ashamed of.

The thought stopped him in his tracks.

He'd been living with guilt and shame for four years. When had he stopped agreeing with the negative things people said about him?

The click of Carolina's heels on the tile floor alerted him

to her approach. It was obvious from the fake smile she wore that some of her bravado had left her. Taking her hand in his, he escorted her outside. He'd rather do a whole lot more. Hold her, shelter her, tuck her away in a safe corner and put her under constant guard. Anything to protect her from harm.

"I'm parked over here." At the cruiser, he opened the passenger-side door. She made a face.

"You haven't been in an official vehicle before?"

"Not in the front seat. Once or twice in the back." One corner of her mouth tipped up, and she was suddenly her old self again, if only for a moment.

It required every bit of his professional training not to grab her and bring his mouth crashing down on hers.

The ride to Bear Creek Ranch took about twenty minutes. They didn't say much during the drive. For his part, Neil was saving up until they reached her cabin, where she'd be trapped and have no avenue of escape except running. And he'd bet, in those shoes, he'd catch her in two seconds flat. When he did, he'd give her a big piece of his mind.

Pulling up in front of her gate, he helped her out of the cruiser.

"Would you like to come in for a minute," she asked with the tiniest trace of insecurity.

Just like that, all Neil's intentions went out the window.

"Yeah, sure." Just a warning, he decided, no lecture.

One step inside the cabin, she turned to face him. Two steps, she was in his arms again, all soft curves, sweet-smelling skin and needing comfort. Three steps, their jackets were off and his mouth was where he'd wanted it to be since he walked into the conference room. On hers. Taking, giving, demanding, relenting.

Good God, the relenting was insane. Without even trying, she caused him to lose control over and over again.

"I was so scared for you," he said between ragged breaths.

"I broke every traffic law getting to the station after you called."

"I'm glad you did." She arched into him, soft moans escaping her. "I wasn't sure you cared."

He abruptly stopped and pushed her away from him. "I more than care, Carolina. You matter to me. A lot." The vehemence of his admission took him aback.

It did Carolina, too, gauging by the flash in her eyes. He thought he might have gone too far, said too much. Scared her off.

She looped one arm around his neck. With her other hand, she lightly stroked the bristles of his five-o'clock shadow. "Don't talk like that, Sheriff Lovitt, unless you intend to back up your words with action."

Okay, he hadn't scared her off.

"You sure?" Talking wasn't easy, not with his chest pounding and pulse racing. "I won't stop once I get started." He cupped her bottom, lifted her flush against him so she would know exactly what she was getting into with him.

She shifted so that his erection fit more snugly into the junction of her legs. Yeah, she knew.

"For the record," she murmured, "you matter a lot to me, too."

This was insane. He should stop. Once they crossed the line, there was no going back.

Her fingertips dug into his muscles of his shoulders. "Did you bring protection?"

A jolt of sexual energy ripped through him. The hell with going back. There was only ahead.

"I'm an officer of the law." He lowered his mouth, pressed his lips to the shallow dip at the base of her neck and tasted her skin. "It's my sworn duty to protect."

"And you're good at your job." She smiled coyly.

"I haven't carried a condom in my wallet since Lynne and

I dated." He skimmed his hand up her back, kneading the pliant flesh his fingers encountered. "Until recently." Did she understand the meaning of what he'd just said?

"When did you start?"

"The night I dropped you off here." When they'd first kissed. "It was wrong and stupid and—"

"I went out and bought a box the next day. Just in case."

"You did?"

She nibbled at his bottom lip, teased it with her tongue. "A girl can always hope."

The meaning of her words wasn't lost on him, either.

"I guess we're good to go." He grinned.

"All night long."

"I have to pick up Zoey later."

"Then all afternoon."

He could do all afternoon, assuming no calls came in. "There's something else I should tell you." His hand slipped inside her blouse. Her skin was like silk, smooth, warm and inviting. "Along with protecting you, it's also my sworn duty to serve." His fingers dipped into the waistband of her skirt, fumbled for her zipper. "I consider it the most important part of my job."

She shivered and cuddled closer. "Who am I to interfere with your sworn duty? Especially the most important part."

A minute later, she was naked, and he was thanking God the last shred of his good sense had abandoned him.

CAROLINA WOULD HAVE TAKEN Neil to her bedroom, but the couch was closer. She sank into the plush cushions, pulling him down with her. There was something incredibly erotic about her being utterly naked and him being fully clothed— in his uniform, no less. Her bare calf rubbed against his khaki pant leg. The tips of her breasts skimmed the front of his shirt and the pockets with their mother-of-pearl snaps.

The cool metal of his belt buckle nestled in the warm curve of her belly.

Erotic, indeed.

Also frustrating. She wanted him naked, too.

"Take this off." She removed his cowboy hat and flung it…somewhere. "And this."

When she tried to strip him of his shirt, he eased out of her reach. "Not yet." He moved down the length of her body, leaving a trail of goose bumps in his wake. "Not until I'm done."

"With what?"

"You." He plumped her breast with his hand, then took her beaded nipple in his mouth.

She stopped breathing. Stopped thinking. Stopped trying to put into words what she felt and just let myriad pleasurable sensations crash over her one by one.

His talent was unequaled, she thought distractedly as he kissed his way to her other breast. They should erect a shrine in his honor. No, no, she amended as his tongue circled and teased and flicked over profoundly sensitive regions that had lain dormant much too long. She wanted to keep his skills her own little secret.

He nudged her legs apart, causing her to gasp. She'd been so occupied with losing herself in the sensual delights of his touch that she'd failed to notice he'd once again changed positions, sliding lower on her body and stopping only when his mouth was level with her lower belly.

She watched him through half-closed eyes, her anticipation building as he stroked and caressed her most intimate spots. Nothing had ever aroused her more.

He made her wait, damn him, driving her crazy with feather-light touches. When his mouth finally descended on her, she was ready to fly apart. He made her wait for

that, too, expertly keeping her poised on the precipice for...
oh, my!

Her climax was sudden and earth-shattering and seemingly endless. Maybe she just didn't want it to end. Who would? Time, perhaps, to reconsider that shrine.

"What did you say?" he murmured, wearing an infuriating and well-deserved grin.

"Nothing." She moved languorously.

"Yes, you did. Something about a shrine."

Her cheeks instantly heated. Make that overheated. She was already flushed from head to toe.

"I said that was fine."

"It was more than fine." He got up and started undressing.

"Okay. On a scale of one to ten, it was a—"

Carolina's mind went blank, wiped clean by the sight of Neil shirtless. When his pants and briefs followed, her system poised on the verge of shutdown. It wasn't merely a five-year abstinence that made Carolina appreciate Neil's honed physique and impressive arousal. The man was Greek-statue worthy.

He dug the condom out of his wallet before tossing his pants aside.

"I'll take that." She held out her hand.

His grin went from sexy to dangerous in the span of a heartbeat. "You sure?"

"Very."

He dropped the condom into her open palm. She promptly set it on the end table.

"I thought—"

"All in good time," she promised before he could say more. Taking his hand, she guided him down beside her and welcomed him with a kiss that went from sweet to demanding in three seconds flat. She heightened their shared excitement by reaching between them to cup and stroke and fondle every inch of him.

When he moved over her, she pushed him back. "Not yet."

He grunted in protest but relented and let her have her way with him. She left the very intense pleasure of his mouth to explore other parts of his body. Neck. Chest. Abdomen. Thighs.

"Carolina." Her name was a hoarse whisper that seemed to tear from his lips.

She replied by taking him fully into her hands, then into her mouth.

He hung on for another thirty seconds before demanding, "Put the damn condom on."

"Soon." He'd made her wait, and turnabout was fair play.

Neil, however, wasn't patient and, in her opinion, a spoilsport. Without warning, he hoisted her up onto the couch and into his lap so that she straddled him, one leg on each side. He reached for the condom. She beat him to it, ripping it open with a flourish.

Then, thank heaven, he was inside her, fulfilling every single one of the fantasies she'd indulged in since the day of her sister's wedding. And she had a very vivid imagination.

Neil didn't talk, not that she expected he would. He let his body speak for him, but Carolina couldn't resist murmuring into his ear about how good he was making her feel.

Neil cupped her bottom, thrusting harder and deeper. She adjusted to the new rhythm, adding a little of her own. He swore, which Carolina took as an indication he liked her innovativeness, then gave himself over to a violent shudder.

She cradled his head and held it to her breasts. Kissing the top of his hair, now damp with sweat, she rode the remainder of his release with him, rocking them both until he was spent at last.

When his ragged breathing slowed, he sweetly nuzzled

the underside of her breast, repeating her name. A rush of tender emotions filled Carolina, and her throat unexpectedly closed. The great sex hadn't surprised her. Considering the sparks that had flared between them, it was a given. What had taken her by storm was the intensity and depth of her feelings for him.

Then it hit her. She didn't just like Neil, wasn't simply attracted to him. She was falling for him. Completely.

What now?

Would he regret what they'd done? She sure as heck didn't. Would he tell her that, despite everything, they weren't getting involved because of his stupid hang-ups about danger and all the other BS he'd handed her? If so, she had the perfect answer.

Rather than panic and drive herself batty by attempting to analyze what was going on with her and Neil and where it might lead, she relaxed. Or tried to. Fear that they would lapse into an awkward moment kept her from enjoying herself.

Then Neil hugged her. His arms came up, circled her and pulled her close so that her breasts lay flat against his chest and his face fit perfectly into the side of her neck. She couldn't help but respond. Slowly, bit by bit, her limbs turned to liquid and her heart to mush.

"I'd like to do this again," he mumbled. "Soon."

"Right away soon?" She thought she detected a slight stirring beneath her, and he *had* mentioned all afternoon.

"I wish." He gave a robust groan when the radio attached to his shirt crackled and a disembodied female voice spewed codes that made no sense to Carolina. "I have to return to the station."

"Are you still on duty?" She should have realized that.

"Technically, yes."

The thought made her feel exquisitely naughty.

"Drats." She rose from the couch to get dressed. Sort of. She stopped at panties and her blouse, which she only partially buttoned. He seemed to like ogling her cleavage and legs, so she indulged him.

At the door, he swooped her into his arms for a goodbye kiss. Then two, then three. They were starting to feel like hello kisses when he set her aside.

"I have to go."

"Call me?" Afraid she sounded a bit anxious, she affected a lighter tone. "If you want."

"You know I want." His hand pressed into the small of her back.

That was better.

"I didn't plan this," he said.

"Me neither." She snuggled deeper into his embrace. "But I'm glad it happened." A profound pause followed.

Like that, the doubts Carolina had previously dismissed returned to plague her.

"Just in case you don't know it," she said breezily, "this is the part where you jump in and enthusiastically agree with me."

"I'm glad. Believe me." He spoke with such conviction she couldn't help but be relieved. "But I'm also concerned."

"About where this is going?"

"That, too."

"Don't ruin the mood, Neil, by bringing up work and the mine and danger."

"I worry about you."

Because he cared. Hadn't he told her as much? Twice, if she remembered correctly. "I worry about you, too. You're far more likely to land in trouble or get hurt than me."

The change in his expression was instantaneous.

"Let me guess," she said. "Lynne told you the same thing."

"Let's talk about this later. I really need to stop by the station, then pick up Zoey."

She bristled—she couldn't help it. His excuse was a valid one but smacked of a brush-off.

"All right." Feeling suddenly vulnerable, she fastened the rest of the buttons on her blouse. The shield was a flimsy one at best and no defense against Neil.

To prove it, he swooped her up into an embrace, slipped his hand inside her blouse and fondled her breast as if to say the hell with her and stake his claim. A Neanderthal and chauvinistic move if ever Carolina saw one.

That didn't stop her from loving it.

"I'll call you," he said determinedly, his fingers making all sorts of unspoken promises.

If not for the very tenuous thread of pride she clung to, she might have dissolved into a puddle.

"I have to go out and won't be home later."

"I'll track you down."

She believed him, and the lovely little tingle in her middle bloomed into a full-fledged fluttering. This silly, girly-girl stuff had to stop. It was so not like her.

He bent his head for another goodbye kiss. Carolina knew it would truly be the last when his radio went off again and she heard the female voice distinctly say, "Bear Creek Ranch." She thrust away from Neil. "What's going on?"

He didn't answer her question. Pressing a button on his radio, he spoke into it. "On my way."

"Neil."

"Later." He was out the door in a flash.

"I'm one of the owners." She chased after him, mindless of the cool temperature and that she was only half-dressed. "I have a right to know."

"The mining site's been broken into, and the equipment belonging to the Arizona Geological Society vandalized."

Neil rounded the cruiser and yanked open the driver's-side door.

Carolina spent exactly two seconds deliberating what to do. "I'll meet you there. I just have to get dressed."

"No!" He stood with one hand on the open cruiser door. The other, balled into a fist, rested on the roof. "Stay put. You got it? Don't you set foot within a mile of that mine until I give you the all clear." He didn't wait for her to reply. Jumping into the cruiser, he sped off, leaving a plume of dust behind.

Stay put? Not on her life.

No sooner was she inside than she got on the phone and called Jake.

Chapter Twelve

"Carolina! Hey, where you off to?"

"The sub shop." She waited for Adrian, the station's techie, to catch up with her. "Want me to grab you something?"

"Mind if I go with you?"

"Not at all."

She felt no discomfort issuing the invitation. He hadn't asked her out again or shown any interest in her for weeks. Come to think of it, no man had. Was she giving off some sort of unconscious vibes since... She'd started to think *hooking up with Neil,* but that wasn't exactly right.

He hadn't called her since their afternoon together three days ago, as he said he would. Probably because she'd shown up at the mining site that night with Jake and her sister Rachel. They weren't allowed near the tunnel, and though Neil spoke with them, it was in an official capacity only.

Hard to imagine he'd been in her arms a mere hour earlier.

His eyes, however, had spoken volumes. They let her know he wasn't happy she'd defied his instructions to remain home.

And he hadn't called since.

It was obvious he didn't want her interfering with the investigation, didn't want her reporting on it—too late for that—and didn't want her leaving her cabin.

Well, forget it. Listeners were eating up her reports, and

the station's ratings had escalated through the roof. The owners were pleased, giving her a special acknowledgment at the last staff meeting, and insisted she continue until further notice. On top of that, Jake's administrative assistant had reported reservations at the ranch were exceeding projections. The family couldn't be happier.

If only Ward were as pleased with her. Since the phone call and the threatening email, he'd been acting even more out of sorts.

What was it with her and men lately?

Adrian appeared to be the exception. He increased his pace to match hers and headed toward the door.

"Let me get that." He rushed to open it for her.

"Thank you." She refrained from staring openmouthed. Adrian was cute and charming in a nerdy kind of way. Gentlemanly manners weren't his style.

At the curb, he placed a hand on her arm and halted her when she would have crossed the street.

"Jeez, Adrian, what's up with you?"

"Nothing."

"Seriously. You're no Boy Scout, and I'm no old lady."

"A car was coming."

"The light was red."

"The driver might have run the light. You can't be too careful."

She laughed. "Quit joking, and tell me what's going on."

He was too ingenuous to hide his guilt. "Ward asked me to watch out for you."

"Ward?" She was dumbfounded.

"He's worried about you."

"Oh, pull-eeze." She looked around, wondering for half a second if there were any hidden cameras in the area. "Ward's not exactly a role model for a concerned boss."

"You're wrong. He was really upset when you got that email."

"He wasn't the only one."

Carolina still couldn't open an email from a sender she didn't recognize without enduring a bout of nervous anxiety. She hadn't talked about it with Neil yet, but there had to be a connection between his phone calls and hers.

"He didn't think you should go to the sub shop alone," Adrian said.

"What?" Her boss was totally flipping out. What could happen to her in the middle of the day, in the middle of town and with people everywhere?

Then she remembered. Neil's wife, Lynne, had died under just such circumstances.

Carolina immediately shook off the thought. That was New York. Not Payson.

"Whatever the reason," she said to Adrian, "I'm glad you came along. I like the company."

"Good report this morning. I heard the guys from the Arizona Geological Society might have seen a vehicle leaving the scene."

"A white Ford Suburban. They passed it on their way back to the mine. Didn't catch the license plate, unfortunately."

"Must be a hundred white Ford Suburbans in Gila County."

"Exactly. And this one's probably stolen anyway."

They reached the sub shop counter and placed their orders.

"What about gold? Did the investigators find any?"

Adrian was sure asking a lot of questions. Up until now, he hadn't been all that interested in her stories on the illegal mining.

"They've given us a preliminary report." She was purposely evasive. The family had agreed to wait to announce the investigation results until they received the final report and decided what to do.

They chatted about work until a harried clerk called out, "Number seventy-two."

Carolina and Adrian retrieved their sandwiches.

"You want to eat here?" he asked.

"Can't. I have to finish up my draft on tomorrow's report so Ward can okay it."

Adrian took her arm again at the corner and held it while they crossed the street. She didn't know whether to be amused, flattered or annoyed.

"What are you reporting on next?" he asked.

"I'm interviewing the team from the Arizona Geological Society. Getting a follow-up from them on the vandalism." Jake had spent half of yesterday afternoon on the phone with the ranch's insurance company, making sure the team's equipment would be paid for. "I wish I had something new to report." She might if Neil ever called.

"Have you been out to the mining site lately?"

"Not since the night of the vandalism. We're not allowed. The police have it cordoned off again."

"Too bad you couldn't do a live broadcast from there."

Carolina's feet came to a grinding halt. "What a great idea, Adrian! You're a genius."

He grinned sheepishly. "No, I'm not."

"Seriously. That's a fantastic idea." She was already picturing the live broadcast in her head. "I can't believe I didn't think of it."

"I mean, it's not really my idea. Ward was talking about a live broadcast during your report this morning."

"He was? How come he didn't mention it to me?"

Was he attempting to keep her out of harm's way again? Or were he and Neil in cahoots?

"I'm going to hit Ward up the second we get back. Sug-

gest we include the interview with the team from the geological society."

"What about Sheriff Lovitt?"

"What about him?"

"Won't he object?"

Did everyone at the station know about her and Neil?

"He may." That was an understatement. Neil would blow
his top and get all sheriffy on her. "I can deal with him."

Could she?

Carolina and Adrian parted ways at the receptionist's
desk.

"Good luck," he told her.

"Thanks." She'd need her fair share to pull this off.

THERE HAD BEEN a total of seven articles to date about Neil in
the Payson paper and sixteen letters to the editor, a couple in
support but mostly not. He sat at his desk, reading the latest
article when he should be tackling the mountain of reports
awaiting review. Nothing new had been printed in the paper,
just the same old stuff about Lynne and the IA investigation. So as not to show bias, the paper had also inserted a
paragraph—a *tiny* paragraph—about his exemplary service
to the county since coming to Payson.

If he were a regular subscriber, he'd be getting pretty tired
of reading about Neil Lovitt by now.

He set his half-eaten lunch aside and flipped to the editorial page. Only two of the letters were about him today, and
of those, just one appeared negative. A fifty/fifty ratio. The
percentages were getting better. He had Carolina to thank
for that, at least in part. Her positively slanted reports on his
investigation of the illegal mining operation had cast him
in a good light.

His own efforts also helped. Before Lynne's death, Neil
had been a good cop and a good investigating officer. He

was glad to discover he hadn't lost his skill...or his enthusiasm for the work.

More than ever, he remained convinced someone with an ulterior motive had it in for him, though he still didn't know who or why. If they could get even one small break on the case, chances were folks—and the newspaper—would forget all about his past.

A copy of the geological society's preliminary report had been faxed over to him from Bear Creek Ranch that afternoon. The results weren't what he'd expected, and he'd be interested in learning what the family's plans were.

Not that Carolina would tell him. They hadn't spoken since he left her cabin after making love with her. His fault. He should have called her. But everything had become so complicated so quickly.

She must hate him.

He really needed to man up and call her.

He laid down the newspaper and reached for the phone. Face-to-face would be better, but he had an open house at Zoey's school tonight and didn't want to wait another day before talking to Carolina. His hand was just lifting the receiver when Otis strolled into his office.

"Hey! What are you doing here?" Neil returned the phone to its cradle, fighting a mixture of disappointment and relief.

"I escaped Patty's clutches."

"Good for you."

"Actually, she has a meeting over at the Historical Society and dropped me off out front." The sheriff sat down in the visitor chair. "She figured I couldn't get into too much trouble in an hour."

"She doesn't know you well, does she?"

Otis's loud laugh filled the room. "If I'm lucky, their speaker will run over, and I'll have an extra hour to chew the fat with you. Could happen. He's the assistant curator from the museum."

"Really?" Neil had been in contact with Mr. Dunstan several times over the past week.

"He's talking to Patty's group about the early mining that went on here. Everyone's interested, naturally, what with the illegal digging at Bear Creek Ranch. And not just locally. We've had a flood of new tourists lately."

Neil knew that from the increase in traffic citations.

"Well, if anything, it's good for the economy. Who said crime doesn't pay?" Otis laughed again and rocked back in his chair. He studied Neil at length. "You look good behind that desk."

The change in their usual positions hadn't been lost on Neil. He'd experienced a fleeting moment of discomfort when Otis had first entered the room.

"The chair's a little roomy. Might be a bit more than I'm capable of filling."

"Don't underestimate yourself, Neil. You're doing a bang-up job."

"I'm not sure about that. And besides, I won't be sitting here much longer."

"Who knows? I have to retire eventually." Otis's features fell slightly. "One thing this heart attack has taught me, I won't be around forever."

"You have a lot of years left."

"I may not want to spend all of them in that chair. I've shortchanged Patty something awful during our marriage. She's a good woman, a good wife, and deserves more than I've given her."

"She loves you, Otis."

"Don't know why." He shook off his display of emotion with a grunt.

Neil tapped the folded newspaper beside his desk blotter. "Have you read the latest?"

"Ridiculous drivel."

Neil took that as a no.

"What you need to do is find out who the hell's behind the illegal mining."

"I was thinking the same thing myself right before you walked in."

"Any progress?"

For reasons he couldn't explain, Neil hesitated telling Otis about the preliminary report from the geological society. Not that he didn't trust Otis, but the fewer people who knew about the team's findings, the better.

"Not much," he told Otis. "The wheels are moving slow."

"Good! Maybe we can draw this out a little longer, just until the economy in this town turns all the way around."

"Yeah," Neil said pensively.

Without meaning to, Otis may have hit on something. Everyone assumed the motive behind the illegal mining was to extract gold for resale on the black market. What if it wasn't? What if the purpose was to generate interest and bring tourists to Payson? Who would have the most to gain in that scenario?

The first names that came to mind were the owners of Bear Creek Ranch. The place where the illegal mining had occurred.

Neil set that thought aside and, for the next fifteen minutes, he and Otis discussed the department and how Neil was progressing with the deputies.

"Not good, but better," he said. "Like me, they're laying low, waiting for you to return."

"You can add Patty to that list. She's plumb tired of having me constantly underfoot."

"R.J. might be responsible for bringing the men in line. He's been a good supporter."

"He's just a good man all-around."

"You got that right."

Otis braced his hands on the arms of the visitor chair and hoisted himself out of his seat. "I'd better get a move on. Let you get back to your lunch."

"I'm glad you stopped by."

"Me, too." He surprised Neil by reaching across the desk and shaking his hand. "You've conducted yourself well during this mess and deserve to be congratulated. Makes me glad I recommended you to the county commissioner."

"Thank you, sir." The compliment touched Neil.

After Otis ambled out of the office, Neil picked up the remaining half of his sandwich and the newspaper, flipping to the editorial page. He ate on automatic pilot, his attention completely focused on the more positive letter to the editor.

At the last paragraph, he paused then reread it. The letter writer mentioned a number of Neil's accomplishments during his year-and-a-half as deputy sheriff, including the time he'd administered CPR to a heart attack victim living in Bliss Canyon. If not for his action, the elderly woman might have died.

Neil hadn't considered himself a hero, he'd simply been doing his duty. There'd been very little notice of the incident after it happened except for a brief mention in the newspaper that excluded Neil's role. He'd liked it that way, having no wish to draw attention to himself.

Which told him the person who wrote this letter either had amazing resources or was there the night he'd responded to the call. That limited the possibilities to someone on the hospital staff or the other two deputies on duty that night, Hank and R.J.

If Neil had to guess the author of the anonymous letter,

he'd pick R.J. Neil didn't know whether to thank his deputy or chew him out.

Reading the letter made him realize not everything about the job of acting sheriff was bad.

His intercom abruptly buzzed, shaking him from his thoughts. "Yes."

"Sorry to bother you, Neil." Mary Twohorses was on the line. "Can I speak to Otis?"

"He left a few minutes ago."

"Oh. I must have missed him."

"Can I help you with something?"

"No, it's all right. I have Ward Preston from KPKD holding. I'll tell him Otis left already."

Neil hung up, unable to dismiss the nagging feeling that had come from nowhere. Why would Carolina's boss be calling Otis? And how did he even know that Otis was at the station? Neil tried to focus on the pile of reports but his mind kept returning to Otis and Carolina's boss and any possible connection. Not that the two men couldn't be friends, but as far as Neil knew, they never had been.

A few minutes later his intercom buzzed again.

"Sorry, Neil," Mary said again. "But a call just came in, and I thought you should know about it."

"What's going on?"

"Carolina Sweetwater and a crew from the radio station have shown up at the illegal mining site. They're attempting to do a live broadcast."

Chapter Thirteen

Neil bolted from his chair and grabbed his hat off the credenza. "Call my babysitter for me and tell her I may be late. If she can't pick up Zoey from the riding stables, let me know."

"You got it!" Mary stepped back in the nick of time. Otherwise, he might have trampled her.

He took the old Jeep rather than his cruiser. The four-wheel-drive vehicle didn't disappoint him. Arriving at the mining site, he parked beside the radio station's brightly painted van and cut the ignition. R.J. and Hank were already there. From what Neil could see, they were making little headway with Carolina and her two-man crew.

The ground underneath his boots crunched as he tromped up the slope. He stopped on a level area about twenty feet away from the mine entrance and the yellow caution tape Carolina and her crew were trying to breach.

Refusing to be intimated, she stood tall and strong and fierce, a look of grim determination on her face. Her lavender skirt—*lavender,* for Pete's sake—hugged her legs, making a ridiculous contrast to the green trench coat she never seemed to be without.

Quite frankly, she took his breath away.

He should have phoned her before now. Maybe then the impact of seeing her wouldn't be having such a profound effect on him. Or maybe not. In the next instant, their gazes locked, and they engaged in a nonverbal standoff Neil doubted he'd win.

Could she and her family have staged this whole event just so she could use the reports to advance her career and the ranch could benefit from the increase in business?

No, he didn't think so. Seeing her rooted there, ready to take on the entire sheriff's department if necessary, he knew her motives were purely journalistic and nothing personal. KPKD might be a small radio station serving a small market, but Carolina brought a big market attitude to her job.

"R.J.," he called. His deputy came running, leaving Hank in charge of crowd control. "Report."

"Ms. Sweetwater insists that, as one of the property owners and a representative of the media, she has a right to be here."

"I bet she does." Neil reassessed the situation. "I'll talk to her."

"Want me to radio for backup?"

Did his deputy think he'd need it? "Hold off. See if I can't handle her myself."

R.J. nearly split a shirt seam laughing.

Neil wasn't amused. "I appreciate the vote of confidence."

"She's a corker, that one." R.J. attempted to wipe the smirk from his face with the back of his hand.

How much did his deputies know about his and Carolina's relationship? Neil didn't know or, he realized with a slight start, care. When had his feelings on that subject changed?

More importantly, why?

"Corker or not, the law is the law." Neil eyed Carolina.

As if anticipating his next move, she stood even taller, the flaps of her coat waving in the breeze.

Neil was more than ready for a showdown and did a little posturing himself. "By the way," he said to R.J. before moving on, "thanks for writing that letter to the newspaper."

"What letter?"

"The one to the editor. It was in this afternoon's edition. Your support means a lot to me."

R.J. pushed his hat back and scratched his head. "You say it was a good letter?"

"Yeah. Real nice."

"Well, I'll be damned."

"What?"

"I didn't write that letter, Sheriff."

Neil frowned. "I thought maybe you did. It mentioned me giving CPR to that old woman in Bliss Canyon."

"Hank did it."

"What?"

"He bragged to the guys about writing a letter to the paper. We told him not to. Course, that's cuz we figured he'd take the low road." R.J.'s face broke out into a huge grin. "Guess we were wrong."

Neil gave his head a small shake. Hank wrote the letter? He gazed up the slope to where the deputy stood, his broad figure effectively blocking any entrance to the mine shaft.

There had to be a mistake. Maybe the letter was written by someone at the hospital. But how would anyone at the hospital know about the other incidents mentioned? Now that Neil thought about it, Hank had been on every one of those calls.

But the deputy didn't like Neil. Didn't respect him. He resented Neil for getting the appointment he felt had belonged to him.

"Let's get this over with," Neil said.

Still grinning, R.J. followed Neil up the hill. "This ought to be real good."

About ten feet from Carolina and her crew, Neil stopped

again and motioned with a small jerk of his head for Hank to join him. The deputy responded. Still built like the re-cord-breaking halfback he'd been in junior college, he lumbered over, his features cross, his beefy hands knotted at his sides. "Yes, sir."

Sir? That was new.

"I'd like to encourage these fine folks to leave with as little trouble as possible," Neil said.

"Carolina won't go without a fight."

Since when did Hank refer to Carolina by her first name? Neil's hackles rose, though he refused to show it. He didn't have exclusive rights to Carolina's first name, even if he wanted them.

"Nice letter to the editor." R.J. socked Hank in the arm. "Way to go, pal."

Hank's stern features softened momentarily, then grew dark again. "I don't know what you're talking about."

"Right," R.J. scoffed.

"Shut up." Hank elbowed R.J. hard in the ribs.

Neil wasn't sure what to make of their antics. "Hank?"

"Yes, sir."

Sir again? "Did you write the letter?"

"Well…" The young deputy faltered. "Didn't seem right that folks were talking trash about you."

Neil swallowed his shock. "I appreciate it."

"I don't always agree with you, sir, but we need to stick up for our own. If we don't, who else will?"

"Call me Neil." He put out his hand.

Hank shook it. "Yes, sir. Neil."

"You two watch the mine entrance." It was time to get this job done. "I'll see if I can't defuse the situation."

"Sure you don't want me to radio for backup?" R.J. visibly held in a chuckle. Neil couldn't tell but he thought Hank might be hiding a smile, as well. So much for maintaining a position of authority.

"Get after it," he barked.

R.J. and Hank strode over to the yellow caution tape barrier and positioned themselves behind it. All eyes were on Neil as he approached the group.

"Ms. Sweetwater." He addressed her calmly and professionally. "Can I help you with something?"

"My team and I would like access to the mine for a live broadcast." She sent him an icy stare.

He didn't wilt. Ice he could handle. It was her fire that robbed him of his senses and turned him to putty in her hands.

"I'm sorry, Ms. Sweetwater," he said in his best cop voice, "but this is a crime scene, and we can't risk contamination."

"We have a right to be here."

"You can conduct your broadcast from the base of the slope but not here." He could tell from her expression she hadn't expected him to concede even that much.

"We prefer to do it from the actual crime scene." She formed her lips into a stubborn pout.

Given the chance, he'd cover her lips with his and kiss her until pouting was the furthest thing from her mind. Unfortunately, he'd have to wait for another day. Like tomorrow. When he told her in private just how idiotic her little scheme was.

"Will it make a difference? Your listeners can't see the mine. You could be broadcasting from the dining hall at Bear Creek Ranch for all they'd know."

She inhaled sharply. Neil had found her hot button. The geeky guy beside her giggled, then choked when she glared at him.

"No need for you to be insulting," she said to Neil.

"No need for you to be stupid," he fired back. "There's

evidence in that mine that could lead to the identification and arrest of the criminals behind the illegal digging. I can't allow you and your crew to stomp all over it."

"We will not stomp—"

"If you don't leave now, I'll have the three of you arrested."

"Just try."

"Don't push me, Carolina." Somewhere along the way, Neil realized, the battle had become personal. "I'm not joking around."

She didn't give an inch. "I suppose that means an interview with you is out of the question."

"If that's what it takes to get you to leave, then yes."

"No, thank you." She pulled herself together. "I don't need to negotiate for an interview."

Her words were reminiscent of the ones she'd uttered during an earlier argument, only that one had been about their relationship.

Wasn't this one, too?

"My men will help you down," he said through a very tightly clenched jaw.

"We're not leaving. Not until—"

In the next instant, a gunshot rang out.

"Take cover!" Hank shouted, and dived for Carolina's two crew members, taking them both down at the same time. The trio hit with a loud, bone-crunching thud.

Neil didn't think. He grabbed Carolina and tossed her to the ground, covering her with his body. More bullets whizzed past their heads. Four, five, six. Neil could hear them pinging off the rocks just above them. The blood in his veins instantly froze, and he was thrust back in time to the deli and the day Lynne died from a stray bullet.

It took all his willpower to remain rooted in the present.

If he didn't, if he let the memories get a stranglehold on him and affect his judgment, he might not be able to keep Carolina and the others safe.

"ARE YOU ALL RIGHT?" Neil raised himself up slightly on one elbow.

Carolina lay beneath him, warm and breathing, but that was no guarantee she hadn't been hit and was slowly bleeding out.

"Yes," she squeaked.

"Don't move. You hear me? This isn't the time to argue."

"I won't."

Her face, just inches from his, was stark white, and her lips trembled. Good. For once, she'd probably behave.

"R.J.?" he called.

"Over here, Sheriff. I'm fine."

"Hank?"

"We're all okay."

That was a relief. The bullets had been close. *Very* close. They were lucky no one was shot.

Lucky, or intentional?

The gunfire had come from nearby. Just over the ridge. They should all be dead, but they weren't.

"You want me to call for that backup now?" R.J. asked from behind a boulder where he'd taken cover.

"Yes. And everybody stay down!"

Neil didn't have much hope the shooter would still be in the area when their backup arrived. And he'd bet when they located the spot the shooter had fired from, not one piece of evidence would be there. Not even a hair follicle.

If he'd had any doubts before, this afternoon had erased them. The criminals they were dealing with were professionals.

"There's a rock sticking in my back." Carolina shifted.

He pinned her with an arm across her chest. "I don't care if it's sticking in your...never mind. Don't move until I give you the go-ahead."

"Neil?" she whispered.

"Yes."

"That was scary."

His heart constricted. "I know, sweetheart." He'd been scared, too. Out of his mind. Every time he blinked, he saw the image of Lynne's blood splattered all over the side of the building. "But he's gone now, and you're okay."

"You sure he's gone?"

"Not so sure that I'm going to let you up before our backup arrives." He could hear R.J. radioing in for assistance and Hank attempting to calm the two crew members.

"Adrian, Miguel," Carolina called out. "Are you all right?"

"I'm fine. Miguel's having a meltdown."

"So what if I am? We almost died."

"Yeah, but we'll be front-page news," Adrian answered. "Think of the publicity."

"That's the spirit," Carolina answered.

"Keep quiet," Neil ordered. "We don't know if the shooter is still out there and what he'll do."

All was silent for several minutes. Neil tried to twist the upper half of his body around so he could scan the area.

"Thank you." Carolina's warm breath caressed his cheek, distracting him.

"For what?"

"Saving me." She lifted her head and kissed him. Soft, sweet and tender.

Because he could have lost her today, because he'd wanted to kiss her so badly earlier and couldn't, because everything he'd worried would happen to her *had* happened, he kissed her back, and to hell with what his deputies and her crew thought.

She clung to him as if this was their last moment together. Maybe it should be. Once again, his job had put a person he cared about in danger.

Unable to continue gazing into her liquid hazel eyes, he averted his head. "Your coat's dirty."

She seemed unaware of his distress. "A small price to pay."

"Hey, Sheriff," R.J. called. "I think I can make it to the mine shaft. You want me to try? I might be able to see the road. That shooter didn't walk here."

"Stay low."

"Will do."

Neil listened to the sound of his deputy crawling across the ground, listened harder for any movement in the distance.

"What do you see?"

"Nothing," R.J. responded. "Not even a dust cloud. I'm thinking he's clean gone." A few minutes later, he announced, "Here comes our backup."

Neil felt Carolina relax. He wished he could do the same. Whoever had shot at them was still out there and would likely try again. Only next time, the shots might not be warning ones fired over their heads.

Fifteen minutes later, Carolina's crew was safely ensconced in the rear seat of a Payson Police Department cruiser and seemed quite content to wait there.

Carolina wasn't patient. She was supposed to be sitting in the front seat but kept hopping out, only to be firmly escorted back. If she'd had her way, she and her crew would be doing the live broadcast that had brought them to the illegal mining site in the first place. When she'd called her boss, however, he had demonstrated good judgment and vetoed the idea.

"Hi, Carmen." Neil had phoned his babysitter to inform

her that he'd be delayed. "I know it's a lot to ask, but can you pick Zoey up at the stables?"

"No problem, Sheriff."

Sheriff. He involuntarily tensed. If he weren't acting sheriff, none of this would have happened. Carolina wouldn't have almost died.

"Thanks. I'll pay you double."

"Well, I won't refuse," Carmen said. "Tuition for next semester's coming up, and I can use the money."

"See you later, then." Neil disconnected. He was more than happy to pay Carmen extra for her services. An idea had started forming in the back of his mind, and if everything came together, he might not need his babysitter's services anymore. He wanted to compensate her as much as possible before then.

"You ready to head back to the station?" a detective from the Payson Police Department asked Neil. The two agencies continued to work closely together on the illegal mining investigation. Neil would be required to give them a report along with one for the sheriff's department.

"Let's go." He almost made it back to his cruiser.

"Neil?" Carolina materialized beside him.

How did she get away from the cruiser? He glanced around, trying to see who wasn't doing their job.

"You need to get back." He reached for her arm.

"What's going to happen?" The tough exterior she presented to everyone else cracked, revealing a rarely seen vulnerable side.

"You'll be taken to the Payson police station to give a statement."

"Not tonight. I mean, with us."

"I'll call you."

"Like you did the last time?"

He deserved that.

"How about you come over—" she moved to stand near him "—and we talk in person?"

The gesture was subtle but he understood it. She was giving him the opportunity to touch her, possibly hug or hold her, offer the reassurance she needed.

Too bad he couldn't do it.

"That's a good idea. Are you free tomorrow after lunch?"

"I'll make sure I am." She reached for his hand. "I'm looking forward to it."

She wouldn't be if she had any idea what he planned to say.

Chapter Fourteen

"I'm fine," Carolina insisted.

"You sure, sweetie?"

"Absolutely." Her sisters, Rachel, Corrine and Vi, hovered around her like a trio of mothers leaving their children at preschool for the first time.

The idea of them lunching together in the ranch's dining hall had appealed to Carolina, but as it turned out, the noise and commotion of a hundred other diners simultaneously eating their meals grated on her nerves. Every time someone dropped a plate or scraped a chair across the floor, she jumped.

All in all, she'd rather be at work. Her boss, however, had insisted she stay home the rest of the week. As a result, she was fighting off a chronic case of anxiety as well as her sisters' irritating yet well-intentioned coddling.

She was also worried about her job. Ward probably would take her off the mining story. He'd come close after she'd received the threatening email. He might even decide to let her go altogether. After yesterday, she'd become something of a liability to the station.

"You could have been killed," Vi repeated her earlier scolding in proper older-sister fashion. "What in the world were you doing out there to begin with?"

"My job." Carolina didn't let her sister's sharp tone annoy her. Vi always came on strong.

Besides, the previous evening and night had been wretched for Carolina. She was usually one to rebound quickly. Being used as a moving target by some sicko creep had been more than even she could handle.

She really wished Neil had accompanied her when she'd given her statement. Without his comfort and protection, the seriousness of her close call had hit her hard. Returning to a dark, empty cabin after a grueling interview at the police station had driven the point home.

Her cabin had always been her sanctuary. A safe and secure haven she could retreat to with no fears. Instead, she'd spent a sleepless night ducking around corners and avoiding windows, the ping of ricocheting bullets resounding in her ears. Thank goodness Rachel had stayed with her. About three in the morning, Carolina had finally drifted off into a restless sleep, only to wake up shortly after dawn, more exhausted than when she'd gone to bed.

Neil was right. She'd been in far more danger than she realized and should have listened to him. When she saw him—any minute now—she'd tell him that and a whole lot more.

Like how crazy she was about him and how there weren't any obstacles they couldn't overcome together.

"You have to eat," Rachel chided.

"I am."

"Not enough. You haven't had anything substantial since lunch yesterday."

It was true. Carolina had missed dinner because of being at the police station, and breakfast, too. Much as she'd tried, the idea of putting even one bite of toast in her mouth had caused her stomach to roil in protest. The chicken noodle soup sitting in front of her was going down a little easier.

"See." Carolina lifted her spoon high and took another bite.

Great. While she'd been stalling, the soup had grown cold.

Would she ever be able to relax again? Not hear the bullets or relive the horror? She didn't dare tell her sisters about her anxiety. They'd insist she see a therapist when all she needed was time. And Neil. He was better than any counselor's advice could ever be.

She'd been too hard on him for sure. Her insistence in doing a live broadcast from the mining site had endangered Adrian's and Miguel's lives as well as her own. She couldn't have lived with herself if something had happened to them.

Which must be exactly how Neil felt about Lynne.

Carolina wanted to thump herself in the head with the heel of her hand. Honestly, how shortsighted could she be? The line between caring and controlling wasn't nearly as tenuous as she'd thought.

"Carolina!" Vi complained. "Eat."

"Okay, okay."

Without warning, the noise level in the dining room dropped to near silence. Carolina's heart began to flutter in fear. She clutched the edge of the table and automatically looked around to see what had caused the disturbance. The answer was obvious.

Neil stood near the entrance. Tall, strong and in full uniform, he made an impressive image.

Carolina couldn't believe how much safer just seeing him made her feel. No shooters would dare lurk behind a dark corner with him there.

He removed his aviator sunglasses and scanned the dining room. She sat up straighter, resisting the urge to wave girlishly. She needn't have worried. His instincts were right on target. Diners scrambled to clear a path as he came over.

"Good afternoon, ladies," he said, touching the brim of his cowboy hat when he reached Carolina's table.

"Hi." She couldn't believe how soft and shaky her voice came out. "These are my sisters, Vi, Corrine and Rachel." She pointed to each of them. "And this is Neil. Sheriff Lovitt," she added, upon seeing her sisters' conspiratorial grins.

"Nice to meet you," Vi said, "but I have to go."

"Yeah, we're needed in the kitchen to…to…take out the garbage," Rachel added.

Corrine's lame excuse followed the others.

"Please don't leave on my account," Neil said smoothly, and turned to Carolina. "Can we chat for a few minutes? Somewhere else besides here? That is, if you're done eating."

"I am." Carolina stood and together they left the dining hall. She was certain every pair of eyes in the room was fastened on them.

Outside, he surprised her by taking her hand. His fingers felt warm and firm and magically chased away the nervousness that had plagued her since the previous evening.

"Would you mind walking a bit?" he asked, something not quite right in his voice.

So much for alleviating her nervousness. "There's a foot trail that runs along the creek," she said. "It starts there, on the other side of the parking lot."

They walked in relative silence, though it was anything but silent around them. Guests were everywhere. Strolling to and from the dining hall. Swimming in the heated pool. Playing horseshoes or badminton. Riding horses or ATVs up and down the main road.

The atmosphere changed upon entering the wooded area and the trailhead. As if a thick curtain had fallen around them, Carolina and Neil were thrust into a serene calm that was broken only by the distant ruckus of children playing.

"How are you doing today?"

"Good." Her laugh came out with a slightly desperate edge to it. "I've been spending the morning trying to figure out how I can work all this into my next report."

He dropped her hand. Not a good sign.

They came to a more secluded area with a small bridge. Beneath it, the creek babbled as it rushed over rocks and around bends. Neil made no move to cross the bridge.

"I called Zoey's grandparents this morning, my former in-laws." He appeared to choose his words carefully. "She stayed with them the year after Lynne died."

"I remember you telling me."

"They're coming out for a visit in a few days."

"How nice. Zoey will be thrilled."

No answer.

Carolina began to worry in earnest. "How long are they staying?"

"A few days. Bud has to get back to work."

"That's a shame for them to come all the way from upstate New York and not stay longer. They don't get to see Zoey often."

"They're taking her back with them."

"Oh!" That was unexpected.

"She's safer with them."

"After yesterday, I don't blame you for being cautious. But sending her away seems a bit extreme."

"It wasn't a random shooting."

"I know that."

"Next time, the shooter may not miss."

"Trust me, I'm not going to the mine again."

"Damn straight you're not. If I have to tie you to your desk chair, I will."

He probably meant that in a caring way, but for some reason, his tone rubbed Carolina the wrong way. "I'm not that crazy to put myself in danger again."

"What makes you think they were after you?"

"I'm...I'm the reporter on the story."

"And I'm heading up the investigation for the department. You may not think Zoey's life is in danger, but I do."

Carolina hadn't thought of it that way.

Dear Lord, the situation had spiraled so far out of control. As soon as she got home, she was going to call Ward and remove herself from the story. No career was worth risking people's lives.

Hadn't Neil told her that very thing time and again?

"How does Zoey feel about going away with her grandparents?"

"She doesn't know, and she won't until they're ready to leave."

For a smart man, he was pretty dumb. "She won't want to go."

"She won't have a choice."

"Neil, think about this. She's not a toddler anymore. She's a bright, astute young girl who won't understand why her father's sending her away."

"I'll explain it to her."

Carolina moved to stand in front of him and placed her hands on her hips. "How are you going to do that without telling her about her mother?"

"I don't know yet."

"You could try the truth."

"She's not ready."

"Her, or you?"

"I've made my decision. Zoey will be safe. That's what matters the most."

"And two thousand miles away."

"It's temporary."

Well, at least there was a light on the horizon. By his own admission, he'd been an emotional wreck the last time he'd dispatched his daughter to live with her grandparents. Carolina would hate for him to have to go through it again. "When are you planning on bringing her home?"

"After Otis returns to work."

Two months. He could probably survive, and she would do her best to help him navigate the rough patches. But could Zoey survive without her dad?

"Or I may leave her there until I can join her."

"Join her?" Awareness stole slowly over Carolina, leaving chilly footprints up her spine. "Not bring her home?"

"I'm going to submit my resignation."

It felt like the ground shifted and rolled out from beneath her feet. Neil was leaving?

"What about us?" she asked lamely.

"I have to think of Zoey."

"Yes. Which you aren't doing and haven't from the beginning." Hurt and surprise mingled inside Carolina, giving her voice a brittle edge. "You've only been thinking of yourself and your own guilt."

"You're wrong. I'm thinking of you, too."

"Pardon me if I don't agree."

He grabbed her arm, not roughly but desperately. "You were shot at yesterday, Carolina. If you'd been hurt—killed—it would have been my fault."

"Like it was your fault Lynne died?"

"Yes."

"That was an accident."

"An avoidable one."

"You can't control everything and everybody."

"I can this. And I won't be responsible for another person losing their life on my account." He drew in a shuddering breath. "I want you, Carolina, make no mistake. But more than that, I want you alive and safe. The only way to accomplish that is for me to stay the hell away from you."

She withdrew from his grasp. "That excuse is starting to sound really tired." She knew he believed what he said, but if she heard it one more time, she'd scream. "You can't keep running away, and you can't keep sending people away. Sooner or later you're going to have to confront your problems. Only if you wait until later, your daughter may not be there. I certainly won't be."

"I was hoping you'd understand."

"You hoped I'd make it easy for you by not creating a stink."

"Trust me, you making a stink was a given."

His attempt at humor didn't amuse her. If anything, it widened the wound in her heart and caused her to strike out at him. "Can't you see what you're doing? You're so damn worried about keeping Zoey and me safe, you're losing the very thing you're trying to preserve. Our love for you."

There. She'd said it.

"I haven't lost Zoey's love. Not yet. And I don't plan to." He spoke with conviction. "Which is another reason we have to leave Payson. I can't risk her finding out about her mother."

Had he not acknowledged her admission that she loved him on purpose or had it gone unnoticed?

No, Neil wasn't obtuse.

She suddenly felt stifled by an overwhelming sense of déjà vu. Once again, she was being dumped by a man because of his job. The same feelings of hurt and rejection and anger she'd felt before came rushing back, only much stronger. Probably because they'd never entirely disappeared.

"Have it your way," she said, sniffing. "Be alone. At least you won't have to fight with your guilt anymore."

"I never wanted to hurt you, Carolina. You have to believe me."

She did. Neil's thinking might be skewed, but he'd been

straight with her from the very beginning about how he felt. She'd walked into their relationship with her eyes open. The only mistake she'd made was to think she could battle his ghosts and win.

"Contrary to popular opinion," she said, struggling to compose herself, "I won't create a stink. You'll get what you want, Neil. Your daughter will be safe, living on the other side of the country. I'll be safe, too, out of your life for good. I hope it makes you happy."

"It doesn't."

Small solace. "Then you have no one to blame but yourself." She squared her shoulders. "Forgive me if I don't walk back with you." Hell would freeze over before he saw her cry. And she would be crying. For days. "Have a good life. Wherever you wind up."

"I really wish it could have turned out differently."

She gave him one last look. "It could have."

Walking away, she decided Neil had just lost the best thing to happen to him in a long time.

But then, so had she.

So much for her life-redirecting plan.

Chapter Fifteen

"A milk truck's blocking traffic?" Rowdy Rodgers made a silly face. "I didn't think they used those anymore."

"An eighteen-wheeler hauling milk," Carolina corrected him. She wasn't in the mood to joke with the deejay. "It stalled in the middle of an intersection, and the driver can't get it started again. There's a mile-long backup, so it's best to avoid that side of town if at all possible."

"Talk about sour milk."

Rowdy frowned at her when she didn't respond to his jest and gave her a what's-up-with-you look.

She shrugged him off. "Authorities estimate another hour before traffic clears."

"Well, thanks for the update, Carolina." His inflection more than his actual words dismissed her. "I can't wait to check with you at nine."

She exited the control room a minute later. Rowdy had good reason to be annoyed with her. She'd been no more fun to work with during the four earlier reports she'd given. In fact, her entire family was fed up with her glum mood the past five days.

Carolina had neither seen nor heard from Neil since leaving him behind on the foot trail at Bear Creek Ranch. Not that she'd expected to. Once he made a commitment, he stuck to it. Damn stubborn New Yorker. It was a shame his commitment hadn't been to resolve the issues between them.

She knew from her niece Briana that Zoey's grandparents were in town visiting, because they were picking her up from riding lessons. How long had Neil said they'd stay? A few days? Zoey would be leaving soon, possibly forever. Carolina would have liked to see her before then to say goodbye but she doubted she'd get the chance. Too bad.

For all of them.

She made her way to her private cubicle, intending to enjoy it while it lasted. Now that she'd been demoted back to morning traffic reporter, she fully expected to return to her old cubicle, the one she'd shared with the afternoon traffic reporter.

A painful lump lodged in her throat, but she didn't cry. Been there, done that, thank you.

The thing was, she missed Neil. And his daughter and the reports on the illegal mining. Other than a few scary moments—okay, hours—she hadn't felt so good, enjoyed her life so much in years.

She suspected it had been the same for him, too.

"Hey, Carolina." Ward stopped her before she entered her cubicle. "You have a minute?" He looked awful. Drawn, older. As if he hadn't slept in days.

"Sure." She changed direction and followed him, expecting to be reprimanded for not playing along with Rowdy during the broadcast. Fine. Let Ward fire her. She didn't care anymore.

A bald-faced lie, but it sounded good.

Ward led her to the conference room. Definitely a reprimand coming. He closed the door behind her, and they sat down at one end of the long table. Carolina couldn't help but recall the last time she'd been in this room. It was right after she'd received the threatening email. Neil had taken her home, and they'd spent the rest of the afternoon making love.

Enough! She gave herself a stern mental kick and tried to concentrate on what Ward was saying. The poor man really did need to get some sleep before he fell apart. Even his hands were shaking.

She decided to cut him some slack. "I promise I'll joke more with Rowdy."

He gave her a blank stare. "What?"

"Rowdy," she prompted. "The traffic reports."

"I don't care about that."

"You don't?"

"I want to discuss the, uh…" He took a breath, a shallow one. "I'd like you to do a final report on the illegal mining operation."

He was just full of surprises this morning. "Why? You said yourself it was too dangerous."

"This one will be different." He spoke slowly, and his appearance became even more drawn. "The people responsible for the illegal mining will be behind bars soon."

"The authorities have caught them?" Carolina couldn't believe it.

"They're about to." His voice sounded odd.

"Ward? Are you all right?" She was really starting to worry.

"I'm very sorry you were shot at, Carolina. That was never the plan. Never what I agreed to."

"What are you talking about?" A sick, scary feeling formed in the pit of her stomach.

"Last May, my son, Len, was driving home from his senior prom. He'd been drinking. Pretty heavily."

"I don't understand what your son has to do with any of this."

"It all started with him and that night." The battle waging

inside Ward was evident on his face. "Len didn't normally drink, but you know seniors and prom night. Sheriff Herberger was coming back from a call. He's a big supporter of the school's football program. He recognized Len and pulled him over. At the time, I thought it was the luckiest break in the world."

"How so?"

"He could have given Len a DUI and hauled him to jail. He certainly deserved it—the kid broke the law. If Sheriff Herberger had, chances are Len would have lost his scholarship to ASU. Instead, the sheriff called me to come pick up Len and never reported the incident."

"That was nice of him." Carolina knew from her own experience as an occasionally wayward youth that the sheriff had a soft spot when it came to children and teenagers. Maybe because he and his wife Patty weren't able to have any of their own.

"I told him if he ever needed anything, anything at all, he had only to ask me." Ward cleared his throat. "I had no idea at the time what such an open-ended promise would cost me. What it might cost other people."

Carolina shook her head. None of this made sense.

"Sheriff Herberger contacted me when he was still in the hospital after his heart attack," Ward said. "He told me he was collecting on my debt. I couldn't say no. Not after what he'd done for Len. And, at first, what he asked for wasn't so bad."

"Which was…?"

"Apply pressure to Neil Lovitt. Attempt to discredit him by doing a story on his involvement in his late wife's death."

"Why?"

"To distract him."

"From what?"

"Investigating the illegal mining operation on your family's ranch."

"I'm confused."

"Sheriff Herberger's involved."

"You can't be serious!"

"He may even be the one behind it. I don't know everything. He intentionally kept me in the dark."

She recalled Neil's comment about the operation requiring brains and money and that the brains were local. No, it couldn't be! Sheriff Herberger was a family friend. County Sheriff for over twenty-five years.

"You're wrong."

"I wish to God I were. He knew about the mine from old maps belonging to his wife's family. He's been sneaking onto your property for the past year. He even went so far as to help an engineer from Mexico cross the border illegally. In exchange, the engineer put the crew together and oversaw the digging."

Carolina lifted trembling fingers and pressed them to her mouth. The rational part of her brain wanted to reject everything Ward said. "What about the dead phone calls and the emails?"

"I'm sure he's behind those, too. And the shooting at the mine site. He had contacts on both sides of the law." Ward's eyes filled with despair. "When you, Adrian and Miguel were shot at, I knew Otis had gone too far."

"I have to tell Sheriff Lovitt."

"Which is why I called you in here. I want you to break the story wide open."

"What about Len?"

"We talked for hours last night. He doesn't like this any more than I do and is ready to deal with the consequences. He feels responsible for the predicament I'm in. If he hadn't been drinking that night—"

"He didn't hire a thug to shoot at innocent people." The idea that her uncle's lifelong friend was capable of such an atrocious act horrified Carolina.

"No, he didn't," Ward said, his voice thick with regret. "He's a victim, like the rest of us. Which is why I'm telling you this now. Sheriff Herberger has got to be stopped."

"You might be arrested, too."

"At least I'll be able to sleep at night again."

Carolina appreciated the sacrifice Ward and his son were making. Confessing their involvement took courage. "I'm going to call Neil right now." She rose from the table.

"Be careful." Ward walked her to the door. "You have no idea what Sheriff Herberger is capable of, what lengths he'll go to."

Something else Neil had told her. If only she'd listened.

Still in a state of disbelief, she hurried down the hall to her cubicle. Lifting the phone, she called the sheriff's office.

"I'm sorry, ma'am," a young male voice on the other end of the line said after she'd asked for Neil. "He's not here."

"This is Carolina Sweetwater. It's very important I reach him." She almost said it was a matter of life and death. "Can you patch me through to him?"

"I'm afraid not. He's unavailable."

"Unavailable as in out of range?"

"Can someone else help you?"

"No, thank you." Hanging up, she dialed Neil's private cell phone.

He picked up on the first ring. "Carolina." It was clear he hadn't expected to hear from her.

"Neil, I have to talk to you. Right away. Can we meet someplace?"

"I can't. I'm on my way to the school. They called. There's a problem with Zoey. I don't have all the details, only that—"

"Sheriff Herberger is the one behind the illegal mining operation."

"What?" Disbelief rang in his voice.

"It's true." She talked fast, recounting what Ward had told her.

"I've got to go," Neil said tightly when she'd finished. "I'll call you later."

"Okay." She disconnected and sat there, undecided about whether to begin work on her story or phone her family. Before she could make up her mind, her cell phone rang. The caller ID flashed Neil's cell.

"Hello!"

He didn't return her greeting. "I'm en route to the Payson Police station. I've tried reaching my in-laws but they're not answering and Carmen's in class. Would you mind going to the school and checking on Zoey for me? There's no one else I trust to take care of her."

"Of course. I'll leave now." She opened her desk drawer and retrieved her purse.

"Thank you." He paused. "You have every right to tell me no after the way I've treated you."

"Zoey's more important than any argument."

When Carolina arrived at the school office, she was immediately escorted to the office where a crying Zoey was waiting. The vice principal quickly advised Carolina of what had happened. She was surprised at the trouble Zoey had gotten into—pushing and shoving another student wasn't like her—but not surprised at the reason. She'd warned Neil of this very thing.

"I don't want to go live with my grandparents," Zoey wailed, clinging to Carolina. "He can't make me."

NEIL FORCED HIMSELF to slow down as he drove the main road through Bear Creek Ranch. Though quieter than the other

day, guests were still out and about, heading to their cabins
as dusk faded into evening. It felt like months rather than
days since he'd last been here. How would Zoey react when
she saw him? How would Carolina?

He didn't deserve her kindness, not after the hurtful
things he'd said to her. He'd have understood if she refused
to help him. But she hadn't. She'd put her personal feelings
aside for Zoey. In hindsight, he'd been right to break off with
Carolina, if only because he didn't deserve her.

She'd checked in with him twice since picking Zoey up
from school, informing him that she'd been in a minor play-
ground altercation. That fact alone stunned Neil. Zoey was
the shyest, most complacent child he knew. Carolina indicated there was more to what happened but refused to go into
details, insisting he take care of business first, then come to
her cabin to fetch Zoey.

"Business" had taken over six hours and would probably
require months to wrap up completely. How long until the
town recovered was another question.

Carolina and Zoey were sitting on the porch swing, bun-
dled up in what looked like an old quilt, drinking something
out of mugs. Neil guessed hot chocolate. With her many
nieces around, Carolina would have that on hand. When he
stepped out of the Jeep, he detected a faint aroma of food
coming from inside the cabin. Whatever she'd fixed for dinner—spaghetti?—smelled good.

They watched him approach, Carolina with obvious relief and Zoey with trepidation. As he opened the gate, something small and furry sprang from the blanket, raced up the
fieldstone walkway and greeted him.

If gnawing on his bootlaces could be considered a greeting.

"Where did you come from?"

The little dog yipped loudly. No, not a little dog. A puppy.

With oversize paws and ears and a tail that wouldn't stop wagging.

"Spike, down." Carolina stood, pushing the quilt over Zoey.

Neil kept walking. The puppy refused to let go. Growling, it hung on to his laces with sharp little teeth. "You went dog shopping."

"Seemed like a good idea."

"Spike?"

"I wanted to give him a tough name to grow into."

"I can see the killer instinct already."

The puppy stopped chewing and gazed up at his new owner adoringly.

"Zoey helped me pick him out."

In response, his daughter clapped and called, "Here, Spike." The puppy spun around so quickly, he lost his balance, then raced back up the porch steps to leap into Zoey's arms. She gathered him to her chest, nearly crushing him in the process.

Separating them was going to prove difficult.

"Is everything okay?" Carolina asked.

"Ward was brought into the station." Neil spoke softly so Zoey didn't hear. "Based on his statement, Otis was arrested."

"I'm sorry."

They all were. "He's refusing to talk, even with his attorney present."

"What will happen to him?"

"He'll strike a deal, eventually. Name his accomplices. His wife's apparently involved."

"Patty!"

"When she heard about Otis's arrest, she turned herself in." Neil was still trying to wrap his mind around that.

"I'll go inside and set the table," Carolina said, "so you and Zoey can talk."

"I'd rather you stayed."

"Seriously?" She seemed to be asking more than the obvious question.

He hoped his reply conveyed more than the obvious answer. "Yes."

Zoey, with Spike in tow, scooted to the far end of the swing. Neil sat down. The chains holding the swing creaked under his added weight.

"You want to tell me what happened at school today?" From the corner of his eye, Neil saw Carolina retreat to a dark corner of the porch.

"I pushed Hayden down on the sidewalk."

"Why?"

Spike offered his support by raining dog kisses all over Zoey's face.

"'Cuz he's a brat and said mean things to me."

More taunts about him shooting Lynne? Poor Zoey.

"Even so, you shouldn't have done it." He might be sheriff, but apparently his daughter felt entitled to take the law into her own hands.

All at once, she started to sob. "I don't want to go away with Grandma and Grandpa."

Okay, that came from left field. "Who told you?"

"Grandma. She said I had to start packing when I got home from school today."

Damn. He wished his mother-in-law had waited for him to break the news to Zoey. Well, nothing he could do to change that now. He tried for a positive slant.

"You always like visiting them."

She flung herself at him, trapping Spike between them. "I don't want to go."

"Is that why you pushed Hayden down?"

"He told me good riddance to bad rubbish." Zoey raised a woeful expression to him. "What's rubbish?"

"Nothing you have to worry about." He stroked her hair and patted her back until she stopped crying.

"I like it here," she said around a hiccup after her crying ceased. "I don't want to move."

How did she know his plans? More grandparent interference? "I like it here, too."

"Then let's stay."

"It's not that simple."

"Grandpa says moving isn't the…" She scrunched her mouth to one side. "The slu-tion to everything."

He needed to speak to his in-laws about what they discussed with Zoey. "It isn't. I just want to keep you safe." And other people safe. "My job is dangerous."

"Carolina says you caught the bad guys."

Was *everyone* having conversations with his daughter now? Conversations, he realized, he should be having with her himself.

"The bad guys aren't all caught, but they will be soon."

"Then we can stay," Zoey announced happily.

"Oh, sweetie." He hugged her again, tighter this time.

"I don't believe you shot my mommy."

"Were the kids at school teasing you again?"

"Yes."

"Well, if we move, they won't anymore." Until someone else found out about Lynne.

"What happened to my mommy? How did she die?"

"I told you. It was an accident."

"Were you there?"

"Yes."

"Was I there?"

"Yes."

He glanced over at Carolina. She leaned against the railing, all but her face hidden by shadows. He didn't know it was possible, but the love and devotion shining in her eyes changed his entire way of thinking in the span of a single heartbeat.

He didn't want to leave, either. If he were honest with himself, he'd admit that what he longed for most was a permanent home. A caring wife, one who both delighted him and drove him nuts. Another kid or two. To be sheriff, a job he'd be damn good at. And, okay, it was true, a dog. Preferably one that didn't chew on the end of quilts or drink out of mugs.

If he looked around him right now, all those things were within easy reach. He just had to let go of the past and embrace the future.

It wasn't nearly as hard as he'd imagined.

"Yes, Zoey, you were there. You were just a baby, sitting in your stroller. You, your mommy and I were having breakfast at an outdoor deli."

"What's a deli?"

He looked over again at Carolina, who encouraged him with a gentle smile. As he told Zoey in simple terms what had happened the day her mother died, Carolina wiped away tears with the sleeve of her sweatshirt. Neil felt each tear as, one by one, his burden was lifted.

When he finished, Zoey raised herself up on her knees and wrapped her small arms around him. "Don't feel bad, Daddy. It wasn't your fault."

For the first time, he believed it.

She pulled back, patted his cheek, then kissed it. "I love you."

With those three words, Neil's fears, carried for four long years, dissolved. His daughter didn't hate him or blame him for her mother's death. She'd demonstrated a capacity for compassion well beyond her tender years and understood his feelings of guilt better than anyone except...

Boy, when he was wrong about something, he was really wrong.

He got to his feet, Zoey clinging to his side. Carolina had accused him of being a man of action and few words. He hoped his actions spoke for him now. Raising his free arm, he held it out to her.

Fortunately for him, she was good at reading nuances.

Catching her as she flung herself at him, he lifted her onto her tiptoes in order to kiss the socks off her.

Spike tried to get in on the act by jumping up on Neil's leg.

"Zoey and I have decided to stay," he told Carolina, his arm fitting snugly around her waist. Now that he had her, she wasn't going anywhere.

"Is that a proposal?"

He laughed. Subtlety wasn't her style.

"I'd get down on one knee but the dog's in the way."

"The answer's yes!" She gave him a smacking kiss on the lips. "Yes, yes, yes." Abruptly sobering, she pulled away. "That is, if Zoey's okay with it."

They both looked down. Zoey had picked the puppy up off the floor.

"Does this mean Spike gets to be my dog, too?"

"Absolutely." Carolina radiated happiness. "Are you up to training him?"

"Yes, yes, yes," she mimicked Carolina and twirled the puppy in a circle.

Neil thought that seemed like a good idea and did the same to Carolina. "I love you, Carolina Sweetwater."

Her laughter was like a balm, repairing the last tear in his damaged heart. Good. He wanted to be whole and new for her and his daughter and the life they would all share together.

Epilogue

The sound of squealing tires and spitting gravel rendered nearly every one of the thirty-eight happy and raucous wedding guests silent—for maybe twenty seconds. When it was obvious no one was hurt, the celebrating started up again.

So did Carolina's heart. It was her PT Cruiser, now decorated with balloons, paper flowers, streamers and "Just Married" penned with white shoe polish in the rear window that had barely missed being in another parking lot fender bender. And the driver was none other than Briana. Would her niece ever learn to be more careful?

Neil had wanted to drive the department's old Jeep to the resort outside of Payson where they would spend the night before leaving tomorrow to catch a flight to Lake Tahoe and the condo they'd rented for a week of skiing—Neil knew how, Carolina was going to learn. They also planned to do a lot of snuggling together on the living room floor in front of a roaring fire. Preferably naked. Well, it was their honeymoon, after all.

"Hello, Mrs. Lovitt." Neil drew her away from the crowd and into his warm embrace. "Or are you keeping your maiden name now that you're famous?"

"I'm not famous," she joked back. "Not outside of Payson."

"It's only a matter of time."

He could be right. Being the one to break the story about Sheriff Herberger and the illegal mining had given Carolina's career a tremendous boost. She had Ward to thank for that.

Too bad she couldn't do it in person. After cutting a deal with the prosecutor in which he was given a significant reduction in charges in exchange for his testimony, Ward and his wife quietly left Payson and relocated to Tempe, where they would be closer to his son. Ward had used the very last of his pull at the station to make sure Carolina was given the position of roving reporter.

Until yesterday morning, she'd thought that was the best possible news. Then the home pregnancy test she'd taken came back positive. Neil still didn't know. She was planning on telling him during one of those evenings spent cuddling on the floor in front of the fire. If she could hold out that long.

She brushed a tiny speck of lint off his lapel and straightened his red rose boutonniere. "You look good, Sheriff Lovitt."

They'd opted for a small, simple wedding with Neil wearing his dress uniform.

"Acting Sheriff Lovitt," he corrected her.

"Not for long."

"I have to win the election first."

"You will." She had no doubt.

Shortly after Sheriff Herberger was arrested, he was removed from office. Sadly, his health took a turn for the worse. The last Carolina had heard, he was in the hospital again, his trial postponed. Justice would eventually be served, but it saddened her that someone who had once been a pillar of the community and a close family friend had fallen so far.

Greed did that to people, she supposed—and resentment. After serving in the department over a quarter century, he'd had only his pension to show for it. Deciding that wasn't enough, he'd chosen to supplement his retirement income with illegally obtained gold after discovering a map to the mine in his wife's family heirlooms.

He should have hired a more qualified expert to check out the mine before assuming a life of crime. He would have saved himself a lot of time and money and possibly years in prison.

The reports from the Arizona Geological Society were conclusive: there would be no historic gold strike on Bear Creek Ranch. The only wealth to be made from the illegal mining operation was the fifteen percent increase in revenue as tourists flocked to the ranch's newest attraction. To mark the grand opening of the mine site, Carolina would be doing a live broadcast on location shortly after returning from her honeymoon with Neil.

He'd promised to be there. As he'd promised to stand beside her for the rest of their lives in the vows they'd recently exchanged.

"I'm going to miss you, Daddy." Zoey grabbed Neil's much bigger hand in her small one. "Hurry home."

"I'm going to miss you, too, pumpkin pie. Be good for your uncle Jake." His voice was husky with emotion.

"I will."

She and Spike were staying with Jake, his wife and his four daughters for the week. Carolina could only imagine how chaotic their house would be—and how full of love.

It was how she wanted their life to be, too. And after seeing the pregnancy test results, she was certain it would be.

Neil released Zoey, but instead of running off, the little girl turned to Carolina. "I'm going to miss you, too."

"Same here, kiddo." She bent down and gave Zoey a kiss on the cheek.

When she attempted to straighten, Zoey held on to her and whispered, "Do you think Daddy would mind if I called you Mommy?"

Carolina's heart melted on the spot. "I don't know. Why don't you ask him?"

Talk about a wonderful wedding gift!

"I will," Zoey said shyly. "When you get back."

"Okay."

"What was that about?" Neil asked when Zoey joined her new cousins for yet another photo op.

"Something between Zoey and me. She'll tell you later."

"Come on." He took her arm. "It's time to go."

"What's the rush?"

"I want to get you alone."

Neil was indeed a man of action, as he'd proved many times. And right now, what his eyes said to her was infinitely sexier than the few words he'd uttered.

Darting through a shower of bird seed, they waved goodbye to their family and friends. Rather than get in the passenger side of her PT Cruiser, she snatched the keys from his hands, sauntered around the front of the car and, shoving her long train aside, slid in behind the steering wheel.

"I'll drive."

Wearing a dumbfounded expression, he climbed in beside her.

Carolina smiled. Men like Neil needed to be shaken up every once in a while, and she intended to do just that for the next fifty or sixty years.

* * * * *

Read on for a sneak peek of
HAVING THE COWBOY'S BABY
By Trish Milburn
Available September 2013 from
Harlequin American Romance

Chapter One

Skyler Harrington smoothed her new cream-colored pencil skirt as she took her seat at the corner table at La Cantina. She pointed at the enormous platter of nachos that sat on the table between her and her two best friends, India Pike and Elissa Mason. Elissa was in the midst of grabbing a nacho laden with beef, sour cream and gooey cheese.

"Glad to see you all waited for me," Skyler said.

India nodded toward Elissa, who was now stuffing said nacho into her mouth. "She threatened to start gnawing on her arm if we didn't get something to eat pronto."

"What?" Elissa said around her food. "I was starving. You try unloading a truckload of shrubbery and see if you're not hungry."

She had a point. While each of them owned her own business, Elissa's plant nursery required more physical labor than India's clothing boutique or Skyler's inn.

"Plus," Elissa said as she pointed another nacho at Skyler, "you were late."

Skyler's forehead scrunched as she reached for her phone to check the time. It was exactly one minute after six, and she knew she'd been at the restaurant more than a minute already.

Elissa laughed.

Skyler lifted her narrowed gaze to her friend, who was teasing her yet again about her preference for being places on time, or better yet, early. "I don't know why I'm friends with you."

Elissa smiled. "Because I'm so lovable."

"That's debatable."

"You let her get you every time," India said.

"One of these days maybe I'll figure out what she finds so funny about my punctuality."

"You call it punctuality, I call it inability to go with the flow," Elissa said.

"I can go with the flow." It made her twitchy, but she could do it. "I'm not as big of a stick-in-the-mud as you seem to think."

"Oh, really? When was the last time you really let go and didn't plan your day out to within an inch of its life?"

Skyler opened her mouth but then couldn't think of an answer that wouldn't prove Elissa's point. "I have a lot of responsibilities, people depending on me."

"And we don't?"

"Hey, I'm not that different from India." At least India before Liam Parrish strode into town with his cowboy boots, a Stetson and two very long legs. India's well-ordered life had gone topsy-turvy in two seconds flat. Not that Skyler blamed her. Liam wasn't just good-looking. He also was a really good guy and would become the closest thing Skyler had to a brother when he and India got married in a few weeks.

Skyler grabbed a nacho and scraped most of the toppings off of it back onto the platter.

"You're getting rid of all the good stuff," Elissa said.

"A little goes a long way. Now I'll actually be able to taste the chip."

Elissa rolled her eyes. "Can't even eat a nacho without overthinking it."

"I'll remind you of that when your arteries get clogged with cheese."

Elissa just smiled, stuffed another nacho in her mouth and *mmmed* her taste buds' appreciation.

Skyler didn't know whether she wanted to throw something at Elissa or give in and eat a heaping nacho herself.

After the waitress took their orders, Skyler turned her attention to India before Elissa had the chance to start bugging the living daylights out of her again.

"So how are the final plans for the wedding going? Is there anything else you need me to do?"

India's eyes lit up at the mention of her upcoming nuptials, causing Skyler's heart to warm. After everything she'd been through, India deserved to be happy.

"I don't think so. You've done so much already, both of you."

"It's not every day your best friend gets married to the hottest guy in town," Elissa said.

On that point, Elissa and Skyler could agree.

"I wish it was tomorrow," India said.

Skyler smiled. "That anxious to make an honest man out of Liam?"

India laughed. "If there was more to do between now and then, I'd be fine. But the waiting might kill me. You know what would really help?"

"What?"

"Another project."

India and Elissa exchanged a look that made Skyler nervous. "Why do I feel like I've missed something really important?"

"Your thirtieth birthday is two days away and we haven't planned what we're going to do," India said. "That would keep my mind occupied."

"It doesn't take that long to look up movie times in Austin," Skyler said.

India raised an eyebrow. "I think the occasion calls for more than a movie."

"I happen to quite like watching Jeremy Renner and his awesome arms."

"Well, I can't argue with you there," Elissa said. "But India's right. We can do a movie anytime. I was thinking of something more exciting."

"Of course you were."

Elissa sighed and leaned back in her chair. She glanced at India. "I told you she wouldn't be up for anything interesting."

The sudden overwhelming urge to prove her friend wrong rose up in Skyler. "Fine. You know what? You all can plan whatever you want, and I'll do it."

Elissa barked out a disbelieving laugh. "Yeah, right."

"Really. I'll let you plan the whole thing." The moment the words were out of her mouth, she wanted to call them back and pretend they were never uttered. But if she backed out now, she would never, ever hear the end of it. Blast Elissa for causing her emotions to override her common sense.

The smile that spread across Elissa's face told Skyler she'd just made perhaps the biggest mistake of her life.

"Is it Christmas?" Elissa asked. "Because it feels like Christmas."

"Don't gloat," India said, but she looked like she was having a hard time keeping from smiling, too.

Skyler really knew she was in trouble when their food arrived and Elissa didn't immediately attack her quesadillas. Instead, she was scrolling through something on her phone.

Skyler picked up her fork and stirred the contents of her taco salad. "You know it's rude to have your face buried in your phone when you're with other people, right?"

"This is important business."

"A mulch emergency?"

"I'll have you know I'm doing research, with a little help from Verona."

Skyler stopped with her fork halfway to her mouth, warning bells clanging in her head. "Verona?"

"Yes, you know, my aunt."

Skyler narrowed her eyes. "I don't trust you or your aunt."

"Why not? You have to admit she got it right with India and Liam."

"Yes, but that doesn't mean I want her anywhere near my personal life."

"Verona does more than matchmake, you know."

"What, she's giving you tourist suggestions? I've lived in Texas my whole life. Pretty sure there aren't that many places of interest I've not been to."

Elissa waved off her concern. "Hush. Eat your salad."

Knowing that short of snatching Elissa's phone from her there was nothing she could do, Skyler refocused her attention on her meal. Her stomach growled in response. She'd been so busy during the day that she hadn't taken time for a real lunch, nothing beyond the bag of apple slices she'd snagged from her fridge on the way out of her apartment that morning.

Sure, since her apartment was located at the inn, she could have gone to get something else to eat or ordered something from the kitchen, but a staff meeting had led to several phone calls, which had flowed into going over a contract for fresh produce. The next thing she knew, it was time to leave to meet her friends for dinner.

When Elissa set down her phone, the satisfied smile on her face didn't bode well for Skyler.

"What do you have up your sleeve?"

"Who, me?"

Skyler slowly rested her fork on top of what was left of her salad. "You shouldn't try to sound innocent. You're not very good at it."

Elissa shrugged. "Who wants to be innocent anyway when there's so much fun to be had?"

"I'm afraid to ask what kind of 'fun' you have in mind."

"I wouldn't tell you anyway."

"Um, it's *my* birthday."

Elissa finally looked up after she took a bite of her dinner and swallowed. "And birthdays include surprises."

"You know I'm not a fan of surprises." They'd rarely turned out well in her experience.

Surprise! Your dad's gone to Alaska to fish.

Surprise! He's back again with no warning and who knows for how long.

Surprise! Your mom had a heart attack and died.

"You'll like this one."

Skyler doubted that and considered booking a last-minute vacation for one to the Caribbean.

"And no, we're not letting you weasel out of this, so stop trying to concoct a way to do just that." Elissa gestured toward Skyler's head as if she knew exactly what she was thinking. She probably did.

"Sometimes it's highly annoying that you know me so well."

As Elissa and India laughed, Skyler felt like kicking herself all the way to El Paso and back for giving them just enough rope to hang her with.

SKYLER WAS ON the verge of asking Elissa again where the devil they were going when she spotted a sign on the side of the road just as Elissa started to slow down. Hill Country Adventure Sports.

"Please tell me this isn't our final destination, that you're delivering plants or something."

Elissa glanced at her from the driver's seat of the SUV. "Nope, this is the place."

Skyler turned halfway to look at India and Verona in the back. "Tell me she's kidding."

India shook her head. "It'll be fun."

Skyler looked from one friend to the other, wondering if they'd been body-snatched. Because the Elissa and India she knew wouldn't go this far. "Are you smoking crack? There is no way I'm jumping out of a perfectly good airplane."

"Yes, you are," Elissa said as if Skyler was being silly. "You only live once."

"Yeah, and I'd like to live beyond today, thank you very much."

"They're not going to push you out without a parachute, dear," Verona said.

"It's tandem diving," India added. "You jump with an experienced diver who is trained."

Elissa took her hand off the steering wheel long enough to wave away Skyler's concern. "They've done this a million times."

"All it takes is one time when it doesn't go as planned."

Elissa shook her head as she parked next to a long building that contained an office and several hangar bays for small planes. "I knew you were a compulsive planner, but I didn't know you were a chicken."

"I'm not. I'm sane."

Ignoring her protests, everyone else got out of the car and headed toward the office. She wondered what they'd do if she flatly refused to budge. It was her birthday, damn it. She ought to be able to choose what she wanted to do and not do. And skydiving was way up on the "not do" list.

But the longer she sat in the SUV, the more fidgety she grew. Hurtling through thin air was definitely not on her bucket list, but she didn't like that the mere thought of jumping could get the better of her, either. She wanted to believe she could do anything even if she chose not to, but she'd given her friends permission to take this decision out of her hands. Big mistake, but one she was going to have to swallow.

She cursed under her breath as she opened the door, shut it none too gently and closed the distance between her and her so-called friends.

"I'm so sorry," said Jesse Bradshaw as she got close enough to hear him speaking to Elissa, India and Verona. "I must have caught a stomach bug. I can't dive today."

Oh, hallelujah, birthday wishes were granted!

"That's too bad," India said.

"Man, we'll never get her out here again," Elissa said before she noticed Skyler.

Something was off about her friends' responses to the news that Jesse was sick, but she couldn't put her finger on it.

"She can still go up. My cousin will just be the diver, not me."

Skyler fought the urge to run all the way back to Blue

Falls. "I didn't know you had a cousin, Jesse." She scanned the area but saw no one else but the pilot, next to a small red-and-white plane on the tarmac, and the jet-fuel delivery guy.

"Yeah, he's in town visiting. I just called him a few minutes ago. He's on his way. He wasn't expecting to have to dive today."

"Oh, I don't want to put anyone to any trouble," Skyler said.

"It's no trouble."

The sound of a pickup heading toward them on the gravel entrance road drew everyone's attention.

"That's him now," Jesse said.

A red pickup truck that looked like it had seen better days—better decades—rolled to a stop next to Elissa's SUV, leaving a cloud of gravel dust in its wake.

When the driver stepped out of the truck and strode toward them, Skyler thought there had to be some mistake. This guy looked about as much like a skydiver as Verona did. With worn jeans, scuffed boots and a dark brown cowboy hat, he would look more at home on a cattle drive. When he nodded at her friends and said, "Hello, again," Skyler definitely knew something was up.

"This is all a big joke, isn't it? I'm being punked."

"Well, that's not usually the reaction I get from the ladies," the guy said as he stopped a couple of feet away, his lips stretching into a mischievous smile.

Skyler gave him a raised-eyebrow look before shifting her attention to the other three women. "Seriously, what is going on?"

Before they could answer, the guy laughed. "Don't worry, I don't dive in the boots."

She glanced at him. "Just the hat?"

"Nah. I'd lose it as soon as we jumped."

"Lucky for you, there won't be any jumping today."

"But we've already paid for it," India said.

"Then I suggest you get your money back." When Skyler glanced at Jesse, he had an apologetic look on his face.

"I'm sorry, but there's a no-refund policy on the deposit unless canceled by inclement weather," he said.

Skyler sighed heavily as she looked up into the bright blue sky devoid of clouds. You couldn't ask for a more beautiful day, unless, of course, you were hoping to avoid plummeting to your death.

"Come on, Jesse," the still-nameless cousin said. "You can allow the refund."

Surprised by his siding with her, Skyler met his eyes. "Thank you."

"Ah, come on," Elissa said. "Everyone I know who has done this has loved it. Heck, Jesse jumped with McKenna Parks's eighty-seven-year-old grandpa last week, and the old guy is ready to go again. Right, Jesse?"

Jesse, to his credit, looked uncomfortable being put in the middle of their disagreement. But he nodded. "He wanted to go back up as soon as we hit the ground."

She knew Elissa was daring her, effectively taking away any nonchicken way of backing out of the dive. Skyler shifted her eyes to Jesse's cousin. "Just how many dives have you done?"

He smiled. "Enough."

For a moment she let herself appreciate how that smile only added to how good-looking he was. Good-looking, ha! The man was three-alarm-fire, drop-dead gorgeous.

She snatched her gaze away from his. She did not need to be thinking about dropping dead, or about how Mr. No

Name looked good enough to lick up one side and down the other. Her face flamed, and for once she was glad to have fair skin and red hair. It made blaming the flush on the sun totally believable.

The guy leaned close and used a faux whisper to say, "Don't worry, beautiful. I promise you're safe with me."

She wondered how many times he'd used that line. Because the cowboy was a flirt and most likely a class A player.

The longer she stood there with everyone looking at her, the more she had to fight fidgeting. She closed her eyes for a moment and pulled together all the fragments of her courage. "Fine, I'll do it."

It was smart to face your fears, right? At the very least, she could stick her tongue out at Elissa after it was over.

"Just give me a few minutes to suit up, and I'll give you the ride of your life," her dive partner said.

Skyler glanced at him in time to see him wink. She'd never admit it out loud, but she felt that wink all the way to her toes. She shook her head and rolled her eyes as he walked away. When Jesse followed him, Skyler spun toward her friends.

"So, what do you think?" Verona asked.

"What do I—? This isn't one of your matchmaking schemes, is it?"

Verona's eyes widened. "How could it be? We didn't find out about Jesse being sick until we got here."

Skyler wasn't buying it. She wasn't exactly sure what was going on, but she got the distinct feeling it was more than it appeared on the surface.

"For the record, I know you all are up to something."

"But you're going through with the dive, right?" India asked.

"Do I have a choice?"

"No," Elissa said with a boatload more cheer in her voice than the occasion called for. "We're giving you the experience of a lifetime."

"I could have handled canoeing, maybe a wad of dollar bills and a strip club, but no, you all give me the skydiving cowboy and a potential coronary."

"You're in perfect health," India said.

"And that skydiving cowboy is yum-my," Elissa added.

"I don't care what he looks like as long as he keeps me from going splat against the ground. And just so you know, if I die, I'm coming back and haunting all of you at the most inconvenient times."

When the skydiving cowboy came back outside, followed by his cousin, he looked more skydiver than cowboy. With the Stetson gone, she was able to see more of his short dark hair, angular jaw and dark eyes. If she'd met him somewhere else under different circumstances, he would have definitely caught her eye.

What was she doing? She had to concentrate on surviving the next hour, not lusting over this guy who probably got laid more than carpet. Reluctantly, she followed him toward the plane, her stomach churning.

"So what did they convince you to do?" she asked.

He glanced at her, genuine confusion in his expression. "Jump out of an airplane?"

She stopped walking halfway to the plane. "You met them before, right?"

"Yeah, yesterday at the café. Why?"

Skyler shook her head. "Never mind." She glanced back in time to see her friends smiling from ear to ear. "I am going to kill them." She didn't realize she'd said the words loud enough for anyone to hear until her diving partner laughed.

"Killing's over too quickly," he said. "Payback's better."

"You know, you're right. And I can be very creative."

His mouth quirked up at one edge. "That right?"

The innuendo caused her skin to tingle all over, and that only made her more determined to find the perfect payback for her friends. But first she evidently had to throw common sense to the wind and take a literal leap of faith.

The next few minutes went by in a blur as they boarded the plane, the pilot took off and they geared up for the dive. As they approached the designated point for the jump, Skyler felt as though she might throw up.

"It's okay. Once you're out there flying, you'll forget all about the nerves." He sounded so casual and relaxed, as if hurling one's self from an airplane was no big deal.

"Somehow I doubt that."

"Trust me."

"Trust you? I don't even know your name."

"Tell me yours and I'll tell you mine," he said, mischief in his voice.

"You have a line for everything, don't you?"

"Yep."

"Well, at least your honesty is refreshing." She glanced toward where another guy slid the side door open to reveal nothing but sky. She swallowed hard as cowboy dude moved up behind her and did whatever it was he had to do to connect their gear together.

"Logan Bradshaw," he said, his voice rumbling in her ear.

"What?"

"My name, Logan Bradshaw."

"Oh. Skyler Harrington."

Her heart leaped into her throat as he urged her toward the open doorway.

"Ten seconds," the other guy said.

Oh, Lord.

"Well, Skyler Harrington, you and I are going to go out after this is over," Logan said.

And then he pushed her out the door, and she greeted her birthday with a scream.

Don't miss
HAVING THE COWBOY'S BABY
By Trish Milburn
Available September 2013 from
Harlequin American Romance

HARLEQUIN®

American Romance®

ROMANCE THE ALL-AMERICAN WAY!

Use this coupon to
SAVE $1.00
on the purchase of
ANY
Harlequin American Romance book!

Available wherever books are sold, including most
bookstores, supermarkets, drugstores and discount stores.

✂

SAVE $1.00

ON THE PURCHASE OF **ANY**
HARLEQUIN® AMERICAN ROMANCE®
BOOK.

Coupon expires October 31, 2013. Redeemable at participating retail
outlets in the U.S. and Canada only. Limit one coupon per customer.

52611067

5 65373 00076 2   (8100)0 11875

HARCOUPWBLCM

WIN *Vegas*

A **TRIP** TO

& **TICKETS**
TO CHAMPIONSHIP
RODEO EVENTS!

Who can resist a cowboy? We sure can't!

You and a friend can win a 3-night,
4-day trip to Vegas to see some real
cowboys in action.

Visit
www.Harlequin.com/VegasSweepstakes
to enter!

See reverse for details.

Sweepstakes closes October 18, 2013.

NO PURCHASE NECESSARY TO ENTER. Purchase or acceptance of a product offer does not improve your chances of winning. Sweepstakes opens 7/22/2013 at 12:01 AM (ET) and closes 10/18/2013 at 11:59 PM (ET). Enter online at www.Harlequin.com/VegasSweepstakes. Open to legal residents of the U.S. (excl. Alaska, Hawaii, Overseas Military Installations and other U.S. Territories) and Canada (excl. Quebec, Yukon Territory, Northwest Territories and Nunavut Territory) who are twenty-one (21) years of age or older. Void where prohibited by law. One Grand Prize available to be won consisting of a 3-night/ 4-day trip for winner and guest to Las Vegas, Nevada (12/05/13 to 12/8/13); tickets for winner and guest for two single performances at championship rodeo events; and $700 USD spending money (Total ARV: approx. $3,990). Odds of winning depend on number of eligible entries received. Full details and Official Rules available online at www.Harlequin.com/VegasSweepstakes.
Sponsor: Harlequin Enterprises Limited.

Home to the Cowboy
AMANDA RENEE

It seems as if all of Ramblewood, Texas, is far too
up-to-date on Tess Dalton's love life, or rather, recent lack
thereof. She thought the trip home would help heal her
heart—instead, it just puts her face-to-face with the first
man to crush it.

Cole Langtry is determined to fulfill his father's dream
and he doesn't have time for distractions, especially of
the heartbreaking brunette variety. But when one
remarkable little girl finally brings Tess and Cole
together, it's hard to remember why they've stayed apart.

**Available August 6, 2013,
from Harlequin® American Romance®.**

HARLEQUIN®

American Romance®

A Navy SEAL's Surprise Baby

by

LAURA MARIE ALTOM

Fatherhood is the last thing on navy SEAL
Calder Remington's mind. On the job, he's a
hardworking hero; in civilian life, he's a carefree
bachelor. When he finds a baby—*his* baby—on his
doorstep, he's got no choice but to be a dad. He needs
help, and that's where supernanny Pandora Moore
comes in. She's perfect in every way and Calder can't
deny that he's attracted to her. But Calder can't help
wondering if she's hiding something. He never
imagines that the truth may tear them apart—just as
they dare to imagine a future together.

**Available September 3, only from
Harlequin® American Romance®.**